UNTIL PHILOSOPHERS BECOME KINGS

UNTIL PHILOSOPHERS BECOME KINGS

Book One

A Novel

Chris Thomas

ISBN: 099656070X
ISBN 13: 9780996560702
Library of Congress Control Number: 2015910830
Chris Thomas, Denver, CO

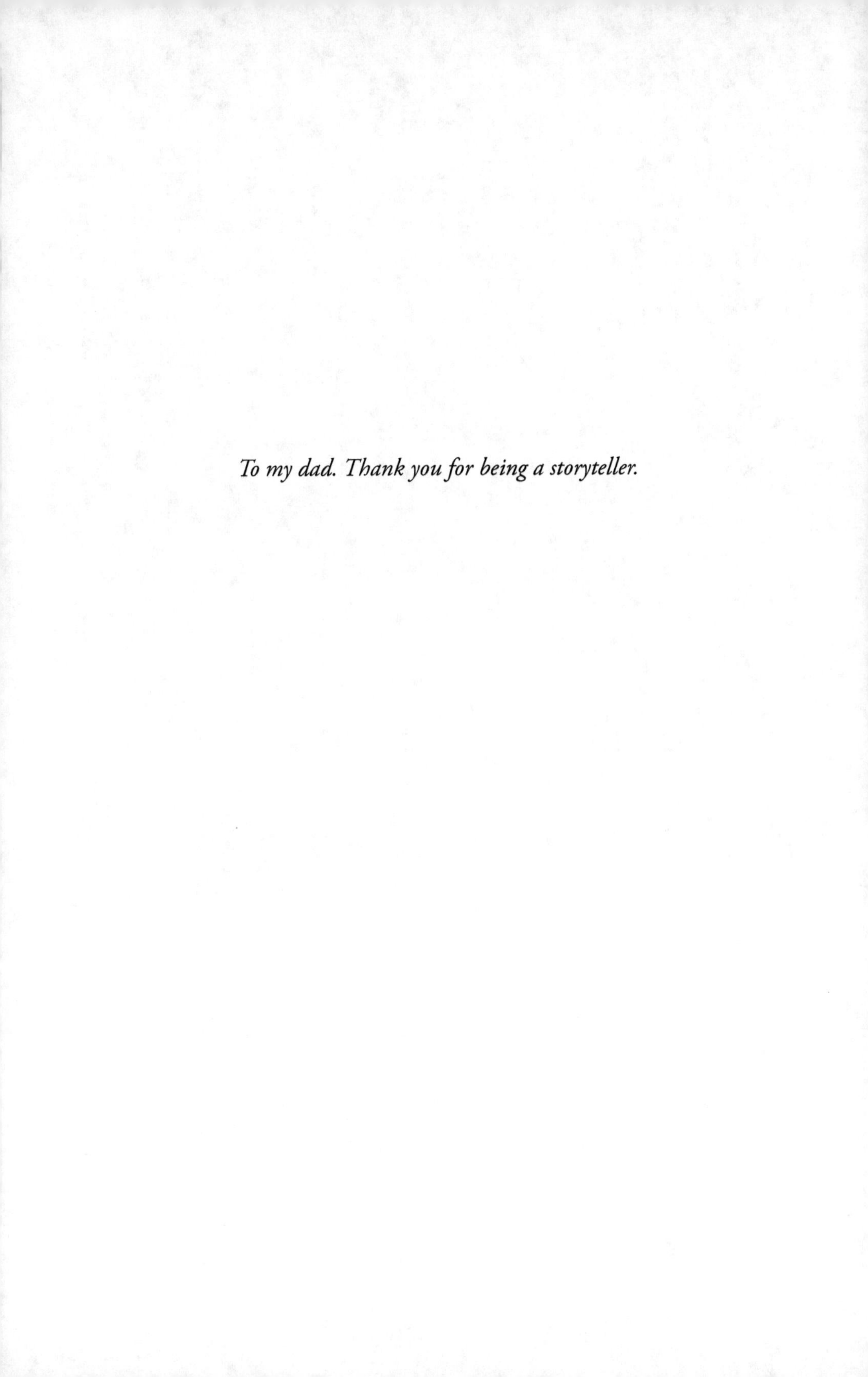

To my dad. Thank you for being a storyteller.

Acknowledgments

My heartfelt thanks go to the following people for taking the time to read various drafts of the manuscript as I took this quixotic journey and for providing me their valued opinions and support: Mic and Mindy Gumb, Neal and Nora Quitno, Ted Baird, Art Cudworth, Scott Guetz, Karen Gumina, Sue McIlvennan, Harvey Brandt, Phil Schwartz, Pete Graham, and Ellen Diana. Also to my brother Dan Thomas and my sister Tere Thomas, for not only reading the manuscripts but also for having the honesty to tell me what they really thought, and my sister Kathy for her reality checks. Lastly to my wife, Nan, and our three kids, Sarah, Wil, and Sam, for their belief in me and the dream.

"The society we have described can never grow into a reality or see the light of day, and there will be no end to the troubles of states, or of humanity itself, till philosophers become kings in this world, or till those we now call kings and rulers really and truly become philosophers, and political power and philosophy thus come into the same hands.... For it is not easy to see that there is no other road to happiness, either for society or the individual."

—Plato (427 BC–347 BC), *The Republic*

Prologue

Mexico City
A Tuesday, twelve years ago

As Deputy Attorney General Jacques Pablo Alvarez left his office in the Department of Public Security and Justice Building in Mexico City, he was glad to finally be heading home; it was nearly six, and he was late. His father didn't visit the capital city often, preferring to live and run his businesses from his ocean-side home in Baja, and Jacques cherished his infrequent visits. Because his new job placed him squarely in the sights of the cartels he was now responsible for prosecuting, he couldn't drive himself—not that he could remember ever driving a car or going anywhere unaccompanied by his bodyguards. This was Mexico, after all, and, as unfortunate as it was, if you were from a wealthy family or you were fighting the cartels—and he was—you needed personal protection. Several thousand kidnappings occurred each year in Mexico, with several hundred a month in the city of nine million alone, so one had to take precautions.

The private elevator from the Justice Department's executive floor opened onto the secure loading area of the underground garage, where his armored limousine and capital police protection detail waited for him. The older of his two longtime bodyguards held the limousine door open for him as he took his usual seat before they joined him. The Justice Building sat on the southwest corner of the world's second-largest public square; Jacques's motorcade exited the secure garage and entered the heavy ring of slow-moving traffic that snaked around the perimeter of the Zocalo, as the square was known.

He glanced at the two men sitting opposite him, thankful they were there as usual. His father had selected Francisco and Raul Ortega to watch over him when he sent him to the capital to enter Saint Matthew's Jesuit Preparatory School, an exclusive private academy for the sons of the wealthy and powerful in the country. As a twelve-year-old, Jacques was embarrassed at first by them and then went through a period when he simply ignored them, as one might ignore an old chair in the corner of a room. But over the last twenty-five years, he not only had noticed and appreciated them, but they also had become his closest friends. Closer even than Emilio and Alberto Rodriguez, the two sons of another of the country's wealthiest families who had befriended him during his first few confusing, frightening weeks at Saint Matthew's.

His new job brought back some of those forgotten feelings, as well as new feelings of frustration, as he began to realize not only the enormity of the task he had been promoted to but also the difficulties those challenges were presenting. Ramon Castillo, Mexico's attorney general, had gone out on a political limb to promote one as young as he to the very visible position of deputy attorney general for organized crime; at thirty-eight years old, he was the youngest ever to hold this position. Jacques was tall, slim, and handsome, with short dark hair, even features, and a firm chin. His looks and new appointment already had powers in Castillo's party talking about his bright political future, if brought along slowly and carefully. For years, men in their forties and fifties who had served in the Justice Department for longer than his twelve years had held his new position. But too many of those men were found to be unreliable in one way or another, with weaknesses that made them targets for coercion and the temptations offered by the very deep pockets of the cartels—that or they simply lacked the courage to do their job and take on the cartels, knowing that to do so would invite retribution.

For the last twelve years, Jacques had worked as a federal prosecutor in the Justice Department and never lost a case he could get to trial. The problem then and now that was so frustrating was getting cases to trial. The higher up in a cartel a criminal was, the greater the difficulty. The principal problem was the loss of evidence and witnesses as cartel members sat in jail waiting for their day in court. As a trial date approached, the government's case often was lost before it could start when witnesses recanted previously sworn affidavits or came up dead or missing. Kidnapping children was the most effective method the cartel used to change hearts, minds, and testimony. In Jacques's own heart, he could hardly fault an arresting officer, or other material witness, for lying in order to free a child, and there was no protecting them all. The cartels reached into all levels of the government and appeared increasingly untouchable. Truth be known, Jacques was spending more time prosecuting policemen and judges than cartel members, and he was sick of it.

Prior to entering law school, he had earned a degree in philosophy. From his studies, one particular thought by Plato motivated him above all others after he chose the law and public service in particular: "Any man may easily do harm, but not every man can do good to another."

Jacques desperately wanted to be a man like that. His father was just such a man. From his father he had learned that as members of the wealthy and privileged class in a Catholic country, their family had an obligation to help others in need in as many ways as they could. As a family, their needs were taken care of for all generations to come through the proceeds of their many successful businesses. His father had quietly created a family foundation to support many causes and organizations and, despite his efforts to avoid attention, was recognized throughout the country for his generosity. But more than his father's philanthropy, Plato's words inspired a higher calling in him, a much more far-reaching goal than simple giving. With his new position in the justice department, he could do some good, and for so many more people in so many ways, by pursuing and removing from society the criminals who were killing so many innocent people in his country, especially in the northern states.

As Jacques's motorcade finally exited the Zocalo and slowly made its way through the congested evening traffic to the west of the central square of Mexico City toward the great Bosque de Chapultepec—the huge park with the many beautiful old neighborhoods that ringed it—his thoughts focused on his father rather than the troubles he was having with his new position. He was determined not to let his frustrations ruin the evening with his father. He had asked his chef to prepare something special, and he and his father would dine and talk well into the night, as was their custom during his father's visits since Jacques had graduated from law school. He was worried about his father. More and more he sensed tension and great unhappiness in him, and his visits were becoming less frequent. His father was clearly troubled, and it was probably the estranged relationship with his mother that his father was finding difficult to discuss with him. Jacques's parents had lived apart for years now, the result of some deeply personal problem between them not shared with him or his sisters. He knew with each passing year his father was growing lonelier. His mother had mostly raised him; as a result, he had grown up with her family's surname, Alvarez, rather than his father's, Peña. When he had asked his father about this when he was a teenager, his father simply had said it was what his mother wanted.

In other cultures, perhaps his parents would have legally parted. But that wasn't possible in Mexico, given the norms of society as well as his mother's almost fanatical devotion to the church and the scriptures. His father's many business interests had kept him traveling all over the country and the Western hemisphere for as long as Jacques could remember. But even if his father's travels hadn't kept him away for long periods, his sense was that his parents' relationship wouldn't have been different. His mother was in many ways a saint, but her deep devotion to her religion made her difficult to live with as a son. He could only imagine the emotional distance and the resulting pain his father must have endured as a husband.

His father had never been a weak or jealous man—quite the opposite—but how could a husband compete with God? It wasn't something a son wanted to think about his mother, but Jacques had come to believe that what love she could share was reserved exclusively for God. He was sure he had disappointed her when he hadn't entered the seminary and chose to attend law school instead. His mother would have liked very much to have a priest in the family, and there was a time when he had considered it. But although he was devout, he had never had felt the deep, passionate calling he supposed those who did take the vows must have felt.

If his father's unhappiness wasn't due to his relationship with his estranged wife, it could only be his worry over his only son's involvement with the most dangerous people in Mexico. There was no question in his mind that his father's attitudes had changed when he had become the country's chief prosecutor. He knew his father was proud of him and the position he had attained, but a sadness also had surfaced.

Jacques dismissed any thoughts about his father's various businesses as being the source of his unhappiness. The businesses were so numerous and so diverse in their nature that no economic downturn could affect the family's wealth. When Jacques was twenty-one, his father had arranged a meeting for him in the capital city with a group of lawyers and accountants who took him through summaries of the family's investments. He would inherit control of everything after his father's death, he learned, and his father wanted him to be aware of their holdings as well as their philanthropic responsibilities. Jacques was flabbergasted at the extent of what they owned and the wide variety of businesses his father had created. He had known about the very successful salt company in Baja, as well as the two cruise-ship lines, because his father had taken him through the mines once when he was young and still living in Baja, and he had crewed on several of their ships during summer breaks from school. But he had no idea they owned as much land in ranches and farms as they did.

There were the other real-estate holdings as well—shopping centers and arcades, hotels and restaurants. And in several major cities in the north, such as Chihuahua, Hermosillo, and Monterrey, entire city blocks of retail establishments were under the family's control. His father's business interests were breathtaking in scope and diversity, and all were carefully watched—and to a great extent managed—by the stodgiest and most respected of Mexico City's law firms and public accountants, whose principals sat on the board of the private family umbrella corporation. While Jacques's father was personally involved in his businesses, the most senior of lawyers explained to Jacques that in the unfortunate but inevitable circumstance of his father's passing, he wouldn't have to give up his chosen work in the law to assume the mantle of leadership of the family businesses. All that would be required was his presence once every three months at a board meeting where, as chairman, he would preside. In the meantime, the stodgy accountants would continue to read the columns of figures and do whatever ciphering it was they did, and the money would keep flowing in, all carefully watched by the old lawyers for their enormous fees.

After that meeting, Jacques seldom thought about the family's businesses, despite the quarterly reports sent to him, although he did reminisce occasionally about the times he had spent on his father's cruise ships when he was a teenager. His father had insisted he work in the summers to better appreciate all they had as a family. Some of Jacques's fondest memories were of working with his friends the Rodriguez brothers during their summer breaks from Saint Matthew's, and later, from the National University, as deckhands and eventually waiters on the cruises offered by his father's shipping companies.

He enjoyed the family cruises the most. As he'd been brought up in great wealth, living at guarded estates with his own personal bodyguards, it wasn't until he was fifteen and working his first cruise that he began to realize how other families lived. It was a cultural and personal awakening to see how other families interacted. As he worked more summers and saw more families, he came to the conclusion that his family's privileged life was very strange. His family relationships, while loving in their own way, were so different from what he observed in others. He was twelve when he was first sent away to school, and he came to realize that he didn't live with his family so much as visited them. Not having been previously exposed to any other way of life, and being mostly surrounded by classmates and friends at school from similar circumstances, he had grown up thinking that was how all families lived and how their children grew up. Working the cruise ships, however, had disabused him of that belief. Many families in other cultures seemed to spend all their time together, and he envied that.

Regardless of how different Jacques's life was, he grew up worshiping his father and was devoted to him. Despite their many forced separations, all through school—at a soccer match, a class play, or debate; anytime he was involved in an activity of consequence in his young life—he would look into the audience or across to the stands, and there his father would be, knowing how important the event was to his son. Afterward there would be a dinner perhaps, sometimes just a ride to the airport, and then his father would be gone. But for the few precious hours when it really mattered, his father was there.

Jacques's mother, by contrast, was never there, even though she had raised him and his two younger sisters mostly alone, with just the help of the church. For as long as he could remember, church schools and church functions had been the foundation of their family relationship. Although he initially was very unhappy about being sent south from the family home in Baja to Mexico City to attend Saint Matthew's, prep school ended up being a welcome relief. Even with the Jesuits' structure and rules, when compared to the suffocating religious attitudes of his mother, he felt free for the first time.

The motorcade finally was picking up speed, having reached the broad expanse of Paseo de la Reforma and its eight lanes of traffic. The great boulevard angled southwest, away from the city center and through the newer developments, with their high-rise apartments and offices towering over the older classical buildings. Jacques didn't want his father worrying about him, and he intended to discuss his new security detail with him until he put that worry out of his mind, if that was what was troubling him. He had Francisco and Raul, and he knew they reported to his father regularly. Since his promotion to deputy attorney general, he also had his capital police protection in two chase cars that went everywhere he did.

His estate in Lomas de Chapultepec, La Casa Rosada, had been a law-school graduation gift from his mother, but he knew his father had quietly arranged for it. The walled grounds and his personal guards who lived there protected him. Jacques had been protected for so long that the trappings of his protection had become like the air around him. He simply never gave it any thought, except in the context of his friendships with his two personal guards. The younger of the two brothers, Raul, had become someone he thought of as an older brother. Raul, only six years his senior, had guided him through many of the mysteries of life while growing up; Jacques had returned that gift of friendship by helping Raul become a better man. He forced his bright but basically uneducated protector to read more, and eventually he coaxed him into taking classes and helped tutor him to his own first degree in philosophy. They were now as inseparable as any two brothers. If Jacques couldn't convince his father of his safety, he felt strongly that Raul could. Although there were others in the government who hadn't escaped the reach of the cartels, he was certain they would never touch him.

The motorcade turned off Reforma and entered the beautiful old Lomas de Chapultepec residential area with its narrow, treelined streets and impressive mansions and estates. They reached the gate to La Casa Rosada, literally the Pink House, called so because of the color and hue the stucco took on at sunrise and sunset, when the sunlight was at its deepest and most beautiful. The old stately mansion sat back on the grounds, protected from prying eyes and unwanted visitors by twelve-foot-tall stone-and-stucco walls surrounding the several acres of the estate. His father's limousine and his body guards SUV's were parked in the long curving driveway in front of the great house. After Jacques's driver pulled up beside it, he got out and went in through the impressive front entry, followed closely by Francisco and Raul.

His father was standing by the bar in the formal living room, a drink in hand. Smiling broadly, Jacques walked quickly up and embraced him. Handshakes were exchanged between his father and the Ortega brothers before they discreetly made themselves scarce. They knew how important the infrequent times Jacques and his father could be together were, and they respected the moment. Jacques's manservant behind the bar prepared a glass of his favorite whiskey for him, and he joined his father in a toast to his mother and sisters.

For a man who had spent so much time away from his family, his father was very sentimental about family whenever they got together. Jacques looked hard at his father, for he could not remember having seen him look so deeply troubled. He noticed that his father tried to hide this fact with small talk about his wife and daughters, so Jacques decided to be patient. Whatever was bothering him he would draw out over dinner. Since his college days, the ritual of sharing a fine meal alone with his father had provided some of his fondest memories, and he knew his father enjoyed this simple pleasure as well. Anxious to relieve his father of whatever was troubling him, he suggested they go in to dinner.

The formal dining room, like all the large first-level rooms of the mansion, was an impressive architectural space, with a tall ceiling and rich moldings with handcrafted details that gave the space depth and a visual richness. An antique crystal chandelier hung over the polished formal table for sixteen, which was beautifully set for two at one end. Jacques had selected an exquisite Bordeaux from his cellar that morning, and it had been decanting since. He took his spot at the head of the table, something his father had insisted upon when they had taken their first dinner together in the opulent room years earlier; his father sat to his right in the traditional place for an honored guest. Jacques poured the 1996 Chateau Pichon Longueville Comtesse de Lalande and offered another toast to the family members not present, while his old butler, Reynaldo, served dinner. When the main course was brought in, his father looked at Reynaldo and politely told him they would like some privacy and would serve themselves. The butler nodded and said he would see to it.

Jacques watched his father when he made his unusual request to Reynaldo and was glad of it. His father wanted privacy to talk, and this was good in his mind. If what his father wanted to discuss was indeed about his parents' relationship, it would be uncomfortable for them both, but he wanted to ease his father's mind of whatever was bothering him. Jacques loved his mother but worshiped his father and would side with him in any circumstance. His father took a very large drink of his wine, which Jacques found troubling, as he could see his father clearly was struggling to summon the strength to say whatever it was he needed to talk about.

His father gently wiped his face with the linen napkin, replaced it in his lap, and clasped his hands on the table as if to calm himself. He looked intently but sadly at Jacques and softly said, "Son, you know my pride in you knows no limits. Your having graduated from the national university and then law school is very special to me. In each instance, you were the first in our family to do so. I'm also proud of your courage and desire to serve the people of this country. For my own deeply personal reasons, and in my own way through our family trust, I also have been trying to serve the people. I was so proud when I read about your new promotion…but…at the same time; my feelings for you and your successes are overwhelmed by my choices and failures in life, which you must now know about. I'm deeply ashamed of my past, our family's past, and what it could mean to you. For thirty years I've avoided this day and what I now must tell you, knowing full well that some day it would be necessary."

What in the world is he talking about? Jacques wondered.

"Good God, Father, what is it? Whatever it is, we'll deal with it together. A young man's transgressions three or four decades in the past don't define the man. You've done so much in your life for so many—just tell me what's bothering you."

His father looked at him, his eyes glistening, his expression reflecting a deepening despair. "There are some mistakes a young man makes that he never can walk away from, no matter how badly he might wish to do so a lifetime later. These mistakes often lead not to isolated events a man simply can put behind him after many years but sadly to paths that are irreversible and end up defining his life. That's the path that I've been on and that I've tried to protect you, your sisters, and your mother from. But as your position in the government grows, I fear I can no longer protect you…except with the truth. And son, it's a hard truth, one that will be difficult for you to accept."

Jacques sat in confused silence, staring at his father, his concerns prior to dinner turning to anxiety with the direction the conversation had taken. Whatever was on his father's mind was nothing he'd been imagining.

"Father, we can face the truth, no matter how hard you believe it is."

His father placed both hands flat on the table and was looking down, as if he truly were ashamed. He raised his gaze and looked intently at Jacques.

"You're aware of the many businesses I've built or acquired over the last three decades, but it's our root business that you must now know about, the foundation that provided me the means to build our many respectable businesses. I no longer can live with the possibility that in your new responsibilities, you'll discover I'm nothing more than one of the criminals you seek so passionately to eliminate. The shame would be too devastating to bear. So, my son, I'm here to surrender to you."

Jacques was stunned. He wasn't sure exactly what his father was trying to tell him, but the possibilities were flashing through his mind like sheet lightning in a summer thunderstorm, his understanding as obscured as those brief moments of light in a darkly clouded sky. His anxiety turned into an icy ball in his gut as possible explanations formed in his mind. Hesitantly—actually afraid, he realized, of the truth—he said, "You said, 'surrender,' Father, as in turn yourself in, as if you're guilty of a crime. You did something illegal thirty years ago and used the proceeds to start your business—is that it? If it is, I don't care—not if it happened thirty years ago, illegal or not. You've done too much good with your life; surely you've made up for any perceived crime with your life's work. I love you, Father, and would forgive you for anything."

"No, no," his father said softly, pathetically, shaking his head. "You aren't hearing me—not thirty years ago, but every day for the last thirty years. Don't you understand? My family, your family, the family I've kept you safely from all these years are traffickers. And as we sit here, our family members in the north are busy doing what they do, and I'm their leader. With the businesses I've set up over the years, we transport illicit drugs north, and I successfully use those businesses to launder the profits."

His father's admission hit him like a tidal wave, and he couldn't speak; even breathing seemed difficult. His mouth hung open in shock, his eyes wide. In almost a whisper, Jacques said, "This can't be the truth, Father, not you. You're nothing like the criminals I prosecute—nothing! Why are you telling me this lie?"

With the truth finally out, his father seemed to shrink in his chair, his once-solid shoulders sagging as if he were exhausted or defeated. He was staring at his clasped hands on the table and then mustered the courage to look up at his son and continue, his words coming slowly.

"It isn't a lie, son, but sadly the truth. You can't imagine how I wish it were all a lie, how I wish my life were different. It's true to say that in most ways, our family isn't like those you prosecute, as we've never harmed the truly innocent. But we do associate with those who have. We are what I said we are—that's why I'm here to turn myself in. I only ask that before you take me into custody, you allow me to call my brother, the uncle you hardly remember, and tell him what I've done. I want him and the rest of our family, the cousins you haven't seen since you were a boy, to have the chance to leave the country and seek lives elsewhere. I alone will suffer the punishment for our family's crimes. I only became involved to keep my brother from getting into trouble all those years ago. I must protect him in this as well."

Jacques felt numb; his hands were trembling slightly, and he couldn't will them to stop. His mind was trying to process what his father had just revealed, but nothing he'd said made sense to him. His father had said the truth would be hard, but this was unimaginable. He couldn't accept what he was saying; he wouldn't. Still in obvious denial, and in a state of quiet desperation, Jacques said, "Father, I'm aware of all the serious traffickers in the country. How involved can you be if I don't know about you? The names Alvarez or Peña aren't associated with any known cartels—I'm certain of this. You must be exaggerating your crimes; you have to be."

His father's expression was heartbreaking to him. "No...I'm sorry... but I'm not. From the beginning, where others used force and violence, I used cunning and intelligence. Where others have been clumsy and careless, I've been careful and organized. You know well of the Mendoza cartel of Chihuahua—of this I have no doubt. Yes?"

Jacques was surprised by the question and the familiarity his father seemed to have with the name of one of the country's most ruthless cartels. "Yes," he said. "I'm well aware of the existence of a Mendoza brothers' cartel in Chihuahua," he snapped, something he'd never done before with his father.

His father was taken back momentarily, surprised at the emotion from his son, but deep down he understood. Leaning forward again in his chair, he went on. "The Mendozas are my creation—they and several more groups just like them. They were my brother's boyhood friends, and, like them, my brother was always involved in petty criminal acts. It was the Mendozas who first made contact with the Columbians and tried their hand at moving their cocaine to America. Your uncle wanted that life, and nothing I could say would dissuade him. I used my head to keep him safe and out of jail. I could see they would all end up in jail or, worse, dead. So I figured out ways to transport the drugs so they wouldn't get caught. That's the crime I perpetrated to try to save my younger brother from himself—that and successfully hiding all the money.

"I realized from the beginning that the Mendozas would attract attention, as they are and always have been careless, brutal, and stupid. So I showed them how our family could move their products north undetected. Then I arranged the business so the authorities, if they looked, would see the Mendozas and not us. And that's what we've done all these years with them and the others who unknowingly serve us. I've done my best to keep our family safe and, more important, to keep our true family name unknown to the authorities. But as the government becomes stronger in its attempts to eliminate the trafficking, more of those whom I have fronting our illicit business will become known to you, and you will prosecute them. And as you do, the greater the chances will be that I'll be revealed for what I am.

"Over the last few years, I've thought from time to time about talking with you and trying to convince you that I'm different, that our business is different, perhaps persuade you to join me, but this all must end. With your rise in the Justice Department, I've read the articles about your potential, your destiny. I want you to have that life, an honorable and just life that you've earned."

"Father, I don't—"

"Please, please, this is difficult for me. Let me finish…I'm a criminal, a trafficker in illegal drugs, but I believe I am different. You were right to think that, and you must believe me. We aren't murderers, but the same can't be said for our business partners, who've committed every abomination known to your mother's God. I have co-opted all manner of police and prosecutors, but only after they came to us first with their hands held out, seeking money in exchange for their assistance. I never wanted this, any of it, but once I started it, there seemed to be no way out. I admit there was a time when I thought I was smarter than the others and could somehow control it, keep it from hurting people. But that was an arrogant fool's dream.

"I've tried to do good with what I've built, to give back to the people for being a part of this terrible business, but all that I have is built on a lie. So do with me, son, what you must. I won't have another moment of peace until you do. All I ask is that someday, knowing the entire truth of my life, you'll find it in your heart to forgive me."

Jacques silently stared at his father for a full minute, trying to process the hell he'd just been exposed to; his mind was a kaleidoscope of images and possibilities but no coherent thoughts. Finally, quietly, his emotions spent, he asked, "What is it you expect me to do, Father? Take you down in the morning and prosecute you, then lock you up for the rest of your life? How could you believe for a second that I'm capable of such a thing?"

The tears that had been gathering in the corners of his father's eyes finally trickled down his cheeks as he said softly, "You must. You have no other alternative. It's only a matter of time before the authorities discover me, and I don't want your life ruined because of my choices. With young men like you and your friends the Rodriguez brothers gaining positions of greater responsibility, the government in time will gain the upper hand against the cartels, and I'll be revealed."

Jacques slowly stood up and looked down at his father, the reality of the moment crashing down on him, crushing any rational thought. Without saying another word, he turned and walked unsteadily out of the dining room and up the main staircase to his bedroom suite. His father had planned to spend the night and return to the north in the morning. At this very moment, Jacques didn't care—he couldn't care—as his world spun out of control. He locked himself in his suite, sat on the couch in his sitting room with his head buried in his hands, and wept.

The night crawled by as he alternated between pacing and sitting, trying to see his way through the disaster his life had just become. It was nearly

6:00 a.m., and his head snapped up; he had been dozing—for how long he wasn't sure. He was sitting at his writing table, loose papers and scribbled notes everywhere—nothing but deep thoughts, terrible thoughts, penned in a fit of self-pity. The subcompact Glock 29 that Raul had given him as a graduation gift from law school years before was still there, on the corner of the desk. Raul had intended the gift as personal protection, the last line of defense in an unsafe world. Instead, ironically last night, it had dangerously become the opposite, as Jacques imagined that it had spoken to him: *I'm your only friend, and I can stop the pain and end this nightmare.*

He had spent the better part of the dark night staring at the Glock, his thoughts as cold and black as the steel it was made from. He reminded himself that suicide was a mortal sin, and a violation of his faith. He also thought of the anguish his mother would suffer if he did the inconceivable. But the hard truth was that he simply didn't have the courage, if that was what it was, to commit such a terrible act. That and memories of his mother finally silenced the black thoughts as the handgun pressed against his temple. Slowly the gun was lowered, the safety reset and the lethal, cold object was set aside, to be returned to the closet, where it had sat undisturbed for years. He spent the remaining night and coming dawn examining other hard truths. In the end, one such truth was that he didn't want to die, but neither did he know how to live now that he had learned the truth about his father and his family.

His last thoughts before dozing off had been of his mother. She never could survive a mortal sin committed by her only son. She would at first blame herself, then eventually blame his father and wonder until her last breath what monstrous thing he must have done to incur God's wrath and invite the terrible retribution of her only son's death. She might not even be able to endure the shame of knowing the truth of her husband's secret life once it was revealed or Jacques having to prosecute his father—all hard truths.

Despite their long estrangement, his father was after all still her husband in the eyes of God—truly the one flesh—and she would be humiliated by his life's misdeeds. Jacques was lost with nowhere to turn, with his father—his moral compass—no longer in a position to help him see his way. He'd never in his life doubted the fundamental goodness in his father, and, despite his father's revelations, he still believed in it; he had felt it as his father had struggled to tell him the awful truth. He also never had doubted that from the position in life his father had provided him, he could "do good to another," as Plato had written—or, as he saw it, a great many others—by remaining beyond the long reach of the cartels and fighting them for the people who couldn't fight back themselves. But life can be cruel, destinies and dreams capricious and elusive things; the mercy of the benevolent God his mother said he could always trust in seemed nowhere to be found. Despite his dreams and everything he had worked for, the long, insidious reach of the cartels had found him, and in such an unimaginable way.

In his struggle to see his way forward, and just as the sun started to make its appearance through the delicate decorative filigree of the antique cotton drapes of his bedroom windows, it was a thought from Burke, not Plato, remembered from his studies years ago, that came to him: "The only thing necessary for the triumph of evil is that good men do nothing."

Do nothing. It was at that moment, with that long-forgotten thought from a second-term philosophy class, that Jacques realized perhaps the hardest truth of that long, painful night: doing nothing was a choice he simply didn't have, yet evil might succeed anyway. He had to choose. It was one or the other, good or evil, no matter how hard that once-simple choice had surprisingly become for him, for good now had more than one meaning to him; black and white were now less clear, obscured by shades of gray he never had contemplated.

He stood and stared at the rising sun for a full minute, the beauty of the pink light filtering through the surrounding trees incongruous in the face of the reality confronting him, then nodded slowly in understanding. He went to the door, unlocked it, and slowly walked out of his suite.

Jacques was barefoot but still in his suit pants and shirt from the night before, the coat and tie long since thrown against a wall, the shoes and socks in some forgotten place. He walked down to his father's room and quietly knocked on the door. His father, the drug trafficker, the cleverly concealed cartel leader, answered, also still dressed in a portion of last night's attire. It was clear he hadn't slept much either; he looked ashen, evidence of tears still in his eyes. His father turned and slowly walked back to the table in his sitting room; from his posture, he looked to be a thoroughly defeated man. A fresh coffee service was there, and he sat back down in front of the cup from which he'd been drinking. Jacques followed him and sat opposite his father at the small table and looked at him. Neither could hold the gaze of the other; instead, both looked down at the table. In those initial moments, each was unable to face the pain he saw there.

Jacques felt crushed, body and soul, but he knew what he had to do. He was an officer of the court; there was right, and there was wrong. And then there was his father. In the final analysis, after all the soul-searching, after looking for any other answer, including his own death, he finally realized that for him—this morning and every morning to follow for the rest of his life—there could be only one answer, one path forward. He looked up at his father, reached over, gently touched his hand, and said softly, "Two questions, Father: who am I, and what is my family name? Then tell me more about our business and how I am to help you."

1

Rogelio Sanchez State Detention Facility
El Paso, Texas
A Tuesday morning, twelve years later

The midnight-to-eight shift at the new addition to the state detention facility in southeast El Paso usually was boring and uneventful for the eight officers who worked it. The new wing was highly automated, with several layers of overlapping, redundant security systems to keep the inmates right where they were. A single guard sitting in an impregnable glassed-in control room within each of the four cellblocks could view and control all twelve cells by himself. Four of the eight officers sat in these bulletproof fishbowls, which projected into the larger dayrooms, and did just that. Cells were arranged on three sides of each dayroom so the guards personally could see every cell from their safe perches in addition to watching the banks of monitors that took feeds from the dozen CCTV cameras located strategically throughout the block.

The shift supervisor sat in the command center and watched those who watched, while the remaining three guards of the shift walked the complex, exchanging positions every couple of hours with the others to keep the routine from dulling everyone's senses. All inmates were secured in their cells during the night, and access to the cellblocks was controlled from the glassed-in control cubicles through secure sally ports. All one had to do on the midnight-to-eight was watch the monitors and have a good book. At least this morning they would have something to do.

When the guards came on at midnight, word had been left for them that the three pairs of prisoners in cells one through three of cellblock A were finally to be moved to their permanent federal home at Fort Bliss. Located in a far corner of the huge army post in the middle of the southwest Texan high desert, the cells of the new isolated maximum-security prison just marginally met the Supreme Court's established standards regarding cruel and unusual punishment. Unlike the El Paso facility the six were leaving, the federal maximum-security facility was real incarceration, with each inmate subject to true solitary confinement. The one hour each day prisoners would be allowed out of their cells was only to shower, receive a change of coveralls, and get thirty minutes of "outside" time in a small high-walled courtyard with steel bars overhead. The six inmates making the move to their new quarters had no idea of the desolation they were headed to.

The guards of the midnight-to-eight did. The several deeply Christian members among them would say a quiet prayer for them as they left, for they knew from their training that the human animal, no matter how tough he or she purported to be, craved and needed human contact. After three or four years of the type of solitary confinement they were off to, these inmates likely would cease to be functioning human beings. Whoever went in not a danger to himself or others would be made so inside.

Exactly at 4:00 a.m., the lights were turned on in the three cells that held the transferees, and the six prisoners were rudely rousted out of their bunks. After their legs and wrists were shackled, they were locked into pairs and led shuffling down to the central sally port in the bowels of the detention facility. Right on schedule, a US Army prisoner-transport van pulled up to the main exterior security-door CCTV camera, and the driver produced the proper identification to be allowed entry. The shift supervisor in the control room pushed the correct buttons, and the bright bluish hue of the high-output light fixtures both inside and out came on full; then the large overhead door of the sally port slowly followed its tracks upward and opened. The van pulled into the cavernous space, where three guards stood with the prisoners. None of the night-shift guards recognized the two burly military policemen who climbed out of the van, but that wasn't unusual. With the huge expansion of the base in the last several years to handle all the troubles at the border, there were new faces by the thousands. The paper work was reviewed and signed, the prisoners were loaded up, and the van left the way it had come.

Thirty minutes later, the shift supervisor in the command center picked up the ringing phone, identified himself, and was surprised to hear the voice of Captain Teddy Gonzales of the El Paso PD on the other end of the line, especially at this time of morning. The captain told him there had been a traffic accident and then a shooting twenty minutes earlier involving a Fort Bliss provost marshal transfer vehicle, and two of his black-and-whites were on their way back to the state facility with the four prisoners found at the scene.

"Four prisoners?" the surprised shift supervisor said. "Six were being transferred, Teddy."

"Well, four's all we found," said the captain. "We got them headed to you in a couple of my cars. A wounded MP and the other guard are on their way to the hospital at Fort Bliss in an army ambulance. Get the missing two identified and give their information to my guys so we know who the hell to start looking for."

Once the four prisoners still in custody were returned, it took the shift supervisor all of one minute to identify the two missing prisoners. The first was Carlo (last name unknown), a fifty-year-old drug trafficker with no record or identity that could be found in any criminal database. Nevertheless, he had been caught during a raid on a distributor the local cops had been watching for some time and had been identified by others picked up in the raid as the boss as well as a dangerous, brutal man. He was arrested and thrown into the El Paso City Jail, only to quickly escape with what had to have been inside help. He was quickly recaptured after he was found falling-down drunk in the company of a prostitute he had hired and bragged to about his escape. The hooker, looking to score some much-needed points with the local cops, turned him in after he passed out. The police were unsure exactly who among them had helped him escape, so he was sent temporarily to the state detention facility until they could root out the traitors among them. The other escapee was Ray Espinoza, a twenty-year-old trafficker and murderer, also with little other history in the computers. Both were considered dangerous, high-value, cartel-connected illegals and were to be held in detention at Fort Bliss until their cases could be resolved; at least that had been the plan.

At 8:00 a.m., just as he went off duty, out of curiosity and out of concern for a fellow professional, the shift supervisor called Captain Gonzales to check on the condition of the MP shot during the escape. The captain informed him that he also had been concerned and had called the Fort Bliss hospital to inquire about the wounded MP, but no one seemed to know what he was talking about. All their ambulances were accounted for, and none had made a run into El Paso that morning. Captain Gonzales said he was following up on this, but he appeared to have a real mystery on his hands, and the captain hated mysteries, especially when traffickers and murderers were involved. The long reach of one of the Mexican cartels had to be involved in this, which was always dangerous for everyone but especially for American law enforcement.

The escape of the two new fugitives, as viewed from their perspective, had begun when they, along with the four other inmates, had been advised at dinner the evening before that they were to be transferred to the new federal detention compound at Fort Bliss early the next morning. This wasn't welcome news; Fort Bliss was a vast military post with far more security than the state detention facility in which they were being incarcerated.

After being awakened and ordered to dress, Ray and Carlo were placed in wrist manacles and belly chains, then coupled together and shuffled out of the cellblock into the sally port of the detention facility and loaded into the military van for transport to Fort Bliss. The transfer vehicle was a typical Chevy heavy-duty van with three bench seats behind the front driver and guard seats. There were heavy mesh security screens on the windows, and a similar heavy mesh panel separated the two military police guards from the prisoners. Both the driver and guard carried standard military-issue M9 nine-millimeter Beretta handguns in their waist web gear, and the guard also carried a short-barreled Mossberg M500 twelve-gauge pump-action shotgun. Five of the six prisoners were groggy due to the early hour of the transfer, and most dozed as the van started to make the short drive from the state facility to Fort Bliss. The one exception among them, however, was quietly alert and filled with great anticipation.

Five minutes and three miles from the detention facility, as the van was traversing a quiet warehouse district en route to Fort Bliss, it was hit broadside by a beat-up pickup that had come out of nowhere. The van skidded across the intersection and crashed into a power pole adjacent to an alley behind a run-down warehouse. The panel that separated the prisoners from the guards was knocked loose, and the driver and the guard were stunned by the impact of the collision and the deployment of the airbags. Ray and Carlo were sitting in the first seat behind the guards and were knocked sideways. Seeing the loose security panel, the young Ray moved fast, pulling a surprised and disoriented Carlo along with him, and grabbed the shotgun from the stunned guard and forced him and the driver to hand over their Berettas and the keys to the restraints. They ignored the pleas from several of the other prisoners to unlock their chains, and once Ray and Carlo were free of their restraints, they made for the side van door.

As Ray was pushing Carlo out of the wrecked van, the guard riding shotgun made a move for what appeared to be a backup handgun, and, to Carlo's surprise, Ray shot the guard with the guard's Beretta and then leaped out of the van after Carlo. They hurried down the alley for several blocks until Ray recognized they were behind a Goodwill thrift store. He dumped the gun he had used in an adjacent trash bin and told Carlo he should do the same. Carlo wanted to keep his, but in a quick, hushed conversation, Ray convinced him that a fast, quiet escape was their only option, especially after the shootout they'd just been through. Carlo finally reluctantly agreed. They found an unlocked window at the back of the store and shimmied through. In just a few minutes, they had shed and hidden their orange jailhouse-issued coveralls and changed into decent slacks, dress shirts, and sport coats. They found a petty cash box in a drawer in the office and a set of car keys hanging on a nail by the rear door. The keys were to a Goodwill collection truck parked in the alley. When they emerged from the back of the store, they looked good, like a couple of typical office workers getting an early jump on their workday.

With Ray behind the wheel, they left the alley in the truck with twenty-eight dollars in their pockets. Ray told Carlo he thought they had at least two or three hours before anyone would show up for work at the store, more than enough time to get miles away and ditch the truck. It had been less than thirty minutes since they had departed the sally port of the detention facility, and in that time, they had managed to get free and get clothes and cash and were miles away, driving west and north on I-10, headed for Las Cruces, New Mexico, twenty miles across the state line. Except for the shooting of the one guard, the escape had been fortunate, quick, and uncomplicated.

Once out of El Paso proper, Carlo, who was almost thirty years older than his young cellmate, took the lead. He told Ray his family business in Mexico maintained a safe house in the area, and he would get them there, where they could stay until nightfall and then make their way south, which was their only possible safe destination. Ray knew before becoming Carlo's cellmate and spending the last three months in jail with him that he had been arrested for narcotics trafficking in El Paso and was somehow involved in one of the Mexican cartels.

As they approached the Las Cruces city limits, they followed the signs for I-25 north, and Carlo directed Ray to the largest shopping center in the Las Cruces area, just off the interstate at the north end of town. They parked the truck in the large parking lot and headed to a restaurant at the edge of the lot, eventually joining the other customers who were gathering for an early breakfast. Dressed as they were in their Goodwill outfits, they looked like the couple dozen professional workers who had stopped in to have their morning coffee and breakfast and scan the newspaper before heading off to work. Carlo called his local contact from a pay phone in the restaurant, and he and Ray sat and ate breakfast while they waited.

When Carlo quietly announced a short time later that his man had arrived outside, they paid their bill, casually left the restaurant, and walked to the rear parking lot. Ray was surprised to see that Carlo's business contact wasn't the dangerous-looking cartel member he was expecting—a type he was all too familiar with—but rather a grandfatherly-looking man in his sixties who neither looked nor acted like a member of a drug organization. Carlo introduced him as his cousin Alonzo, who, to all appearances, looked to be the simple farmer he actually was, dressed as typically as any other farmer in his flannel shirt, worn but clean denim overalls, and broken-in work boots.

The F-150 Ford pickup he had arrived in had definitely seen better days, and after loading his two passengers into the front seat with him, Alonzo drove them to the safe house not ten miles away. Located on a rural fifteen acres covered mostly with pecan orchards, the small, clean stucco house with its inviting front porch and adjacent well-kept barn looked like the many other small farms that dotted this part of the lower Rio Grande Valley south of Las Cruces. Alonzo, who farmed the few acres and grazed a few head of cattle in the pecan orchards, had only one function within the family business—the safe harboring of other members as they passed back and forth through the border security area, for which he was paid a modest but welcome income. Under a portion of the barn, accessed from a tool room inside, was a basement area that contained a bunk room, a bathroom with shower, and a small living room. Although there were no windows, the space was clean, dry, comfortable, and secure. Other than providing cartel members a safe place to rest, eat, and clean up, no cartel business was conducted there. As such, the safe house had gone unnoticed by drug and immigration law-enforcement authorities. Until now.

Now Ray knew of its existence, and as soon as he could contact Bennie Santiago, his control agent in the DEA for his undercover operation, the authorities could begin to keep the farm under surveillance. It was at that moment, after months of patient and dangerous undercover work, that DEA Agent Ray Cruz—or Espinoza, as he was known in his false identity—began to believe that Bennie's plan, as simple as it was in concept, would pay off with good, actionable intelligence. The entire plan had depended on his establishing a relationship with Carlo and then Carlo buying the staged escape that Bennie had orchestrated. Given the nonstop excited chatter from the none-too-smart Carlo during the drive to Las Cruces, especially about

Ray having to "shoot" the one guard, Ray was sure Carlo had been fooled. The trickiest part of Bennie's plan for him, after the crash itself, would be convincing Carlo to toss the weapon if he took one, before he could discover it was loaded with nothing but blanks. Fortunately, he had managed to do that and not raise any suspicions.

Alonzo drove his rusty F-150 directly into the barn and dropped off his two passengers. Around lunchtime, Alonzo's wife delivered a simple meal of tortillas, beans, and a very nice homemade green chili washed down with some tasty cold American beer. Over lunch, Ray learned from Carlo that Alonzo and his wife had migrated north from Carlo's hometown near Chihuahua, Mexico, more than thirty years ago, raised a family—all citizens of the United States since they were born here—and eventually became citizens themselves. Carlo finally admitted to Ray that his family was involved in drug trafficking, had their own organization, and required safe sanctuaries like his cousin's farm in the southern United States. Carlo had been dispatched to southern New Mexico years earlier to remind his distant relative that he owed a debt of honor to his family for their help over the years. With the caveat that there wouldn't be violence or the distribution of drugs on the farm, Alonzo agreed, and the cartel had honored his request.

Once darkness fell, Alonzo again loaded his two passengers into his pickup and headed west on I-10 toward Deming, New Mexico. He turned south on State Highway 11, passing through the isolated town of Columbus, three miles north of the Mexican border. A mile south of town, Alonzo turned east off the two-lane asphalt highway onto what looked like a seldom-used road that gradually climbed into some low foothills. The night was dark, and the headlights from Alonzo's pickup barely lit their way as they bisected nothing but rolling barren desert. Slowly the shadowy shapes of structures emerged, and they pulled into the dirt-and-gravel drive of a run-down adobe-and-stucco house. The collection of rusted-out cars and trucks in the adjoining lot suggested its occupant was either a junk collector or ran some sort of salvage operation. The only light illuminating the incredibly stark landscape was provided by Alonzo's old truck and a quartering moon in the night sky. Carlo embraced and thanked his distant cousin, and then he and

Ray watched in silence as the red taillights of the pickup disappeared into the near-total darkness as Alonzo made his way back west to the highway.

Ray turned and glanced down the slope to the south; the Mexican border lay less than two miles away across the arid landscape, and, on this clear night, in the distance beyond the new imposing border fence, he saw the streetlights and porch lights of the small town of Las Palomas, Mexico. He was anxious but also excited. The code name for his operation was Trojan Horse for the obvious reasons; however, there was never a guarantee that even if he could establish a friendly relationship with Carlo in jail that Carlo would do as Bennie had hoped and schemed and take him south into his cartel. Ray had watched all day for any sign from the outgoing but dangerous Carlo that he might just be eliminated for the obvious security reasons, but no such signs were evident. Carlo genuinely liked him—he could just tell. A dim porch light came on at the house, and Carlo turned and headed for the front door, so Ray quickly followed. Carlo often spoke of how easily he went back and forth across the border. As he joined the older man on the front porch and they entered the dilapidated house, Ray knew he was headed to Mexico.

2

Near Las Palomas, Mexico
Tuesday evening

Carlo embraced the sole occupant of the house and then introduced Ray to the older man, whom he simply called José. Like his cousin Alonzo, José was a taxpaying American citizen, who, in this case, was paid by the cartel to run a dilapidated salvage operation as a front to the business's true function: an embarkation or debarkation point to and from Mexico. This second safe house was also unknown to the authorities but now too would be put under surveillance. José provided them with some bottled water and a flashlight to help them on their journey south. After saying a quick goodbye, Carlo led Ray south and west through the deepening darkness into what seemed to be a dry stream bed that wound and twisted down through the shallow hills of the high desert toward Mexico.

Even with all the focus recently at the border on the hastily erected detention camps and the thousands of aliens being processed weekly and returned to Mexico under the new immigration law, the eight-thousand-officer-strong US Border Patrol, augmented with an additional six thousand specially trained mobile troops of the US Army out of Fort Bliss, couldn't watch every inch of the nearly two thousand miles of wall and fence that made up the just-completed Border Security Structure (BSS). To the border guards and army troopers whose job it was to patrol its many miles, most of which were located in extremely hot, arid, inhospitable landscapes, it was simply known as the BS wall or, more bluntly, when the officers were absent, the "bullshit wall."

For all the millions of dollars of taxpayer money that had been spent on its hasty construction and upgrades in the last twenty-four months, there were serious holes in the wall, and the cartels knew where they were. Prior to the enactment of the new law, this part of the border was protected with nothing more than a ten-foot-high steel plank fence topped with barbed wire, with the occasional metallic sign attached in English and Spanish telling anyone who might come across the pitiful barrier in the middle of the desolate setting that they were to "Halt!" or "*Parada!*" and not cross the fence—as if a few words had the power to discourage the desperate stream of people who had come north over the years seeking a better life. Four members of the Border Patrol had been stationed in Columbus then, but for every one illegal they ever caught, ten or twenty got through, usually after paying a small unreported fee.

In the months since the new immigration law had been passed and funded, the shoddy old barrier in this remote part of the border had been replaced during the crash construction program by the US Army Corps of Engineers with double fifteen-foot-high fences of steel mesh topped with four strands of razor wire that projected out from the top to discourage would-be illegals from climbing over. As if somehow that weren't enough in the mind of some Washington bureaucrat or planner to discourage those attempting to enter the United States undocumented, the new fences were crowned with seemingly never-ending coils of razor-sharp stainless-steel concertina wire that sparkled under the harsh sun of the desert like jewels in a royal tiara. What Homeland Security and Congress didn't know, however, was what the Corps of Engineers hadn't done when they'd replaced the pitiful fence with the expensive, intimidating-looking new one. In their haste to meet the strict construction deadlines, the construction battalions, or the civilian subcontractors who worked for them, hadn't discovered or eliminated many of the very old, well-used tunnels that had been carved into the clay formations beneath the arid desert and that began and ended several hundred feet on either side of the border.

Carlo led Ray south down the stream bed until they came to a typical-looking rock formation along one bank that pinched into the old, dry stream.

Carefully concealed among the large boulders was the entry to the old smugglers' tunnel that Carlo used to pass back and forth under the border. With Carlo providing the occasional light, Ray followed him down the tight shaft into the darkness, slipping and sliding until his footing finally gave way, and he bounced down the last three or four feet to the bottom of the narrow tunnel. With the dim illumination from the flashlight, Ray saw they were in a very rough five-foot-diameter earthen tunnel whose shape disappeared into the darkness to the south. Hunched over due to the low headroom, Carlo led the way for hundreds of feet until the tunnel ended at an earthen face with a crude wooden ladder leaning against it.

Carlo pointed the light toward the shaft overhead and told Ray to go on up until he hit a wooden ceiling and then push it open. After he did as instructed and the ceiling panel gave way on its rusty hinges, he found himself on the floor of a small, dark, narrow room. Carlo followed him through the opening, and his light revealed they were in what appeared to be a kitchen pantry, as three of the four walls were lined with shelves stocked with canned goods. Carlo went to the far end of the room, flipped on the light switch, and, under the glow of a single sixty-watt bulb hanging from the ceiling, turned to Ray and quietly said, "Welcome to Mexico, my friend. Now that we're safely back in our homeland, maybe I'll have a chance to repay the debt I owe you."

"You owe me nothing, Carlo," Ray responded just as quietly. "Where are we?"

"In the house of another friend." He pointed straight ahead. "Through that door is the kitchen. There was no way to let my man know we were coming, and he's a very nervous type and sleeps with his pistol, so we must be quiet. After all we've been through, it would be shitty to be shot by one of my men in one of my houses."

"Houses" plural, Ray thought. *Three so far. Whatever Carlo is, he isn't just some small-time trafficker. Bennie was right; he must be part of a bigger, more sophisticated group. Nice guess, Bennie.*

Carlo lay on the floor as if nothing were out of the ordinary and soon fell into a deep, sonorous sleep, making so much racket that Ray feared

Carlo's friend would be alerted and start looking for the source of the noise. He didn't sleep a wink; between his worrying about what would happen in the morning, Carlo's snoring, and his listening for the sleeping friend with the handgun, sleep wasn't possible.

Just after sunrise, Carlo woke up and, after yawning and patting Ray on the shoulder, told him to stay where he was and said he would get his friend. Carlo slowly stepped into the kitchen and, not seeing his friend, called out loudly, "Gilberto! Wake up, asshole, and fix me some breakfast."

After a few seconds, Ray heard friendly greetings, and then Carlo looked into the pantry and told him to come out. He slowly walked into the kitchen to find a smiling Carlo with his arm around the shoulders of a wiry older man with long gray hair and a beard. The old man was holding an old-fashioned long-barreled .38 Special in his dangling right hand and, even in the presence of Carlo, still had the twitchy eyes of someone who was always very nervous.

"Ray, this is an old friend, Gilberto. We call him El Gato, for he once was as quick as a cat before age and too much mescal slowed him down. Gato, meet my new friend, Ray, who got me out of the American jail."

"It's a pleasure, young one. Thank you for saving my old friend."

Ray simply nodded as they shook hands.

"Gato," Carlo said, now more serious, "we need some food, and then you must take us to the Chihuahua house."

"Of course, Carlo, of course. There's enough food in the refrigerator for a nice breakfast, but the van is at the garage—bad radiator; it will be ready by noon."

Ray could see Carlo wasn't happy, but Carlo let it pass. "Call your mechanic and tell him you must have it sooner. I want to be in Chihuahua by this afternoon. Do you have a cell phone, one of the new ones?"

Gato nodded. "Yes, it's never been used."

"Give it to me. I need to let my brother and cousin know I'm out of jail."

As Carlo made his call, Ray tried to eavesdrop without looking too obvious about it. There wasn't much to overhear. Carlo called whomever he was talking to Eduardo and said he was in Las Palomas and would be in Chihuahua later that day. Eduardo already seemed to know that Carlo and another man had escaped from jail and apparently asked Carlo about that.

"His name is Ray Espinoza," Carlo said. "He was my cellmate for the last three months, and we were being moved to a new prison together. He saved my life when I was in jail, and he's responsible for getting me out."

Whoever was on the other end said something more, but Carlo told him he would explain everything once he got to Chihuahua and then hung up. While Ray and Carlo had a simple breakfast, Gato left to deal with their transportation. It was nearly three in the afternoon, and Carlo was plenty agitated before the old man returned with his rusted-out van, got them loaded, and started out for Chihuahua. It was just over three hundred miles and took five hours before they finally arrived, dirty and tired, at what Carlo called the Chihuahua estate. Ray was sitting in the backseat, using all the powers of his intellect and training to record everything he saw as the van left the highway west of Chihuahua. They followed a narrow paved road up into the foothills until they came to a formal entry gate to a walled estate with dangerous-looking armed guards watching their approach. They appeared to recognize old Gato's van, and, after looking in and seeing Carlo, the guards quickly let them through. Gato slowly drove up the long, winding private road through a forest of small, twisted pines. As they reached the top of the hill, the asphalt road became a circular drive that passed under a beautiful stucco-and-timber porte cochere that extended from a grand house in a large clearing. As they stepped out of the van, they were greeted by several more heavily armed security types who warmly embraced Carlo. Carlo put his arm around Ray's shoulders and led him into the sprawling house.

Everything about the modern hacienda told Ray there was immense wealth here. An uncle of his was a talented carpenter and home builder back in Sacramento and he had worked many summers for him, so he recognized the unbelievable quality of the tall hand-carved wood entry doors as he stepped through them into the foyer. The floor tiles appeared to be handmade also, and the details in the ornately plastered walls had been done just so to set off and frame the fine works of art that hung there. Small, nearly invisible lights illuminated the art in ways Ray had seen only in the one or two fine museums he'd been to in San Francisco. Large hand-carved wooden beams on the ceiling of the foyer seemed to point them toward the main room of the hacienda.

The great room was very large, and the height of the room drew Ray's eye toward the peaked ceiling. From the centermost intersection of timber beams hung an elegant crystal chandelier. At the far end of the room was a massive stone fireplace framed by a cut-stone mantel and matching hearth. Standing in front of it, with warm smiles, were Carlo's brother and cousin. There were others in the room as well; four hard-looking men in fine clothes stood discreetly off to the sides with the focused looks and subtle tension of men whose responsibility it was to see that no harm came to the men they were there to protect.

Carlo walked directly to the strangest and most imposing-looking figure and embraced him, then turned and introduced him. "Pablo, this is my friend Ray Espinoza, and I owe him my life. Ray, this is my cousin and the leader of our family business. He's known as El Condor de Muerte, but you may call him Jefe."

The Condor of Death—pretty dramatic, Ray thought. *Bennie never mentioned anyone down here by that name. But from what Carlo said on the drive here, this guy's a player.*

The Condor, a small tight smile on his face, extended his hand and nodded slightly. "Thank you for returning my wayward cousin to me and his brother Eduardo." With a glance to his left, he said, "Eduardo, this is Ray Espinoza, our Carlo's savior, it seems."

Ray took the Condor's extended hand while nodding at Eduardo, who simply nodded back. The Condor's eyes, concealed as they were by slightly tinted oversize glasses, appeared black and cold. The Condor was several inches taller than Ray, perhaps six feet one or two, very trim, and athletic looking. His wild shoulder-length hair was absolutely white, as was his heavy beard. Ray's first thought was the man looked like the archangel Gabriel from his Sunday-school days, only updated to modern times to include the almost Elvis-like sunglasses he wore and the fine suit of clothes. A member of what he concluded was the security detail passed out heavy crystal tumblers that held a clear liquid. Once everyone had a glass, the Condor looked at Carlo, and then to Ray, and said, "A toast, my friends. To my cousin and boyhood friend, welcome home. And to Ray Espinoza, thank you for your courage in setting him free."

They touched glasses in salute, then drank, and so did the others. Ray recognized the drink as fine aged tequila. After the toast, the Condor turned to him and said, "You must be tired and hungry from your journey, especially after traveling such a distance with El Gato in that rattrap he drives."

The others, their serious countenances broken for the first time, chuckled and smiled. "Raul will take you to where you can get something to eat. Then you'll be shown where you can clean up and sleep."

Carlo turned, warmly embraced Ray, and then stepped back. "Thank you for getting me home, Ray. I'll come get you in the morning. Sleep well."

With that dismissal, he followed the one named Raul from the great room, down a side hall, and into a large commercial-looking kitchen. There were several informal dining tables there and two guard types sitting and having coffee. As Raul walked up to them, they stood, clearly out of respect for whatever position the man held in the organization.

"Have one of the cooks get this man whatever he wishes to eat," Raul told them. "Then take him to the southwest casita and show him where he can clean up and sleep."

Raul turned and looked at Ray with a neutral, unsmiling expression that revealed nothing about him or his intentions. "Please be comfortable and order what you wish," he said. "We'll speak more tomorrow." He nodded, then turned and walked out.

Ray hadn't eaten anything since breakfast, so he was hungry, but with the intimidating introductions to Carlo's cousin and brother, he had lost his appetite. Nevertheless, in order to appear unworried and collected in front of the two guards, he asked for whatever was easiest for the cook to fix. A few minutes later, he was devouring a tasty Mexican omelet dish and a cup of coffee. The two guards never lost their grim looks or said a word the entire time they watched him eat. Finished, Ray stood, and one of the unfriendly-looking guards did likewise and silently led him outside through some French doors, across a fine stone-paved patio, and down a path through the scrub pines and undergrowth. The path was dark, and Ray was on guard until they came to a pleasant-looking stucco cottage that stood against the tall perimeter estate wall. The guard opened the unlocked door to the casita and stood to the side to allow him to enter before speaking for the first time.

"This casita isn't being used. Take any of the beds you find. Everything you require to clean up will be in there," he said, pointing to what was apparently the bathroom. "If you get up before the others tomorrow, it would be best if you waited for someone to come get you. If you wish to return to the main house sooner, stay on the path. There are always other guards around, and those who don't know you would question who you are—some would shoot before asking questions."

With that, the guard abruptly turned and left, and Ray was alone. He watched the man retreat into the darkness, and for the first time in several minutes, he started to breathe normally again. Expecting the worst, he had been tense the entire time they were walking through the darkness to the casita. Months before, during his briefing sessions, Bennie had told him bluntly that if the plan worked and he managed to get into a cartel, the most dangerous period would be the first few hours. There existed the very real possibility that, in the interest of security, he might be shot and killed out of hand. Ray had been less worried about this possibility when he'd been in Carlo's company; he knew his friendship with Carlo, viewed from Carlo's perspective, was genuine. No way did the brute, ignorant Carlo suspect him of being an undercover agent. However, the brief encounter with his cousin, the Condor, and his older brother, Eduardo, had unnerved him. Ray's first impression was that they were smarter and far more dangerous than Carlo. Even the mostly silent one, Raul, gave him pause to remember Bennie's warnings from months earlier. Regardless of Carlo's feelings, Ray had been worried that the smarter leaders might do the sensible thing from a security point of view and simply eliminate him as a potential threat.

After he'd spent several minutes in the dark, just watching and listening, his sense was that the others had accepted Carlo's introduction of him and he was safe for the moment, so he took advantage of the modern bathroom to clean up and take a long, hot shower. It was, Ray thought, the first time in three months that he had showered alone and not in the large gang shower of the jail. Three long months—it had been necessary to spend that much time in lockup to establish trust, and then a friendship, with the burly, tough-looking Carlo. That was the unique part of Bennie's plan, the extended time in lockup—that and Bennie's advice to let Carlo come to him and not the other way around. Ray had kept his distance, and, as Bennie had predicted, the more gregarious older man finally had approached him, and they slowly became friends. Although Carlo was much older than he was (Ray was twenty-six but passing himself off as a twenty-year-old), Carlo thought they were of a similar background and from the same part of Mexico, based on the background story that Bennie had crafted and that Ray had passed on as the two of them lay in the bunks of their cell at night and talked to pass the time.

As Ray slipped into one of the comfortable beds in the casita, he hoped he would see the morning. His instincts told him he was in. Despite Carlo's obvious limitations, he was a serious player in this group, and Ray was his friend and had saved him in the prison yard not a month earlier during a particularly violent fight with some Anglo trash. Potential violence while Ray was undercover in jail was a possibility he and Bennie had discussed during his preoperation briefings. Bennie had been very clear about this; Ray was to maintain a low profile and stay quiet and not risk antagonizing others in the population. His basic nature and police training made this easy to accomplish, but unfortunately, his cellmate was a loudmouthed, stupid, aggressive son of a bitch, which made confrontation almost inevitable.

The inmates were allowed only sixty minutes a day in the yard and only in small groups, but Carlo had managed to quickly piss off every white guy in the population and instigated the fight in the yard that almost resulted in his getting a shiv between the ribs. Ray's powers of observation were keen, and he saw the assailant coming from twenty feet away. It hadn't been difficult to blindside the pissed-off trailer-park trash and disarm him before he could stick Carlo. The guards quickly controlled the altercation, and after they confiscated the white trash's pick and searched the others for more weapons, all the prisoners were returned to their cells and locked down.

Carlo, no stranger to fights or attempted murder, recognized that if it weren't for the help of his cellmate, he would be badly wounded or dead. He solemnly told Ray he was grateful for the help and vowed to return the debt of honor when and if he could. It had been luck—it had just happened—but Carlo was grateful and showed it, and Ray believed that would count for something. Bennie had thirty years of experience running undercover operations, so Ray figured his boss knew what he was talking about when he had said the first few hours in a cartel would be the most dangerous. But it didn't really matter now what Bennie thought or what his instincts were telling him. He had played his part convincingly so far, but his fate was in the hands of Carlo's cousin. But as cold as the Condor's eyes had been, and despite the quick dismissal from the others, something—and he couldn't put his finger on just what it was—told him he was in.

Unable to sleep because of all the thoughts and possibilities spinning around in his head, he spent a great deal of the night sitting on a wooden chair on the small front stoop of the casita, thinking and looking at the heavens. The night was perfect, the sky crystal clear, the air warm and still. It was so dark he could hardly see his hand in front of his face. What little light there was came from a crescent moon slowly disappearing beyond the mountains to the west. He couldn't remember ever having seen so many stars or feeling such awe at a sight. It was at times like this, alone and in the presence of something as infinite and beautiful as the night sky, that the occasional thoughts he had about his spiritual beliefs took hold. In this moment, however, he quickly brushed aside any notions he had about God or divine protection, feeling in his present situation they would appear as nothing more than what they were—the transparent hopes of a frightened soul stuck in a dangerous place.

As Ray's thoughts returned to nothing more than the millions of stars pressing down from above, he felt as if he could reach up and touch them, but they were as distant to him as he was to Bennie. He felt truly alone for the first time in his life. He was anxious, unsure whether he had what it would take to remain convincing and survive within the cartel. But he also knew he must get past his doubts, because as improbable as it may have seemed at times during the planning, Bennie's strategy had worked, and he was in.

3

The estates of El Condor de Muerte
The northern states of Mexico
Day one through eighty

Ray did live to see the new day and many more.

He was napping on the couch in the small living room of the casita on his first morning in the cartel when the thick, round-shouldered Carlo burst through the front door yelling, "Good morning!" and something about needing a big breakfast right now. Nothing about Carlo was subtle or refined. He was built like a bull and led a careless lifestyle, which, coupled with his limited intelligence, had landed him in trouble his entire life. This was evidenced by the behavior that had gotten him caught not once but twice in El Paso, making him Ray's cellmate. True to his word from the night before, however, his "friend" Carlo was here and took him up to the main house and introduced him to the other guards and servants in the dining room as the young man who had saved his life and then had helped him escape from jail in the north. Because of Carlo's obviously high position in the organization, Ray was accepted, if not initially trusted, by the others.

He spent the next twelve weeks working as one of Carlo's personal bodyguards and was part of the larger group that made up the twenty-man entourage that traveled with the Condor de Muerte. He learned that the sprawling hacienda near Chihuahua was one of three the Condor stayed in while running his drug empire in northern Mexico. All were similar looking and located near the capital cities of the northern states of Sonora, Chihuahua, and Nuevo Leon, each of which shared a border with the United States. In addition to the Chihuahua estate, there was one outside Hermosillo and another outside Monterrey.

The surreal, dangerous situation Ray found himself in had been set in motion only seven months earlier. He had met Bennie while working on a joint operation with the DEA as an undercover member of the Sacramento Police Department's drug unit. The success of their joint operation led to an offer from Bennie to join the DEA and his covert special operations unit. Everything that followed happened quickly; there were only a few months of orientation, training, and background research before he assumed his undercover identity and Bennie had him transferred to the El Paso detention facility. Bennie secretly had arranged with the warden for Ray to be Carlo's cellmate, which had led to his friendship with Carlo, their escape from jail to Mexico, his inclusion in the cartel, and now his role as a member of the entourage of a man he now knew was one of the most secretive, powerful cartel leaders in all of Mexico.

Because he couldn't write anything down, Ray had taken to remembering key intelligence or special events by associating them with a day. Day one he was in and had learned who all the major players were; on day four, he had traveled to the Hermosillo estate and learned of the Monterrey estate, and so on. The job of an undercover operative was to develop intelligence, and almost every day since his successful infiltration, he had picked up some valuable piece of information that would be useful to Bennie and the DEA in prosecuting the Condor's associates and businesses in the United States. The problem was that he couldn't contact Bennie as often as they had discussed. Bennie's plan assumed that if Ray was successful, he likely would be a very low-level soldier within the cartel, free to do whatever he wished when not performing assigned duties. That, however, hadn't been the case.

The four bodyguards who protected the Condor were the highest ranking of the soldiers in the cartel. Second only to them were the personal guards to the Condor's cousins and two chief lieutenants, Carlo and Eduardo Vargas. Ray was rarely ever alone in his duties as one of Carlo's guards. And to complicate matters further, each estate had a security room jammed with sophisticated electronic equipment that was manned full-time by at least two men. Instant communications were reserved for very few individuals in the Condor's organization. Only a handful of the soldiers within the entourage—and the four members of the Condor's small inner circle, as his bodyguards were referred to—were allowed to carry cell phones. Get caught with a personal cell phone, and you'd likely be placed against a wall and shot. Obviously, with all the enemies the Condor had cultivated in building and running his empire, he was taking no chances that some lower-level soldier or servant would profit by turning traitor and reporting his real-time location to the police or another cartel.

In addition to the security measures at his estates, the Condor traveled everywhere with a technical staff of two who were in charge of an array of sophisticated-looking laptop computers and other electronic equipment. Along with receiving and sending messages and providing what seemed like a never-ending stream of information for the Condor, the techs provided electronic scanning and monitoring of all frequencies everywhere the Condor traveled. All communications into and out of whichever hacienda the Condor was occupying were monitored by the two mysterious men. Ray wasn't an expert in gadgets, but to his professional eye, all the gear that moved with the Condor appeared top-notch and highly sophisticated, especially what he believed were satellite-capable computers that definitely weren't off-the-shelf products. He thought this electronic sophistication was very unusual for a cartel leader, which was another of the developing indicators that the man wasn't your typical criminal. In the twelve weeks Ray had been inside the cartel, he hadn't been able to learn what all the technical staff was keeping track of or monitoring; he could just tell they seemed to be in communication with many people and did what they did twenty-four seven. This attention to electronic security made it nearly impossible for him to contact Bennie, and he had successfully done so only on two brief occasions, both times within the first four weeks he was inside.

His first successful contact with Bennie came on day fourteen. After two weeks of moving between two of the three large estates, one morning, while at the Hermosillo estate, the Condor and most of the entourage piled into the black Escalades the Condor typically used when they moved and drove off. Carlo didn't go with them, so that meant Ray didn't either. When he asked Carlo about this, Carlo said the Condor had business all over the country, and sometimes he flew, so he was off to meet his plane. The Condor was gone for almost two weeks, and the atmosphere around the Chihuahua estate that Carlo and Eduardo had relocated to with the entourage was more relaxed. Security was still tight, but the soldiers were less tense when the Condor wasn't around.

Late on day fourteen, Carlo mentioned to Ray that they were going into Chihuahua for a little fun. Carlo had an interest in a whorehouse there, and several of the girls were his regulars. Ray quietly said it had been some time since he'd had a woman, but he was thinking that perhaps he could find a way to contact Bennie. Carlo burst into a big smile and told him his drought would end that night. Ray, Carlo, and a driver went to town and pulled into the parking lot of a two-story apartment building several blocks off the city center in an area of dive bars, cheap restaurants, and tattoo parlors. They entered the building and went to a large first-floor apartment, where Ray was shown his choice of girls. He selected a shy young one, not because he was attracted to her but because he was certain she looked more frightened of him than he was feeling about the situation he was in. Everything worked out; Carlo insisted they all drink and party together for a while with their women, and he had no choice but to join in. The driver and Carlo were heavy drinkers and soon got pretty drunk before heading off to their rooms with their women.

Ray was lucky and drew a first-floor end room with his girl. He could see no way not to have sex with the young woman and not raise suspicions, so he did so. While it was enjoyable, it was difficult for him to concentrate while he was plotting how to sneak out for a few minutes and contact Bennie. When he was finished, he got dressed and told the still-frightened young prostitute to stay where she was; he wasn't done with her yet, he said, but he needed something better to drink. He slipped out of the room and went out the end hallway door, unseen, and then across the street to a bustling retail strip area. He found a liquor store and bought a small bottle of a fancy-looking tequila he'd never heard of before, and, from a vendor next door, he bought two prepaid cell phones. Carlo, assuming Ray didn't have money, had paid for everything, as he always did, but Ray had come south with two hundred dollars' worth of pesos that Bennie had given him, which he'd kept hidden for occasions such as this.

Ray slipped into the shadows of the parking lot next to the apartment building and called the number he'd memorized. As expected, after some electronic clicking that he'd been briefed would be part of the encryption system, he reached Bennie and made his initial report, covering everything that had happened to date. The notable intelligence was that he was in a cartel that Bennie apparently knew nothing about. He passed on the names of all the principal players he knew of but told Bennie the best he could do for a name for the Condor was Pablo Vargas, and that was assuming his last name was that of his cousins. He described the safe houses they had used, the tunnel, and also some general information regarding the three northern estates. Finally, he told Bennie how difficult it would be to get messages to him given the security arrangements, but he would try. After hanging up, he quietly broke up the cheap cell phone as much as he could and tossed the pieces in a nearby trash can and returned to his room to find the young woman right where he had left her fifteen minutes earlier. He stripped once again, and, after sharing a drink with her, he did what was expected of him, pleased he had gotten away with his contact report.

The routine was the same at all the estates when the Condor was off doing whatever he did on his secretive travels, with Carlo and Eduardo appearing to run the day-to-day business. Ray spent all his time at Carlo's side as he traveled the local area visiting hidden or disguised factories for meth, warehouses for bricks of cocaine, or fields of poppy and weed that seemed to be everywhere, concealed in the open by legal crops being raised on vast farms the family controlled. The Condor returned several weeks after Ray and Carlo had gone to the whorehouse, and Ray went with Carlo to meet their boss and his private plane on a deserted rural road. To Ray's professional eye, the man always appeared preoccupied. Carlo and Eduardo updated him on business, but in reality, the Condor didn't seem all that interested in the details, which puzzled Ray. Another aspect of the Condor's behavior that bothered him was that as the leader of what appeared to be a large, complex organization, the Condor met with very few people, in or out of the cartel. That job also was left to the cousins and contributed further to the mystery surrounding the Condor.

A week later, the Condor disappeared again for two more weeks. It was during this second absence, on day thirty, that Ray got the chance to go into town again with Carlo. He had his same girl, who seemed very happy to see him, and repeated his moves, only this time telling her he had to make a security sweep. During this second call, he provided Bennie greater details regarding the locations of the three estates, described the routine of meeting the Condor's plane, and gave an overview of the general trafficking operations. Most of the information had to do with sites in Mexico. He knew Bennie didn't trust his Mexican law-enforcement counterparts, so any action on these sites would be put on the back burner for a bit. But it still was all valuable intelligence.

For Ray, most of the days he spent undercover in the cartel were boring. They spent a lot of time hanging around whichever estate they currently were occupying and going out to dinner a lot when the Condor was gone, but they hardly ever left when he was there. Each of the three estates had a permanent staff that cooked and cleaned, and a contingent of guards lived at each estate and patrolled the grounds and the walls. The dozen trusted retainers like Ray, who were included in the entourage that traveled among the estates with the Condor, were charged with the responsibility of doing anything and everything the Condor or his cousins ordered or required. More often than not, this meant performing very menial tasks such as guard duty or errands, picking up dinner from a favorite cantina, or driving visiting business associates of the Condor to and from the estates. But there were times when orders were for far more serious tasks, such as the occasional kidnapping or, worse, executions. Ray had witnessed both extremes in his short tenure with the cartel and thanked God he hadn't been ordered to kill anyone. If that had happened, he would have refused the order, which probably would have resulted in his death.

The one execution he had witnessed was extremely difficult to bear. Day thirty-eight started out routinely for him; the Condor, Eduardo, and Carlo were enjoying a luncheon on the trellis-covered patio of the Chihuahua estate with three very fortunate junior lieutenants from a recently brutally acquired cartel who had been chosen to live and continue to oversee operations on their part of the border. Now, of course, their business operations would be on behalf of the Condor. Eduardo was explaining their new duties to them and the need for total loyalty when four of Eduardo's men dragged a prisoner onto the terrace. As one of the guards assigned to Carlo, Ray was standing behind him when the man was brought in. The Condor proceeded to tell his three new associates that their former leaders had been careless in their operations and had been selling product for quite some time to the American DEA, and the proof of their negligence was standing before them. The man was a corrupt DEA agent out of Texas. After telling the three frightened lieutenants the man's life story and the double cross he had been caught in, the Condor nodded to the men who had brought in the corrupt agent, and he was dragged off the terrace, placed against an adjacent stone wall, and shot, one bullet to the head, but not before the Condor told him he would be seeing his family soon in the afterlife. Such were the intelligence capabilities and the tactics of the Condor.

Ray had stood frozen in horror during the execution. Even though the agent was a criminal and a traitor to the DEA, Ray made no move to try to help a brother agent and simply stood at his post behind Carlo, hoping his professional mask was sufficiently containing the terror he felt as the agent was hauled off and executed in front of him. The first rational thought Ray had following the execution was to try to manipulate Carlo to entrusting the job of killing the agent's family to him and perhaps save them somehow, remain covert, and maybe even hook up with Bennie and pass along what he knew so far. After lunch, as they were leaving the terrace, he volunteered to Carlo that he would be willing to return to the United States and do what was required with the man's family. Carlo smiled, patted him on the back, and told him that wouldn't be necessary; he had men already in place in Texas who could take care of traitor's family, if that was what the Condor wanted. Ray was puzzled at Carlo's response, and it showed, so he asked him, "Are they not to be killed, Carlo, as the Condor said?"

Carlo put a big beefy arm around Ray's slim shoulders, looked around as if checking to be sure no one could overhear him, and responded quietly, "That traitor by his own hand has killed several others, both in the business and the American DEA. He was a greedy pig trying to work both sides of the fence and would kill anyone who came between him and his money—a very bad man, even for our business. But killing that traitor's family is not necessary and not something Pablo does anyway—they're innocents in this matter. What was required was to make those three gutless pigeons now working for us *believe* the family was to be killed. No, now that they've seen the traitor shot, no more violence is necessary. A very bad man is dead, and these new men will be loyal and do as they are told. That's how Pablo does things, but we'll keep that to ourselves, eh, Ray?"

After Ray went to bed that night and thought about everything that had transpired, he knew he had learned another interesting fact about the Condor and his organization. It was apparent that what made the Condor a cut above the trash Ray was used to seeing in the drug underworld was his collection and use of information. There was also the use of psychology, the aura of the mysterious Condor that the man orchestrated. The Condor clearly had an extensive intelligence network that allowed him to take over other cartels, and then, using incredibly simple methods, he made his point with the lieutenants of his new acquisition to cement their loyalty. The one man killed was a murderer and a traitor, yet his innocent family was not to be touched. This was not only interesting but, from his experience, also unusual behavior for a cartel leader.

As the Condor came and went from his mysterious travels and the days passed, Ray came to understand fully the routines, both when the Condor was present and gone. He settled into his part of the routine and felt fairly safe for a while. Undercover work required total concentration every moment one was awake; a covert operative couldn't survive even one mistake. In this assignment, Ray was lucky in that he spent almost all his time around Carlo, and while he was a dangerous brute, he wasn't the least bit intelligent.

He had street smarts, and Ray recognized and respected that, but when it came to him, Carlo had a big blind spot. All he saw when looking at him was a young man he liked and who had saved him in jail. With those thoughts in Carlo's mind, there was relative safety for Ray, and he knew it.

Eduardo, however, was far different. The more Ray was around the older brother, the more he realized just how intelligent he was, maybe even educated formally. He and the Condor required a lot more focus and concentration to fool. Ray usually said very little and did nothing to draw attention to himself. He followed orders and performed every task assigned to him quickly and well. Eduardo really ran things when the Condor was gone, and although Ray saw a lot of Eduardo, he had his own protection, and he and his guards mostly did their own thing and paid him little attention. The big problem, of course, with being one of Carlo's trusted guards and a confidant was that Ray was hardly ever alone, which meant no communications with Bennie. He shared a casita with three others in Carlo's detail, took almost all his meals with Carlo, and, on the rare occasions when he didn't, there were always others around. If that didn't limit his movements enough, this all took place on the estates where the electronic spooks were always doing whatever it was they did. Ray was trapped.

He had carried the second cell phone he had purchased at the time of his first report around with him for two weeks until he made his second report. He wouldn't do so again; it made that two weeks far more dangerous than they already were for him. The likelihood of being caught with the cell phone was dangerously high, and there would be no explaining it. He could always buy a cell phone when another moment like the trips to see the women presented itself, he told himself at the time; however, the bleak reality was that so far, eight weeks since his second report, the moment never had come. Carlo stopped going to the whorehouses after their second visit. There was a similar brothel in Hermosillo that Carlo also had an interest in, he learned, but Carlo simply stopped going there too and was drinking less. Carlo's changed behavior wasn't the only difference Ray noticed. The atmosphere around all the leaders seemed to be subtly changing. Trained as he was to observe people's body language, routines, and mannerisms, Ray sensed something was up. He didn't have any hard evidence, just his intuition, but it never had let him down.

Today was Friday, day eighty of his mission, and the suspicions he had that big events were in the works began to be confirmed. Meetings took place all day just between the cousins, and he could tell that Eduardo in particular was tenser than usual and obviously dealing with or planning something when he had seen him this morning. Ray's guess was confirmed when Carlo took him aside and told him what was planned for that evening. Men were going to die—bad men, to be sure, on Ray's scale of good and evil, but he had been instilled with a sense of justice and the rule of law, which meant warrants, arrests, evidence, and trials. He had arrested many criminals in his young career and had seen them severely punished by judges and juries, but all of it had been done under the name of and for justice. Tonight there would be cartel justice, and it would be sudden and violent. The only good news, if there was any, was that he wouldn't be one of Carlo's shooters.

Late in the afternoon, Ray joined Eduardo, Carlo, and a dozen of their guards in the Escalades and proceeded south down Federal Highway 45. Fifty miles from Chihuahua was the small town of Lazaro Cardenas, where they left the paved four-lane highway and drove east to the tiny village of Rancho El Nido. They pulled to a stop in front of a modest-looking cantina and got out of the Escalades. A tense Eduardo briefly explained their purpose for being here, then gave Ray and the other soldiers their assignments. They were here to meet the two oldest of the notorious Mendoza brothers, the leaders of El Puño Terrible (the Terrible Fist) cartel, old business partners of the family. Rodolfo and Arturo Mendoza had been childhood friends of Carlo and Eduardo's father, Enrique, and their uncle Armando, the Condor's father. Enrique and Armando had taken them under their wing years earlier in the most violent neighborhood of Chihuahua, the Hoyo del Infierno (Hell's Hole), and protected them. The third and youngest Mendoza, Rico, was closer in age to Carlo and Eduardo, and they'd been friends while growing up together.

The relationship between the families began to change when Armando was unexpectedly killed, and his son, a man the Mendozas had thought was long since dead, showed up out of nowhere. He was a strange one to look at, with his long white hair and beard. Enrique explained to the Mendozas that it had been his nephew, the young Pablo Vargas, protected all these years from exposure to the day-in-day-out operations of the business by his father, who had in fact been their source for much of the information that had helped them out all these years. This impressed the Mendozas initially. After rejoining the family, the lost son continued to be a great source of information regarding the police and prosecutors especially and, like his slain father, was well educated and knowledgeable about their business.

Things continued for a while as before, but several years later, after Enrique died from natural causes, Eduardo and Carlo told the Mendozas they were deferring to their cousin Pablo for leadership of their part of the organization. That was when things started to change dramatically. For one, the young Vargases were never around Chihuahua much anymore. It used to be that they lived as they always had in the Chihuahua area, but that changed under the leadership of Pablo Vargas. More often than not, the Mendozas had no idea where their partners were most of the time. Second, there had been occasional but persistent rumors about a new player in the state of Chihuahua—El Condor de Muerte, they heard he was called. They mentioned this to Pablo Vargas, who simply said he was aware of the Condor, and the Condor was aware of their interests, but as there were no conflicts between their businesses, they shouldn't worry about it. With each passing year, as awareness of an organization headed by the mysterious Condor de Muerte quietly grew, the Mendozas occasionally confronted Pablo Vargas about this potential enemy, only to be told that the Vargas family had a business relationship with the Condor similar to theirs, and therefore there would be no trouble. While the Mendozas stayed aware of the growing reality of a powerful cartel run by this unknown Condor, they were never overtly threatened, so they trusted their friends.

What the Mendozas didn't know, of course, was that Pablo Vargas was the Condor and that the cartel of El Condor de Muerte and that of the Vargas brothers were in fact one and the same. Furthermore, the Condor was the one supplying the Mendozas their product—through other proxies—which they then delivered to the Vargas brothers for shipment to the United States. The Mendozas believed they were running a very efficient transshipment business of their own, when they were nothing more than highly visible shipping agents of Vargas-owned drugs from the south to the north of Mexico, unknowingly dancing on the ends of strings like puppets, controlled by the puppet master that was the Condor.

The Vargas family was moving ten times more product out of South America than the Mendozas were involved with. They had no idea they were very small "suppliers." Their chief job in the Condor's organization didn't appear on an organizational chart, nor had it ever been discussed and agreed to. The Condor's father, their old friend Armando, long ago had recognized their many weaknesses and was well aware of the dangers their personalities and personal habits would bring to any organization involved in trafficking. So Armando had set them up initially as a front or decoy. If he helped them succeed, they would attract every police and government organization in the area, as indiscreet as they were. Keeping the police looking over there while Armando and Enrique did their thing quietly over here had been the idea, and it worked. Armando originally assumed his young, dumb friends eventually would get caught, and that would be the end of his little diversion, and he would have to establish business relationships with others. But it became relatively simple to set up information networks in the local police and the courts, especially when the civil servants were paid as little as they were to try to rein in such a dangerous and evil business. While other gangs like the Mendozas were killing off local and state police and justice officials, Armando was buying them off—offering them protection in return for information. Through his network of informants, he was able to mostly protect the Mendozas from themselves and keep them established as one of his most visible and reliable diversions. But where Armando Vargas had some empathy for his old childhood friends, his strange-looking son had none.

The Mendozas arrived at the cantina thirty minutes after Ray and the others. The two brothers, along with their two personal guards, went inside to meet with Carlo and Eduardo. From what Carlo had told Ray earlier in the day, a private room in the back of the cantina was sometimes used for private meetings between the two families. Carlo had posted Ray and another young soldier outside, near the back door of the cantina, when they'd first arrived. While Ray knew what was happening inside, it didn't reduce his tension. It wasn't so much the specific moment that was bothering him—the fact that cold-blooded murder was taking place and he was doing nothing to stop it—it was what this event meant to the changing bigger picture as he saw it. *Why is this happening now?* he wondered. *And why is the Condor killing his father's old friends?*

After Ray had been nervously standing around for a while, Carlo finally came out from the back and told him and the other guard to go in and report to Eduardo. They did as ordered and, upon entering the dimly lit room, were stunned to see the Mendoza brothers with catastrophic head wounds, bleeding out on the unfinished wooden floor, as two of Carlo's shooters kept the Mendozas' two chief bodyguards restrained. Carlo and his other men rounded up the rest of the Mendoza guards from outside without a fight, and, several minutes later, they brought the other disarmed retainers into the back room as well.

As the collection of nervous guards stared down at the bodies of their dead employers, Eduardo began by telling them that if he'd wanted them dead, they already would be. He explained to the frightened group that it had become necessary for the Vargas family to tighten up their business, which meant the elimination of the Mendoza brothers. They had run a bad operation, he said, and were drawing more and more federal attention, which could no longer be tolerated. He then told them he knew they were good men, working for careless ones, and therefore weren't responsible. To Ray's surprise, instead of killing them, Eduardo was trying to recruit them.

The oldest guard and leader, who had been Rodolfo Mendoza's top man for many years, was as surprised as Ray was. Only Ray was concealing his astonishment, whereas the old guard could not. In his relief at having avoided what he had thought was going to be certain death, the older man looked around at his men, who all nodded slightly. "I do wish to work for you, Señor Vargas," he said, "and I know I speak for the others. They're all good, loyal men. They will follow me, but what about Rico? He isn't right in the head and will go crazy when he learns of this."

Eduardo looked stoically at the older, dangerous-looking guard. "Rico is as dead as his brothers. Our people in America took care of this several hours ago."

The guard showed visible relief and then said, "Tell me what you wish us to do."

Eduardo fixed him with a hard look. "Tomorrow, any of you who want to join us go to this address." He handed the leader a card. "We have men there who'll be expecting you. I give you my word that no harm will come to you if you join us."

He then told them there were cleaning buckets and supplies out back, and they were to clean the room and bury the bodies out in the desert. As Eduardo, Carlo, Ray, and the others turned to leave, Carlo looked at the leader and said, "The family that owns this cantina has no idea what has happened here. They are to be respected and left unharmed. Harm them, and you'll have me as an enemy."

The leader of the Mendozas' guards nodded and said they would do as ordered, and with that, the Vargas's left their completely relieved new employees to their grisly task.

Because of his friendship and position with Carlo, Ray rode in the middle Escalade, along with Eduardo and his driver, as they and the others headed back toward Federal Highway 45. The small town of Lazaro Cardenas was five miles to the west of the cantina, and the highway ran past the town on the other side. Ray thought they would be driving back to the estate in Chihuahua, but just short of town, the lead SUV turned north on a narrow, dusty road. After a mile, they came to a small, non-towered dirt airstrip where an eight-passenger, twin-engine King Air sat in the gravel parking area, the right engine running. As they pulled up, the door on the left side of the twin turboprop opened, and the Condor descended the steps and waited.

Eduardo, who was riding in the front beside his driver, turned and looked at Ray. "It's important that Carlo and I get to Monterrey quickly tonight with Jefe. You, Javier, and the others meet us there. I'm sorry we can't take you on the plane with us."

"As you wish, Eduardo," Ray said.

Eduardo and Carlo got out and, after embracing their cousin, followed him up the steps and boarded the plane. The door was pulled closed, the left engine restarted, and the pilot taxied the aircraft to the end of the dirt strip and quickly took off to the north. Ray watched the plane as it climbed out of the area, and then he turned and had a word with the other drivers. As he got into the front seat of the Escalade alongside the young driver, he said, "To Monterrey, Javier. It'll be a long night. Let me know when you want me to drive."

Javier nodded, and they started out on their six-hour drive; it would be two or three in the morning before they arrived. As Javier drove, Ray sat quietly, staring out at the passing landscapes and trying to make some sense out of the Mendoza assassinations.

Day eighty was one Ray would remember. The tempo of events was clearly changing. It was as if events were building toward a climax or a conclusion of some sort; only he hadn't known of anything specific until today's hit. The changes he had observed in the behavior of the Condor and Eduardo during the week had been bothering him, but now, with the Mendoza murders, his anxiety level was rising. Their deaths were particularly troubling, but for reasons he'd never have imagined three months before. In his time inside the cartel, Ray had come to know that while they were a pain in the ass to the Vargas's, the Mendozas served a purpose. But more than that, they'd been their father's friends. Old family and friendship ties meant something to these people—until today. To suddenly kill off the Mendoza brothers was so contrary to the culture he had come to understand that the Condor seemed to believe in. As twisted as it might appear to an outsider, Ray now understood that deep, long-lasting friendships did exist in the world of drugs and violence in which he now found himself. But that was changing. Something big was happening—that was for certain—but what? What had made the Condor do such a thing?

4

The Emilio Rodriguez estate
Colonia Polanco Chapultepec, Mexico City
Sunday morning

For the citizens of Mexico suffering at the hands of the cartels and wondering whether anyone in the government or anywhere else really cared, the answer was yes. Emilio Rodriguez cared; however, the number of people in the Mexican capital who did and had the power to act were few and getting fewer, as they too were dying. As the director of the Federal Investigation Agency, or AFI, as the Mexican equivalent to the American FBI was known, Emilio got up every morning with one thought on his mind: to continue to take the fight to the cartels and traffickers that were intimidating and murdering their way across Mexico, depleting the available resources his country was able to bring to bear on the deportation disaster along the northern border.

Emilio and his older brother, Alberto, who headed up the national police, had been appointed to their positions two years earlier by then newly elected President Ramon Castillo. The president was an old political pro who had come up through the Justice Department and brought Emilio and his old law-school classmate and friend Jacques Alvarez along with him. Alvarez was now the secretary for public security; and the Justice Department, the national police, and the AFI reported to him. Alvarez had wasted no time reorganizing the national police and the Justice Department. Emilio, as the country's chief investigator, now reported to and coordinated with his older brother, Alberto, making their organizations that much more effective. With themselves and their old friend Jacques now in top government positions, for the first time in years the Rodriguez brothers believed they actually would make progress in their war against the cartels.

Emilio, Alberto, and Jacques Alvarez had been close friends ever since they'd met as teens at Saint Matthew's, a private Jesuit prep school in Mexico City. All were the sons and heirs of old, respected, hugely wealthy families that were part of the privileged class of Mexico. What distinguished the three from others of their class was their desire to serve their country publicly in capacities that exposed them daily to potential cartel retribution. All three friends went from Saint Matthew's to the National University, and Emilio and Jacques moved on to law school with an eye toward eventually being prosecutors. Alberto studied public administration and police sciences and established a career in law enforcement. They all entered public service and, due largely to their talents and ambitions, rose quickly in their respective fields. All three attracted the attention of Castillo as he was working his way up in the Justice Department, and he used his influence to promote them in their fields. Years later, after his election to the presidency, Castillo moved them into the top leadership positions of their departments in his administration, making them responsible for taking on the cartels.

Unfortunately for the people of Mexico, sixteen months into his one and only six-year term, Castillo suffered a debilitating stroke, and the Permanent Presidential Commission, the official governmental body responsible for dealing with presidential succession, had no choice but to select an interim president to serve out his remaining term. To the surprise of the Rodriguez brothers and Jacques Alvarez, the commission selected Attorney General Rafael Fernandez as president. Fernandez had gained a great deal of notoriety as a Sonora state prosecutor in the fight against the cartels, but Secretary Alvarez was more senior in the cabinet and, to anyone who knew both men, was the far-superior intellect and leader. Petty politics, however, ruled the private discussions of the commission, and Fernandez was their pick. Several on the commission also had their sights set on the presidency, and the last thing they wanted was to see a talented Alvarez serve out Castillo's term of better than four years and then get elected to his own six-year term. Attorney General Fernandez would be beatable in four years but not Jacques Alvarez.

While disappointed not to see his close friend become president, Emilio was still excited about the possibilities for success against the cartels that he, Alvarez, and Alberto could manage. Working as closely as they did in their government jobs gave the brothers opportunities to implement a few radical ideas known only to them to try to expand their intelligence take on the cartels. The cartels' greatest advantage over them was their ability to buy off informants at every level of government with their huge illicit fortunes. With the intelligence on government plans and actions the cartels purchased or acquired through coercion, they were able to stay a step ahead of the government's efforts to combat them. Emilio and Alberto hoped to alter this equation through an intelligence effort of their own that they privately financed outside their official offices. It was a fight Emilio unfortunately wouldn't see to a successful conclusion.

Emilio, his wife Elena, and their two youngest children were dressed and preparing to leave for mass when his valet stopped him and said he had a call from President Fernandez. Emilio stepped into his study off the foyer to take the call, surprised not only that the president was calling on a Sunday morning but also that he had called him at all. Usually it was his friend, Secretary Alvarez, or his brother who called with anything important. The president was terribly sorry to interrupt his morning, he said, but some important information had come to him through sources other than the AFI, and he needed Emilio's immediate review and comment on the information. Emilio told the president it would be no bother at all to postpone mass and drive to Los Pinos, the president's official residence, and he would be there in twenty minutes. Emilio returned to the foyer, where his wife and kids were patiently waiting, and gave them the news. He would take the waiting cars and go meet with the president, and they would attend mass together later in the day, perhaps even go out for a nice dinner afterward. Emilio kissed his wife and children, went out the front doors, and informed his head of security of the change in plans.

As was typical for affluent citizens and important people in the government, especially those whose business it was to take on the cartels, Emilio traveled in armored limousines with a minimum of two chase cars and six heavily armed bodyguards. Kidnapping was the major threat they were prepared to prevent, but assassination also was a risk. For all his great intellect, and while he was aware of all the potential threats, Emilio deep down believed he'd risen high enough in the government to be an untouchable target for the worst criminal offenders in Mexican society. Few serious attacks had been made on high federal officials; it was as if the cartel leaders, however ruthless and ignorant they might have been, understood the enormous potential downside to raising the stakes in their war if they moved beyond state-level officials in their violent crimes. Emilio's life and career had been marked by a series of brilliant legal actions and public policies; it was tragic he could be so wrong about the appetites and plans of some of his enemies.

The team of assassins lying in ambush outside the gates of his estate west of downtown Mexico City had reconnoitered the area carefully and planned their attack professionally. The residents of a neighboring estate, an old prominent attorney and his wife, as well as their personal domestic staff of five, were all dead, murdered by the assassins during the night so they could have the run of the grounds as they set up for their attack. The six different shooters, spaced at intervals along the top of the tall privacy wall of the neighboring estate across the narrow, treelined residential street, had selected their fields of fire carefully. The training they had received as soldiers in Mexico's military years before had made them experts in the attack they were about to launch as Emilio's motorcade rolled through the heavily protected gates of his estate.

Equipped with a *Ruchnoy Protivotankovyy Granatomyot*—the world's most common handheld antitank grenade launcher—the assassins launched the first of the RPGs, which struck Emilio Rodriguez's armored limousine squarely at the base of the windshield, shattering the bulletproof glass and killing the driver instantly under a fusillade of shrapnel propelled by the significant explosion and resulting shock wave. Emilio surely must have had last thoughts despite the surprise attack, but they would have been fleeting, as the second small missile passed through the gaping hole left by the first and detonated deeply in the limousine's interior. The force of the 2.5-pound high-explosive round killed Emilio and his chief aide instantly. Identification of the few remains would have been difficult had the occupants of the vehicle not been well known to the investigating authorities.

As quickly as the attack had begun, it was over. The highly paid assassins withdrew according to their well-thought-out escape plan before the echoes of the shattering explosions had died away. The smoking hulks that once had been expensive armored luxury vehicles continued to burn, fouling the pristine Sunday-morning air of the exclusive Mexico City residential area, as the high-pitched wails of distant sirens drew near.

Several miles away and twenty minutes later, Alberto Rodriguez was alone in the sitting room of his master bedroom suite when the call came in. The commander of the capital police force said he had the sad duty to inform the head of the federal police that his brother had been assassinated as he was leaving his estate. His officers were cordoning off the area and securing the scene for the impending investigation, and he offered Alberto his most profound condolences.

"What of his family, Commander?" a deeply shocked Alberto asked quietly, his heart heavy.

"Safe, sir, and under the protection of a dozen of my men within the estate. They were in their home and not in the motorcade."

Alberto closed his eyes and thanked a merciful God for that. He knew Emilio and his family regularly attended mass together at this hour, and it was a miracle that Emilio was alone in his motorcade. The police officer in him wondered how that was possible, and he planned to look into that question, but getting Emilio's family out of danger was clearly his first responsibility, especially after he had just failed his brother so tragically.

Upon hearing the news, he knew the attack had to be retribution by the one calling himself the Condor, who unsuccessfully had tried to coerce him several days earlier and threatened his family in the process. Until just recently, Alberto had read or heard very little about a gang or cartel leader called El Condor de Muerte. Mostly there were just rumors and few facts, until the clandestine intelligence operation he and Emilio were privately running began to reveal the Condor's existence.

Alberto had been surprised that an unknown criminal—and, he assumed, a small-time player in the grand scheme of things—had made such an attempt to coerce him. He felt good about having gotten his own wife and children safely to the United States, all the while supposedly being closely watched by the Condor and his people under the threat of violence. The Condor had underestimated him last Friday, and he cleverly and boldly had sent his family away to safety. But it turned out Alberto also had underestimated the Condor, and Emilio had paid the price for his arrogance. That was a painful reality he would have to live with for the rest of his life, and he vowed not to make that mistake again.

He knew now that he must do for his brother's widow and her children what he had failed to do for Emilio—protect them and get them to safety. He picked up his private cell phone and made the necessary calls, setting into motion the process to ensure their safety. He then had to get to the US embassy and see a military officer he knew there, for there were certain discussions he couldn't have over any communication system belonging to his country.

Quarters No. 1, Fort Bliss Army Base
El Paso, Texas
Sunday morning

Lieutenant General Manuel "Manny" Rodriquez, United States Army, hung up the telephone and looked intently out the window of his kitchen, trying to process the news from Alberto of his cousin Emilio's assassination. As hard as it must have been for Alberto, he also felt as if he had just lost a brother. His emotions bounced back and forth between great sadness and extreme anger, and he was having trouble deciding which he felt at the moment. As a soldier with a half dozen battle stars adorning the many campaign ribbons he wore on the chest of his uniform, Manny had seen far more than his share of violent deaths. Yet the assassination of his cousin Emilio hit him especially hard. He turned to his wife, Beth, who was quietly sitting at their breakfast table, having heard only one side of the conversation, and filled her in. As a strategic planner of battles in his many years in the army, he would wait until his cousin Alberto sent him the details on the assassination and then would analyze the data and let Alberto know what he thought. Perhaps he would see something in the reports that would help Alberto catch those responsible for Emilio's assassination. It was something he dearly wanted to do.

Manny and his family had taken occupancy of Quarters No. 1 at the sprawling military reservation outside of El Paso soon after he had assumed command of Fort Bliss two months earlier. This morning's tragic news really had started two days before, when he was winding down his workweek in his office late Friday afternoon. His command sergeant major had buzzed him on the intercom and said a call had come in on the secure military communication system (MCS) from a man saying he was Alberto Rodriguez, the general's cousin. Manny was surprised—not to hear from Alberto, as they kept in close touch, but because his secure military line was his means of contact with his superior commands, such as the chief of staff of the army in DC or the commanding general at the US Army Forces Command (FORSCOM) in Atlanta, as well as his subordinates. He was puzzled how his cousin could be calling him on his secure military network. He took the call nonetheless, and, after the requisite electronic clicking sounds that indicated the call was being processed by the encryption systems, he said, "Al, good to hear from you, compadre, but you have me at a disadvantage—how the hell did you get this number?"

"Hola, Manny. I'm sitting in the office of Colonel Montoya, the military attaché at your embassy here in Mexico City, who has graciously placed this call on my behalf. It was most urgent I speak with you, and in the securest of ways."

"Well, please tell the colonel I'm grateful for his assistance," Manny said. "What's on your mind?"

"Maria and the children are en route to your base in one of your country's DEA business jets. They should be there within the hour. There was an attempt to compromise me earlier today, and with it a very real threat against the lives of my family. Considering the source of this threat, I had no choice but to act quickly. I managed to have Maria and the kids evacuated from our estate by helicopter late this afternoon and taken directly to General Ramos Airfield outside the city and placed under guard. An official from your DEA was in Mexico City, consulting with us on issues of mutual concern. Through him I contacted Theodore Mills, your DEA director, and he was most kind to accommodate my request that my family be flown to safety in your country. I was told Señor Mills will be contacting you in this regard, as I requested they be flown to your base."

"Jesus, Alberto," a very alert, concerned Manny said as he sat up in his chair. "Everyone's OK, you say?"

"Yes. They're all a little shaken up, but the flight should settle them down. Hasn't Señor Mills contacted you?"

"This is the first I've heard about this," Manny said, "but don't worry about that. We'll see that their flight gets the clearances they need, and of course Maria and the kids will stay with Beth and me."

Alberto let out a sigh of relief. "*Gracias*, Manny. It's been a long, bad day."

"Can you tell me the nature of the threat?"

"Yes, but not at this moment or in this way. I don't mean this as a sign of disrespect or distrust toward Colonel Montoya or his offices, as they've been most helpful, but this is something that can only be discussed face-to-face. As soon as I can arrange it, I'll come see you and my family and explain everything to you then."

"Not a problem," Manny said. "Call me when you can, and in the meantime, don't worry about Maria and the kids. We'll take good care of them."

"Gracias, Manny. Good-bye."

"Adios, Al." Manny placed the receiver in its cradle, reflected for a few moments on the seriousness of what his cousin had just told him, then yelled, "Sergeant Major!"

Command Sergeant Major Jefferson Green, all six foot four, two hundred fifty pounds of him, opened the general's door and walked briskly in, stopping at attention precisely two steps in front of his desk, and said, "Yes, General?"

To Manny, his senior noncommissioned officer looked exactly the way a command sergeant major with thirty years of service should look—erect in bearing, with a totally squared-away personal appearance; always crisply dressed, even in his dungarees—and nothing on the base, much less in the ranks, missed his sharp, experienced eye.

"Jeff, call the base tower and tell them that in about an hour, a DEA business jet inbound from Mexico City will want permission to land, and I want it granted. I want the aircraft taxied and parked in one of the hangars out of sight, and I want this kept quiet and secure."

"Yes, sir, immediately. With respect, sir, does the general desire that I should know what the fuck this is all about, sir?"

Manny shook his head and chuckled. He and Jeff had served together on many occasions over the last twenty years, beginning with Manny's first deployment in the Middle East during the first war with Iraq. Jeff had been one of his platoon sergeants back then and had helped patch him up after a firefight with the Iraqis had left him badly wounded. As a staff sergeant twenty years ago, the sergeant major had little use for young, West Point educated, ring-knocking infantry officers, thinking most of them were a walking pain in the ass with lieutenant's butter bars on their shoulders and not an ounce of sense above that. But the young Lieutenant Manny Rodriguez had proven to be the exception to that holy writ. Then Staff Sergeant Green was only too willing to admit that the lieutenant had maneuvered their troops skillfully and with great courage under fire and had saved lives, including his. As far as the sergeant major was concerned, the years had proved there wasn't a finer commander in the army, and he was proud to serve under him. As Manny rose in the ranks and held various command positions, he often had selected Jeff to be his top sergeant. Unless he turned down the position to remain at Fort Bliss with his general, in two years Jeff was slated to be the next command sergeant major of the US Army, the top enlisted rank, and posted to Washington, DC.

"Jefferson, old buddy," Manny said, "when I find out exactly what the fuck is going on, you'll be the first to know. All I do know is that the family of my cousin Alberto in Mexico City was physically threatened today, and it was necessary to get them the hell out of Dodge."

"Yes, sir, of course. Sorry as hell to hear that. I'll meet the plane personally, sir."

"Thanks, Jeff, but I'll go. Probably a good idea if you go with me, though. Also, I'm expecting a call from the director of the DEA in Washington, so put it through immediately."

Jeff nodded, did a perfect about-face, and left the office as Manny punched in the number of his residence on his base phone. A few minutes later, as he was on the line explaining to Beth that they were going to have company under unusual circumstances, Jeff stepped back into Manny's office and picked up the receiver to the secure telephone on the general's desk, punched a button, and announced tersely into the set, "Director Mills, please hold for the general, sir."

He pushed the Hold button and stood there clutching the receiver until the general was finished with his call. Manny told Beth he'd get back to her, took the receiver from Jeff, and punched the correct button. After a few introductions, Manny told the DEA director in Washington that he'd just been on the phone with his cousin and was aware of the situation. Director Mills filled him in on who exactly would be on the jet, and they agreed to talk again soon. Manny hung up and sat quietly for a few moments, reflecting on everything he had just learned and realizing he was deeply disturbed. Alberto always had been one of the coolest customers he knew, so he was taken aback by the tone of his obviously distressed cousin. He shook off his ill feelings, and he and his sergeant major went to the airport to meet his cousin's family. True to Manny's word, that terrible Friday ended with Alberto's family safely settled in with Beth and the kids.

The forty-six-year-old Lieutenant General Manny Rodriguez struck an imposing figure, even when dressed in the nylon-and-cotton camo army combat uniform he usually wore around the huge grounds at Fort Bliss. Still an athletic and trim six feet two and 210 pounds, he was viewed by almost everyone who knew him personally or professionally as a true modern-day warrior. Manny's father Henri was the brother of Alberto and Emilio Rodriguez's father Ernesto. Henri had come to the United States upon his graduation from the National University in Mexico City to pursue graduate studies in international business at the University of Texas and had decided to stay. He had met Manny's mother on the first day of classes, and that had been that, as they say.

Manny had many interests while growing up, but early on, during high school, he dreamed of nothing else but a career in the army and eventually easily earned one of the two appointments granted to the senior US senator from Texas at the time. From the first day he entered the parade ground at West Point, he knew he had found a home, and he excelled at every level. By his fourth year, he was named brigade commander, the top cadet rank, and graduated third overall in his class. As brigade commander, he earned the right to have his choice of duty assignments and picked the Airborne Infantry and Ranger Schools. Manny gave his choice of specialty in the army a lot of thought and concluded that the light infantry was where he wanted to be.

Advancement in the US Army is available to all and largely dependent upon the intelligence, education, experiences, and skills of individual officers. The very best young officers followed a proven similar path up the command ladder, from small unit commands to senior staff positions and eventually to the command of battalions, regiments, and divisions. During the slippery climb up the ranks, more education was required for the few who had earned the right to be selected to attend the army's advanced officer schools. In addition to the army postgraduate schools, officers with their sights on general rank also earned postgraduate degrees at other universities in a variety of subjects intended to round out their personal and professional experiences. This rigorous path up the ladder for the most part identified the truly best and brightest of the officer corps and resulted in senior officers of enviable educational and command-experience backgrounds. Most of the officers who achieved the lofty position of general officer had earned it, for anything less than outstanding fitness reports anywhere along the climb could derail a career as quickly and decisively as a head-on collision with a train.

From Manny's first command as a platoon leader assigned to Bravo Company, First Battalion of the Seventy-Fifth Ranger Regiment at Fort Benning, his career followed an aggressive path up through the ranks. He assumed command of an infantry company in Desert Storm, in what history now calls the First Persian Gulf War, when his captain was injured in training and couldn't carry out his duties. He was seriously wounded and decorated twice for leadership and courage as a result of several night actions he had conducted as the acting company commander against elements of the crack Iraqi Republican Guard. For Manny, however, the best thing to come out of his first unit-command experience wasn't the Distinguished Service Cross or Silver Star medals he had earned—and the recognition and respect that went with such high honors—but rather his close friendship with Jefferson Green. Nevertheless, because of his cool, courageous leadership during the deadly actions in the harsh desert, his career had been brilliant and noticed.

As a highly decorated junior officer, Manny quickly received promotions and choice assignments. During a two-year staff assignment in Washington, DC, while recovering from his wounds from Desert Storm, he had the opportunity to further his education and did so by earning a master's degree in international relations from Georgetown University. For the next twelve years, he continued to receive early promotions and assume commands in increasingly higher and more important positions in the army. The years also saw him involved in nearly every overseas deployment made by the US military. Manny's actions as a combat commander in Somalia, two more tours in Iraq, and one in Afghanistan saw him decorated time and again for his leadership and courage under fire. Between overseas deployments, he continued to further his education with appointments to the US Army Command and General Staff College in Fort Leavenworth, Kansas, where he earned a second master's degree in military arts and science, and then the US Army War College at Carlisle Barracks, Pennsylvania, where he received his third postgraduate degree, a master's in strategic studies.

On the twentieth anniversary of his graduation from West Point, Manny achieved a significant accomplishment in the life of a career military officer when the president nominated him to the rank of brigadier general. His appointment didn't go unnoticed within the military establishment, for it was a remarkable achievement to have reached flag rank in just twenty years, and he was the first of his academy class to do so. Since his appointment as brigade commander at the Point, he had been on a fast track to the "star" he received. His courage and leadership in battle earned him even more respect and admirers in the upper ranks, and at the time of his appointment to brigadier general, there didn't exist in the US Army a more highly decorated, battle-tested colonel, and there were few better-educated ones.

Despite Manny's training and experience, as well as the awesome military power he now commanded, he felt completely powerless as he stood in the kitchen with Beth. One thing his new command quickly had taught him was that the enemy he was charged with containing, the brutal and elusive cartels of northern Mexico, were as dangerous as any he ever had fought. The miserable part of the assignment was that all he was empowered to do was contain or intercept and keep the bastards south of the border. Of the fifty thousand troops under his command, only the six thousand troops of the recently organized US Border Corps were doing any effective soldiering. And then there was little they actually did except make their general presence known with endless patrolling up and down the nearly two thousand miles of wire. This dirty, thankless task was augmented by the intelligence take from his squadrons of Predator drones that patrolled the skies each day and watched for the elusive enemy from overhead. *Glorified camp guards*, he thought more than once—only the camp was Camp USA.

South of Manny's picket wire, real fighting was going on against the cartels of Mexico, and his cousins were at the front lines of that battle. These heavily armed criminal organizations were rampaging and killing all over northern Mexico, protecting their profitable business interests, and it was his cousins with their police forces and law books who had been doing the real fighting—only now, one of them was dead. It didn't take three silver stars on your shoulders to understand that the good guys were losing—and losing big—down there. They were outgunned, outfinanced, and, as far as Manny could see, outfoxed when it came to intelligence information, the absolute bedrock of requirements for an effective combat leader. The Mexican authorities, and his cousins in particular, were constantly looking to expose and prosecute traitors in their own camps, bought off with small pieces of the billions the cartel leaders reaped in profits every year, if the report given to him recently by the DEA was to be believed—that, or as with the very recent attempt with Alberto, officials were being coerced into turning dirty to keep their families safe from retribution. Very few of the Mexican leaders carrying the fight to the cartels could pick up the phone and get their families safely tucked away on a secure US base, as Alberto's family now was.

Deep in thought as he was, Manny didn't hear Beth at first as she broke the silence of the somber moment. He turned away from the kitchen window and said, "I'm sorry, honey. What did you say?"

"I was just asking about the funeral. Everything seems such a mess. Will there be one down there?"

Manny shrugged. "Normally, sure, babe, but as you say, things are indeed a mess down there. I really don't know what Alberto will do. He'll want to have one, of course, but the security arrangements will be a bitch, especially if we go down there with Maria and the kids. We'll just have to wait and see."

As he turned back toward the window and stared off into the distance, he felt his grief turn to anger. *I have to find a way to help Alberto, but how?* he thought. *I don't make policy—I just enforce it. But I swear to God, I won't just sit here on this side of the border with my thumb up my ass and watch him get killed too.*

5

The estate of El Condor de Muerte
Monterrey, Mexico
Monday morning

Ray woke up early. He showered and shaved, dressed in one of the gray two-piece suits Carlo had bought for him soon after he had joined the cartel, and quietly left the casita he shared with three other guards of the entourage. He made his way up the path to the main house, entered through the rear doors into the kitchen dining area reserved for the staff, and grabbed a cup of coffee from the large urn the cooks always had ready. The actual shift change for the guards would occur in another hour, and his station would be wherever Carlo was. Ray made a habit of relieving one of the overnight guards in the main hall earlier than scheduled in order to further cement his relationship with the others and also to give him a place to quietly contemplate events, commit to memory any important intelligence he learned, and calm himself and prepare for the coming day.

He went into the impressive main hall of the hacienda and quietly walked up its stately length toward the well-guarded north wing, where the Condor's suite and those of the four members of his inner circle were located. He nodded in recognition to the older guard standing post there and offered to relieve him. He had no doubts the older man would accept; standing at this post from two until seven in the morning was boring and tiring. Those chosen to guard the north hall did so with a great sense of seriousness and purpose but also out of fear. One didn't doze off at such an important post and get caught by Francisco or Raul, the Condor's two senior and most-trusted guards.

As the older guard walked off, grateful for the early relief, Ray leaned against the wall and closed his eyes to gather himself. Today was day eighty-three in the cartel, and with each passing day, he found himself having to muster additional concentration and control to maintain his cover. He and Eduardo's young driver, Javier, had arrived in Monterrey early Saturday morning following the mess with the Mendozas and had been given a rare day off. Yesterday had been quiet and spent entirely on the estate, but with the Condor around, things would be happening—Ray was sure of that. He was tired, not physically but mentally. In order to make those around you comfortable and accepting, *you* had to look comfortable; that was one of the basic tenets of staying covert. The problem was that Ray was feeling anything but comfortable. He was surrounded by highly intelligent, observant people—successful people in their own way—who paid attention to details as much as he did.

The Condor and his cartel were mostly unknown to the DEA; this fact still stunned him. From his preparation prior to his insertion, he was aware of the six major cartels and a dozen lesser but still dangerous ones that operated in Mexico. The cartel Ray was in wasn't on anyone's radar, yet it was clearly equal to—or perhaps even stronger, more cunning, and dangerous than—those he had studied. For certain there were three cartels on Bennie's list—such as the now-dead Mendozas—that were nothing more than fronts for this one. People smart enough to engineer that sort of organization over many years were smart enough to sniff out a covert operative in their midst. That thought was never far from Ray's consciousness; as such he was having trouble sleeping at night.

He was a quiet man by nature but even more so since he had infiltrated the cartel. To his luck and amazement, from what he could determine, the other guards and staff had simply written off his reticence to youth and shyness, while the leaders had commented on his seriousness and respect for one so young. Ray stopped wondering how the various groups had arrived at their particular conclusions about him and gratefully accepted them; their erroneous conclusions were keeping him alive. He hadn't come close at all to falling out of character, but it took a lot of energy to make that so.

He had been giving the assassinations of the Mendozas a lot of thought since Friday night. The ambush and murder of the brothers must have served a purpose greater than what he had overheard Eduardo telling the captured guards. Even in the short three months he had been in the cartel, he realized how crude and careless the Mendozas were. Their bad habits had just made them that much more visible to the government and obscured the influence and importance of the Condor that much more. The perfect smoke screen, and you eliminate it? It didn't make sense to him; therefore, he reasoned, there had to be a greater purpose, a more important reason or objective, but what was it?

More than ever, Ray was convinced there were more serious plans in the making. Even with the Condor and his inner circle of four guards and two senior communications technicians away, Carlo and his more cerebral older brother, Eduardo, were spending a lot of time in the Condor's study in private meetings. Eduardo in particular was growing more serious. Ray was reasonably sure he was in charge of running the Condor's intelligence network; he shook his head at that thought. In truth he had no idea what sort of intelligence-gathering operation the Condor and Eduardo had up and running, just that there was one and it apparently was very effective. In all the operations or actions Ray had observed, this cartel's enemies or competition stood little chance because of information available to the Condor. *Ducks in a barrel*, he'd thought on more than one occasion.

As an experienced undercover operative, Ray knew the value of patience. He would wait, observe, and learn, and then, if all went well, somehow report. Whatever the Condor and his close associates were planning would become known in time, and he would have even more valuable intelligence to pass on when the opportunity presented itself. Not being able to communicate with Bennie was wearing on him, but that was a reality he had to accept. To force an opportunity to communicate was too risky, as the Condor's security apparatus was too sophisticated. The people around their leader took protecting his safety very seriously. Ray would wait it out, hoping an opportunity would come, and soon.

The Condor was here, which meant everyone would be on their toes, more serious in all their actions or responsibilities. His aura did that to people. Ray had given a lot of thought to just what it was about being in the Condor's presence that affected people so strongly. For visiting business associates and entourage members alike, the aura around the Condor created fear. Over the last twelve weeks, Ray had deduced that much of that aura was, for lack of a better description, an act. The man on occasion acted—he *wanted* others to fear him, yet Ray's sense of the man was one of distracted or preoccupied civility. He didn't sense evil in the man, which was a strange feeling to have about a cartel leader, but he trusted his intuition.

The Condor was an enigma to him. Ray was certain he cultivated that perception, but as to why, he could only guess. Even his self-created name seemed to be all about perception, a metaphor no doubt for the majestic bird, so beautiful in flight but a carrion eater on the ground, typically feasting on the large carcasses of the dead. Even with the absence of evil, Ray couldn't help but to think that the carrion for the Cóndor de Muerte seemed to be the countries where he conducted his illicit business. Still, there was far more to the man than first met the eye. While he had proved to be ruthless when he wanted to be, as demonstrated by the execution of the dirty DEA agent he had witnessed, the act wasn't capricious or random. There was always calculation in the Condor's actions, all done for a purpose, leading to other seemingly more important actions. This brought Ray back around to Friday's murders of the Mendozas. The more he thought about it, the more troubled he became.

He was deep in thought when he heard someone approach from the kitchen end of the mansion. He looked up and saw the large, round-shouldered Carlo, a wide smile on his face, lumbering up to him. Carlo wasn't tall, but he was thick, with strong shoulders, beefy arms, and a menacing presence if you didn't know him. When he was with his friends or relatives, however, the man almost continuously smiled. It bothered Ray a great deal that Carlo was so likable. He wasn't intelligent like the Condor, Eduardo, and the mysterious Raul, but he was cunning and street smart, which made him dangerous in his own way. Ray was grateful for the unabashed affection Carlo had for him; within that camaraderie was safety, such as it was for him.

"I thought I would find you here," Carlo said softly as he walked up. "You made Jesus very happy with the extra hour of sleep he'll now get. Come…let's have some coffee before the others get up. I have a few things to go over with you. I'll send one of the others to take this post."

Ray followed the older man toward the staff dining area. After Carlo sent one of the other guards they found there to the hall, they sat down and ordered breakfast from the young woman serving them before Carlo went on.

"Jefe has an important meeting later today with a couple of assholes we do business with, Barega and Vasso. Both believe they run their own businesses, but, as with the Mendozas, it is we who control them. As is usual with these meetings, Eduardo will be the Condor's second, and each will be allowed one security man. The rest of us must stay outside on the streets. It's understood that weapons aren't allowed at the meeting, but it's permitted for each security team to check the others. There's no offense in this; everyone understands the need for security. Francisco will, of course, be the Condor's guard, and Raul usually acts as Eduardo's, but today I want to change this. When I meet with Jefe and the others this morning, I'm going to ask that you be Eduardo's security."

Ray was surprised and suddenly very anxious. The last thing he wanted to do was spend any more time than necessary around the Condor and the other leaders; they were just too damn smart. He shook his head. "Me, Carlo? This seems too important. I wouldn't know what to do, how to act."

Carlo smiled his big, toothy grin. "You're perfect for this, more so than you know. I say this with respect—you aren't dangerous to look at, but I know how dangerous you can be. I remember well how you handled that trash in the prison yard and protected me; you would do well to remember that too. You have good instincts, and you have your knives, my friend. I don't trust the two my cousin will be meeting, and I want him protected today and Eduardo protected as well. That's why I want you as his second. You don't look threatening, so I believe you'll be able to get your knives past the security check. I wanted you to know my plans so that when I call for you later, you'll be prepared. You can do this, Ray. It's important."

Ray didn't like the idea of his participation in this at all, and he was certain that despite his training, some of his consternation showed on his face, but it wasn't revealing in a dangerous way to Carlo. He knew what Carlo saw in his face was to some extent to be expected of a new member of the cartel when he was asked to do something important for the first time.

"I'll do whatever you wish, Carlo," Ray calmly stated.

After breakfast, the Condor gathered his inner circle with Carlo and Eduardo in his study. As was his duty as a personal guard to Carlo, Ray took up a position outside the closed door and, like the other guards in the main hall, waited.

Several hours passed before the door opened. Carlo made eye contact with him, indicating for him to come in. The Condor was sitting at his impressive desk with Eduardo and Raul. The others of the inner circle, the older and serious Miguel and Francisco, and the younger and always cross-looking Luis, were standing against the opposite wall, arms folded, watching as usual. Ray followed Carlo and stood before the Condor's desk as Carlo returned to his seat. The Condor had an almost warm smile on his face as he looked up at him.

"Good morning, Ray," he said evenly. "It seems my cousin doesn't think too highly of the business associates I'll be meeting later today and has asked that you be included in our party as security for Eduardo. He's told me of your skill with knives. Is this true?"

"It is true that I prefer knives to guns, Jefe, and carry two on me."

"Show me, please," the Condor said conversationally.

Ray slid the sleeves of his suit coat and shirt up enough to reveal the scabbard on his left arm, which held his Heckler & Koch four-inch auto-opening switch knife, then took off his coat and turned around so the others could see the much larger scabbard strapped over his shirt in the middle of his back, which held his fourteen-inch Jungle Master bowie knife with its nine-inch serrated blade. In the first few days after Ray was brought into the entourage, Carlo had offered Ray his choice of several Glock .40-caliber pistols kept at the hacienda. He declined, choosing instead the two knives that were available from Carlo's private arsenal. Knives had been sort of a hobby to Ray, and as a result, he was very quick and skilled at handling any number of different types, especially the four-inch auto-opening H-K, which was exactly like the one he had back home. After he had joined the police force in Sacramento and started to work undercover, having a well-hidden knife or two had been like a having a security blanket.

"You see, Pablo, no one will think to check either place for a weapon," Carlo offered.

The Condor looked unconvinced and unconcerned to Ray, then confirmed this when he responded, "Perhaps, but I still don't see the need for weapons. Vasso and Barega simply don't have the intelligence to harm me, and if they were planning something, I would've heard about it. Little happens in their groups that we're unaware of."

"And yet," the reserved Raul said, speaking up for the first time, "how many times have I heard you say, 'Never underestimate our enemies'?"

The Condor smiled genuinely at his close friend. "OK, OK, you're right, Raul. Always be prepared."

The Condor turned to Carlo. "If you want Ray as Eduardo's man cousin, he goes." He then turned back to Ray. "So, young man, are you OK with this? Don't be offended, but you seem a little uneasy."

Goddamn it, Ray thought. *Focus, asshole. Get control.*

"I consider it an honor to be asked to protect Eduardo, Jefe, but I have not been in one of your meetings before, so I'm not sure what I'm supposed to do, how I should act."

The quiet, scary-looking Eduardo spoke up. "All that's required is that you observe. I respect my brother's concerns, but Pablo's right—the men he's meeting are afraid of their own shadows. We've heard nothing of a sinister or dangerous nature from their camps. This meeting will be quite routine. Follow Francisco's lead; he's done this many times. When in doubt, simply look at him, and he'll let you know what he wants."

Ray looked over at Francisco; he had yet to exchange a word with the older man. Francisco was every bit as reticent as he was, perhaps even more so, and in the three months Ray had been in the cartel, he was certain he'd never seen the man smile. Francisco simply made eye contact and coolly nodded, which Ray did also in response. The Condor leaned back in his executive chair and in a friendly tone said, "We leave at four thirty for the drive to town. Carlo will provide you further details. Thank you, Ray. You may go."

Ray nodded and left the study, once again taking up a position in the great hall. If he could have screamed out loud at what he believed was his poor performance before the Condor, he would have. Two other guards in the hall had looked at him briefly as he came out of the study but then returned their gazes elsewhere, paying no attention to their fellow guard. Ray leaned against the wall and shut his eyes for a few seconds to play back the entire event. He was a professional and felt certain he had controlled his face, but the observant Condor must have seen something in his eyes. That was as far as his thinking got him, and there was no discerning anything from the Condor's eyes because Ray could barely see them, shaded as they always were with the ever-present photochromic sunglasses he wore.

I showed emotion, Ray thought. *I can't believe I did that, and he saw it! Why does that man fluster me like that? Admit it...you were scared shitless. Jesus, get a grip. The man's smart—you know it—so work with it. Nothing's been revealed. A new guy would be expected to be a little nervous with his first important assignment. But you'd better focus, or the next guy placed against a wall and capped will be you, dipshit.*

The rest of the morning and early afternoon were spent in the usual routines. Members of the inner circle came and went, as did one or the other of the two senior communications wizards. It was just after four before Carlo came out of the study, grabbed Ray by the shoulder, and said, "Time to get the caravan ready."

As was typical for any movement involving the Condor, travel to the meeting would be in black armored Escalades. There were a total of fourteen men in the Condor's entourage for this trip, so they would be using four of the six available luxury SUVs. All the men were armed except for the Condor and Eduardo. Francisco, of course, would surrender his weapon before entering the meeting site, and Ray, hopefully, would get his knives through the security check. As was his custom, he rode in the second SUV with Carlo.

The three cartel leaders arrived with their entourages within a few minutes of one another at a private club near downtown Monterey. Vasso's and Barega's motorcades pulled up to the front awning of the upscale swim-and-dining club, and they and their seconds and security people went in the front door. The Condor's motorcade pulled up to the curb on the street that bordered the rear of the club. The Condor and Eduardo, with Ray and Francisco close behind, followed Carlo and two of his men through a back door Carlo had a key to, through a storage area, and then into the walled terrace area of the club, with its lush, manicured landscaping surrounding an inviting-looking pool. A large round table was set up under several tall palm trees. The well-dressed club manager welcomed the Condor personally as Carlo and his men took a quick look around. With a wink to Ray, Carlo and his men turned and left the way they had come. As the manager and the Condor were exchanging pleasantries, the other two cartel leaders with their seconds and personal bodyguards came through the glass doors of the club's main dining room and approached the Condor.

To Ray's trained eye, the smiles on the faces of the two well-dressed leaders were forced. Their security people, while dressed professionally, were tough-looking men who, his instincts told him, were far more accustomed to the streets in the worst parts of Monterrey than the upscale club setting where they now found themselves. As the three principals, their seconds, and the club manager quietly chatted, Ray followed Francisco as he nodded in recognition to the other security types. A pat down of sorts was conducted, with members of one cartel frisking the members of the others. Given how Ray carried his knives, the weapons fortunately were missed, much as Carlo had said they would be, and he started breathing easier. It was apparently true that his youthful appearance didn't generate any feeling of danger in the minds of the other guards, for their looks, as best as he could determine, were dismissive, even insulting, as if they could hardly believe that one so hard and experienced as Francisco would have a kid like him around.

After the initial embraces of greetings and small talk with the club manager, the principals sat down at the large table. Ray and the other security people stood a discreet distance behind them as the club's staff served an array of tapas and beverages, and then, after the waitstaff was politely excused, the principals settled in and began what sounded to Ray like a civilized discussion of their differences. His basic instincts, as augmented by his police training, made him particularly adept at reading the eyes and body language of people, especially criminals. The seating arrangements at the table had the Condor's second, Eduardo, sitting to his right, and the particularly violent and stupid cartel leader Ramon Vasso sat to the Condor's left. This put Francisco, who stood behind the Condor, between Ray and Vasso's chief security man.

As the discussions went on and the cartel leaders civilly worked out their differences, Ray's peripheral vision and attention were focused on Vasso's man standing to Francisco's left; all his subtle body actions suggested to him a man who was very nervous—too nervous for the situation, in his opinion—and working himself up to some action. The man's eyes constantly darted about, and beads of sweat had formed at his sideburns and were running down the sides of his face. More concerning to Ray was that every so often, he would subtly unclasp his hands from in front of him and lightly touch the side pocket of his suit coat. He had no doubt the man was carrying a weapon that somehow had been missed in the searches, but, more important, his intuition told him the man was waiting for an opportunity to use it. Since it was highly unlikely that he was going to attack his own principal or the second, it was clear to Ray that the Condor was the target. Carlo's instincts, at least about Vasso, had been on the mark. Francisco, meanwhile, appeared completely oblivious to the actions of the man standing not three feet to his left. But by using the large Francisco to screen his glances, Ray was able to watch the man closely.

Ray stood with his hands casually clasped in front of him, which allowed for extremely quick access to his H-K, if necessary. He observed the man close his eyes and take a slow, deep breath as if to calm himself, and then the man swiftly reached for his jacket pocket as he lunged forward. Ray was ready for him and shot past a stunned Francisco, surprising the assailant, who indeed was going for the Condor. Ray's H-K was propelled out of his sleeve by a simple spring actuator in the sheath and opened before the assassin could clear the small-caliber handgun from the hip pocket of his suit coat. Ray aimed his thrust for the attacker's right arm in an effort to disable his shooting ability, but the un-choreographed, sudden and rapid movements of himself and the assassin resulted in a miss when the assailant turned slightly toward Ray in his surprise. The H-K glanced off the man's arm and sank deeply into his upper chest as they fell to the patio. From the look of shock on the assassin's face as it quickly changed to a frozen death mask, Ray instinctively knew he had killed him.

The security man behind Vasso's second apparently had been waiting for his coconspirator to strike before he also attacked, but Ray's momentum had smashed the first assassin into the second as he lunged forward a second after his partner. The second assassin was knocked off balance, allowing Francisco the time to finally react and smash a blow to the side of the second attacker's head. The explosion of a single shot resounded as Francisco and the assassin also collapsed to the patio in a tangled heap. The sharp report of the shot seemed to snap Ray out of his adrenaline-induced state, and he looked down as he slowly pulled his knife from the dead assailant's chest. *My God,* he thought as an awful feeling overcame him, *what have I done?*

6

The estate of El Condor de Muerte
Monterrey, Mexico
Late Monday night

As quickly as the attack had started, the sudden scrambling and screams of warning stopped, and when they did, both of Vasso's men lay dead on the patio stones, as did Francisco, who lay astride the second assailant, his large, dead hand attached like a vise to the man's throat. The second man had managed to get off the one shot, and it had caught Francisco in the chest, killing him, but not before he broke the man's neck in their fall. Ray gathered his senses, jumped to his feet, and placed his H-K at the neck of a terrified and shocked Ramon Vasso, who was frozen in horror as he saw the results of his failed attempt to kill his powerful adversary.

The third cartel leader, Gerardo Barega, as well as his people, appeared to be stunned by the attack. They remained essentially where they were, sitting or standing on the opposite side of the table. The Condor, assessing that the immediate danger was over, turned to Barega and said, "You're either with me or against me, Gerardo. What's it to be?"

A stammering, clearly terrified Barega swore on the soul of his mother that he had no idea Vasso had been planning an attack and vowed to assist the Condor in whatever action he insisted on.

"There are no problems between us, Gerardo, that can't be settled as businessmen," the Condor said. "If you're with me, have your men take this trash and dispose of it. I'll deal with Ramon and his treachery myself."

The Condor turned to Vasso's second and gave him a choice: join him now and send his men away or die with Vasso. The second glanced at his terrified boss, then at the bodies on the patio, and nodded his acceptance. He made the call and ordered his people outside the club to leave. Barega and his men gathered up the dead assailants, wrapped them in oversize pool towels, and, leaving by way of the rear storage door, took the bodies with them. Eduardo placed a call after Vasso's man called off his soldiers, and the other members of the Condor's entourage, led by a clearly pissed-off Carlo, joined them. They carried Francisco out and gently placed him in the back of one of the Escalades. Vasso was tied up and stowed in the backseat of another Escalade; Ray sat next to him, his knife at his throat. Eduardo handsomely paid off the club manager and his staff and quietly, but with menace in his tone, warned them all to keep their silence.

The Condor's entourage returned to the estate, where everyone else was on high alert after a call from Carlo. The Condor had a quick private word with Eduardo, who, along with several of his men, took Vasso and his second off toward a casita located in a remote corner of the estate. Ray was certain he never would see Vasso alive again. They were still standing under the porte cochere when the Condor turned to him and, with a small smile and genuine warmth showing on his face, motioned for him to follow him inside.

To any observer, Ray had appeared ruthless and calm during the entire ordeal, but his appearance belied the truth. He had been scared shitless during the brief attack and for the tense minutes afterward, and his mind was racing as he followed the Condor into his private study. His initial attack had been all instinct and had happened so quickly that there had been no time to really think, just react. He never intended to kill the assailant; he just wanted to keep him from killing the Condor. But as he followed the Condor to his private study, the implications of what he had done were beginning to hit him, and it took all the control he could muster to keep his breathing even and his hands steady. The Condor led him through the heavy double doors of the study, which were immediately closed behind them by an agitated Raul and the other two remaining members of the inner circle. The Condor casually walked to a built-in bar on one side of the large, handsomely decorated office, poured two tumblers of old Herradura Anejo tequila from a crystal decanter, and then turned and handed one to Ray.

"I salute you, my friend, and give you my thanks," he said as he calmly raised his glass to him in a toast. "Like my cousin, I owe you a debt of honor I fear I won't be able to adequately repay. Tell me, how did you know that man was going to try to kill me? In my short discussion with Barega, his security man said he happened to be looking across the table when Vasso's man attacked, and he said you intercepted the bastard before he had taken no more than a step."

Without really thinking, probably a result of the adrenaline rush he was still feeling, Ray responded with the truth. "It was in his eyes, Jefe, and in the way he stood. There was reason to be alert, but he was more—he was too tense. I'd been watching him for several minutes. I felt he was armed, even though no weapon was found during the search. When he made his move to his weapon, he was careless—he didn't notice me; he was looking only at you. He thought he had the advantage of surprise but saw my attack too late and paid for his stupidity with his life."

This brief answer to the Condor's question was the longest conversation Ray had ever had with the man, or any man in the cartel, for that matter, except for Carlo, in the twelve weeks he had been inside. Before this moment, he had spoken almost exclusively with Carlo and with very few of the others, limiting his conversations to short questions or answers. No one could really draw any conclusions about him or his intelligence, as he said so little. As Ray was speaking, the Condor maintained a warm, friendly expression that eventually turned more to one of curiosity or interest.

"You intrigue me, my young friend. You handled yourself not only with great courage and skill but also with obvious intelligence, and you speak well. You clearly have some education that Carlo hasn't shared with me. Tell me about this."

Shit, what did I just say? Ray thought. *God, what did I sound like? "Education," he said? What do I say now? Quick—think! Keep it short and simple.*

As his panicky thoughts flashed through his mind, as casually as he could, he took a healthy swallow of Herradura to buy some time and calm himself. He hoped the Condor hadn't seen his hands shaking. He then remembered a part of the legend that Bennie had created for him and had him commit to memory, and he responded with the first coherent thought that came to him.

"In America, Jefe, when you are still young and are arrested for small crimes, you do not go to prison—you go to a school that is also a jail. The better you did in school, the better you were treated and the faster they let you go. I didn't like being in jail. The family who took me in after my parents were killed spoke English, so I learned it as well. The women who raised me could read, so I learned to read also. In jail I found I liked the lessons, even though I pretended not to. I was stupid to get caught and sent to jail. I knew if I learned more, I wouldn't be caught so easily again. I don't do well in jail, Jefe, even if the jail is for children."

The Condor gave Ray another warm smile as he nodded in understanding and then said in perfect English, "You're wise as well as courageous."

He turned and reached for the crystal container and poured them some more tequila. "Tell me of the knives," he continued, "your skill with them. Carlo mentioned that you refused a pistol and selected the knives instead when you joined us. I'm curious…why such weapons? And please, respond in English."

As Ray took a swig of his tequila to help him collect his thoughts before going on, he couldn't help being surprised by the Condor's nearly perfect English.

"I can use a gun, but knives were easier to get," he said. "Guns can easily be bought in America, Jefe, but they are expensive, and I did not have any money when I was younger. I needed to be able to protect myself in the places where I lived, so I learned how to use a knife."

The Condor nodded as if he understood. "Ah, yes, and it was your blade that saved my life today." He paused, his warm expression becoming more serious, and then he went on. "Tell me of Francisco."

Ray was puzzled by the question, and it showed, but he collected himself once more and said, "Francisco, Jefe? I do not understand."

"Francisco was standing next to the assassin who attacked, yet he didn't take action until after you had. How do you explain this?"

Jesus, he thought, *where's he going with this?*

"I cannot know for sure, but I do not know your business and was watching the men standing around the table and not listening to what was being said. Francisco was with you for many years; he must have known your business. He probably was listening so he could help you with your problems with the others."

Ray noticed the look in the Condor's eyes becoming sadder as he spoke. When the Condor responded, his voice was softer, and the words came more slowly.

"You're kind to the memory of Francisco. As close as I was to him, and as loyal as he was to me, his age was starting to slow him down. It was only a matter of time before I was going to have to replace him. He did know my business, but there was also a time when Francisco would have seen the attack coming, just as you did this evening."

In what was clearly to Ray a moment of genuine sorrow, the Condor paused, closed his eyes for a second, and took a healthy pull on his drink before looking compassionately at him.

"I will miss him greatly," he said. "He truly was like an older brother to me, and now I've lost him. He was at my side for over thirty-five years, as a friend and protector. We will lay him to rest tomorrow, here on the estate. He had no family outside of us. We were his family."

The clearly emotional Condor took another drink and then cleared the tightness in his throat with a small cough before going on. "Tell me, Ray—what of Barega? He says he was surprised by the attack and swears he had nothing to do with it. Do you think he was involved in this treachery?"

Ray was still trying to adjust to the humanity being displayed by the obviously emotional leader, whose grief was confusing him. The man's entire countenance was upsetting the preconceived notions he'd had of the Condor as a cartel leader, and he had to quickly focus and think.

Shit, this is a minefield. There's no question that asshole was a part of this, but would a young guard know this? It was his men who searched the killer. Do I tell him this? Don't get too clever here—just answer the question.

"I do not wish to offend if he's your friend, Jefe."

"Go on, Ray. What is said in this room is between friends. Barega is no true friend. Tell me what you think, not what you think I want to hear."

Ray decided to plunge ahead, even if it revealed him to be smarter than perhaps the Condor suspected. "He must be involved, Jefe. Of that I have no doubt."

The Condor raised an eyebrow. "And why is this so? What makes you so certain? Was there something in his eyes, perhaps?"

Ray shook his head. "Not his eyes, Jefe. It was more simple than that. When we were checked for weapons before the meeting, it was Barega's men who searched Vasso's. To get my knives past the search was easy; they were checking for guns in the places you would carry such a weapon. But the assassin's gun was in his coat, where it should have been easily found, and it wasn't. So either Barega's men are very bad at their jobs, or they let the weapon pass through."

The Condor was smiling and nodding in either agreement or perhaps amusement; Ray wasn't sure which at the moment.

"You're unusually bright, Ray, and very observant. That's exactly the conclusion I've come to regarding Barega. Eduardo should know more by morning; he's questioning Vasso as we speak. Should he discover that Barega was involved, what would you advise me to do?"

Ray was surprised again by the question. "Jefe, I'm just one of Carlo's guards. I do not know your business."

"Tell me what you would do, Ray, if you were in my place. Please, we're friends here, you and I, and I want to know."

Ray paused and took another large drink of his tequila, draining his glass and trying to quickly think out what he should say next. He was a smart guy and knew it, but after his actions and all he'd said so far, to pretend he was simpleminded and not answer the man's question could only raise suspicions in one so clearly intelligent as the Condor. He decided he would demonstrate intelligence, as this was far closer to his real personality, and therefore the likelihood of tripping up actually seemed less. During his briefings, Bennie had told him that the best cover for an undercover operative was a persona very close to the truth. Ray's instincts told him he was stepping over a line somehow by merging his undercover persona closer to who he really was, but he could see no other path forward with what he'd already said. He looked the Condor in the eye and went on. "I would let him think he was a friend, Jefe, use him when I needed him, and then kill him when it was best for me."

The Condor again nodded. "A wise course, perhaps, but there's also danger there, I think. Do you know what that danger is?"

"I think so, Jefe," he responded with just a little hesitation. "If Barega feels he has fooled you into thinking he was not acting with Vasso, he will think you weak and try to kill you again."

Again the Condor nodded, and he was also smiling, as if pleased that Ray had figured out the obvious. "Very good, very good, for that's also how I see it. We *will* use him, as there are things to be done that we can have Barega do for us. When my plans are complete, and he has served us, we'll agree to meet with him again. He will, of course, plan to assassinate me at that meeting, but we'll be prepared. I say *we*, Ray, because starting tonight, I wish for you to take Francisco's place in my security detail."

Ray was dumbfounded and couldn't hide the surprise that showed on his face as he tried to figure out what to say next. The distance the Condor typically put between himself and others had served him well. The thought of being one of his close bodyguards sounded dangerous, so he said the first thing that came to him. "I'm honored, of course, Jefe, by your trust in me. But the others, Carlo and Eduardo and their men, would never understand. I'm new to your business and young. I was lucky today, and Vasso chose his guards badly—that's what happened."

The Condor smiled a small but reassuring smile. "Don't worry about this. The others will accept whatever I decide, and their men will do likewise. And while life *is* full of chance, as to the events of today, Ray, *Res ipsa loquitur*. Do you know what this means?"

"No, I do not understand those words," he said, not lying or playing dumb this time.

"They're from the Latin and mean, 'The facts speak for themselves.' You were alert and observant, and when action was necessary, you were deadly efficient. The man you killed—Zandro Guzman was his name—wasn't just another security man and wasn't poorly chosen by Vasso. To the contrary, he was a feared, deadly lieutenant who served Vasso for many years and certainly had killed often for him. Yet you bested him—he with a gun, you with only a knife. He had the element of surprise, and you still defeated him."

The Condor stepped closer to Ray and placed his free hand on his shoulder. "You underestimate yourself, I suspect, because of your age, but you need to be more confident. You've proved your value to me, and you must accept my request. I require your instincts and service, especially now that I've lost Francisco."

The Condor paused, his warm look slowly turning serious, his voice becoming softer, even though they were alone in the study. "There are very important parts of my business that I must keep from Eduardo and Carlo, yet more and more as my plans move forward, I'll need one with your eyes, skills, and intelligence when we must go south. Starting tonight, you'll travel with me as one of my aides and part of my security. We must return to the capital city soon, and when we do, I'll want you close by, as the most important parts of my plans must be executed from there. You've earned this, my young friend. But as a member of my inner circle, it's important for you to remember that where we go and what we must do remain in the circle. You must never discuss our travels, or our business, with Carlo or any of the others. All our lives depend on this. Is this clear?"

Ray was very stressed at the turn of events and trying hard to maintain the appearance of control. "Yes, Jefe, of course. And Carlo and Eduardo will understand? I wish to serve, but I do not want to cause bad blood."

"I'll speak with my cousins," the Condor said, "but I assure you, you have nothing to concern yourself with. The skills you showed today have earned you great respect. You already have Carlo's respect, as well as his friendship and loyalty for your actions while you were imprisoned together and during your escape. And have you not considered that Eduardo owes you his life as well? For certainly after killing me, Guzman or the other assassin would have killed him next, and he knows this. It seems that all three of us now owe you a great debt. My cousins are honorable men and will understand my wishing to repay that debt of honor. I'll have a word with Raul and have your things moved up here to the hacienda. Raul will take Francisco's place as head of my inner circle, and you'll replace Francisco. But for now, come…Let's have dinner together. Tomorrow you'll go with Carlo to see a friend of mine in the city who's a fine tailor. Where we're going, you must fit in and look professional, which means some new clothes. And he'll understand your need for a looser fit at your sleeves, right, my friend?"

The Condor smiled warmly and patted Ray on the back and with a nod indicated he should lead them to his private dining room. Before they entered the dining room, the Condor had a quick word with Raul, who was still standing sentry with Luis and Miguel. While Raul went off, the other two followed them and stood just outside the door. During dinner, the Condor wanted to know everything about Ray that he was willing to talk about and spoke to him like a friend rather than his leader. His entire manner changed from that of a mysterious, terrifying presence to that of a man of warmth and friendship. Ray found this terribly confusing, as if, before his very eyes, the man were undergoing a metamorphosis he didn't understand. Despite his great reservation to do so, he was drawn into a personal conversation with the man. Fortunately, before sending Ray south with a false identity, Bennie had been very careful to provide him with a "legend" to support his identity, so he carefully shared his meticulously prepared background with the Condor.

There had indeed been an Espinoza family from the Hermosillo area who had immigrated illegally to America some eighteen years earlier, and there had been a young boy. They were involved in a fatal traffic accident soon after arriving, and, unfortunately, the boy was killed also. But the record of his death was concealed and his identify saved by the intelligence division of the DEA until such time as it could be used. Ray was amazed to discover during their dinner conversation that the Condor seemed to know all the details regarding the genealogy of his Ray Espinoza legend and the extended family who still lived in the Hermosillo area. How he had managed to live to see the morning of his first night at the estate was now explained in his mind. Clearly the Condor believed he was Ray Espinoza of Hermosillo and had satisfied himself to that fact after Carlo's call from the border and before they arrived at the Chihuahua estate that first night. Another question Ray needed to get to the bottom of was just how the Condor had found this kind of information out and in so short a time.

As they were finishing dinner, they were joined by the Condor's cousins and Raul, who quietly told the Condor that everything was arranged. The Condor got up from the table, so Ray did also, and then the Condor surprised him once again by quickly embracing him and thanking him again for saving his life. There was no doubt in Ray's mind that the Condor appeared very emotional as he turned away and quickly embraced the others as well. Then, without another word, he walked out. Carlo came over, smiled, and poured Ray another drink. The other two gathered around Ray as well, and, after several toasts, Raul showed him the way to his own private suite, just two doors down from the Condor's private apartment.

After saying good night to Raul, Ray closed the door and stood there for a minute, stunned at the day's events, looking blankly around his large private room. The entry was part of a sitting area, almost a small living room, with the bedroom beyond. He slowly walked through the finely appointed space and checked out the private bathroom and shower; the opulence amazed him. For months, he had shared small spaces with dangerous men, always on his guard and in character—and never alone. Even in his off hours, when he would have liked to unwind, lessen the great tension he always felt, and be himself for just a second, he never could. Privacy was a luxury reserved to a few important people within the cartel, and now, surprisingly, he was a part of that exclusive group.

He stood looking at his king-size bed and then slowly sat down, reaching out and feeling the texture and softness of the thick, colorful comforter.

He looked at his hand as he slowly brought it up to his face; it was shaking. One had to look closely, but the tremors were there. He had an impulse to hide his hand, to keep others from seeing this small outward manifestation of the feelings he was suppressing, but he didn't have to. For the first time in weeks, Ray was truly alone—alone and now one of the trusted and privileged. *Unbelievable*, he thought, shaking his head. *Simply unbelievable. What the hell do I do now?*

7

The estate of El Condor de Muerte
Monterrey, Mexico
Late Monday night

As Ray sat alone in his suite, his newfound privacy gave him the needed solitude to reflect on the magnitude of the day's events. Someone under Raul's direction apparently had moved all of Francisco's personal belongings out and Ray's few belongings in as he was having dinner with the Condor. Everything he owned was either neatly arranged in the armoire or in the adjacent set of drawers. After sitting for a few minutes on the edge of the bed in a bewildered state, he finally undressed and slipped under the thick, soft comforter. His first impulse had been to shower, to try to wash the terrible events of the day off him, but he was too exhausted to do anything but lie down.

As tired as he was, he couldn't sleep. His body was numb and spent, he suspected as a reaction to the incredible adrenaline rush he'd experienced earlier, but his mind was racing. In the five years Ray had been a cop, he'd never killed anyone. The fact that it was unintentional didn't quiet his mind; that he had done it with a knife made it far more personal. He never once had thought about just how personal killing with a knife would be. He had been close enough to hear Zandro Guzman's last gasping breath, and the memory made his skin crawl. He remembered feeling the knife grazing bone as it plunged deeply into Guzman's chest. It was a snapshot indelibly planted in his mind, and he wouldn't soon forget it. He only hoped he eventually would learn to live with it.

The fact that Ray had killed a man who no doubt had committed many crimes, even murder for his leader, didn't mitigate the fact that a fellow human being was dead by his hand, which weighed heavily on his conscience. He hoped his father would somehow understand. He hoped God would as well. Although he hadn't been to church in years—not since his parents had made it his choice, and not theirs, that he attend—deep down he still believed. The everyday realities of the world he worked in made it hard for him to maintain his faith, but he did. The seemingly unrepentant killings that were so typical to the drug trade appeared like such sport for the participants. It was hard to swim in the pool of shit Ray found himself in and not wonder each day where this God was. *Why doesn't God just strike them down?* he thought. The realities of the drug business made a concept like faith a hard sell.

It was one thing, Ray thought, for a cop to have to kill in order to protect his life or that of a fellow citizen in the course of his duties. On an intellectual level, he understood the "live by the sword, die by the sword" crap he remembered from his catechism classes, but he had killed one criminal to protect another. The irony of it all wasn't lost on him. He paused in midthought; something had been bothering him, and until that moment, he couldn't put his finger on it, but suddenly the obvious became clear. For the first time since the attack, it occurred to him that if the assassination attempt had been successful, he wouldn't be lying in this fancy room, thinking about all this shit—he'd be dead too. Did that fact justify his actions? He thought about it for a second and supposed that question would be answered in due time by a higher authority, but for the time being, the secular side of him said, *Fuck it. Better Guzman than me.*

As difficult, or perhaps impossible, as justifying the killing would be when Ray eventually was debriefed by his agency, his quick actions had saved the Condor, and as a result, he was trusted now more than ever. The Condor had known everyone in his immediate entourage since he was young. They were his family, for the most part, or deeply trusted old friends, such as Raul. The Condor had known his Ray Espinoza cover for only twelve weeks prior to today, but as a result of the failed attack, he felt he was as close to the Condor as any of the others, perhaps more so. Apparently saving the man's life had that effect.

The events of the last several days, beginning with the murders of the Mendozas and ending with the move to this private room, gave Ray reason to pause and really consider what he was into. He was between a rock and a hard spot, and he knew it. The simple facts, when viewed from a detached perspective, were that he was isolated and on his own illegally in a foreign country, was out of contact with his control agent, and was making decisions and taking actions that were way above his pay grade. He had no clue how to solve the problems he was facing. Nor did he know how he could ever explain to Bennie what had been required of him in the first twelve weeks he had been inside the cartel. The idea that he would be dismissed from the DEA—perhaps even jailed for the one murder he had done nothing to stop or today's murder by his own hand—was a growing possibility in his mind. That would mark the end of a promising young career in law enforcement, and he didn't think he could live with that.

On the one hand, his covert penetration of the Condor's cartel couldn't have been any deeper or more successful than it was. It was a miracle he had achieved it and in such a short time. Whether or not it was a miracle, he was in a position of great personal trust, next to one of the most powerful and secretive—and therefore most dangerous—drug lords in all of Mexico. It was an unparalleled clandestine achievement, one that certainly would be written up in the DEA training manuals if—and this was a big if, he thought, for perhaps the hundredth time—he ever managed to get out of this mess alive, a prospect that seemed less and less likely with each passing day as he was drawn in closer and closer to the Condor. To have learned all that he had learned in the last twelve weeks and not be able to pass the information on to Bennie was the same as having learned nothing, he reminded himself. He was trapped by the success of his operation and his increasingly close proximity to the Condor.

It was late; Monday had become Tuesday, now day eighty-four of his mission. *Jesus,* he thought, *eighty-four days. When will this end? How do I get out? Hell, can I even survive this?*

As Ray thought about the last three months, he was unable to sleep. He sat up, leaned over, and refilled his glass from a bottle of fine tequila he had found as he was checking out the nightstand earlier. He had thought of Francisco when he found the bottle and the solitary old crystal tumbler beside it. He wondered whether the older man also found it necessary to drink alone to force sleep. Did being close to the Condor do that to a man, even one as hard as Francisco had been?

Ray had never known Francisco—or, more accurately, Francisco never bothered to get to know him—but he thought of him now and regretted that he had died in the attempt on the Condor's life. With all the emotions he was feeling, he suddenly felt great sadness for Francisco and took a long drink of the smooth, clear liquid before his thoughts returned to the Condor. Even with the body of knowledge Ray had accumulated on the man, he had learned today the Condor was not only a very intelligent man, as he always had suspected, but also formally educated.

Res ipsa loquitur—the facts speak for themselves. Fucking Latin from a cartel leader? What am I missing here? he thought, shaking his head in wonder.

From the first night, Ray intuitively felt there was something different or special about the Condor, and it drove him crazy that the truth of the man eluded him. Now that he was to be part of the inner circle, he would be required to be with him almost every minute of every day. He knew he would learn far more than he had, perhaps even the elusive truth. There had to be more to the man than he showed. Intelligence gathering was his job, and his job in many ways had just gotten far more interesting, but—and this was a big but in his thinking—maintaining his cover had just become far more difficult.

He reached toward the nightstand but paused to appreciate its beautifully detailed leather-and-copper inserts. The nightstand, like all the furniture in his suite, appeared to be handmade. He picked up the heavy crystal tumbler of fine Herradura Anejo and swallowed another stiff drink. It was difficult to keep his hand from shaking as the smooth, warm, fiery liquid spread through him. Without question, Monday had been the worst day of his young life, worse even than watching the rogue DEA agent being killed in front of his eyes six weeks earlier. *He* had killed a man today and, in so doing, saved the life of a cartel leader. While his conscience tried to reconcile the tragedy that had occurred by his own hand with the success that it had brought him within the entourage, he closed his eyes and said a silent prayer for the assassin he had bested, no matter how evil the man might have been.

Ray sighed deeply; the tequila was starting to have a positive effect, and he slowly felt the tension in his neck and shoulders ebb away. He was still amazed that Bennie's plan had worked. The operational concept was simple but dangerous and the outcome very unpredictable. In and of itself, spending an extended length of time in jail posing as a criminal was dangerous. But he had seen the genius and the potential for success in Bennie's thinking. Trying to wheel and deal one's way into a cartel by posing as a buyer or seller was dumb on its face because *everyone* the cartel came into contact with outside their particular groups was seen as a likely enemy. Better to have a known and trusted member of the group befriend you and willingly take you in and vouch for you. Establishing a relationship that close was the hard part. Somehow Ray had managed it, but the challenges kept piling on and on, and the danger to his survival was growing as a result.

In the tightly controlled, secure environment that the cautious, alert Condor maintained at all three of his northern estates, would he be able to get the valuable intelligence he was collecting out to Bennie? As of tonight, his opportunities for communicating with him had gotten worse, he feared, and they'd been nearly impossible before. Could he maintain the facade he had created over the last twelve weeks, standing as close to the Condor as he now would be? To fool Carlo and the other guards was one thing; to fool the Condor was quite another. The guards, like Carlo, were a tough, ruthless lot, to be sure, but they were very uneducated and not that observant. The Condor, on the other hand, was dangerously smart and seemed to see everything.

The Condor was right about another point as well. After the Condor had retired to his suite following dinner, and after he had shared a last drink with Raul, Carlo, and Eduardo, as he was leaving the two brothers, not only was there no hint of jealousy at his promotion, there was indeed a new level of admiration and respect in their mannerisms and attitudes toward him, a feeling of inclusion he hadn't felt before, especially from the reticent Eduardo. As Ray said good night to them, they each quietly had said, "*La noche buene, gran cuchillo*" ("Good night, great knife"), which he had thought nothing about at first, given the events of the day. As Raul walked him to his new suite, he kindly placed his hand on his shoulder and said, "By morning, what Carlo just said will be all over the estate, I'm afraid, so you might as well accept it."

"What, Raul? I don't understand?" he had asked quizzically.

"Your new name, El Cuchillo."

El Cuchillo, the Knife; Jesus, that was the last way Ray wanted to be remembered. He shook his head slowly at the thought, took a final look around his luxurious room, drank down the last bit of tequila, and then turned off the bedside lamp. He would need all his wits in a few hours as he began his new duties with the Condor, which meant he had to sleep. It was likely that tomorrow would dawn far more interesting and far more dangerous, as he would now be traveling with the Condor wherever he went, charged with protecting him—so many unknowns, so little sleep, a lousy way to start a new day.

Ray closed his eyes and hoped that with the help of the tequila sleep would come, but it came slowly. He kept seeing the same scene: the man in the black suit lunges for the Condor, and he lunges for him, his switch knife plunging deeply into the man's chest in the ensuing chaos, killing him instantly—the same scene over and over.

Despite his deeply troubled conscience, he managed to get a few hours of restless sleep before he awoke with a start. It was still dark, but his internal clock told him it was early morning, near sunrise. He lay still in the darkness, allowing his mind a moment to adjust from the sudden shift of dream state to consciousness. He was grateful to be awake; perhaps now his mind would stop replaying the scene of Guzman's attack and the image of the man's death. He was disoriented for a second, and his head was pounding. With the rising tension he felt as the weeks dragged on, he was experiencing more and more headaches; this one, he knew, was tequila induced.

Ray's first coherent thought was, *Where am I?* He looked around; once he remembered his new surroundings, his second thought was, *What do I do now?*

Staying covert meant blending in and not drawing attention to himself. Now that he was to be one of the Condor's four principal aides and a personal bodyguard, that would be impossible, and that could only mean trouble. Even more troubling was that the Condor seemed to genuinely like him. The stone-cold, gray, almost-black eyes he attributed to the Condor's look were warm, and the Condor had been sincerely friendly last night. Saving the man's life had brought unexpected and unwanted benefits.

How the hell am I supposed to handle this? Ray wondered. *The less said to the man, the better, but he seems to rely on the detail for friendship more than he does for safety. I can't just ignore him. Think, and keep it simple. Learn what you can over the next couple of weeks, get to Mexico City, and ditch these guys. That's what I'll do. First chance I get, I'm getting my ass to the US embassy and contacting Bennie.*

It was a certainty that he would learn even more about the organization as he traveled with the Condor. The dangers to him, however, were getting out of control, and it was time to focus on just getting out, new information be damned. But he still was curious about some of the things the Condor had told him last night. In the twelve weeks Ray had been inside the cartel, he had done little else but accompany Carlo wherever the business had taken him and the Condor in the northern states. This would now change; the Condor's reference to going to Mexico City and executing his plans from there was an intriguing and interesting line of investigation for an undercover operative, and he knew it, despite his growing trepidation—that, and now he would be going on the plane.

For several weeks each month, the Condor and the four members of his inner circle left the estates and went off on their own, accompanied only by the two communication techs. No one outside this inner circle knew where they went. It was never openly discussed among the guards, just whispered about occasionally in small circles whenever the Condor or his cousins weren't around. After joining the cartel, and after the Condor had left for the first time, Ray had casually asked Carlo where they went. Carlo smiled and simply said, "The Condor likes the sea."

Almost always, Carlo accompanied his cousin to his departure point when he took these unexplained trips and picked him up on his return. As part of Carlo's detail, Ray did likewise. The routine for these trips was essentially always the same. The typical caravan of three or four heavily armed black SUVs would leave the estate they happened to be occupying at the time and drive out into the country, away from whichever city they were near. They would be on the move for thirty or forty minutes, seemingly turning randomly from time to time onto smaller, less traveled roadways. Eventually, the rear vehicle would suddenly stop and block the road they were on, while the remaining two vehicles continued on for another mile or so. They would then stop, with the lead vehicle blocking the road from the opposite direction. The section of road was always straight for that mile, an inconspicuous makeshift runway.

Soon after this all occurred, an unmarked, sleek, unusual-looking turboprop plane would appear out of nowhere, make a fast pass over the road at a very low altitude, do a quick 180, and then set down and taxi right up to the Condor's Escalade. The Condor and his inner circle of six men would quickly slip out of the SUVs and into the plane. Then the pilot would do another quick 180 in the middle of the road, and the aircraft would accelerate rapidly down the road and streak off at a very low altitude toward the west. In total, the plane was never on the ground for more than five minutes. The Escalades would turn around, and the caravan would return to the estate as if nothing unusual had happened. On his first trip, witnessing the Condor's departure, Ray committed the details of the plane's appearance to memory and passed them on in his second report to Bennie, for whatever good it would do.

What set the plane off from other private twin-engine planes he had seen was an added pair of small wings on its nose and the fact that the two engines on the wings faced backward. Ray had never seen this before, but it gave the plane a distinctive look—very cool, he thought at the time. The second time he was allowed to accompany Carlo, they met the Condor's plane on a different stretch of deserted road. He'd been close enough to the feathered engine nacelle to read what he suspected was the plane's manufacturer and type: Piaggio 180 Avanti. He'd made it a point to remember this also. Surely there would be sales or maintenance records on such an obviously expensive private plane. The last thing he committed to memory was the speed. On its approach and takeoff, the Avanti was faster than any other small plane Ray had seen or been in.

The Condor was never gone for more than two or three weeks, and when he returned, it was always to a different section of untraveled road or a non-towered airstrip and a different estate than the one he'd left several weeks before. Ray was reasonably sure that outside of the four security men of the inner circle and two electronic techs who always were at the Condor's side, only Carlo and Eduardo actually knew where he went. As the newest member of the inner circle, he now would know as well.

This realization excited him but also increased his anxiety. The unknown was like that, especially if you were undercover. Dull, boring, innocuous routines were a salve for an undercover operative. Constantly changing dynamics and making the required adjustments to them were what usually caught up with covert operatives and eventually got them killed.

Even though the sun wasn't up yet, he got out of bed and headed into the large, finely appointed bathroom to grab a shower. He pulled opened the heavy, frameless glass door to the shower and shook his head as he entered the beautifully finished space. Although Ray was your basic middle-class guy, he did have some experiences with luxury accommodations. He had stayed in some pretty fancy hotels during a couple of trips to Las Vegas and the week he'd spent on Maui after he'd graduated from college, but he'd never seen a shower like this. It had to be six or eight feet square, with stone-covered walls of polished granite or marble, and had three gold or brass-colored shower heads. The only other time he'd seen so many shower heads in one place was the shower off the locker room at his high school or the gang shower in the prison in El Paso. He turned the only wall valve he could find, also gold, and all three heads shot very warm water at him under a great deal of pressure.

It's a shame I'm hanging out with a bunch of traffickers. I could get used to this, he thought.

He adjusted the heads so that all three converged on one particular area of the shower, stepped under the stream, and let the hot water wash over his back and shoulders. He felt awful. He had drunk too much tequila last night too fast, and his head was reminding him of this. Drinking while covert was maybe the dumbest thing an operative could do. But yesterday had been hard, and drinking was the price he had to pay for having a conscience.

As the soothing streams forced the tensions and the tequila of the last twenty-four hours from his body, Ray again reviewed the extended conversation he'd had last night with the Condor. Extended conversations with anyone while undercover were, generally speaking, a risky thing. To do so with someone like the Condor was goddamn foolish, but he'd had no choice. The man had elected to speak with him, thank him, and do so in private. Except for the brief introduction his first night, he hadn't exchanged a dozen words with the leader in the ensuing twelve weeks, until their long talk over dinner last night.

With the exception of Carlo and Eduardo and his immediate inner circle, the Condor seemed to meet few people in person and said little to anyone else. It was as if he were more a figurehead than a hands-on leader, somehow above the gritty daily routines required in the trafficking business. His greatest attribute, it seemed to Ray, was that he somehow could conjure up intelligence on the other cartels or the government whenever he desired. Despite Ray's growing feelings to get out somehow, he was determined to get to the bottom of that riddle. The Condor's second-greatest attribute was the psychological impact he had on nearly anyone who came in contact with him. Great mystery was associated with the Condor, and with this mystery came the ability to strike fear, even terror, into others.

Until last night, Ray had just nodded his recognition on the rare occasions he made eye contact with the man, or as much as one could make eye contact with him, given the photochromic lenses in his oversize glasses. Even when the man was inside, his glasses were slightly tinted, which made reading his eyes difficult. The distance the Condor placed between himself and others had suited Ray just fine. Even a semifriendly nod from the man had been a chilling experience rather than a cordial one. This was a man, after all, who, with a nod of his head and a few whispered words, could have you placed against a wall and shot, and the shooters wouldn't question the order for a second. Usually, when covert, Ray sought to make himself invisible, always listening and watching, always quick to do whatever was asked of him. There was safety blending into the furniture. Obviously, because of his new position, that anonymity and the safety that went with it were now gone.

He dried himself off, noticing that the towels, like everything else in his new surroundings, were of the highest quality, very thick and soft. After helping himself to the small basket of shampoos, lotions, shaving cream, and disposable razors sitting on the stone vanity beside the sink, he grabbed a quick shave and then put on clean shorts and a T-shirt before strapping on the two leather sheaths that held his principal weapons. He finished dressing in the nicest of the dark-gray, loose-fitting, two-piece suits Carlo had bought for him weeks before and went to the wide corridor outside his rooms.

There was always a twenty-four-hour roving patrol of guards on the grounds and in the hacienda. One of Eduardo's men stood post in the hall this morning, and Ray nodded to him as he approached. As a former member of Carlo's detail, he often had stood this same post.

Quietly he greeted the much older, harder-looking guard. "Good morning, Jesus. I'll watch things here. Why don't you get us some coffee?"

The guard simply nodded his acceptance of what clearly had been an order. It apparently didn't matter to him that Ray was far younger than he was and had been with the entourage only a few months and not the ten years that he had, for Ray was now a part of the Condor's inner circle, and he wasn't. The Condor decided on all matters within the cartel, and he had selected the younger man to be near him; Jesus therefore did as he was told. After the events of the previous day, any petty jealousy he may have felt at the apparent injustice of one so young and so new to the cartel being elevated so high in the hierarchy didn't exist. Jesus had total respect for Ray and, if truth be known, was even a little afraid of him. Jesus occasionally had killed for his leaders, but it always had been at a distance and by ambush if the other man was dangerous. The killing he had done close in was always of the unarmed and pitiful. Jesus never had confronted a dangerous, armed enemy face-to-face and bested him, as his new young associate had the previous day. And he didn't even carry a pistol. No, if El Cuchillo wanted some fresh coffee, he was only too happy to go get it.

It was still very early, and the other members of the Condor's detail wouldn't be up for at least another hour or two. As Jesus headed off to the other end of the hacienda, Ray took the opportunity the solitude of the empty hall gave him and tried to get a handle on his emotions as he prepared to face his first day as part of the inner circle.

The Condor was difficult to read. On the one hand, he was what he appeared to be, a ruthless drug trafficker who could have a person killed on the spot simply to make a point. On the other hand, in their private conversation the night before, it became clear that the man he was conversing with was highly intelligent and highly educated and, for lack of a better description, refined or polite. This surprised Ray greatly and upset what remained of his preconceived notions about the man.

Prior to the events of the previous day, which had resulted in his promotion to the inner circle, Ray had only observed the Condor from a distance. But he knew that despite appearances—the flowing, wild, white hair, for example—there was a very serious, wary, cautious man behind the ever-present sunglasses. But Ray hadn't been able to make an appraisal of the man's intelligence until last night. He had assumed he was street-smart, and he respected those who had graduated from that school, but it had taken only a few minutes into their extended conversation for him to realize the Condor was at least as educated as he was and likely far more. The Latin reference still bothered him.

He knew the Condor hadn't been pleased when Carlo had brought him, a complete stranger, to the Chihuahua hacienda that first night; his cop instincts had sensed that. Ray never had heard of El Condor de Muerte until they were on the road between Las Palmas and Chihuahua his first day in

Mexico. No such name had come up in any of the briefings Bennie had conducted regarding the principal cartel leaders in Mexico. He intended to discuss that hole in his intelligence briefings with Bennie, if and when he ever got out of this mess. He only hoped that the little information he had managed to get out had allowed Bennie to start plugging the hole in this part of the DEA's overall strategic picture.

As they had driven to Chihuahua that first day, Carlo had explained in great detail that his father, Enrique, and his uncle, Armando, had started their family business years before, trafficking in Columbian cocaine, then moved into weed, methamphetamine, and heroin as the years passed. Carlo and his cousin Pablo, apparently the Condor's childhood name, were the closest of friends when they were kids. When they were ten, Carlo's uncle moved his wife, Pablo, and Pablo's sisters out of Chihuahua to a part of the country far removed from the rival cartels and the drug culture and told no one where they were. Eventually word spread that the family had been kidnapped.

Everyone associated with their business assumed that Armando's family had sadly been the victims of foul play at the hands of their enemies and no longer thought much about the missing family. Carlo still had seen his cousin Pablo from time to time, always on visits to an ocean-side estate. He didn't know where he was, and he never cared. All that mattered was that he had been reunited with his best friend and had an entire ocean to play in. Just after they turned twelve, Carlo didn't see his cousin again for twenty-eight years. Carlo told Ray he never had never forgotten his cousin, but, over time, he had reached a point where he didn't think about him much either.

Everything changed, Carlo explained, when Armando was assassinated ten years ago. Carlo and Eduardo had accompanied their father as he took his brother's body by private plane west to the Pacific Coast. They landed at a dirt strip late in the day and were met by Armando's widow, the aunt they hadn't seen in years, and their cousin Pablo, now forty and unrecognizable as the grown version of the childhood friend Carlo had once known. The man who embraced him warmly and thanked him for bringing his father home had flowing white hair and wore photochromic sunglasses—a necessity given an extreme sensitivity he had to light, he explained. The voice and certain mannerisms were vaguely familiar, Carlo recalled, but nothing else. Following the small family funeral on the grounds of the ocean-side estate, Pablo returned with Carlo's family to Hermosillo and Chihuahua and became involved in the business. He explained that he had been helping his father with intelligence from the safety of an anonymous life in Mexico City, out of view from their enemies, an arrangement his father had planned from the beginning.

Every couple of weeks, Pablo returned to his mother's estate on the ocean with just his personal guards, staying a week or two each time. He explained to his cousins that he had businesses on the coast and in the south that his father had created for the family, and he had to stay involved with them while they remained in the north. The arrangement, he said, was what his father had set up to ensure the safety of the family.

In the beginning, Carlo told Ray, Pablo watched and learned about the aspects of the business that his uncle and cousins ran. But in a matter of months, it was clear to him and the others that in addition to having inherited his father's intelligence, Pablo seemed able to produce information on their rival cartels that allowed the family not only to avenge the assassination of Armando but also to strengthen and expand the family's business. Pablo also was able to point out to his cousins who in the local police could be turned and used by the family. When he had to, as demonstrated by the revenge killings against his father's assassins, Pablo also showed he could be ruthless. A year after Pablo had rejoined them in the north, Carlo's father died of natural causes, and Pablo seamlessly took control of the business. Carlo and Eduardo were more than happy to cede control to their long-lost cousin. With his arrival came greater safety through the information he was able to produce, as well as greater wealth.

Heavy footsteps coming up the hall in the quiet morning brought Ray out of his deep thoughts and back to the present as Jesus returned with two cups of coffee. Ray thanked him and told him to go get some breakfast and some rest. He would stand at the post until the rest of the house was up and the regular guard changed occurred. Jesus nodded and went off to the kitchen, grateful to have the opportunity for an early breakfast and then some sleep. As Ray watched Jesus walk off, he figured he had an hour to prepare for the coming day; he hoped it would be enough. The closer he got to the Condor, the more questions he had and the more his tension level increased.

8

Crystal City Marriott
Washington, DC
Monday night

Frontier Flight 455 bound for Washington, DC, hurtled through the clear but darkening sky at Mach .80 and an altitude of forty-one thousand feet, the rolling farmland and occasional towns of northeastern Kentucky passing silently below. Although it was rapidly growing dark at ground level, there were still the remains of the day at the plane's altitude. The air was calm, which was more than could be said for the somber, serious-looking passenger in seat 12A. Special Agent in Charge (SAC) Benjamin "Bennie" Santiago was a career DEA field agent with an impeccable record of achievement. At five foot nine and an increasingly softening 180 pounds, the fifty-four-year-old still had his thick head of hair, thanks to the Hispanic heritage of his father, although it was slowly going to gray.

He was clutching his powered-down encrypted iPhone as if the harder he squeezed it the more likely the message he dearly wanted to receive miraculously would appear. Even though he knew there would be no reception, he was tempted to turn on the phone, if for no other reason than to test the fiction that, in doing so, the Airbus 320's navigation systems would get so screwed up that the flight would wind up in Baltimore instead of DC. As was his nature, he decided to do the right thing and wait until the plane touched down at Reagan National before turning it on and hope against hope that there would be a message from Ray. It had been more than eight weeks since he had last heard from his top undercover agent in Mexico, and with each passing day, his concern for Ray's safety grew. As Bennie stared blankly out the window at the lights of the small, unnamed towns they were passing over, he thought, *Hell, I don't even know if he's still alive.* That thought chilled him to his bones.

He had come to know Ray Cruz as an undercover operative during a routine joint-task-force operation with the Sacramento police's drug unit six months earlier. At five ten and a very athletic 165 pounds, the twenty-six-year-old Ray still looked like—and had the reflexes of—the eighteen-year-old All-Northern California High School shortstop he had been eight years earlier. Ray had what women called an angelic face that not only made him very attractive to the ladies but also made him appear younger than his years, an asset for undercover work. With his baby face; slim, athletic build; smooth, clear, brown skin; and short hair, Ray could still pass for a twenty-year-old, way too young to be a cop and therefore too young to arouse suspicion. Add to the equation that Ray was one of the smartest, most intuitive young cops he'd ever worked with, and Bennie knew when first working with him that he was looking at a potentially great undercover operative and had offered him a job. Frustrated with his department's efforts in the fight against drug criminals, and intrigued by the kind of work Bennie was offering, Ray had accepted.

The intelligence division of the DEA knew some of their offices along the border with Mexico had been compromised by the cartels. To what extent and who all was involved was unknown, but too many operations were going bad; too many informants and DEA agents were getting killed; and the flow of drugs was continuing almost unabated for there not to be serious security problems. Bennie personally had been tasked by the new director of the DEA, Theodore Mills, to set up and run an independent, very black special operations unit (SOU) and also had been directed to report only to him and the new director of intelligence, Charley Willis. None of the current field SACs or the agents in their offices would be made aware of his unit. As a widely recognized senior SAC who often had run special investigations for the past director, Bennie would continue to oversee in-progress operations conducted by DEA field offices, but his SOU would be a closely held secret. His mission had two primary objectives. The first was to try to penetrate the northern cartels and, if successful, gain information that could help in interdiction. But more important, the mission was to identify traitors in the southwest DEA offices.

Bennie, Theodore Mills, and Charley Willis had joined the DEA within a few years of one another back in the early 1980s. The agency was still in its infancy then, still learning how best to accomplish its mission. Their friendships grew close as their career paths crossed over the years. All had differing areas of expertise and accomplishments; Ted was always the most political and organized of the three, Charley the most cerebral, and Bennie the most talented at operations on the street. The three had worked successfully together for many years in the Southern California field office, so it was no surprise to other long-tenured employees of the agency that the Los Angeles Mafia, as the trio was jokingly called, had achieved the lofty positions they now held within the DEA.

The only real surprise over the last year was that Bennie had turned down the position of operations director in DC, the number-three leadership slot in the agency, to remain in the field. However, in addition to his classification as special agent in charge, he also was designated as special intelligence assistant to the director. In this newly created position, Bennie could come and go as he pleased within the agency, protected as he was with the director's cloak. He had been given carte blanche to select all agents within his special unit and was provided a nearly unlimited budget from Mills's confidential funds.

Bennie's idea to slip Ray into the prison population of the new detention facility in El Paso for an extended period had been a risky one for all the obvious reasons; a lot of violent—potentially deadly—things happened in prison. However, Bennie's gut told him if Ray could pass himself off as just another illegal and a trafficker, and if he could gain the confidence of one of several suspected cartel leaders being held in El Paso, they had a real chance to infiltrate a cartel in a way that Ray wouldn't be doubted. All Ray had to do was stay alive while in prison.

The captured leader Bennie had selected for Ray to get close to was a mystery. Given the information they'd gathered from others swept up with Carlo when the local police had picked him up, the DEA knew he was well connected and an obvious leader of one of the northern cartels. But beyond that, they had nothing on him in their databases, not even a last name. This made him far more interesting than the others Bennie was holding, and he decided Carlo would be the Trojan horse to take Ray inside whichever cartel he was a part of—thus the code name for the operation. There had been no guarantees that Ray would get close enough to someone like Carlo while in jail to gain his trust, nor was there any guarantee that Carlo would take Ray to the cartel after he arranged their the escape, but it was worth a shot. Almost every other operation the DEA had undertaken to infiltrate the cartels had failed—and failed miserably.

After Ray's orientation and cramming sessions for his first assignment, as they flew from Denver to Albuquerque together, he told Ray there would be only two people privy to the details of the first operation plan he had conceived, and the two of them were knocking back a few Coors together at thirty-seven thousand feet. No one—not even the director or Charley Willis—would know all the details of Operation Trojan Horse, only that an operation had been mounted. That was how tight Bennie intended to keep the operation; that was how he intended to keep Ray alive.

He envisioned that should Ray manage to successfully penetrate a cartel, it would likely be on the periphery or at a low level that would allow him freedom of movement and the ability to communicate in a safe, regular, prearranged way. But that ended up not being the case. Remarkably, Ray was at the heart of what was starting to feel like one of the more powerful cartels in the north-central border states, and if that wasn't problematic enough, the cartel Ray had infiltrated was unknown to Bennie and the rest of DEA. As bad luck would have it, Ray was close to a very intelligent, careful, dangerous man who obviously took seriously the need for secrecy, intelligence, and security. While potentially a treasure trove for intelligence, it also made Ray's situation incredibly risky.

This particular cartel and its leader were largely ghosts to the DEA. There had been some intelligence—whispers, really—regarding a powerful renegade cartel run by a mysterious man referred to only as El Condor de Muerte, the Condor of Death, or just the Condor. What little intelligence

Bennie and the agency possessed had come secondhand from captured members of other cartels that had been destroyed or reportedly taken over by this Condor. To Bennie's knowledge, no DEA office had ever apprehended anyone from this mysterious Condor's cartel until Carlo Vargas. Even then it wasn't known until after the escape and Ray's successful penetration of the cartel and his first report what Carlo's last name was and whom he worked for.

To Bennie, it seemed farfetched at first to think that any one cartel leader could consolidate or eliminate other cartels in an organized way, as Ray had reported in his first contact. But after studying the patterns of the increased level of intercartel violence, Bennie realized that what at first appeared to be unrelated widespread violent activity could in fact be interpreted as someone or some group systematically killing off other cartels over a wide area. That thought chilled him, especially with Ray being covert right in the middle of things.

The last ninety minutes of the flight dragged by, and Bennie was relieved when the Airbus finally descended and started its twisting approach to Reagan National a few hundred feet above the Potomac. Seconds after the pilot greased the landing and started the taxi to the gate, Bennie had his phone on and checked his messages. To his disappointment, there was nothing from Ray. He made his way down the Jetway with his carry-on bag and computer and headed toward ground transportation, thinking he couldn't get to his hotel and inside a bottle of single-malt Scotch quick enough. Despite his father's heritage, from his mother's Scottish heritage he had acquired a taste for really fine Scottish malt in lieu of the beers or tequilas so often associated with Hispanics. To his surprise, as he passed into the main terminal, he saw his boss, Charley Willis, standing casually outside the secure area, apparently waiting for his arrival.

Smiling, Bennie approached him. "To what do I owe this honor? Isn't it way past your bedtime?" he asked his old friend as they shook hands.

The professorial-looking intelligence director of the DEA, with his mussed, graying hair and horn-rimmed glasses, smiled back and said, "Well, it's a little late, but I was at the office and knew you were due in about now, and I knew I needed a drink, so I figured you might also after a four-hour flight. I don't suppose you lucked out and there was actually some of that old smoky whiskey you like so much on the flight, and you started without me."

Bennie chuckled. "I was shit out of luck, as usual. I'd rather dehydrate than pay five bucks a shot for the eight-year-old blended crap they peddle on the airlines these days. God, how I miss the good old days of first class and choices of booze. No, I was saving myself for the Marriott and the bottle of Macallan Twelve I intend to buy from room service and charge to the agency. Care to join me?"

"Sounds like a plan," Charley said, smiling once again. "My car's in the VIP lot across the street. You know the way."

Small talk filled the short drive from the airport to the hotel as they caught up on family news and general happenings in the agency. The DEA maintained several rooms at the Crystal City Marriott on a permanent basis for visiting special agents such as Bennie. The hotel was close to DEA headquarters, and the arrangement guaranteed that rooms were always available. The rooms also were secure, as a team from the technical branch of the DEA made regular sweeps to ensure they were electronically clean. Thanks to the proximity of Reagan National to the hotel, it wasn't twenty-five minutes later that Bennie and Charley were sitting in his room, preparing to have their first drinks.

Standing at the small bar area, Bennie poured the fine Highland malt whiskey, added a single small cube of ice to chill it slightly without turning the amber liquid cloudy, turned, and handed a glass to his old friend. Charley removed his suit jacket and stretched out in the one large, soft chair in the seating area, his feet crossed and resting on the coffee table. Bennie kicked back on the couch, sipped his whiskey, and looked at his friend, waiting for him to say what was on his mind.

After sipping at his whiskey, Charley asked in his typically casual, friendly way, "You want to tell me what's happening in Mexico with Ray Cruz?"

Bennie was pretty sure the status of Ray's mission was why he had been summoned back so suddenly to DC, and now he had his confirmation. He set his whiskey down and said, "Truth is, Charley, I haven't heard a goddamn thing since the second call, when he reported the details of the three estates this Condor fellow uses. But you already know Ray also mentioned that all communications in and around this guy are sophisticated and closely monitored. So I'm choosing to believe that all is well, and he's just being very, very careful. In his shoes, I would act accordingly."

Charley nodded. "Of course. Any way you can verify this? Other sources, perhaps, maybe one of our contacts in the federal police down there? Surely they must have more on this Condor than we do. Maybe they're even watching him and could get us a visual on Ray."

Bennie took another sip of single malt and let it sit on his tongue for a second, savoring the taste and using the pause to gather his thoughts, then shook his head slowly and swallowed.

"Not a thing we can do here but wait. Ray dummied into the bull's-eye. He somehow managed to get very close to the leadership in this cartel, and while commendable, this obviously has limited his actions. That Carlo guy I stuck Ray in jail with is obviously a far more important person to this outfit than I ever would've thought, given his careless behavior. Who the hell could've known? Ray will get word to me when he can—that I know about this kid. Put yourself in his shoes. He's immersed twenty-four seven in who knows what kind of environment. You have to assume, based on what little he's already told us, that there's hardly ever a moment when he isn't in the company of others, and the others are all bad guys. He's not allowed to make even one mistake—not one. If he does—if he falls out of character and raises suspicions or is the least bit careless in talking with us—he's dead. Every time I think about Ray and where I put him, hell, Charley, I can't look at myself in the mirror."

"Don't be so hard on yourself," Charley said, concern for his friend evident in his tone. "You've run undercover ops before, and we're a team on this, including Ray when he signed on in Denver. It's not like we didn't discuss the risks."

Bennie shook his head. "This is different. All we've done in the past was establish the occasional business relationship with a cartel, posing as buyers or potential distributors. We've always had backup around in case the shit hit the fan—only now I got a guy in a spot so deep I can't tell you where he is, much less back him up. Truth be told, until now our operations have been stupid. No one really trusts *anyone* down there, and then strangers like us come in posing as new potential business partners, and we expect the cartels to accept us, to trust us? There's a very good reason we're losing this battle right now—we've only dealt with cartels or organizations that were dumb enough to actually believe us. We've been picking at the margins, and we get marginal returns as a result. We've never had a penetration such as this, so we've got to take this slowly and rely on our guy to do what he can, when he can."

Charley nodded as if he agreed. "What *can* you tell me, Bennie?"

Bennie shrugged, and Charley could tell he was frustrated. "I've spent the last couple of months trying to pull what little information we've heard or thought we've heard on this particular cartel together and make sense of it. I'm convinced we're inside an outfit that's been systematically cleaning house on the other cartels in north-central Mexico. A major player, in other words—only until the last twelve weeks, a major player we had very little knowledge of. I'm reasonably sure that this Condor has killed off no fewer than a dozen of the minor players down there and two or three bigger ones. Think about that for a second, Charley—how organized and careful must you be to have been around long enough to know what's going on down there, then get into a position to whack some of the competition, yet not be on the radar of Mexican or US authorities? That's really hard to pull off if that's what's really happening."

"Agreed," said Charley.

"We have bad guys from a half dozen different organizations locked up at Fort Bliss," Bennie continued, "who've all corroborated in some small detail the fact that the organizations they were with were taken out by another group in surprisingly brutal, effective attacks or with timely police actions. What's troubling is that the police actions seem to be well coordinated with the intercartel fighting. This suggests that entire police units are in fact working with or for a cartel. My analysis is that these other groups weren't victims of random warfare between rival traffickers, but that this is the result of a more calculated, organized, systematic plan.

"As to the federal police, under no circumstance do I want them involved with what I have going on. There isn't one son of a bitch in the northern states I currently trust. I don't want them to ever know about my guy inside. I mean, just yesterday one of the top justice officials down there had his ass blown up in downtown Mexico City."

As was his manner, Charley hadn't interrupted or questioned his friend's analysis. Some guys had a real feel for what was happening on the street, and in his thirty years in the agency, Charley never had known anyone with better gut instincts than Bennie.

"Yeah, that kill was an awful shame and a blow to the Mexican government," Charley said as he slowly shook his head. "Emilio Rodriguez was one of the real good guys in the Mexican part of this fight. He was the equivalent to our FBI director, so this was a serious hit. As you know, Bill Johnson over in foreign operations was cooperating with the guy and his brother, Alberto Rodriguez, the head of the federal police. They were working on a joint-task-force operation, using resources out of our San Diego and El Paso divisions, targeting a half dozen seriously nasty groups, including the Mendoza brothers cartel."

"If you didn't always drink so much of my booze," Bennie continued, "you might recall I set up our tactics on this side of the border to get on top of their distribution network. I didn't know who the players were in Mexico since the reorganization down there, but that end of it was all foreign ops."

Charley smiled at Bennie and then turned more serious, nodding his understanding. "Right, well, Alberto Rodriguez, as head of their reorganized federal police, is the sharp end of the stick down there, right on the front lines. They were doing some good this year until the entire Mendoza operation literally got blasted outside Chihuahua several months back."

Bennie tilted his head and looked quizzically at Charley, then said, "I'd heard the Mexican side of that operation had somehow gone bad, but I've been a little busy, thanks to you, so I haven't looked into the details. You going to tell me what any of this has to do with me?"

Charley smiled, thinking that Bennie never missed a trick. No matter how careful Charley was to soft-soap something, Bennie always could see the other shoe dropping. *A great guy to have on your side*, he thought, as he had many times before.

Charley swung his feet off the coffee table, leaned in toward Bennie, and said more quietly, "Alberto Rodriguez called Ted a couple of days ago and told him he'd been approached by a cartel in a covert manner and given a choice—cooperate with a fellow calling himself El Condor de Muerte or see his family killed. Alberto requested safe passage of his family to the United States to get them out of the crossfire. Bill Johnson was down there, participating in some discussions on joint operations, so Ted had Bill load Rodriguez's family aboard a company jet, and they vamoosed out of there."

Bennie sat up, suddenly very interested. "Did he actually mention the Condor? Are you sure about this, Charley?"

"That's what the man said. So naturally, when I heard this and put it together with the second report on your op, well, it was necessary to bring you here and talk."

Bennie ran a hand through his hair. "Jesus Christ, Charley, you're sure he actually said 'El Condor de Muerte'? He actually talked with him?"

"Yep, apparently he did. Rodriguez received a package with a one-time-use cell phone inside and a note telling him to call or see his family wiped out, so he did. This Condor apparently answered and told Rodriguez exactly where and what his wife and children were doing at that exact moment, even what they were wearing. Apparently this Condor said that if his people saw any indication that the family's security detachments had been given a heads-up as a result of their conversation, he'd order their immediate elimination. This Condor gave Rodriguez no choice, so Rodriguez agreed. He hung up, but before he got home that evening, he quietly arranged for his entire family to be hauled out of their estate on one of their air force's choppers—a slick evacuation straight off the family's tennis court and onto their main military base outside the city. As I heard the story, the chopper was in and out in less than five minutes. Rodriguez had the balls not to alert any of his normal security, what with not knowing whether he'd been compromised from within. As soon as his family members were all delivered home by their respective security details, he got the chopper in and out—a ballsy move. Turns out Alberto and the recently deceased Emilio Rodriguez have a first cousin living up here in the States, and that cousin happens to be the commanding general at Fort Bliss, so that's where we took them."

Bennie shook his head in amazement. "You're right, Charley—a very ballsy move. I'm not sure I could have done what he did."

Charley nodded. "You don't stay alive down there for long in Alberto Rodriguez's position without being smart and gutsy. He acted fast and must have caught the bastard off guard because his family is safe, and he's still alive and on the job. Unfortunately, what Alberto didn't count on was the Condor going after his brother and his brother's family, and his brother paid the price for his underestimating the Condor's ruthlessness and organizational ability."

Bennie had raised his eyebrows at the mention of the connection to the commanding general of Fort Bliss, and he was still a little startled at everything Charley had told him. He picked up his glass and took a big drink, then set it carefully on the table and stared at his friend for a long second.

"OK, Charley, let me try to understand this. Our foreign-ops division was supporting a Mexican-run intervention op with their top Mexican cop, Alberto Rodriquez, against the Mendoza cartel, which, if memory serves me, operated almost exclusively out of the northwest area of Mexico. The op went bad, with great loss of life to the Mexican federals due to poor security on their part, so they obviously have traitors in their midst. Soon after, down in Mexico City, Alberto Rodriguez, gets a 'cooperate or we'll kill your family' call from this Condor guy. Rodriguez protects his family, but the Condor gets to his brother instead, blowing his ass up rather spectacularly, I might add, according to CNN." Bennie stood up and slowly paced the room, rubbing his chin and obviously mulling things over, then returned to the couch, sat back down, and looked at his old friend with a troubled look on his face.

"The timing of the call so soon after the Mendoza bust fuckup may be a coincidence, but it also raises some interesting other possibilities, Charley. It might suggest the Condor was involved with that mess, and the assassination is, or was, a none-too-subtle message to Alberto to play ball. In the meantime, in what we thought was a totally unrelated operation that no one knows about but you and me, I managed to get a guy quietly into a cartel in the northern and eastern states, and he tells us it's run, coincidentally, by someone who calls himself the Condor. So it appears the same guy Ray is next to in the northern states went after the head of the federal police down in Mexico City and then killed the head of their version of the FBI. In addition to being a ruthless prick, he appears to operate with some skill over a very wide area. That about sum it up?"

"In a nutshell," Charley said with a tip of his glass to Bennie.

"Jesus…interesting that you mentioned the Mendozas, Charley. Here's another tidbit for you we just learned yesterday. One of the traffickers we caught in Texas a couple of months back was a top man in the Mendozas' operations up here, or so he claims. Apparently, whatever the Johnson-Rodriguez task force failed to do, someone just did for them. If we believe this guy, the Mendoza brothers are quite dead, including another brother who apparently was living up here on the sly and running their distribution. Seems they were taken out at some high-level summit in the last couple of days."

Charley sat back, his eyes a little wider. "You're shitting me!"

"I shit you not, Charley. The informant calls us on Saturday and says to bring him in. When we picked him up, he had no desire to go back south. Said he'd tell us everything we ever wanted to know if we kept him up here and helped get his family out of Mexico. I don't often see bad guys like him scared, but he was."

Charley was deep in thought, digesting what Bennie had just told him. "This is very troubling new information," he said. "A top Mexican Justice official gets killed in Mexico City because of the pressure his brother is apparently bringing to bear on the Mendoza cartel, as well as his refusal to be co-opted. An operation designed to grab a significant amount of Mendoza product and cash turns out to be a setup, devastating the Mexican portion of the task force in Chihuahua. Now you're telling me Rodolfo and Arturo Mendoza, still feeling pretty happy, no doubt about their recent victory over the police, attend some high-level meeting and apparently wind up meeting their maker, as does their brother. All this within a few days, and…a lot of this action happens in or near Hermosillo or Chihuahua, two of the locations where the Condor has estates he operates out of, according to Ray. That's a lot of dots, and two different sources mentioned the Condor—well, I'm thinking at least some are connected. If that's the case, if this *is* one guy doing all this, he has great intel and a long reach, and he is one ruthless son of a bitch."

Bennie nodded. "There's one other thing that's starting to make a little sense, Charley."

"What's that?"

"With all the shit that goes on down there, if you're a cartel leader, and you know someone is killing off the competition, why on earth would you go to a meeting with other cartel leaders? I mean, if ever anything smelled like a setup, wouldn't that be the scenario?"

Charley shrugged. "Yeah, sure, I suppose, but I'm missing your point."

"My point is, wouldn't you be more apt to accept a meet if you thought you were meeting with a friend or partner, say, someone who had just helped you save some product and cash and take out a bunch of federal guys trying to bust you?"

Charley leaned in toward Bennie again. "Jesus, Bennie, I hadn't thought that through. We're speculating a bit here—for all we know, the Mendoza brothers were hit by a pissed-off brother-in-law having nothing to do with anything, but if your reasoning is on the mark, and my gut says it is, then whoever hit the Mendozas might have set them up first by demonstrating a deep reach into the federal task force, tipped them about the raid, and later suckered them to a meet just to take them out. That smells like great intelligence sources and heady strategy and tactics."

Bennie nodded his acceptance of Charley's point and said, "We need more to go on, but my instincts tell me we're next to a real player." He took another swig of his drink and went on. "You know, I met General Rodriguez a couple of months ago. I was just making my manners to the new commanding general of the base, and he was real helpful, ordering his provost marshal to help me with Ray's escape. Impressive guy, lots of responsibility down at the border, what with that damnable new immigration bill. How is it that he's related to one of their former top prosecutors and Mexico's top federal cop?"

Charley sipped at his whiskey, then set it on the low table. "As it was explained to me by a friend from that puzzle palace across the river in Virginia, the general's father is one of several brothers from a much-respected, wealthy, old family down there. He came north when he was about twenty as an exchange student out of their National University in Mexico City. Did some graduate work at UT in Austin, met and married a gal from there, decided to stay after graduation, became a citizen, and had a family. The rest of his family—his brothers, sisters, and all their kids—stayed home, mostly in and around Mexico City, all solid citizens, apparently. The families have remained close throughout the years as a result of the brothers."

Bennie smiled over his glass at his friend. "Interesting story, compadre, and interesting you have a friend at Langley you'll admit to. How do you know so much about this, and, more important, why are you telling me all this?"

"How I know is one of the reasons I asked Ted to get you up here. I have an old, reliable friend, Henry McDonald—you guys met years ago down in Arizona when you helped me out a couple of times. Why I'm bringing it up should be self-evident."

"Can't say offhand I remember him. I'm over fifty—I can't remember what I had for breakfast this morning. Remind me."

Charley chuckled. "He's the chief of staff to the junior senator from Arizona, Pete Martinez."

Bennie nodded slowly. "Aw, yeah, that's right. Now I remember. Hank McDonald, real direct sort, rude son of a bitch, as I recall. He was Martinez's assistant in the Arizona AG office way back when. Helped get Martinez elected governor, didn't he?"

"Yeah, that, and then he helped him get his present senate seat and a spot on the intelligence committee. Hank's a real political pro. Very loyal, and, despite his directness, he suffers fools about as well as you do, Bennie."

"Why the trip down memory lane? What does any of this have to do with special ops and with what I'm currently doing?"

Charley finished off his drink and set his glass on the table. He knew Bennie wouldn't like where the conversation had to go. "Hank and I get together occasionally, and, over a few drinks, we share information on common concerns." Bennie started to sit up, a frown on his face, but before he could say anything, Charley went on. "Now, before you go and get all excited, Hank knows nothing about you or what you've got going specifically. All he knows is that we have some *interesting* things working down in Mexico, and if I hear anything of interest or importance to our country, I'll let him know."

Bennie sat back and threw his hands in the air. "Jesus Christ! The entire point of how we've set up this op is to ensure operational security and keep Ray alive, then get him out, before we get Justice or anyone else involved. What does anything Ray comes up with on the cartels down there possibly have to do with anything Hank and Senator Martinez could be concerned with?"

"There are connections, Bennie. Settle down, and let me try to piece this all together so you see the bigger picture."

Bennie looked hard at Charley, then picked up his drink and tipped his glass as if to say, "Sorry. Get on with it." He trusted Charley more than any other man he knew, inside or outside the agency.

"Hank has a lot of connections in this town for a guy who's only been here for a couple of years," Charley explained. "He's got a friend on the Mexico desk at CIA—a very good friend, I think, given the intel he shares with Hank—and Hank then shares it with me. Between us, we want to try to make sure the left hand knows what the right hand is doing when it comes to Mexico. Hank recently got the three of us together over a few drinks, and we had a chat about the goings-on down there, from our own perspectives, off the record and quiet. I'm grateful to him for arranging this because, as I've explained to you, we have matters of common interest."

Bennie settled down a bit. "That sounds fine. I've never had a problem with the occasional confidential DC cocktail party, but I'll ask you again—what the hell does this have to do with me?"

"One of the big questions we all have about all the problems at the border and in Mexico in general is why President Fernandez has bungled this so badly, Charley explained. "He had twelve months to prepare for the mass deportations from the United States, required by the new immigration bill, and did very little. There was universal condemnation of the Mexican government's pitiful organization and relief efforts at their border camps, which were uncoordinated and poorly managed, to say the least, before they finally got their act in gear. Why such a slow, poor performance? They've had their fair share of natural disasters down there, what with a hurricane season every year, and have a well-developed emergency services organization. Yet it's failed miserably in this instance to deal with the crush of citizens we're forcibly returning to them.

"Furthermore, all this is from a guy who appears to have made his bones by being a ballsy, well-organized, smart prosecutor. Nothing Fernandez has done in the last year strikes anyone as being very smart. If the deportation issues aren't enough, what followed is even more puzzling and destabilizing. Once the crisis became plainly evident, Fernandez issued one of his presidential 'decrees' he's allowed under their constitution and postponed state and midterm national elections indefinitely, on the basis that the government needed to get the mess sorted out in the north so some four to six million recently returned citizens are lawfully identified and eligible to vote. All this does is piss off a lot of smart but not particularly united politicians who normally don't give each other the time of day. Now they have a uniting cause. It just doesn't add up.

"Hank's friend at the CIA believes Fernandez is being controlled somehow rather than controlling events. If that's the case, that likely means cartel involvement. When you couple all this with the fact that concurrent with the deportation mess at the border you have what appears to be a major uptick in infighting between the cartels in the north, well, the three of us think there has to be a connection."

Charley put his drink down and leaned into toward Bennie.

"What I'm saying, Bennie, is that I agree with your initial assessment of the intel you've collected, and we all three suspect Fernandez is in someone's pocket—that, and I think someone down there is using the mess at the border to consolidate the trafficking. Think about it: the greater distraction at the border on the human tragedy developing as a result of our new immigration policy, the less focus there is on just plain old basic drug-crime investigation and intervention. If we connect the dots, that's a hell of a diversionary strategy."

Bennie was staring at his old friend as Charley paused and sipped his drink before continuing. "I don't want to jump to unsupportable conclusions, Bennie. Our data doesn't definitively support this yet, but hell, tell me you don't see some possibilities here. It's open season down there for the cartels to move dope freely—only what we're seeing is an increase in cartel infighting, which appears to be leading to elimination and consolidation. The few known cartel leaders we're tracking seem very much like your typical drug trash—the fringes or margins, I think you called them—ruthless and motivated, to be sure, but none too bright. But then we have the whispers regarding this Condor, whose existence Ray confirmed, and the tactics and results seem very sophisticated and organized. Given Ray's first couple of reports, I'm starting to believe this Condor is a major player."

Bennie had sat quietly, listening carefully to everything Charley was saying, then said, "I see why you're all worked up about this, and I'm not dismissing it out of hand. I too see some connectable dots, at least enough to press forward on this line of investigation. But I remind you that in Ray's first two messages, he couldn't even confirm a real name for the guy, just the Condor nom de guerre. We have his principal lieutenants, his cousins the Vargas brothers, and I'm trying to quietly run that down. But I can't go very far down that path yet without potentially alerting the Condor to the fact that the DEA is looking into his relatives. We have to go slow here, Charley."

Charley shook his head. "I understand your concerns, but time isn't on our side. A lot of bad things seem to be happening all at once, and that can't be a coincidence. Most of this is speculation at this point. We have no hard intel beyond what Ray has given us, and we have nothing on a connection to Fernandez by anyone. We have no evidence the Condor is anything more than what Ray has told you thus far—a more careful and intelligent trafficker, who possibly has reached out to the head of the Mexican federal police and maybe killed off some of his family. But Bennie, you have to agree that's a helluva reach. It's just not the sort of move a small-timer would make. Directly threatening the head of the Mexican national police is a massive overreach for most of these operators, in my learned opinion. It's like going out of your way to kick over a hornets' nest. Why do that?"

Bennie sat back and sighed as he ran a hand through his hair. "I don't disagree, Charley, with anything you've said. I'd add that if we didn't by chance have Ray in with this particular guy, knowing what just happened to the Rodriguez brothers would mean far less—to us or anybody. It's really bad luck for the Condor that such a coincidence exists. He's no longer in the shadows is what I mean, and he doesn't know it yet—a secret, by the way, we need to protect like our young."

He paused again, finished off his drink, and then, looking intently at his old friend, said, "OK, Charley, you want something, so what is it?"

Charley's expression became even more serious than it had been. "Listen Bennie, the situation is bad down there and getting worse and you understand that better than anyone. But what that means is for the good of the country, we need to share information, and we need information from others, and I know you don't like that idea. We need to know who the Condor is. We need to find the connection to Fernandez, if there is one, and we need to know if the Condor is behind all the intercartel bad blood we've seen lately. What we really need, Bennie, is to hear from Ray."

Bennie looked at Charley, then stood up and walked slowly to the bar and poured himself another drink. He turned to his friend and asked, "Another taste?"

"Yeah, but a short one. I have to get home in one piece."

Bennie returned to the couch and poured a little more into Charley's glass, set the half-empty bottle on the coffee table, and sat down slowly, resignation or frustration evident on his face.

"Charley, not five minutes go by in a day when I don't look and see if I have a message from Ray," he said. "Hell, I'm clutching at my phone so often you'd think I was a cheerleader hoping the star quarterback calls and asks me to the prom. Based on what Ray said in his first two messages, I have to believe he's alive and well but can't get word to me. We have to wait this out, as uncomfortable as that'll be. I can't think of a way to find him, let alone make contact, that won't potentially expose him, and I won't do that."

Charley looked at him for a second and said, "What if I told you I think I could get you one hundred percent secure overhead observation of all three of the estates you've identified?"

Bennie leaned back, smiled, and then chuckled. "No offense, but I'd say you're pissing up a rope. No way is the NSA going to task one of their precious National Reconnaissance Office satellites to watch some houses for us—not unless you have some dirty pictures on that tight-assed admiral who runs the place."

Charley smiled. "Not the NSA, Bennie. You say you're ninety percent sure of the estate locations based on Ray's last call? Well, I can help you get to a hundred and maybe even get you eyes on Ray. Interested?"

Bennie's look instantly turned more serious. "Goddamn right I am. What the hell are you talking about?"

"Lieutenant General Manny Rodriguez and his recon drone assets at Fort Bliss."

Bennie was surprised, and it showed. "Hold it, Charley. Now you're the one shitting me. No way will we get DOD approval to fly some of his fancy birds into Mexican airspace—not without a lot of diplomatic bullshitting anyway—and I don't want *any* contact with the Mexicans. The good general was kind enough to show me his toys a couple of months ago when we first met. He has a roomful of young NCOs playing what look like video games, when in fact they're flying drones up and down the border. The imagery is fantastic from ten thousand feet, both infrared and normal visual, and also his lowlight stuff—I'll give you that—but they stay in our airspace. He was quite clear on that point."

"Well, that may be," Charley said, "but that was before his cousin, his very close cousin, was taken out by a Mexican cartel leader we seem to be next to. No one's looking over the general's shoulder, Bennie, not in that rarified air. I'm betting if we sat him down and shared with him what we and the CIA have, he'd help us and not involve the DOD or State. The guy has been a risk taker his entire career. I know he'd help us. I'm at least going to ask."

"Jesus, Charley, that's asking a lot of him—to violate Mexican airspace and do it on his personal authority? Man, you're talking big cojones, pal. This isn't Pakistan we're talking about. If anyone ever found out, he'd be instantly retired if not locked up in Leavenworth. We're talking a couple-of-hundred-mile penetration into a friendly sovereign nation. But man, oh, man, would I like to have those eyes on those haciendas, so count me in. What do we have to do?"

"What we do, Bennie, is I work on getting us invited to a little barbecue in Arizona over the weekend."

Bennie smiled, leaned back on the couch, and patted his somewhat expanding stomach. "You know me, Charley. I love a good barbecue, but what're you talking about?"

"Hank told me that he and Senator Martinez are heading back to Arizona on Thursday, and high on the senator's agenda is a quiet little dinner and a few cocktails with his old West Point roommate, Manny Rodriguez."

This immediately made Bennie sit back up. "Christ on a crutch, Charley, you're going to involve the senator in all this? Why? Have you ever met one of those self-absorbed political sons of bitches who didn't spill his guts if it meant getting good press for himself? Or simply laid, for that matter?"

Charley was a little taken aback by Bennie's outburst but quickly replied, "Well, first and foremost, Senator Martinez is Hank's boss, and he'd be in the loop anyway. Second, Martinez sits on the Senate Select Committee on Intelligence, so he should know about anything we know, and he's in a position to provide us with information we don't currently have. And third, he's a decent guy and highly motivated to help. They're not all self-indulgent philanderers, for Christ's sake. When the hell did you become so cynical?"

Bennie was clearly upset. "I get more and more cynical every time I pick up a newspaper or watch a newscast and hear one of those windbags shooting his or her mouth off about how secure our borders are now. If they're so goddamn secure, why do I still have a job, a gut ache, and get zero sleep? But sorry, Charley, what the hell...you're right. I don't know any more about the senator than what I read in the papers, and he seems to be a good Catholic boy with good intentions. It's too bad, frankly, that the Mexicans have made such a mess of his immigration bill."

"Senator Martinez is a good man, Bennie, and I think he can help us. Anyway, it's inevitable that he'll be involved. After we fill the others in on the dots we're connecting, I think we can get you some eyes on your haciendas. If nothing else, the senator could maybe ride cover for General Rodriguez to help him keep from getting his ass burned on this deal. Where we go from there I have no clue, but it would be better than sitting around staring at our phones, don't you think?"

Bennie shook his head. "Shit, Charley, I'm just a street guy. You're the brains and always have been, but you know as well as I do that with every new pair of eyes or ears we bring in on a secret, we get another mouth, which leads to another, then another, then another. I don't want to lose this kid."

"Neither do I. Hank, the senator, and General Rodriquez are the kind of men I feel we can trust, and they have sources of information and assets we need."

Bennie stared at his old friend, then shrugged in either resignation or agreement. Charley stood and grabbed his suit coat. Bennie got up and walked him to the door; he suddenly was very tired. Charley turned and asked, "How about I swing by about eight tomorrow, and we'll grab some breakfast, and then I'll take you over to the office?"

"Sure. Sounds good. Thanks. See you in morning."

Bennie closed and locked his door, went to the bed, took off his travel clothes, and tossed them over the chair. After a quick shower, he killed the lights and went to bed. But sleep came very slowly as he thought about everything Charley had said, and he tied it to what he already knew. The more he thought about it, the more he knew Charley was right, and as a result, the more he believed Ray was in a world of hurt, and he had put him there.

In all the conversations he and Ray had had leading up to the operation, he always assumed that if Ray were to successfully penetrate a cartel, it would be at such a low level that he could make contact with him regularly.

He'd just be a fly on the wall, reporting what, if anything, he had learned. It never occurred to him that Ray would wind up inside so powerful a cartel and so close to the leaders that it would limit his room to operate. In his gut, Bennie had always expected there would be a real problem with trust. Existing members of a cartel wouldn't completely trust a new guy, so Ray's inclusion, if at all, would most likely be superficial; he'd just be Carlo's young friend, maybe a glorified gofer or something, a driver perhaps.

Bennie had to admit he'd experienced few feelings of relief in his life as great as the one he had upon hearing Ray's first message from inside the cartel. Being killed outright once he got to Mexico was a real possibility they'd discussed, and it was a risk Ray had accepted. The fact that Ray had managed to stay alive so far, as Bennie hoped was the case, was something he promised himself he'd make sure he did everything in his power to maintain. But he could see that promise would be hard to keep. He'd never felt so helpless about an operation in his life. He knew he was grasping at straws when he had agreed with Charley's plan, but Charley was right—it sure as shit was better than sitting around staring at a blank cell-phone screen. How in the hell had Ray gotten so close? His last conscious thought before finally falling asleep was, *What the hell did I get that kid into?*

9

The estate of El Condor de Muerte
Monterrey, Mexico
Tuesday morning

Ray's first day as a member of the Condor's inner circle was a study in contrasts. He spent an hour alone standing Jesus's post at the end of the hallway, thinking about the previous day and everything that had happened, trying to mentally prepare for the new one. As always, the early-morning quiet gave him a chance to try to order his thoughts and control his emotions. In addition to the troubling questions he had about the Condor, the killing of Guzman was hard to process, yet he had to do it—and quickly, before the house got up. He felt deep remorse over the killing, and that was an emotion, along with any outward appearances on his face and in his eyes, that had to be buried deeply. Given the newfound respect Eduardo had shown him, along with the new name Carlo had given him, it was certain that the others in the entourage would think him the quietly sinister cold-blooded killer his new name implied. The humanity he was really feeling hardly fit that perception and had to be concealed. He focused his mind on what he knew about today's events from his dinner conversation with the Condor. The morning, he understood, would be spent shopping for new clothes; midday was to be devoted to a meeting with the Condor and the others of the inner circle, followed by Francisco's funeral on the estate grounds. After the service, the late afternoon and evening were, for lack of a better description, to be a wake for the departed Francisco.

As the sun came up, the occupants of the sprawling hacienda slowly emerged from their various quarters and headed off to their respective dining rooms for breakfast. By and large, the entourage ate in shifts in an informal dining area adjacent to the commercial-quality kitchen at the back of the great house. From there, the many guards and members of the household staff could come and go via French doors that opened out to a trellis-covered stone terrace. Most living quarters for the entourage, both guards and permanent house staff, were located in the half dozen casitas scattered around the rear areas of the estate grounds. They therefore could come and go to the main house and not intrude on the Condor, who visited the rear areas of the estate infrequently. The more senior members of the entourage, Carlo and Eduardo, and the communication techs occupied quarters in the south wing of the main house. The Condor always came and went through the magnificent front entry hall and spent most of his time in the formal areas of the mansion—the great room, the dining room, and his private study—when he wasn't occupying his four-room suite at the end of the north wing. No one entered the Condor's dining room or study without being summoned, and access to his private quarters was even more restricted.

Raul Ortega, the new head of the Condor's detail, came out of his suite, saw Ray standing at his post, and walked up to him. "Ah, El Cuchillo, what are you doing here? Did you not sleep well? Is there something wrong with your rooms?"

Ray put his game face on. "I couldn't sleep, Senor Ortega. I'm still a little surprised about everything that's happened. But my rooms are the nicest I've ever had…and the shower—it is unbelievable!" His response wasn't a thought-out act. He was genuinely amazed at his new surroundings and didn't hide this fact.

Raul smiled at him. "Yes, the shower is excellent. Wait until you share it with your first woman—they love it. As to your new duties, relax and give the changes some time. Believe me when I say you can handle them."

The entire time Ray had been inside the cartel, until the last twenty-four hours, he couldn't remember Raul having said more than a few words to him—usually in the form of orders—certainly he never had seen him smile. Carlo, despite his easygoing and friendly demeanor within the cartel, looked every bit like the menacing criminal he was. But Raul was the opposite. All four members of the inner circle dressed better than the others in the entourage, for starters, which apparently was expected of those around the Condor. But the slim, tall Raul, with his quietly professional demeanor and handsome features, looked more like a lawyer to Ray, not a criminal or the head of security to a cartel leader.

I need to be careful, Ray thought. *He's obviously trying to put me at ease. Maybe it's sincere now that I'm in the inner circle, but maybe I'm being measured somehow. Keep it short and simple; don't trip up. He sounds different this morning, kind of like the Condor did last night. This guy is smarter than he lets on. Jesus, are they all like that?*

"I didn't know that was allowed...having women at the hacienda, I mean."

"You're part of the Condor's security detail now, El Cuchillo, the inner circle. You'll learn there are different rules for us, and please call me Raul. Only the Condor needs to be addressed formally."

Ray nodded and asked, "With respect, Raul, could you call me Ray and not El Cuchillo?"

Raul smiled again and chuckled. "Of course, Ray, when we're alone as we are now. But when you're around the others, you'll have to get accustomed to your new name. Not only will the others call you this out of respect for what you've done, but also, it's sometimes important that they be reminded of your particular skills. Fear is a weapon, Ray, not unlike the knives you carry. Fear can be more effective than violence and far less expensive. You don't overtly threaten those who know of your skill, but never is it far from their thoughts. You'll learn more about the importance of fear as a tool the more time you spend with us. Come. Let's get some breakfast and go over the schedule."

Jesus, for weeks I've thought this guy was nothing more than a lapdog for the Condor. He's a hell of a lot smarter than I thought. The guy is... what? "Polished" or "smooth" are the only words I can think of to describe him. His entire manner is almost... kind.

Raul led Ray out of the north hall and into the main foyer, where he ordered one of Carlo's men to stand the post near the Condor's suite. They entered the formal dining room, with its polished wooden table and chairs for a dozen, and sat at one end. Immediately, one of the young female servants entered with a pitcher of coffee and another of orange juice and then stood off to the side, awaiting instructions from Raul.

"The usual for me, Juanita," Raul said kindly as she nodded her understanding and shifted her look to Ray.

Ray looked at Raul. "May I ask what the usual is?"

"A peasant's breakfast, Ray: eggs, chilies, some local goat sausage, and warm tortillas."

"I'll have that also," Ray said, turning to the beautiful young woman. There was no mistaking the look in her eyes as she quickly averted them, nodded, and then left the room. She clearly was scared to death of him. Apparently news of yesterday's events was now common knowledge in the hacienda.

God, the way she looked at me, Ray thought. *What have I become? I have no idea who this young woman is, but to her I'm a killer, someone to fear. Please don't hate me, Juanita! Shit!*

Raul poured the coffee and offered Ray a cup, then added cream and sugar to his and looked at him as if to ask, "And for you?" Ray shook his head and silently watched the older man as he drank.

Raul put his cup down and looked at him. "After breakfast, Carlo will take you to town to visit the tailor, Dominguez. He's been making clothes for the family since Carlo was your age. You'll need a half dozen fine suits and all that goes with them: shirts, ties, belts, jewelry, and, of course, the correct shoes. Where we go when we leave the north requires that you look correct, formal. You'll be required to look and play a part that at first you may find difficult, perhaps even frightening."

Ray was nervous in Raul's company and couldn't help believing that some of his emotions were showing, which would only make the situation worse. So he did what Bennie had taught him and used his emotions as part of his character. "I'm already finding it difficult, Raul. What do you mean by 'playing a part'? I question whether I'm smart enough to be part of the Condor's detail."

Raul smiled reassuringly at him, clearly impressed by Ray's candor. "You'll do fine. I'll explain more to you after we leave for the coast. I'd normally suggest to a new member of the circle that you observe and listen at first, but that seems to come naturally to you. All will become clear in time, but know this: after what happened yesterday, had Jefe asked me who should replace Francisco, I would have picked you. You're new here, and you're young; I can understand why you doubt yourself, but I knew Zandro Guzman for twenty years. He was a worthless shit, but he was also a dangerous enemy. I only wish I could have been there myself to see you put him down. No, anyone who could take Guzman with a knife can stand with me. You'll get used to things and quickly, I think. Jefe said you were smart, and I can see that. So relax, watch, and learn. You're a natural for the type of work you'll be required to do for Jefe. Now, as for your wardrobe, Dominguez knows what you'll require and will have one suit for you today before you return to the estate. I want you to wear it back; it will be appropriate for this afternoon. When you and Carlo return, we'll lay Francisco to rest."

Although Raul's tone was conversational, there was a quiet emotion in his statement about today's events that couldn't be missed. Ray's intuition told him to draw Raul out with more conversation, if for no other reason than to get the man more comfortable with him.

"I wish I'd known Francisco," Ray said. "What he did yesterday…it took more courage than my killing Guzman. The other assassin had a chance to see him coming and get off a shot. Francisco killed him with his hands. His strength was greater than my knife."

Raul was looking at him, and Ray saw pain in his eyes. "Yes, Francisco had courage, always did. Even when we were boys, he never backed down from anyone."

Raul paused and looked off in the distance, as if remembering long-forgotten times and the camaraderie of boyhood friends.

Building a relationship with Raul was important to his safety, so Ray asked quietly, "You were friends for a long time, Raul?"

Raul returned his gaze. While there were no tears—the man was far too hard for that—Ray saw sadness in his eyes. "He was my older brother, Ray, and I'll miss him greatly."

Juanita came in as Raul was talking and set their plates in front of them. Neither of them spoke again until they'd nearly finished their breakfasts, which suited Ray just fine. Carlo and Eduardo entered the dining room at the same time, saving Ray from having to say anything more to Raul. He didn't know what to say, really; he had had no clue Raul and Francisco were brothers. He kept reminding himself that these men were criminals; many were murderers; and they all were in the business of moving drugs into America. Yet as he sat among them, they too mourned their dead and celebrated family and friendships.

He found himself feeling empathy for Raul as he so obviously and courageously silently mourned his brother's violent death of the day before.

This is crazy, Ray thought. *Remember who and what you are and who these guys are. Jesus, this could get complicated.*

After Carlo and Eduardo joined them, the conversation turned mostly to everything that had to be done today and who would be doing what. Ray and Carlo left the dining room, and, along with a driver-guard, took one of the Escalades and drove to Monterrey. The tailor, Dominguez, would be waiting for them at his shop; Eduardo had called him while they made the twenty-minute drive into the city. The narrow paved road that fronted the estate wound its way down from the hills until it met Highway 40, which would take them east into the affluent Monterrey suburb of Garza Garcia. Dominguez's shop was located on a nice retail street lined for many blocks with every sort of small shop or specialty store, as well as the occasional restaurant or cantina.

Abele Dominguez looked like a tailor. Even at the early hour—it was just past eight—he was immaculately dressed in a fine three-piece suit. After greeting Carlo and Ray, he removed and properly hung up his coat as he prepared to do his job. He had a gold pocket watch and chain that hung across his vest, green garters on his sleeves, a cloth tape measure hanging around his neck, and half glasses perched on his nose. Ray was surprised to find out from Carlo on their drive to town that Dominguez was a Jewish tailor. He casually had commented that Ray would like his new suits "because the Jews are the best tailors." As silly as it was, it had never occurred to Ray that there were Jewish Mexicans. He decided right then and there that as careful as he had been on this assignment, it wasn't enough. Despite the mission prepping he'd done, he really knew very little about Mexico.

Dominguez began taking all the necessary measurements. "He's to have whatever you've made for Raul or Luis," Carlo told the old man, who simply nodded his understanding and kept measuring.

When Dominguez was finished, he told Carlo he should take Ray to the shoe store down the block and get fitted for new shoes to go with the suits he would be preparing. He said he would call his friend who owned the shop and let him know exactly which styles were required. In the meantime, he would get to his alterations and have one suit ready for them when they returned.

Carlo led them out the front door and down the block to the shoe store. An equally elderly man treated them just as well as Dominguez had. It required only a few minutes to measure him and have him try on a few pairs. The styles surprised Ray. The first several pairs were similar to old-fashioned wing tips. He recognized them because his dad had always had a pair or two, but never in his twenty-six-years had Ray owned a pair. He had always thought of wing tips as "old-man shoes," and here he sat getting fitted for black and oxford pairs. There were also loafers in two colors and several pairs of some basic black shoes that reminded him of what waiters or waitresses wore in restaurants. Not the least bit stylish, but they were the most comfortable of the lot. The elderly shoe merchant boxed up all six pairs, put them in several bags, handed them over, and thanked them for the business. Carlo nodded and took Ray back to the tailor's. A bill for the shoes had not been offered, nor had payment been extended by Carlo—they simply walked out.

They had been gone for only twenty minutes, too soon for Dominguez to have finished his labors, so they went to the Escalade, dropped off the packages, and entered the back of a restaurant across the alley from Dominguez's shop. Even at the early hour, the door was unlocked, and Carlo led them through a small but spotless kitchen into a dark, low-ceilinged space with a bar and a few tables, all covered with red-and-white-checkered tablecloths. This and the general ambience of the small but pleasant-appearing restaurant suggested to Ray that it was probably an Italian one, which, like the revelation that his tailor was Jewish, surprised him. The owner came out of an office adjacent to the kitchen and greeted Carlo warmly but gave Ray a nervous, wary look.

"Benito, old friend, this is Ray. He works with me, and he's my friend. I'd like you to remember that."

"Of course, of course, Carlo. Welcome, señor. What may I get you? Have you had your breakfast?"

"Just coffee, Benito, and some sotol on the side," Carlo told the owner. Before he said more, they sat at one of the tables and waited until Benito had served them and left. "Have you had sotol before?" Carlo asked Ray.

"I don't think so," Ray said. "What is it?"

Carlo smiled. "It's a special local mescal. Pour a little into your coffee—it's a nice way to start the day."

Carlo poured a small amount of sotol into his black coffee, stirred it, and sipped the hot blend. The last thing Ray wanted was a shot of mescal in his coffee before nine in the morning, especially after having drunk half a bottle of tequila the night before, but he nursed his coffee along as Carlo told him about the shopping district they were in and the various businesses that occupied it, all apparently owned by the Condor and the family.

"The Condor's father, my uncle Armando, was a very smart man," Carlo explained. "He started taking our profits and buying up the land and businesses in this area thirty years ago, when business wasn't so good for them. In return for providing us what we need, no questions asked, they get a fine income and protection from any troubles. We own almost everything in the four blocks around us. There are all kinds of businesses, all of them honest, all owned under different names but all controlled by us. The places on this street, like this cantina, aren't as fancy as the places downtown, but they do a good business. Downtown, we own several square blocks as well. Now that you're a part of the Condor's circle, you'll come to know all this. It's his job to watch over our business interests here and throughout the country, while Eduardo and I produce our product and move it into the United States. Your job will be to keep our cousin safe."

Ray never had known exactly what everyone's responsibilities were, and he cataloged the new information from Carlo into his memory. He was astounded at the breadth of the Condor's diversification. The value of the real estate alone that Carlo said the Condor controlled was incredible, and that didn't even take into account the value of his many successful businesses. The amount and quality of information Ray was accumulating was intelligence of the highest order.

After Carlo drank several coffees and told Ray more about the family's business, they left the cantina and returned to Dominguez's shop after stopping at the SUV and picking up one of the new pair of dress shoes. As they came through the rear door, the tailor stood in the back, admiring a dark-blue pinstripe suit on a rack. He was carefully brushing it, making sure it was free of any loose threads or lint.

"Ah, you're back. Good," Dominguez said, speaking directly to Ray. "Step into that dressing room, young man, and remove your clothes, and we shall dress you properly."

Dominguez handed him a package and gently pushed him in the direction of the dressing room. Ray did as told, and then Dominguez pulled the curtain closed. Ray looked into the package and found some new underwear, a T-shirt, and socks. He removed what he was wearing and started to put the new clothes on. The old man handed him the new suit through the curtain as he was doing this, complete with a dress shirt and tie. He put the shirt on, and then the slacks and shoes. As he was lacing up the black wing tips, Dominguez handed him a new black belt to go with the suit. He started to tie his tie but thought it best to let Dominguez show him how, as it might raise suspicion, even in the dimly intelligent Carlo, if he came out with a double Windsor properly in place. He slipped the lovely summer wool suit jacket on over the dress shirt, amazed at the quality of the material and the fit.

His back knife sheath was over his dress shirt, covered only by the new suit jacket. His sleeves were perfect, and his arm sheath was concealed perfectly, yet he still had room to extract the H-K quickly if need be. He checked out his reflection in the full-length mirror on one side of the small room and couldn't believe how he looked. He'd never owned such a high-quality suit before, and his first thought was that he swore he looked several years older.

When he opened the curtains, Carlo smiled with admiration. "Very nice, Ray, very nice."

With a sheepish look, Ray handed the tie to Dominguez and asked the old man if he would show him how to tie it. Dominguez smiled warmly and assured him he wasn't the first young man he had had to teach how to tie a knot. After several tries, Dominguez was satisfied that his new pupil would be able to handle the simple task on his own, while Carlo watched the short lesson with amusement. Carlo thanked the old man after telling him to finish up the rest of the order by day's end and have it delivered to the estate.

He and Carlo headed out the back door, and as they walked, Carlo turned to him and said, "Think you're hot shit now, eh, my friend, with your fancy clothes and your neckties you can now tie?"

Ray looked at Carlo with an almost panicky expression that immediately made Carlo laugh.

"Easy, El Cuchillo, easy. I'm just fucking with you. In case you didn't know, in our little family, you *are* hot shit."

Carlo stopped beside the Escalade, his expression turning serious, and placed a meaty hand on Ray's shoulder. "Listen, my friend, there's nothing more important to us than one another. You saved my two brothers yesterday, and you saved me in that hellhole in El Paso. We're of different mothers, yes, but I consider you my little brother, my family. When we crossed the border together, I told you I owed you my life—well, now I owe you three. Anything I have, Ray, is yours. All you have to do is ask."

Ray said the first thing that came to mind, because in an incredibly ironic way, it was the cold, emotional truth. "Thank you, Carlo, but you owe me nothing. You brought me into your family, which is payment enough."

Even the hard, ruthless Carlo seemed moved by the bullshit sentiment. It was beginning to bother Ray that these people—his targets, as it were—were showing a far more likeable personal side; he felt too close. Back in their cell in El Paso, he had just gotten close enough to be trusted so Carlo would take him into whatever organization he was a part of. It was the only way Bennie would allow the penetration attempt to go forward. But he always had dismissed any talk of friendship from Carlo as jailhouse talk from a cellmate who was grateful for having been saved in a prison-yard brawl. But after the events of yesterday, all that had changed. The emerging awareness that the Condor and Raul were nothing like typical traffickers complicated everything. The reality was that the smarter they were, the more dangerous they became, which made concealing his true identity far more difficult. Getting friendly with these men didn't make his job easier; it made it much harder, the risks even greater.

Carlo went on as all those thoughts rolled through Ray's head. "I know little of the Condor's business when he leaves us, but I know it's important and dangerous. Because of what he does, he's able to provide us with information about our enemies that allows us to survive. You're part of his circle now. Raul told me of your worries, how you think you may be offending me in some way because of your new duties. I tell you, I'm proud of you, El Cuchillo, and proud to call you my brother. Just protect Jefe, as you did yesterday." He squeezed Ray's shoulder and smiled again. "And I meant it when I said you look sharp. Don't be embarrassed that you didn't know how to tie a tie. What the hell—I still don't!"

Carlo threw his head back and laughed heartily at his own humor, and then they got into the Escalade and headed downtown. Along their route, Carlo pointed out the various businesses the family had an interest in. After driving around the downtown area for twenty minutes, when it was clear to Ray that they were finally returning to the estate, Carlo turned to him and said, "When we get back, you'll go to Raul. He'll either be in the study or his suite—we'll know when we get there. He has things for you to do until it's time to honor Francisco. It's time you begin your duties as part of the Condor's inner circle."

Ray looked at Carlo and, as nonchalantly as he could, nodded in agreement. To Carlo, he appeared calm and in control—a special young man with special skills. But inside, Ray's guts were twisted in a knot, and he was as unsure of himself as he'd ever been during the mission. When he had accepted Bennie's job offer, he knew he could wind up in edgy, even dangerous surroundings. But he never had imagined the circumstances he was now facing. Despite Raul's assurances over breakfast that he would do well in his new duties, Ray had serious doubts.

10

The estate of El Condor de Muerte
Monterrey, Mexico
Tuesday morning

Carlo and Ray returned to the estate and pulled to a stop under the porte cochere. Carlo turned to Ray and told him to go inside and report. After Ray entered the great foyer, it was clear from where the guards were posted that Raul was in the study. Ray walked up and nodded recognition to one of the guards standing to the side, who then opened the door without a word. Ray took a deep breath, and then, after a brief pause, walked in as the guard closed the door behind him. The Condor and Raul were sitting at the Condor's large desk with the head of the Condor's electronic-security and information-gathering team, a mousy, bespectacled man named Baca. Miguel and Luis, the other two principal guards and members of the inner circle, sat on an adjacent couch, watching Ray. The Condor looked up from his desk and smiled, taking in Ray's appearance and clearly liking what he saw. The others were dressed more casually than Ray, wearing sport coats and tieless dress shirts in lieu of the fancy suit, dress shirt and tie, and new wing tips he was wearing. The Condor turned to Baca and said, "Take his photograph, and we'll finish after lunch, Geraldo. Then finish his history, get the current updates from the capital, and be prepared to present them at two. I must call in at three."

"Yes, Jefe. All will be ready."

Ray had seen Baca often in the last twelve weeks but had had no idea what his first name was until this moment. To him and the other guards of the entourage, he was always just Baca. Geraldo looked at Ray, nodded an unsmiling hello, and asked him to stand in front of the drapes that covered the expanse of floor-to-ceiling windows that looked out over the estate to the west. When Geraldo was satisfied with what he saw in the viewfinder of the small but sophisticated digital camera he held, he fired off a succession of shots. Without another word, he turned and left, leaving Ray alone, and puzzled, with the Condor and the three other members of his security detail.

The Condor was smiling and watching him. "Geraldo is a brilliant man, Ray. He does for me what no other in Mexico can. But like you, he doesn't say much. Don't be offended if he's short with you—he has great responsibilities." The Condor's tone grew more serious. "Tomorrow we'll be leaving for the west coast and my home there. By the time we get there, you'll have an extensive, detailed personal record in the many computer files of the federal government. Anyone who bothers to check on you—and there will be some who will do so—will discover that you're a decorated, respected young police officer from Hermosillo. If they contact the chief of police in Hermosillo, he'll confirm for the federal officials that you are who their computer printouts say you are. They'll discover, if they look, that you're the nephew of Raul and Francisco, their younger sister's oldest son, and that following in your uncles' footsteps, you've taken Francisco's place on my security detail."

The Condor paused, and when he spoke again, he was more reflective and quiet. "A small circle of important officials inside the government have known Francisco for a long time and will be saddened to hear that he has died. What all this means and why this is important will become clear to you when we reach the coast. Once we leave here, you'll be known as Ray Ortega. It's important you remember this, as that's the name in the history Geraldo will place in the government's computers. Geraldo will have a summary of your new life's history printed out for you so that you can study it tonight. It's important that you know your new identity well."

He then forced a smile. "But enough of that. You've met the others before but haven't had a chance to get to know them. Raul, please," the Condor said as he stood from his leather executive chair and walked over to the bar against the side wall.

As Raul made the introductions, the Condor poured some of the Herradura from the night before into crystal tumblers and passed them around. Ray's mind was racing as he tried to comprehend the magnitude of what had just been so casually revealed to him. By the sound of it, this man Geraldo would be accessing what Ray imagined were secure government databases and inserting into them a false identity with a history that would satisfy the federal police if they looked into him.

Jesus Christ, that's exactly what Bennie did to get me into the cartel in the first place. Now this character is doing it to get me into…what? Why would the federal police or others in the government want to check up on me? You have to remember all this. Are they hacking in somehow without detection, or is it something else? It's so thorough—it has to be something else, but what?

"This old man here is Miguel Rivera," Raul began as he touched Miguel's shoulder affectionately, "who, like me and my brother, has been with Jefe for many years. And the younger one is, of course, Luis Medina, who until your arrival was the youngest of our group and is grateful you now have that distinction. He's been with us for seven years and is the son of Philip Medina, an original member of the Condor's circle, who, like Francisco, fell in order to protect him."

The Condor was passing them all glasses as Raul made the introductions. With drinks in hand, they looked at the Condor as he cleared his throat and offered a toast. Ray saw deep emotion in him, as if he were struggling to maintain his composure.

"My friends," he said in a soft, gentle voice, "I have several toasts I would like to make—first, to our friend and brother, Francisco. We will miss you, old friend."

They each took a swallow of their drinks. "And to my new friend, Ray, to whom I owe my life and those of my dear cousins. You're young, Ray, and you're new to our group, but in the short time you've been among us, you've saved each of us from violence. I find this fact amazing—remarkable, really. We live in a dangerous world, and we conduct a dangerous business, but it's the life we've accepted from our fathers, despite what we may have wished for. You came into our world by chance because you had the courage to take action when circumstances presented themselves and escape from the authorities in America. In doing so, you returned my cousin, my dear friend, to me. Yesterday your attention to your surroundings and your decisive action when it was necessary saved Eduardo and me from certain death. I'm grateful to you and thankful to God for your deliverance. You've earned your place in this group, and here before my oldest and most-trusted friends, I thank you and salute you. What we've lost in our dear friend Francisco we replace with you. Gentlemen, please join me and welcome El Cuchillo to our circle."

"El Cuchillo," the other three bodyguards said in unison.

With that, the Condor moved to Ray and touched glasses, followed in turn by the other three men. They drank and then stood as the Condor poured more from the old crystal decanter that held the aged tequila.

I'll be damned, Ray thought. *I'm really in, but in what? They're so much like any family in the way they honor their dead. Carlo treats me like a brother, and it makes me uncomfortable, but why? I'm clearly safer with his thinking that. Is it because I've been befriended by a criminal, or something else? Bennie said the secret to safety when you're undercover is getting close but not too close. I didn't know what he meant then, but maybe now I'm finding out. And what the hell was the Condor's reference to God and my deliverance? What was that about?*

Ray was still thinking about the little things that were bothering him, as well as the emotion and camaraderie that was evident in the room, when the Condor went on.

"Please, gentlemen, sit. We have some time until we lay Francisco to rest, and I'd like Raul to bring Ray up to date on our plans and movements for this week. But first, let me say how much I admire your new suit, Ray. How did you like old Dominguez?"

Ray popped back into the moment, once again focusing on the Condor. "He's unbelievable, Jefe. I've never before had such fine clothes and so quickly. I can't believe how I look, to tell you the truth."

The Condor smiled warmly at Ray's honesty and then turned more serious once again. "How you look—and how you act—in the coming weeks will be important. In the short time you've been here, it hasn't escaped my attention that you have a special gift, and I'm not talking about your skill with knives. You listen, and you watch. I've noticed this about you; it's a wise man who does so. At first I thought it was simply because of your age and the fact that you were thrown into new, unfamiliar, and perhaps intimidating surroundings in the company of older, potentially dangerous men. But it's far more than that, and I know this now. You possess a valuable skill, my young friend, and you'll need to rely on it once we go west."

God, he's intuitive, Ray thought as a jolt of adrenaline shot through him. *He's been reading me like a book but not seeing the truth. And I thought I was so fucking clever!*

"Did Carlo speak to you about some of our other interests in town?" the Condor asked.

Ray gathered himself from his troubling thoughts, regained his control, and answered after a brief pause. "Yes, Jefe. He showed me some of the places around Dominguez's store and also the businesses downtown."

"Good. There's much, much more, and in time you'll learn what and where and why this is so important. Did Carlo also speak to you about my father?"

"Some, Jefe, and your father's brother."

The Condor's look changed again, becoming almost melancholy, and then he went on. "My father was a special man. This too will become clear to you in time. He had little formal education, yet he was the most intelligent man I have ever known. Everything I am, everything I know, I owe to my father."

The Condor paused and looked thoughtful for a second before going on. "And my mother also—I must be honest here. Despite her limitations, she also has influenced my life, only in far different ways. You'll have the chance to meet her tomorrow. Once we're on the plane, we'll talk more of this. Raul, please review the schedule for tomorrow and the rest of the week."

"Yes, Jefe." Raul turned to him. "Tomorrow morning at eight, we'll go meet the plane and return to the coast. After spending the night at the estate, we'll fly to the capital. Jefe has important business beginning on Thursday. Both at the coast and in Mexico City, we'll be met by others. In the presence of all others, Ray, we of the circle appear as nothing more than the Condor's security detail, but, as you'll learn, we're in fact much more. There's much we do for Jefe, especially when others aren't watching us. The first thing you must learn and never forget is that it's only in the north, here at the three estates, that we refer to Jefe as the Condor. When we're on the plane, I'll explain more, but you must remember this: once we leave for the coast, there *is* no Condor, understand?"

Ray was instantly confused, as nothing Raul had said made any sense to him, but he kept his face passive. "I think so, Raul. How do I address Jefe once we leave?" he asked, glancing at his ever-puzzling boss.

"We'll go over that tomorrow on the plane, when everything will become clear," the Condor answered. He turned back to Raul. "Where is Fernandez?"

"He's in the city all week, Jefe, coordinating with the executive departments on the relief efforts, as you directed. Relief supplies to the camps no longer will be impeded, as you've ordered. Fernandez has mobilized all the medical-relief and emergency-response teams we have and ordered them north. Many will still perish, I'm afraid. He also has ordered another ten thousand troops to the north to assist in the transportation and distribution of supplies and to help maintain order. Most of these troops are being transferred from Sinaloa, as it's the closest to Sonora. We can now move on our enemies in the west as planned."

"Good, good. I'm saddened by the deaths at the camps. I had no idea the sickness could spread so far so fast. More unnecessary deaths I'm responsible for," the Condor said sadly. He shook his head and sighed deeply.

"Don't be so hard on yourself, Pablo," a sympathetic Raul said. "You couldn't have known there would be an influenza outbreak in the camps."

The Condor looked at Raul, shrugged slightly, and shook his head again. "Nevertheless, the chaos at the border was at my orders, but what's done is done. It was regrettably necessary that Fernandez look bad. When exactly is the Gang of Four meeting?"

"Our informants say the exact date hasn't been set," said Raul, "but it'll be soon, near Los Mochis, as usual, and in the usual place they think is so secure. Our people also tell us they're being extra cautious. Eduardo says several of Arellano's lieutenants in Tijuana have gone missing recently, including one of our people who's been inside their camp for years. A great loss, I'm afraid. Arellano suspects his three associates were involved in their disappearance, which is why a final date for the meeting hasn't been set. All, of course, profess their innocence, but that doesn't explain where these men have gone. There's no evidence of foul play—they're simply gone—vanished, as if into thin air."

"What do you make of this?" the Condor asked, clearly saddened to hear that one of the young men he had asked years ago to try to infiltrate their enemies' organizations was now missing and likely dead.

"I am, of course, continuing to look into this, as is Eduardo, but for the moment, I'm unsure. An old score, settled perhaps by others having no connection to our business here or perhaps mischief by one of the Gang of Four against the other? We know it isn't the federals, but other than that, we really know nothing. What we do know is that these missing men are very knowledgeable of Arellano's operations, which makes them valuable. Our man has been a great source, loyal all these years, and comes from a good family. I want very much to know what happened to him."

"So do I," the Condor said. "Have you considered the North Americans?"

Raul nodded. "Yes, Jefe. We've made discreet inquiries of our sources in El Paso, Nogales, and Tucson, but they've heard nothing, and they're in a position to know. I believe this is between us in the south."

The Condor looked grim. "I know neither the federal police nor the army was involved, as I haven't ordered any such actions, so that probably means its local. Perhaps one of the others made a move we're unaware of. Let's not worry too much about this. We'll maintain our schedule and end this. Make the call, Raul. It's time to make District Commander Diaz a hero. Make sure he knows there'll be a summit soon. We'll advise him of the date and place when that information becomes known. Let's see how long it takes him to pass the information up to Alberto Rodriguez."

There was a knock at the door, and Carlo entered to tell the Condor that Father Barilla had arrived, and it was time.

"Thank you. That's enough for now, my friends. Let's go say our farewells to Francisco."

Ray was stunned at the exchange and was using all his willpower and training to keep his face neutral and impassive. *Fernandez? Jesus Christ, did he say Fernandez has ordered more troops to the north, as in the president of Mexico Fernandez? And if they are talking about the president of Mexico, how the hell do they know what he'll be doing all week? How are these people involved with the president? And what was that shit about no longer impeding the supplies? Is that why there's such a mess at the camps? I have to contact Bennie somehow.*

Ray had listened to the entire conversation, trying to remember names and places, but it had all been too much too fast. In addition to the mention of what probably was a reference to the president of Mexico, several other big nuggets of information registered with him, including the mention of the Gang of Four. During Ray's briefings, Bennie had given him a crash course on the overall structure and organization of the trafficking business of Mexico. Of the twenty-four known cartel or gang leaders in Mexico, the four largest, most active, dangerous cartels were referred to as the Gang of Four. Their leaders had arrived at some kind of truce that had resulted in a loose alliance that benefited them all to the detriment of the police in the states of Sinaloa and Nuevo Leon. More than 1,200 policemen or federal troops had been killed in the last several years by the Gang of Four, not to mention thousands of innocent citizens. What Ray had just heard was that the Condor was going to tell some local police commander that the Gang of Four was meeting, and then, based on this tip, the Mexican authorities could plan an attack.

This is unreal! This man, from this study, in one phone call, is going to do what the Mexican authorities apparently haven't been able to do for years—eliminate four major cartel leaders all at once. The Condor kills off the competition and takes more control of the entire drug business. What an operator.

Ray followed the others outside onto the stone-paved terrace. Set up under the portion covered by the trellis was a large but simple wooden coffin on two low tables that served as a catafalque. All the members of the entourage and several of the more important members of the household staff stood together in a loose circle around the coffin. The Condor turned and touched Ray's arm and, in a voice husky with barely concealed grief, said, "Ray, as a personal favor to me, please do Francisco one last service and be one of the pallbearers."

"It would be my honor, Jefe," he responded somberly.

Holding his Bible, an old Catholic priest in familiar vestments stood at the end of the coffin. The Condor, Ray, and the others joined the group, and, with a nod to the priest from the Condor, the short service began. Following the rites, Ray, Raul, Luis, and Miguel, joined by Carlo and Eduardo, picked up the large coffin and solemnly walked it off the terrace and down a path to the west toward the rear of the estate. All the others, led by the Condor, fell in step after them, and they walked through the tangled vegetation on either side of the path until they reached a small clearing near the perimeter wall. Ray hadn't been down this path before, as there were no casitas in this direction. Several headstones marked the graves of others who had been laid to rest here.

I wonder if the old priest knows Francisco was killed at a meeting to discuss the shipment of tons of drugs into America, Ray thought. *Probably doesn't know that, or that I killed Guzman, or that the Condor had Vasso killed a hundred feet from here. I wonder if Vasso is buried here. I doubt it. This looks like a special place, even a family place. Great—a family funeral, and then we get drunk.*

Ray wondered if there was a little cemetery at each of the three estates. He decided he wouldn't be surprised if there was. A grave already had been excavated, and there was a simple platform over the hole. The six pallbearers placed the coffin on the structure and stood to one side. The priest went to the head of the coffin and intoned several more short prayers from either memory or his book, then concluded the service. Most of those attending crossed themselves, and then slowly the entire group retraced their steps back to the terrace, where the house staff was just finishing setting up an elaborate spread of food and a full bar at another table.

"Please," said the Condor, "everyone please get a glass of your favorite drink." When all had done so, he said, "My friends, to our dear friend and brother Francisco. May he forever rest in peace."

The Condor's toast was the first of many that afternoon, and the party lasted well into the night. The Condor quietly left the gathering early in the evening, and Ray noticed. There was no question that the man was deeply hurt by the death of his old friend. The last toast of the evening was given by Carlo, right before he fell over dead drunk. As Ray and several other guards helped Carlo to his room, Carlo grabbed Ray and said that his friend Francisco would have liked the party, and he wished Ray had known him. When Ray returned after helping Carlo, Raul suggested to the gathering that tomorrow was going to be a long day, and with that announcement, the celebration of Francisco's life was over.

Ray, Miguel, and Luis followed Raul through the grand foyer and up the wide north hall to their respective suites. Apparently, toward the end of the day, someone from Dominguez's shop had delivered Ray's new suits, sport coats, slacks, shirts, and all his accessories to the estate. Someone working for Raul then had made sure all the parcels and suit bags were neatly hung or stacked in his room. He also saw several new, fine, black leather travel bags. He took off the new suit he had worn all day and hung it with a care that surprised him. *Jesus, since when have I ever cared about wrinkling my clothes?* he wondered.

Someone else, probably the spook Geraldo, had left a folder on his nightstand. He glanced at it quickly to confirm that it was his new identity and history. Standing only in the new pair of skivvies he had put on that morning, he carefully unpacked and inventoried everything he had. The sheer amount of fine new clothes was staggering. When Raul had seen him to his suite and noticed all the packages, he had told Ray to pack all he could into his new luggage, as Dominguez would be sending more clothes to the estate to make up for the ones he would be taking with him.

Ray carefully packed all the accessories into the large shoulder bag and had all the hanging clothes ready to be packed into the large suit bag first thing in the morning. He headed into his magnificent shower and turned the water on as hot as he could stand. He stood there leaning slightly forward, facing the nearest wall, his arms extended, and let the stinging-hot water hit his shoulders and the back of his neck. As the elegantly finished space steamed up, Ray reviewed every detail of the day until he was sure he had the most important facts indelibly printed into his memory. He especially went over the conversation in the Condor's study prior to Francisco's service.

What does all that stuff about Fernandez really mean? he wondered. *Hopefully tomorrow I'll find out when I'm on the plane to…where? With… whom? Not the Condor anymore, but someone else? What does that mean? Who the hell is this guy? Jesus, every night it's something new, a new secret, or a name, or simply another unknown, like tomorrow's plane ride. Stop thinking about it and get some sleep—you're going to need it. I'd better start figuring out how to get in touch with Bennie. Maybe on the coast or in the city, I'll have a better chance. I hope so. This is getting out of control.*

He turned off the shower and after toweling himself off, he walked to the bed and picked up the folder from his nightstand and read his new history. It was complete and thorough but not flashy. Anyone reading it would think Ray Ortega was a person of perhaps above-average intelligence who was fortunate to have two well-placed uncles. He read and reread the dossier a couple of times and then set it aside. He needed rest now more than ever, but he also needed to be comfortable with the new identity he was now laying over the one Bennie had given him, his situation getting more confusing and dangerous by the day. He eventually fell into a fitful sleep but had uncomfortable dreams punctuated by scenes of graveyards and fancy airplanes.

11

The estate of El Condor de Muerte
Monterrey, Mexico
Wednesday morning

Ray managed to get three or four hours of sleep before waking up before the sunrise. He got up, went to the bathroom, and then returned to bed with the hope of getting the few more hours of precious sleep he desperately needed. But that wasn't possible, as so much had happened in the last several days, making any sleep futile. As he lay in bed thinking, the uncertainties of the coming day only made things worse. Today he would accompany the Condor and the inner circle he was now unbelievably a part of to new places. Today he would be on the plane.

The events of the last several days and the resulting troubling thoughts continued to weigh heavily on him. The Condor was a complete enigma, which was bad for an undercover operative, especially for one who had gotten as close to his targets as he had. The more clarity one had while undercover, the better. Ray's initial impression the first night he had arrived was that the Condor was dangerous and powerful, but there was something different also—an air about him that he couldn't put his finger on at the time. The Condor's caution, intelligence, and the sophisticated electronic security Ray had learned of made him different, but it was something else, something personal, and it wasn't the sunglasses and wild white hair.

In the last several days, Ray had discovered, to his great surprise, that the man was well educated, articulate, and even polite—a real gentleman in private, in his mannerisms and demeanor, as contradictory as that seemed.

Strange characteristics for a ruthless cartel leader, he thought. Every other drug dealer or gang leader he had observed or arrested had been a walking stereotype of what most people thought a criminal such as that would be like. The Condor, however, was the antithesis of that stereotype.

This was further revealed through the Condor's next puzzling characteristic: he was hugely wealthy, which was no surprise considering the billions involved in trafficking, but he was also very organized and diversified in his public businesses. He owned large tracts of valuable real estate and farmland, far in excess of the three great estates he occupied in the north, all of which, Ray learned, were registered with one or another of the many legal businesses the Condor operated.

If all that weren't enough to keep him off balance and guessing, he had discovered two bombshells yesterday. The first was that the Condor was somehow linked to President Fernandez. After thinking about it, Ray knew he would report to Bennie that the Condor was indeed controlling the president somehow. Second—and this was what really bothered him the most—once he hopped on a plane with him this morning and headed off to God knows where, the man no longer would be the Condor but someone else entirely.

Screw it, Ray thought. *I might as well get dressed. I need to sort this out and find a way to get word to Bennie about all this shit. Maybe there'll be an opportunity as we go west and south. I need a fucking plane ride like I need a hole in my head...I hate small airplanes.*

He dressed in the prescribed suit of the day and then quietly left his rooms and went to the formal dining room of the hacienda. As early as it was, two others of the inner circle, Miguel and Luis, arrived individually in the dining room within a few minutes of him. Apparently they also were affected in some way by a departure day. The two senior members of the detail appeared and acted a little different this morning, Ray thought; each was a little more serious and more deliberate in his movements. He was a little disturbed at not having noticed their changed behavior before on previous departure days. He had accompanied Carlo on many occasions when the Condor and his immediate circle had flown off, but he'd always been in one of the chase vehicles and never this close.

What's the big deal? he wondered. *Maybe they just don't like flying in small planes either.*

Several of the maids were serving a light breakfast, recommended and ordered by Miguel, when the Condor and Raul joined them. The Condor appeared normal to Ray, or as normal as he ever appeared. He smiled at Ray and the others, said a quiet good morning, and poured himself a cup of coffee.

"Are you all packed up, Ray?" he asked after taking a sip of his coffee.

"Yes, Jefe, and thank you for the fine travel bags."

"Think nothing of it. Dominguez is making more clothes for you. They'll be here when you return north, so you won't have to bring back what you take south. This will make things easier on future flights."

The five of them were joined by the evidently brilliant Geraldo Baca and the other communication tech, who was introduced to Ray as Lorenzo. Lorenzo also was a nervous type, his eyes always darting about. He handed Raul several pieces of paper and told him, "The overnight report and this morning's traffic."

The Condor looked questioningly over his coffee cup at Raul, who turned to the Condor, saying, "Nothing that can't wait a few hours, Jefe. We can deal with these once we're in Baja."

Baja—this was the first reference to something other than "the coast" that Ray had heard. So apparently the Condor had a house on the sea in Baja. This seemed logical to him. Bennie had briefed him on the primary transshipment routes the DEA monitored out of Mexico, and northern Baja was a prime one. After breakfast, he and the others returned to their rooms and gathered their luggage. Ray had packed before coming to breakfast, so he was the first of the inner circle to get to the porte cochere at the main entry.

Carlo stood there with several of his men and smiled warmly as Ray approached. "Ah, El Cuchillo, you look fine this morning—a handsome suit." He turned to one of the other guards. "Take his bags and put them in the second truck." As the man did as he was told, Carlo put his arm around Ray and drew him in close, saying quietly, "I hope you enjoy small planes, El

Cuchillo, especially fast ones that fly around mountains and not over them. From what Raul has told me, you'll be picking cactus out of your ass before you land!" With that he broke into genuine laughter at his own humor.

"I've never flown before, Carlo," he lied.

Carlo smiled. "Well, enjoy it and tell me all about it when you return."

A frown formed on Ray's face as he thought of a response. He'd been told that Carlo and Eduardo were to know nothing of their travels. Carlo continued before he could answer. He pulled him close again and said, "Don't worry, Ray. I don't wish to know of the Condor's business in the west. I just want to hear about your first plane ride."

Ray was relieved. "Thank you for understanding."

Turning more serious, Carlo whispered, "Remember what I told you yesterday—we are brothers now, and you're a part of the Condor's circle. We'll take care of his business here in the north; you just take care of my cousin in his business elsewhere. Do you have your weapons?"

"Yes, but I can't wear my big knife. The suits fit me perfectly, and you can see it through my coat. I'll need to figure something else out."

Carlo shook his head. "Don't worry about that. Where you're going, your smaller knife will do. Miguel says he'll have a weapon for you, like the others. You must fit in."

By now, the other members of the inner circle and the communication staff started to show up, with the Condor, Eduardo, and Raul appearing last. Eduardo approached Ray, a warm smile on his face, and extended his hand. He was certain the man hadn't ever smiled at him before. Eduardo was as big a mystery to him as the Condor. The more time he spent around him, the more the man changed in his opinion; he was another slyly smart one and therefore also very dangerous.

"Good luck, El Cuchillo," Eduardo said. "You've earned this. I'm happy for you and grateful for my life, thanks to you."

"Thank you, Eduardo. I hope I don't let Jefe or you down," Ray responded respectfully.

"You'll be fine," Eduardo said as they shook hands. "Do what you seem to do naturally: keep a watchful eye and listen." He patted Ray on the back.

"I'll say good-bye here; I'm not going with you to the plane. I'll see you on your return."

Eduardo turned and rejoined the Condor, who was having a conversation with Raul and Carlo. What luggage they had was loaded into one of the three Escalades, and the regular guard force and drivers made up of Carlo's men got into their respective vehicles. The Condor, Raul, and the two technicians got into the middle SUV, while Ray, Miguel, and Luis got into the lead one with Carlo and his most trusted driver. Carlo was carrying a handheld radio. He thumbed a button and asked for each SUV to report in. When the other two acknowledged his request, he nodded to the driver, and the small caravan started down the estate drive. Ray was seated behind the driver on the left side of the SUV and saw that Eduardo was watching him, smiling. Without thinking about it, he touched his forehead and slowly flipped his hand, as if to salute Eduardo, and Eduardo smiled and warmly waved back.

Jesus, he thought after the gesture. *Why did I do that?*

They followed the estate drive down the hill, passed through the heavily guarded entry gate, and drove out, following the winding paved road that passed by the estate and led out of the hills to the northeast. After emerging from the foothills, they passed through housing and industrial areas on the western outskirts of Monterrey until they intersected Federal Highway 40. With Carlo's Escalade leading the way, the three-vehicle caravan stayed on the four-lane highway for half an hour, passing Garza Garcia, which Ray recognized was where he and Carlo had gone the day before to get his new clothes. They passed through the heart of Monterrey and headed into the high desert, east of the Nuevo Leon state capital.

Thirty minutes after passing through Monterrey, they drove past the small farming town of El Capadero and exited the toll road, turning north on a paved road that headed through a sparsely occupied area covered with agricultural fields. After several minutes and a number of turns, they were on another well-maintained dirt road with a line of barren hills to the west. When the road became paved once more, Carlo thumbed the switch on his radio and simply said "Now" into the small device. Ray didn't know it, but the last Escalade in the caravan abruptly stopped and blocked the road behind them. The remaining two armored Cadillac's continued another mile up the road, and Carlo got on his radio again and said "Now" a second time. Their driver slowed down and turned the Escalade sideways across the narrow paved road. Carlo opened his door, as did Luis, so Ray did too, and everyone got out of the vehicles.

Now that they were stopped, Ray could see the obvious reasons this site had been selected. The paved portion of the rural road was on the highest point of a gradual rise, and he could see at least a mile beyond each blocking Escalade to the north and the south, as the dirt portions of the road went slightly downhill in each direction. To their west were the desolate hills, and to the east, sloping downhill gradually, visible for miles, was nothing but cultivated fields.

Carlo walked up to Ray as he was checking out the geography and said, "We own these farms under several different names for as far as you can see. Much of our weed crop is right there in front of your eyes, in the centers of the fields. Pass by on the roads, and all you'll see are vegetables being grown."

He nudged Ray's side and pointed to the north. Ray heard the far-off sound of an approaching aircraft but couldn't at first see the plane itself. Carlo pointed again and said, "There…very low, just east of the road."

Ray realized he was looking far too high above the horizon to see the plane. The curious jet-powered turboprop he had seen before was just a few hundred feet off the ground and approaching fast from the north. It passed them to their east, headed south for four or five seconds, then made a radical, tight, 180-degree, low-altitude turn and flew back toward them, centered on the paved road. The plane flashed over the southernmost blocking Escalade and cut its power. The landing gear appeared, and the slick-looking plane made a fast but controlled landing onto the road.

In the half a minute the sophisticated plane took to finish its rollout and taxi up to the Condor's Escalade, Carlo led Ray to the Condor, and the other guards had the luggage ready to be loaded. Ray saw two pilots in the cockpit, and he sighed in relief. He hadn't flown a great deal in his life, and with few exceptions, it had been on large commercial jets with rolling bar carts and flight attendants. Ray wasn't looking forward to this flight. While not afraid of flying, he was, at a minimum, not comfortable with it. He had jokingly devised three basic rules to flying: first, never fly unless there are two pilots; second, fly only on planes with bathrooms and flight attendants; and last, fly only on planes big enough to have a bar onboard. He was unsure whether the plane adhered to the last two rules, but the strange-looking plane with the two backward-facing turboprops taxiing up to them had two pilots, and to him that was a good start.

The plane pulled up slowly and stopped short of the Condor's Escalade. The left engine already had been shut down on the rollout, and within a few seconds of the plane's stopping, the left side door opened up and the steps descended. The Condor and Raul entered first, followed by the two technicians, then Ray and Miguel; Luis brought up the rear. As Ray was climbing the steps, he couldn't help looking the plane over and marveling at the elegant curving lines of the fuselage. After he ducked through the entry door, one of the pilots was standing in the opening between the main cabin and the cockpit, watching him, evidently wondering who the new face was. Ray looked away from him, as if interested in the small bar and galley on the wall opposite the door.

His first reaction to the plane's interior was one of surprise at its luxury and size. He was following the larger Miguel and realized that, unlike Miguel, he didn't have to duck his head much at all. The smooth, curving, white ceiling was just touching the top of Ray's head, meaning the ceiling was five foot ten or eleven inches high. All the lighting was concealed in moldings where the arching ceiling met the sides, and there were no overhead storage bins, as there were in commercial jets. As he entered the main cabin, he noticed the two computer techs were occupying the first two tan leather seats on the left side—the first seat facing backward, the second forward. They were in the process of pulling a table out of a well on the side, and Ray watched in fascination as they pulled it up and hinged it into place between them. The darkly stained wood surface was highly lacquered, giving it an elegant, finished look.

The Condor took the last seat on the right with Raul facing him, his back to the front of the plane. The Condor motioned to Ray that he should take the other forward-facing rear seat across the aisle from him, and Miguel and Luis took the two remaining seats in the front of the cabin. As Ray approached his seat, he noticed that through the open rear door there appeared to be a small private bathroom. With all the thoughts he could—and perhaps should—have been thinking at this moment as a deep undercover operative in what only could be described as a very tight spot, the first thought he had was, *Good. Except for flight attendants, this plane meets my three rules.*

He sat in the comfortable leather seat and, by force of habit, looked for his seat belt. At first he couldn't find it, and then the Condor said, "Ray, over your right shoulder, at the top of the seat."

The safety belts on the plane were similar to the shoulder straps in his car back home and not the seat belts he was used to on commercial flights. He pulled the belt, which came out of the top of the seat, over his shoulder and across his chest and fastened it to the receptor. Both metal parts of his shoulder strap were a shiny gold or brass color, like the shower heads in his bathroom at the estate. He was secretly taken in by the luxurious look and feel of his seat. He had plenty of room, the way he imagined the first class he'd never flown in must be like on a commercial flight, made even more so by the fact that the seat facing him was empty. One of the five large windows that lined each side of the twenty-foot-long cabin was directly beside him, giving him a great view of the fields to the east. He turned toward the Condor and realized he and Raul were watching him and smiling, clearly amused at the look of pleasure and awe on his face.

Jesus Christ, quit acting like a kid in a toy store and get your game face back on! I suppose one thing is true, though. Bennie said the safest way to maintain a cover is for the cover to be as close to the truth as possible. And this is an amazing plane, so any emotions they see on my face are real.

Before Ray could say anything, one of the pilots' voices came over a hidden speaker. "Jefe, we're secure and initiating our takeoff procedures. Please strap in."

Ray had been busy trying to figure out his seat belt and hadn't noticed when the copilot had closed the entry door and reentered the cockpit. He heard the left-side engine whine as it started back up and saw and felt the plane make a tight 180-degree turn in the middle of the narrow road. The noise level was surprisingly low, apparently the result of the rear-facing props, and the ride was smooth as the plane centered up in the road and the engines were brought up to full power for takeoff. The plane stayed in place as the engine noise grew; there was a slight rocking feeling and then a small lurch as the pilot released the brakes he evidently had been applying as he was powering up.

The sleek plane rapidly gained speed following the initial jump forward. In what seemed only a few seconds, the rumbling of the landing gear down the paved road stopped, and what noise there was diminished as they became airborne. It was about this time that Ray noticed the first and second of what would be many differences between this flight and the few other small-plane flights he had flown. Unlike those other flights, and even the commercial flights he'd been on, the plane was gaining speed quickly but not altitude. After its initial takeoff, the plane climbed shallowly and then seemed to level off, very close to the ground, in Ray's inexperienced opinion, as he stared out the window.

The Condor reached across the aisle and touched his arm. "I understand you haven't flown before," he said. "You must trust me on this—it will grow on you, and I feel you'll come to enjoy it. But I must warn you that we'll soon be flying in what may seem to you to be a radical way. Don't worry about this; it's the way we must fly in order to avoid the country's radar systems and get where we're going undetected. Are you familiar with radar? Do you know what I mean?"

Ray opened his mouth to start to answer, but before a word or breath could escape, the plane made an abrupt turn to the left, and he watched with a feeling akin to horror as he saw nothing but ground flashing past the Condor's window and nothing but sky from his. Just as quickly as the pilots had made the tight left-hand turn, the plane was again flying dead straight and level but still fast and low. Ray realized he had a death grip on his armrests and was amazed he hadn't ruined the new underwear Dominguez had given him.

He noticed the Condor and Raul were reaching down to the sides of their seats, each pressing a button he hadn't noticed before. He watched as they swiveled their seats toward the aisle. The Condor nodded to him to do the same thing. He found his switch and soon discovered it made his seat go forward or back, tilt, or turn about twenty degrees toward the aisle. This allowed the four seats in the rear grouping to somewhat face one another so a more face-to-face meeting could occur. During this time, as the three were adjusting their seats toward one another, the plane continued to make quick turns either right or left—some subtle, some more pronounced.

"Are you OK, Ray?" the Condor asked with a smile.

"Yes, Jefe," he responded, with the grim look and controlled tension in his voice of a first-time flyer. Only he knew he really wasn't a first-time flyer, but it was the first time he had flown like this, and he was terrified and it showed, meeting Bennie's undercover criteria once again.

"Good," the Condor said. "The pilots up front are the best money can buy. They're veterans of our air force and once flew our country's most sophisticated jet fighters. They're well trained and have been flying me for many years. I trust them with my life, so you can also. What we're doing is avoiding the radar coverage of commercial and military radars and also avoiding flying over any large town or city or into the side of some hill or mountain. We're making our way west, and we must do so at a low altitude so the authorities can't track us. Over the years, my pilots have mapped out a number of travel routes across the country from east to west and back from all three estates."

Evidence of what the Condor was telling him became painfully obvious as the plane made a rapid ascent that left him feeling his stomach was several hundred feet below him, followed by an equally abrupt descent that left him feeling light in his seat. The plane would return to level flight for short periods of time, but more often than not, it seemed the plane was turning this way and that.

"We just went over the mountains west of Monterrey," the Condor told him. "That was the sudden climb you felt. We have about a three-hour flight before we reach our first destination. But don't worry—once we get there, we can walk to our second. Tonight we'll be at my seaside estate, and then, early tomorrow morning, we'll fly to the capital. That flight will be more enjoyable for us all, in a larger plane."

"We don't have to avoid the radars again, Jefe?" Ray asked, still gripping his armrests.

The Condor shook his head. "No radars, Ray. We'll be, shall I say, disguised, so we won't need to worry about detection. All will see us and expect us."

Ray nodded as if he understood, but inside he had a million questions.

Disguised? Walk to our second destination? All will expect us? Great, more fucking mysteries—just what I need.

The flight settled down to an extended period of low but straight-and-level flight.

"We can now speak comfortably for about an hour," the Condor said. "We're headed roughly toward Chihuahua and will turn west again about a hundred miles south, then make our way around and through the central mountains. That's the most uncomfortable part of the flight, but it won't last long. Once we're over the central mountains, we'll have another hour of relatively straight flight that'll take us over the coast and out over the Sea of Cortez. We'll then have to get up and over the mountains of Baja, but just as quickly, we'll be back down and out over the Pacific. We'll then turn south and reach our destination. I wanted you to know this, Ray, so you can relax a bit during the flight, knowing in general where we're going and what to expect. This is important, as there's much I need to tell you before we reach Baja, and I want you to remember it. If at any time you don't understand something I tell you, just stop me, and I'll explain it further. Understand?"

"Yes, Jefe. That's where your ocean estate is, Baja?"

"Yes, the southern portion, Baja California Sur. In most ways, that's where my life story begins. Though we lived in Chihuahua until I was ten, Baja was the first real home I remember, my first estate. The three you know about came much later. As my father and uncle became more involved in the drug business, there was much bad blood and fighting among the various gangs for control of the transshipment routes for Columbian cocaine from South America into North America."

"Shipment routes?"

"Transshipment, Ray. These routes are how the drugs of South America and Mexico get into the United States, where the markets are. The safer and more efficient the routes, the more product you can ship and the more money and power you have. The problems, of course, in addition to the federals and the American narcotics police who try to stop us, are the stupid and dangerous cartels we compete with. We get all our product through—and in significantly larger quantities—in ways the other cartels are largely unaware of. The more successful we are, the greater our chances are of controlling the trafficking eventually, and with that control, we can start to help more people. All this success we owe primarily to my father." Ray just nodded, as if he understood.

"He knew of a small, beautiful coastal area in Baja, near the town of Todos Santos, that was then undeveloped," the Condor continued. "A place he went to from time to time with his brother, Enrique, to fish. He bought a great deal of land and hired builders to construct a number of estates—one for us, of course, and others to sell or use for his plans. Other businessmen had started to look at the potential of Baja California Sur as a resort or vacation destination, so my father became one of them, investing our profits, using a different family name.

"My mother didn't know any of this, and certainly neither did I or my sisters as we were growing up. My father had been looking at Baja for some time as a place not only to invest our profits but also as a clever place to ship our product safely into America. Even before he made the move to Baja, he had been investing our profits in legitimate businesses in Chihuahua. While my father had little formal education, he was wise, and he learned quickly. Whereas the other Chihuahua gangs and families were squandering their profits and spending their money foolishly, attracting the attention of the police and prosecutors, my father was investing in legitimate businesses. He hired several good lawyers who could be quietly controlled to set up legal businesses to launder our profits. Do you understand what I mean when I say 'launder our profits,' Ray?"

Ray feigned embarrassment, looked down, and said, "No, Jefe, I don't know what that means."

Raul leaned forward in his seat. "Ray, don't be embarrassed by not knowing this. I also didn't understand it at first. We each have our expertise, the skills we're good at, and Jefe has his. You have many valuable talents, and with our help, you'll have many more. Understand, El Cuchillo?"

"Yes, Raul. Thank you," he said.

The Condor patiently watched the exchange and then smiled and nodded his thanks to Raul before continuing. "Laundering, Ray, is when you take money from the sale of drugs, which is illegal, and put it to work in legitimate businesses. The profits we make on these businesses are legal. We report the income, and we pay our share of taxes to the government. My father had many such legitimate businesses in Chihuahua set up under several corporations owned by a man named Octavio Peña. This was my grandfather's name, my mother's father. He died young, another innocent victim of drug trafficking. He was little known and led an honest if short life, so my father borrowed his name. Whenever my father conducted business or oversaw our family's investments, he did so as Octavio. The bankers and lawyers and government people he dealt with as Octavio didn't associate him with the illegal and dangerous drug business, which they knew nothing about and avoided completely. There was safety for my father in their collective fear and ignorance.

"My father maintained two households in the Chihuahua area: the old Vargas family house in the Hell's Hole neighborhood, where he and my uncle built and ran our trafficking business, and a home in the upscale Campestre area, where he conducted business as Octavio. He didn't socialize with his rich neighbors but was friendly, a man no one really knew well but whom all respected because of his success. My father kept the drug business completely separate from all his other Chihuahua businesses. When he had to attend to one of our legitimate businesses, or come visit my mother and us children, he would leave the barrio and go to a manufacturing business he owned, located in an industrial area with many similar buildings all side by side, all owned by different groups but many controlled by my father. He would drive into one of the buildings as Armando Vargas and then move unseen to one of the adjacent buildings through hidden passageways in the basement. He then would leave from a different building, out onto a different street, and drive to the Campestre looking different, dressed differently, driving a different and better car, and arrive as the prosperous Octavio Peña. When he returned to the barrio, he reversed this trip.

"If ever he had been followed from the barrio, they would find a cold trail, because it might be days or weeks before Armando Vargas ever came out of the building he first entered. With this deception, my father was able to move about freely in Chihuahua's business circles, and no one was the wiser.

"As Octavio Peña, he was known as a lonely man, estranged from his family, but also as a successful, kind, generous one, and his reputation grew in business circles. While he had many business associates in the better parts of the city, none came to know him closely, as he traveled a great deal and didn't forge any deep friendships. In fact, when he was back at our family home in the barrio, he was never more than a few miles from these people but in a neighborhood they would never enter and with a name no one knew. In his deception there was safety."

The Condor leaned in closer to Ray and continued. "The secrets to our family's success always have been our methods of moving our products north, our sources of information, and our deceptions in our personal lives. The police didn't know of us, and neither did the other cartels. As my father and uncle Enrique built the business, they kept very low profiles and didn't compete with the other cartels for the more visible and obvious transshipment routes. My father always devised ways to get the drugs into America in ways that others couldn't see and where there was no competition. Because the other cartels couldn't see how we were trafficking, they had no way to know what to try to take from us. In my father's tactics, there was relative safety for us all.

"My father selected Baja for our family move because he already had established several businesses there as Octavio. Father bought a failing salt company that mined and processed common table salt for commercial and domestic uses. This salt company was sending tons of legitimate product to America. My father brought the necessary family money to the business to be able to purchase the more modern equipment and buy the talents of the best mining engineers and managers to make the Baja Salt Company a great success. We've been shipping tons of salt to North America for many years; my father also used the company to send tons of our special products as well. The Baja Salt Company is a widely known and respected business in Mexico and in the United States. We have major warehousing and distribution facilities in several of Southern California's ports, which we use to receive and distribute our salt. It's also from special areas in these warehouses that a small, loyal part of our organization distributes our drugs. With our salt company as a start, my father was able to expand into even more businesses—the real estate and resorts I mentioned earlier, as well as other investments, such as our cruise-ship lines—and with the success of these businesses, he created even more efficient ways to ship product north."

The Condor stopped and smiled at Ray. "I've been going on and on. I realize this is a lot of information for you. Do you have any questions so far?"

Ray had sat quietly in secret amazement for the thirty minutes the Condor had talked and tried to catalog all the information he was being given and retain it. It was a chore. He was dumbfounded by everything he'd just learned. Just by knowing the name Octavio Peña, the Mexican authorities could identify and hold a great many businesses that were used to launder the cartel's money. The DEA in America could focus on all Peña-owned properties in the United States. The revelation of the salt company as a transshipment route was a major intelligence coup. That was obviously a transshipment route that neither the DEA nor the Mexicans knew anything about. This was a great piece of what Bennie called "actionable intelligence." Ray had suspected that with his lucking into the Condor's inner circle, there would be potentially a fountain of new information available to him, and now that was a certainty. If he played his cards right, he could help the DEA nail one of the most efficient drug importers, if not one of the biggest.

"No, Jefe. I think I understand. I know your father is no longer with us. Are you Octavio now? Is that what I should call you now—Señor Peña?"

The Condor smiled and glanced at Raul, who nodded and smiled back at the Condor; Ray's question was astute, and it further cemented in their minds that he indeed had been a wise choice to replace Francisco.

"When we reach our first destination," the Condor said, "it will be the estate my father created under the name Octavio Peña. At that estate I'm known as Nicolas Peña, a son and heir to Octavio. As his son, I continue to oversee some of the businesses he established. I do this from the Baja estate, rarely in person—mostly by telephone, e-mail, and teleconferencing, meetings where we see each other on computers. Do you understand?"

Ray nodded. "Yes, Señor Peña, and you also own the salt company?"

"Here on the plane, Ray, or when we're alone within the circle, you may still call me Jefe. It's only in the presence of others, at our first destination—and only our first destination—that you'll refer to me as Señor Peña, and even then, Jefe is still appropriate. What's important—the most important thing to remember—is that you can't reveal anything regarding El Condor de Muerte or the three estates in the north once we reach the coast. After we leave our first stop and go south to the capital, you'll no longer refer to me as Peña—but more on that when we get where we're going. I realize this must all sound confusing, but things will become clear in time, so please be patient, Ray."

Ray stared blankly at the Condor, having a difficult time understanding what he'd said.

"As to our salt company," the Condor continued, "the majority owner is my mother, under her family name, Alvarez. Most of our businesses were organized that way and passed on to my mother and me after my father's death. I oversee them, but not as Peña. But we'll speak more about this later when we arrive in Baja. Her estate is our second destination on this trip."

Ray was curious about what the Condor had said earlier, so he asked, "And we'll walk there, Jefe?"

"Yes. My mother's estate and that of Señor Peña are next to each other. It's a long walk, but there'll be no more low, fast flights." The Condor glanced at his watch. "We're approaching Chihuahua, where we'll turn west again and then proceed over the central mountains. This is where our pilots will be required to maneuver us the most. Sit back, Ray, and try to relax. It'll only be about thirty minutes until we return to level flight. There's water or something stronger, if you wish, in the forward bar. Raul and I have some papers to go through, and I have some calls to make. So you'll have to excuse us."

"Should I move, Jefe, to the front? I don't want to drink, but do you wish to speak with Raul in private?"

The Condor shook his head. "No, of course not. I have no secrets from my inner circle. You won't understand most of what we discuss, but you're free to listen. My business is now your business, Ray. I trust you completely."

Normally such a declaration by a target would be welcome news to an undercover operative, but for some reason, Ray had the opposite feeling. All he could think to say next was, "I hope I don't fail you, Jefe."

"You won't, Ray," a smiling Condor said.

The Condor and Raul swiveled their seats back to face each other, and Raul pulled out the table stored in the cabin's side and set it up between their seats. Raul was carrying a leather attaché case with whatever documents they needed to discuss. The acoustics in the interior of the Piaggio 180 Avanti were remarkably quiet due to, as Ray had guessed, the positioning of the two engines on the wings and the fact that the pilots were pushing and not pulling the sophisticated plane through the air. Ray could hear the Condor and Raul clearly, and the Condor was correct—he didn't understand a lot of what they discussed. The main topic seemed to be the upcoming meeting of the Gang of Four and how the Condor and Raul were planning to kill as many members of the loose alliance as they could, all at the same time.

The scope and depth of the planned attack was, to Ray's experienced ear as a tactical planner of raids on drug houses and other facilities, nothing short of spectacular. From the conversation, it was clear that the Condor had penetrated the Gang of Four as deeply as he apparently had the Mexican government. Whoever the Condor had on the inside of the other cartels were in positions of importance and had provided him detailed information on just how the various principals intended to arrive at the meeting place, how many soldiers they would have, and even the existence, in several cases, of emergency escape plans in case some treachery was revealed. The Gang of Four clearly had no idea regarding the depth of the betrayal within their cartels.

Would I report what I'm hearing to Bennie, even if I could? Ray wondered. *What's the moral right here? If I say and do nothing—which, given my situation, is all I can do—the Condor will do us all a big favor by wiping out some of the worst of the assholes. Even if I could contact Bennie, what would the DEA or the Mexicans do? Try to stop the raid? I don't think so. Better the Condor does our dirty work for us and eliminates as many of these people as he can. As long as I can steer Bennie to the Condor afterward, we win—it's best to just go along. Bennie would agree, I think. Now that I know who Señor Peña is, we can get that information to the Mexicans, and they can grab up all the cartel-related businesses down here. And what's this shit about not calling him Peña when we go south? A third alias? Jesus, this son of a bitch is organized. Does he really trust me? I think he does. I was fucking lucky at that meeting. I may never forgive myself or forget killing Guzman, but that's what's keeping me safe and alive and in a position to do some real damage to this guy's network, if I can only find a safe way to contact Bennie.*

The pilot's voice came over the speaker for the first time since takeoff. "Jefe, we'll soon be making our run over the mountains. Everyone, please strap in."

Ray hadn't taken off his seat belt, not even for the hour they'd spent flying level and smooth, but he checked and tightened his belt even more. He was glancing out his window as he was thinking, something he had carefully avoided before now because it was too unnerving to see the ground flash by so closely, when the plane suddenly started to climb, leaving his stomach once more several hundred feet below him. He once again applied a death grip to his armrests and held on tightly, privately thanking Miguel for suggesting he eat a light breakfast. Toast and coffee he could hold down, but if he had ordered his typical breakfast—smothered in the real good green chili the Condor's chef always prepared—he was certain he'd have thrown up by now, all over the luxurious leather seat in front of him.

12

The Peña estate
Baja California Sur
Wednesday, noon

The Baja peninsula had been a hot, dry finger of land with little population for thousands of years. This was especially true for the portion south of the twenty-eighth parallel, Baja California Sur. That began to change in the late 1950s and early 1960s, when sport fishermen from the United States discovered the fertile fishing waters off the peninsula's coasts. In the early 1990s, ambitious developers, shut out of the overdeveloped Mexican gold coast from Mazatlan to Acapulco, saw the potential in the area for large resorts sporting lush ocean-side golf courses, fine restaurants, and five-star hotel communities for the international tourists who would be drawn to expansive beaches and the nearly 360 days of sunshine. With the tourist boom to the lower peninsula came the prospects for a burgeoning vacation-home market near the new hotels and resort developments. As these new developments gained a foothold and expanded, so did the few existing towns, such as La Paz, San Jose del Cabo, and Cabo San Lucas. As these towns grew—expanded by native workers from mainland Mexico drawn to the high-paying jobs and higher standards of living available on the peninsula—more services, such as roads and airports, also were expanded and modernized.

As the sleek twin turboprop made the gradual turn back toward the Baja coast to the east, barely four hundred feet above the placid Pacific, the pilot began to reduce speed, added some flaps, and made preparations to land. Of the several new, modernized airports located on the peninsula available to the seasoned, highly proficient pilot, he had taken great care to avoid them all. He had taken even greater care to avoid the radars located at the airfields.

It was remarkable to the pilot how routine this black flight had become, considering it had originated not from an airport but from a paved rural road thirty miles east of Monterrey. The pilot had flown their entire flight plan "nap-of-the-earth." This meant the plane's altitude was never higher than five hundred feet, except during several points where the interruption of interior mountain ranges or hills had required a quick pop up and over the natural barriers. If an alert operator at one of the many government radar facilities across this part of northern Mexico had been watching his scope at that exact instant, the sweeping image on his screen would have momentarily picked up the reflected blip but never a second time on subsequent sweeps of the scope. Nor would the operator have glimpsed a transponder code emanating from the craft, as it wasn't transmitting one.

The circuitous route the plane flew, while always generally westerly, was a carefully calculated serpentine path that twisted here and there to avoid population centers, small towns, towered airfields, and, above all, known radar-coverage areas. In short order, the fast turboprop passed well west of Chihuahua and negotiated the Continental Divide that ran down the middle-west side of the country. There was no going around the divide, but the sleek plane still maintained its invisibility as it raced up previously traveled valleys and then only briefly popped up and over the top of the range. This part of the flight plan was always the most fun for the former major and veteran fighter pilot of the Mexican air force at the controls of the Condor's plane. Most people didn't know or care that the Mexican air force indeed had a few US-made Northrop F-5 fighters and therefore fighter pilots, but they did. Even the major had wondered about this from time to time—except for occasionally chasing "narc" flights, there was little for the fighters to do. And outside of one brief war with the United States, Mexico hadn't had a real war with anyone other than itself in almost 160 years, and the last one with the United States had been fought on horseback or on foot. Nevertheless, the major loved the flying he was doing for the Condor. He and his copilot were being paid a fortune for their skills and their silence—that, and the Piaggio 180 Avanti was an incredible aircraft and handled like a Ferrari, another fine mode of transportation also manufactured in Italy.

As much fun as the flights were for the major, he also realized they were dangerous as hell and tough on his important passengers. Dangerous because altitude and power were a pilot's best friends, and while the Piaggio 180's two Pratt & Whitney engines provided him ample power, he simply didn't have any altitude on these flights. The flight was tough because the carefully followed flight plan required many abrupt turns and the occasional rapid ascent over natural obstructions that couldn't be circumvented any other way. As the pilots, he and his partner could see and compensate for what they were going to do, like leaning into a curve on his American-made Harley-Davidson motorcycle. But to his passengers, who could see nothing forward, it was brutal—one moment in level, mostly smooth, fast flight followed by surprising two-or three-G turns.

Once the fast, modern aircraft popped over the divide, it hugged a valley pointing toward the west coastline between Huatabampo and Ahome, then headed out over the Sea of Cortez, the part of the Pacific trapped by the Baja Peninsula and the Mexican mainland. About twenty miles offshore, at a precise point in space known only to the sophisticated GPS computer aboard the aircraft, the plane turned due west toward Baja and maintained a heading of 270 degrees. The aircraft was equipped with look-down radar and carefully avoided water vessels of all sizes, from sport-fishing boats to oceangoing cruise ships and merchant ships. Many such watercrafts were dotting the Sea of Cortez, but it was also an enormous body of water. The horizon view from the surface in one of the many boats was only nine or ten miles, perhaps as much as twelve from the upper decks of a larger ship, so it wasn't difficult for the major to avoid flying over the water traffic.

The plane made landfall over Baja at a point thirty miles north of the beach community of Loreto, with nothing but a desolate landscape to observe its passing. There was an attended tower at the Loreto airport, but all radar vectoring was handled by the larger airports at La Paz to the south on the Baja coast and Hermosillo to the north on the mainland. This hadn't concerned the major, given his altitude, as he knew he was invisible in the clutter reflected back to those radars by several of the islands that dotted the sea near this part of the coast.

The plane was momentarily visible to traffic on Highway 1, which ran north and south up the entire peninsula as they flashed overhead, had one been looking in the correct spot for the two to three seconds the plane traveled on its perpendicular path. At its 350-mile-an-hour sustained speed, the plane traversed the fifty-four-mile width of the peninsula in seven and a half minutes. It then flashed out over the Pacific, north of the coastal village of Las Barrancas, and turned south several minutes later in a slow, wide 120-degree turn. The arcing path took the plane south over the Pacific some twenty miles off the coast, wide enough to clear Punta Hughes, the landmass on the west coast of Baja that juts out the farthest into the calm waters of the Pacific, then south and east for another twenty minutes to its final destination.

As the plane began to make the turn south over the Pacific, the pilot announced over the speaker, "Jefe, we're twenty minutes out."

In the passenger cabin, the Condor stood in the aisle next to Ray, a small travel bag in his hand, and smiled at him as he entered the rear lavatory. Before closing the door, he looked at Raul and said, "Will you explain the next step to Ray?"

"Of course, Jefe."

Next step? Ray thought. *How the hell can there be a next step over the middle of the ocean?*

Raul leaned in toward him with a serious expression. "Remember our conversation in the Condor's office when he said you would have to play a part?"

"Yes, I remember."

"Well, we all must play parts, especially Jefe. Your part as Ray Ortega is that of a personal security officer. For his safety and ours, it's necessary for Jefe to alter his appearance, so don't be surprised when he comes out, because he'll look different as he plays his next part."

Ray nodded in understanding, but he was thinking, *What the hell is this guy talking about?*

The door to the lavatory opened ten minutes later, and the Condor stepped out. Despite Raul's heads-up, surprise registered on Ray's face at the Condor's appearance. The flowing, tousled, white hair was now black and pulled into a sleek ponytail, and he was wearing simple, clear glasses in a fine gold frames rather than his oversize tinted photochromic glasses; his warm gray eyes were clearly visible for the first time. His mostly white beard was now shorter, with a salt-and-pepper mix of black and gray. The Condor smiled down at Ray and said, "Aw, El Cuchillo, you're surprised by my appearance?"

Ray was dumbfounded at the drastic change in appearance in so short a time. "I'm…I'm sorry, Jefe," he stammered. "I didn't mean to offend—it's just that you look so different."

"Not to worry, Ray. No offense was made. You're entitled to be surprised. Amazing, though, how just a change in hair color and eyeglasses can transform a man, eh?"

"Yes, Jefe. I wouldn't have recognized you."

"That's the general idea," the Condor said warmly.

Jesus Christ, if I'd passed him on the street, I'm not sure I would've known him! The long white hair is so distinctive, whereas the black hair and ponytail aren't. And he looks ten years younger with the darker beard. Remarkable how much the sunglasses disguised his features. What the hell is going on here? Why is this necessary? Who all knows about this? Just the six of us here?

As Ray was trying to come to grips with the man's altered appearance, at a point in space that the onboard GPS computer told the pilot was his initialization point for the run into the carefully yet simply camouflaged private airstrip, the pilot made a tighter turn to the east and headed toward the land on the horizon, just visible at twenty miles from his four-hundred-foot elevation. A few minutes later, he cut the plane's power and added flaps to give it greater stability at such a low altitude. He made landfall over the coast, flew inland for two miles, and made the final tight 180-degree right turn of his computer-generated flight plan. They flashed over more dry, barren landscape, and then the pilot lined up the plane's nose on a two-lane paved road that to the casual observer was the maintenance-and-delivery entrance to the Baja Pacific Estates residential community located near the southwest. The landing strip itself was disguised in plain view.

Anyone driving by on the main road from Meliton Albanez to Highway 19 simply saw the secure, gated, maintenance-and-delivery entrance to an upscale residential beach community. If allowed to pass through the gate and proceed down the well-maintained two-lane asphalt road, a visitor would drive around and between several small hills in the first half mile, proceed to the southwest dead straight for exactly another mile, and enter the maintenance compound of the development. The compound included the community's sewer-treatment facility, a desalination plant, and several storage and maintenance buildings.

The turboprop not only was the fastest aircraft of its type, but it also had very short field-landing and takeoff capabilities. The mile of paved road on the southwesterly heading—a carefully thought-out, desirable heading, given the prevailing winds in this part of Baja—was more than adequate in length to accommodate the landing aircraft. The pilot adjusted his controls, cut his power some more, pushed the levers that activated the hydraulics that lowered the flaps and the landing gear, and descended onto the make-shift airstrip just as the road snaked out of the low hills beyond the security gate. After landing smoothly at a precise point a quarter of the way down the road, the plane gradually braked and then turned onto a paved drive that led to the first of several large maintenance buildings. The plane taxied into the gaping opening in the end of the first building, and large motorized doors closed behind it as the pilot feathered his engines to a stop.

To anyone in Mexican aviation, this flight hadn't existed, just like the many flights before it. There was no flight plan filed, no fees paid to local officials, no inspections of licenses and paper work. The one-thousand-mile flight had carefully avoided all known radar sites, and on those few scopes that the plane's image had appeared, it had been for only a few seconds. With the plane's maximum speed of four hundred miles an hour and an average ground speed of almost 350 miles per hour, the flight duration had been just under three hours. Of the Condor's three estates, the one at Monterrey was the farthest from Baja and therefore required the longest flight; Chihuahua was an hour closer and Hermosillo two.

Ray almost enjoyed the flight from the time they had departed the main coast and headed out over the Sea of Cortez. Except for the brief climb and subsequent weightlessness-inducing descent over the coastal range of Baja, the last leg of the flight had been smooth and level, with only the occasional manageable turn. He had recognized and anticipated their landing, as the whine of the incredibly quiet engines had slowed, letting him know the pilot had reduced power. Normally one also could glance out the window and see the plane was descending, but not on this flight. They were no lower than they had been for the entire flight, just moving more slowly. Ray had been looking out his window to the south when they had approached the Baja coast and had seen a number of estates, oases of green strung out like pearls on a necklace down the coast to the south. He also saw the maintenance area and the main road of the exclusive housing development, though he didn't know what he was looking at until after they landed. The final 180-degree turn had caught him off guard, and, as he looked down with a feeling of terror at nothing but dry desert rushing so closely by, he decided he never would get used to tight turns at such a low altitude.

As the pilot righted the plane back to level flight, he heard the reassuring rumble as the landing gear came out and a solid clunk as they locked into place. The pilot touched down smoothly, and Ray closed his eyes and said a thank-you—to whom he wasn't sure—just in case someone might be listening.

Raul looked over at him and smiled. "Well, that wasn't so bad, eh, El Cuchillo?"

He responded with the truth. "I'll be happy when I'm off this plane."

"You did well," the new, different-looking Condor said, also smiling. "The first flight is always the most difficult, and the flight from Monterrey is the longest. Now that you've done that, future flights won't be so hard."

Sitting to one side in the large, brightly lit hangar were several gray Toyota Land Cruisers with darkly tinted windows.

"Ray, when we get off, you go with Luis and Miguel in the second Land Rover, OK?"

"Of course, Raul."

Ray followed Raul and the Condor down the aisle and was the last to get off. He quietly thanked the pilot standing in the cockpit doorway, who simply smiled and nodded. *The guy didn't look surprised at the Condor's new look, so he and the other pilot are obviously in on all this. That makes eight.*

He was surprised at how wobbly his legs felt as he walked carefully down the steps built into the main door. The copilot followed him and went to the baggage door near the tail, and his bags were unloaded. The Condor, Raul, and the communication techs got into the lead Land Rover. Miguel climbed into the driver's seat of the second SUV, and Luis had gotten into the other front seat by the time Ray had loaded his bags into the back. Ray was happy to have the backseat to himself so he could try to mentally record his surroundings without having to be as careful as he would if one of the others were beside him. The first thing he noticed was that there didn't appear to be any other people around. The complex of buildings he had observed from the air before their last suicidal turn had appeared extensive, and now he saw it actually was, but where were all the workers? He'd have to find out about that; it was strange.

As the SUVs pulled out of the hangar and headed down the road, Ray started to get his bearings. He knew he was on the lower-west Pacific coast of Baja California Sur, but as to exactly where, he had no clue. Except for the road they had landed on and the maintenance buildings, all he managed to see out the window was desert. With Raul and "Señor Peña," now that they were on the coast, in the lead, they followed the landing strip as it proceeded west and then headed mostly south for a mile through another series of low hills, through another security gate, and into a private estate development that an ornate sign announced as the Baja Pacific Estates. The maintenance area was only a mile north of the first residence but shielded from view by the line of low, sandy hills they'd just passed through.

Of the three other inner-circle members, Ray had yet to get to know and talk with Miguel and Luis as much as he had with Raul; they were still relative strangers to him. He said as casually as he could, "Luis, can I ask a question?"

Luis turned in his seat and looked at him with his typical surly expression. For whatever reason, Ray was certain Luis was the one member of the inner circle who really didn't like him for some reason.

"What is it?"

"Since we landed, I haven't seen any workers."

"The plants back there are highly automated and only need to be watched by the few workers who live nearby," Luis said, and Ray nodded.

The term "residential community," as it was known in the United States, was a misnomer here. The main road—the only road, as far as Ray could tell—led south past large haciendas set well to the west of the road and close to the ocean, with nothing but the native desert between the road and the estates, hardly the upscale-looking neighborhoods of the United States. He saw palms and other kinds of trees in the distance around the homes but little else. The haciendas were well spaced out down the coast, with wide expanses of desert between each of them and the road. To the east of the main road was nothing but desert hills for as far as he could see.

They had driven several miles south and passed about a dozen estates when Ray spotted a tall, white, stucco wall running from the road toward the ocean and a perpendicular run of wall paralleling the road they were on, obviously defining the perimeter of a special estate. After traveling several hundred feet down the road with the tall wall on their right, they reached an ornate gate opening in the wall, the two heavy ornamental metal gates framed by stone-clad columns set back from the road. A brass plaque mounted on each column simply said PENA, letting Ray know they had reached the first destination the Condor had mentioned.

The gates swung inward before Raul's Land Rover reached it and turned in. Miguel followed the lead SUV, and the electrically operated gates closed behind them. Unlike the other estates they'd passed, Ray could see that while there was still a great deal of natural desert from the road to the main house, the paved entry drive was lined on both sides for its entire length with palm trees, framing the road as it headed directly west toward the estate and the Pacific Ocean beyond.

As they approached the hacienda, Ray saw that it wasn't unlike the grand estate in Monterrey. Given the brief family history the Condor had shared with him during their flight, he knew this estate had to be older than the others. Having built homes with his uncle during summers in Sacramento, he strongly suspected the Condor's northern estates were essentially modeled after this one. Within a hundred feet of the main house, they entered an area of lush vegetation of all varieties on both sides of the road and all around the house. A red Spanish-roof-tiled porte cochere jutted out from the main house, and the two Land Rovers followed the circular drive as it passed underneath the impressive structure, where they stopped in the shade provided. Four well-dressed men were waiting for them on the front steps of the hacienda.

Luis turned to Ray and said in an unfriendly way, "These men are part of the permanent house staff, El Cuchillo. Two of them know nothing of Señor Peña's true identity, so be careful with what you say."

"Of course, Luis. Thank you."

As soon as the Land Rover stopped, Ray opened the rear door and observed and heard the four house-staff members greeting the Condor as Señor Peña: "So good to see you, Señor Peña. How was your trip, Señor Peña?" and other such small talk. Ray grabbed his two bags from the back of the SUV and followed the others into the hacienda's grand foyer. The servants were standing by the Condor, looking at him as he waved Ray over. Ray was still stunned by the change in the man's appearance and had to work to put his game face back on. The Condor introduced him to the more formally attired butler and the chef and then two brothers who apparently acted as guards at the Peña estate. After some talk about his travels, the Condor turned to the butler and told him they wouldn't be staying long and would be down in the ocean-side casita, working, and he asked the chef to prepare them a luncheon. The chef said of course he would, and then the Condor nodded to Geraldo, who turned and started toward the rear of the house.

With the communication techs in the lead, Ray, the Condor, and Raul went out through the great room of the house to an expansive patio area with an impressive swimming pool that overlooked the large formal rear yard and the Pacific Ocean beyond. They passed the pool and proceeded down a stone paved path toward the lush, almost arboretum-like grounds that surrounded the perimeter of the yard. Ray saw several stand-alone casitas near the north wall to his right as he tried to commit all the details of the estate layout to memory. He also spotted the red-tiled roof of a larger casita in the southwest corner of the property, where they were evidently going. Even after the long explanation the Condor had provided him on the flight, he was nervous about his immediate future, about where they were going, and what his role would be.

As they approached the casita, Ray knew he needed to get his emotions under control. He couldn't shake the feeling that his mission was getting away from him, as he constantly had to react to the ever-changing dynamics he in no way prepared for. On the one hand, being so close to the Condor and the others of the inner circle ironically offered a small degree of safety because he was so trusted. But the Condor and Raul were just too damned smart, and he couldn't help but feel that at some point, they would see through his facade. Always being on his guard and concentrating as hard as he was required to in his situation was wearing on him. He also was still reeling from the roller-coaster-like flight and the chameleonic change in the Condor's appearance. It was as if the man were a completely different person, and that kind of transformation took skill and intelligence that was extremely dangerous for someone in Ray's position. He believed last night and again this morning that with the plane ride and the proximity he now enjoyed within the circle, he would find greater clarity. But that wasn't the case yet; there were still so many unknowns, and what he did learn on the flight only confused him more, making his situation worse. As they approached the casita, he glanced out over the tranquil-looking Pacific and thought that if he'd known months ago, when Bennie had recruited him, what he knew now; he never would have left Sacramento.

13

The Peña estate
Baja California Sur
Wednesday

The group reached a secluded patio area that surrounded the casita on two sides. Ray could see the casita was perched right on the edge of a bluff, as the estate property tumbled abruptly down to a white sand beach fifty or sixty feet below. They went through the main entry door and then down a hall with a modern kitchen on the left and a formal dining room on the right. The hall opened into one end of the great room, which dominated the main floor with its high-sloping ceilings, and, at the far end, floor-to-ceiling windows revealed the Pacific Ocean beyond. There was a large deck beyond the tall windows, surrounded on all sides by a glass railing that made for an uninterrupted view. In a word, the view was breathtaking. Ray realized, as he took in the entire setting, that the only views into or out of the casita appeared to be to and from the west. What few windows he saw to the east weren't windows at all but rather glass-block-filled openings that allowed light in but obscured any sight from inside or outside the casita.

The Condor didn't stop in the great room as the others did but continued through the dining area into what was obviously an adjacent bedroom suite. A wide spiral stairway separated the dining area from the great room and descended to a lower area. Geraldo and Lorenzo went straight down it, off to do whatever it was they did twenty-four seven.

Almost as if he had been reading Ray's mind, Raul touched him on the arm and said, "Jefe must change. That's his private suite there. Our rooms and the security office are on the lower level for the short time we'll be staying here. We'll wait here for him and our lunch. Please sit. We'll be alone for a few minutes, and there's more you must know."

There were several furniture groupings in the large room, and Raul went to a handsome brown leather couch in the center, so Ray followed. Raul sat, indicating he should also, and then, after appearing to think for a second about what he wanted to say next, he continued.

"What you just witnessed at the main house is more often than not what usually happens—we just pass through. Jefe spends very little time at this estate. Rodrigo, the butler, and Roberto, the chef, along with the brothers Guillermo and Joaquin Sanchez, who handle security here, are the only permanent staff who live on the estate. All others—the maids, gardeners, maintenance people—leave at night. They don't reside here as the staff members do at the other estates. We have a small village down the road that provides housing for all the workers here at the estate and the maintenance facilities. This casita is Jefe's sanctuary when he's here. Within these walls, he has great privacy to do what he must to fulfill his responsibilities. No one is allowed here except us four of the inner circle, as well as Geraldo and Lorenzo, and, of course, the Sanchez brothers when Jefe is present. On the rare occasions that Jefe must do business or entertain others here at La Casa de Peña, he does so in the main house. These functions, mostly large dinner parties or cocktail parties, concern our legal businesses and also some charities that Jefe supports in his role as Nicolas Peña. Whenever he must go where our businesses take him as Señor Peña—be it here in Mexico or north to the United States—he does so from here, flying out of the airport at La Paz. On these occasional trips, Guillermo and Joaquin are his security detail."

This startling revelation piqued Ray's already heightened interest. "We don't protect him, Raul?"

"Not when he goes back to the mainland as Nicolas Peña—that's Guillermo and Joaquin's job. Remember the Condor's story this morning about his father and how he went from being Armando to Octavio?"

Ray thought for a second, recalling the story. "Yes, the two buildings. I remember."

"Good. Well, that's what La Casa de Peña is for—a place where Jefe can change his identity to be able to conduct some of our legal business. It's risky when Jefe has to travel as Señor Peña, and he doesn't travel often as Peña for this reason. When he does, he's seldom seen outside his hotel suite. Most of our legal business is conducted from here and Mexico City. Understand?"

"I think so," Ray said. "Jefe is smart and careful, like his father."

Raul nodded. "That he is, Ray, only so much more than you know."

I need to find out as much as possible about these trips, Ray thought. *Catching the Condor in the open as Peña would make everything much easier.*

"If I may ask, Raul, isn't it dangerous for Jefe to go to the United States?"

Raul shrugged. "Occasionally he must, and I still worry about it, even after he's successfully done it all these years. But he isn't in as much danger as you may think. As Peña he's a well-known, successful businessman in certain business circles; however, little is known or reported about him outside these groups. I mean, who really cares about another successful Mexican businessman? We have significant interests in the United States, legal and illegal. Jefe only deals with the legal ones when he travels. In addition to the family salt business, he has started many new ones; in transportation, for example—trucking and rail and even ships."

Raul smiled as he continued. "Jefe has several successful cruise-ship lines started by his father, one here on the Pacific Ocean side, and one in the Gulf of Mexico serving the Caribbean and the American east coast. We transport more products into the United States in this manner than all the rest of our methods combined."

"Cruise ships?" Ray asked curiously, as if he'd never heard the term.

"Big ships, Ray, like floating luxury hotels. Once we get through the next month or so, after you've been with us awhile and are more comfortable, we'll set up a cruise for you, maybe after you find yourself a girlfriend. You'll enjoy it, I think."

Ray smiled a small smile at Raul and nodded. "Thank you, Raul." *Good God, several cruise-ship lines transporting drugs. I have to get the names. I bet Bennie could figure out which ships they are, maybe even how it's done. This is hot stuff.*

As they were talking, Ray was sitting in one of the side chairs, so his back was to the entry to the Condor's suite. He didn't immediately see him reenter the room, but he heard footsteps and turned around. Despite his four years of undercover work and the great experience he thought he had hiding his emotions when covert, he did a double take as the Condor entered. The surprise on his face was obvious and entirely genuine, for the man walking over to join them bore no resemblance whatsoever to either El Condor de Muerte or Señor Peña. If not for the smile on the Condor's face, Ray could honestly say he didn't recognize the man walking up to him. He had very short black hair, no beard or glasses, and looked younger. Without even realizing it, Ray stood up; he was speechless, his mind racing to grapple with this new situation. Raul also stood and was beside him, clearly amused at Ray's obvious surprise.

The Condor extended his hand, as if meeting him for the first time, and Raul said, "Ray Ortega, I would like to introduce you to Jacques Pablo Alvarez, the secretary for public security for the United Mexican States. Mr. Secretary, may I present Mr. Ray Ortega, the newest member of your security detail."

"A pleasure to make your acquaintance, Mr. Ortega. You come highly recommended by your uncle and my old friend Raul here."

As Ray shook the Condor's hand, he was momentarily powerless to utter any words as a flood of emotions washed over him and thoughts ran through his head.

Christ almighty, Secretary Alvarez! He was detailed in Bennie's briefing papers. He's their top cop; everyone fighting cartels down here works for him! Their FBI, the federal police, fucking everybody. And he's also a cartel leader?

"You OK, Ray?" the Condor said, clearly amused with his stupefaction.

Ray gathered himself as quickly as he could, knowing he was doing a lousy job of reigning in his wild emotions. "Yes, of course, Jefe. I'm sorry again for my surprise…I'm stupid." He looked at the floor as if embarrassed, but it was to try to hide the fact the he was flabbergasted.

"Ray, listen to me," the Condor said, kindly grabbing him by the shoulder. "You have nothing to be ashamed of. This changing of identities…it's not normal, but it's what I must do. Now that you know, you'll be fine. Is this not true?"

Managing to regain some semblance of control, he looked up and responded in what he hoped was a normal voice. "Yes, Jefe. Forgive me. I'm fine now."

"Good. Now that you know my true identity," the Condor said, "it's important, when I'm myself, that you not call me Jefe when others outside the circle are around. And I'm afraid that will be most of the time, especially in Mexico City. There, you must call me Mr. Secretary or Señor Alvarez, OK?"

Ray nodded. "Yes, Jefe, of course. I'll remember."

The Condor glanced at Raul and then looked back to Ray. "Sit down, please. We've thrown a lot at you this morning. But take some time, and after you think about it, I'm confident you'll keep it all straight. Just think before you address me when we're traveling, and you'll be fine. You seem to do that anyway, which is another reason I selected you to be with me. You now understand why I need my security detail and why it's important that I have good men around me. As the Condor, I have many enemies in the cartels, but they know little about the Condor—we've seen to that—and I have plenty of protection with Eduardo's men and Carlo's. But as the secretary, I'm a visible, desirable target to these same men—only half the time they know exactly where to find me. Now, how about some lunch? And I'll tell you more of my life story, which will explain everything to you."

"Thank you. Yes, Jefe, I could eat."

"Raul," the Condor said, "could you call the house and see if Rodrigo has our lunch ready?"

As the Condor was talking with Raul, Ray thought, *In a pig's ass, I can eat. I can't even swallow spit right now. I'm screwed! Wait till Bennie hears about this—if ever. Jesus Christ, I'll bet he won't believe me.*

Miguel, Luis, and the Sanchez brothers pulled up just as the Condor finished speaking to Raul, relieving him of the need to call Rodrigo. The Condor stood and led them into the dining room as Miguel came in the door with the others behind him, carrying packages.

"Miguel, please set up some lunch for Raul, Ray, and me here, and then take the rest downstairs for yourself and the others. We still have some items we must discuss in private."

Miguel nodded and looked to the others, silently ordering them to do as requested.

"And Miguel," the Condor continued, "check in with Geraldo and Lorenzo and see if there's anything requiring my immediate attention."

Miguel nodded again and headed for the stairs. While Luis was setting up the lunch, one of the Sanchez brothers—in his unsettled frame of mind, Ray wasn't sure which one—located some fine crystal wineglasses, opened an old-looking bottle of wine, and poured three glasses.

"Thank you, Guillermo," the Condor said.

Guillermo nodded. "Rodrigo thought you might enjoy this one, Jefe. He just received it and seemed excited about it."

Guillermo set the bottle down between Ray and the Condor. Ray knew little about wines, which he realized was probably sacrilege given how close he had lived to Napa Valley his entire life. While trying to get his emotions under control, he watched with feigned interest as the Condor went through the routine of swirling, sniffing, and tasting the wine.

The Condor smiled at Guillermo. "Please tell Rodrigo he *should* be excited with this acquisition and should try a bottle if he hasn't already. This is most excellent and will pair perfectly with his beef Wellington."

"I will, Jefe. He will be pleased."

As the others were leaving, Ray started to carve at the exceptional-looking steak presented to him, but he was reeling from everything he'd just learned. *He's unbelievable*, he thought. *His transformation from the Condor to Alvarez is so complete. He not only looks totally different—he is totally different. The Condor is obviously a complete act, and man, is he good at it. His eyes—what I could see of them behind those ridiculous sunglasses—seemed so cold as the Condor, and now they're warm, friendly. How does he do it? Even his voice is a little different. And Carlo and Eduardo—what do they know? They probably know he's Peña, but Alvarez? I bet not. And to think he thought this out years ago and set them up at his father's funeral right here, apparently. Carlo told me about meeting him again ten years ago, and he had the white hair—has he really fooled them with his disguise all this time? I haven't seen the Condor as Peña enough to know how different he is in that alias—somewhere between the Condor and himself, I suspect. How ironic that we both have been playing other characters. He had me fooled completely. I'd never have thought that possible, but then, I'm doing it to him. Thank God; I'd be dead otherwise. No wonder he has access to so much information—he's the Holy Grail of information for the entire Mexican government. Bennie and the Mexicans have no clue how dangerous this guy is. I remember Bennie's report on him; one of the real good guys, he said—a real comer, could end up president someday. Goddamn it, how do you take on a guy like that? Bennie said President Fernandez is maybe on his way out because of all the shit at the border that the Condor apparently ordered him to do. So Fernandez only knows him as the Condor? Most likely. Son of a bitch, I need help. This is way out of control. How do you get away from the fucking secretary for public security? That's like our secretary of Homeland Defense and the director of the FBI rolled in to one. How do you hide from someone that powerful down here if he decides to end you? Who am I kidding? I'll never be safe again, here or back home, unless I kill him and the others before they kill me.*

Ray suddenly realized the Condor was saying something to him, but he was so deep in thought that he didn't hear him at first. He felt a momentary flash of panic, like an electric shock coursing through his system. You never went out of character when undercover when others were present, and that was exactly what he had done while deep in thought. But his professional subconscious kicked in, and he popped back into the moment, into his character, and looked up.

"I'm sorry, Jefe. I was thinking while I was eating. I didn't hear what you said."

"That's OK," the Condor said. "It's expected that you'd try to sort through everything you've been exposed to this morning. I asked how your lunch was."

"Oh, ah, it's the nicest I've ever had. I don't know what I'm eating, but it's very good. I mean, I know it's a steak—I have had that before, just not like this."

"Beef Wellington, Ray, a filet mignon in a light pastry, only Rodrigo does it with a simple red wine sauce instead of a Bordelaise. You were frowning as you ate—that's why I asked if you were enjoying your lunch. This may sound like a ridiculous question, given what you've been through this morning and with what you've learned, but is something bothering you?"

God, this guy is intuitive as hell. Be careful.

"No, Jefe. I was just thinking about the flight and what you've said and the…the changes in you. You are an important person. I hope I don't fuck up—that was what I was thinking."

Ray had never before spoken so crudely to the Condor, but fucking up was prominently on his mind, and it had just popped out. "Keep your undercover persona close to your own," Bennie had said. Well, he was as close to Ray Ortega emotionally as he ever would be; both personas were confused and scared shitless.

Raul, who was enjoying his lunch and listening to the conversation, chuckled at Ray's expletive. The Condor leaned back and did likewise. Raul leaned toward Ray, smiling, and said, "Relax, El Cuchillo. I wasn't nearly as smart as you are when I learned of Pablo's plans. I 'fucked up,' as you said, more times than I care to remember. I'm surprised Jefe has kept me around all these years."

"You made mistakes at first?" Ray asked him.

"Of course I did. Unlike you, at your age I was a mouthy little shit and not very smart—always talking, never listening. I thought I was the toughest friend Pablo had. Francisco and I were about your age when Armando, Pablo's father, chose us to be his friends and guards. Pablo was twelve, as I recall. I was eighteen, and Francisco a couple of years older. Here in Baja, we lived at the estate next door, Pablo's mother's estate."

This was new information. Ray looked at the Condor. "Next door, Jefe?"

The Condor had a faraway look on his face, as if he were recalling earlier times, when he and Raul were much younger. His expression changed with the question, becoming more serious, maybe even sad. "Yes," he said. "From the time I was ten, I lived at the adjacent estate, where my mother still lives. It's her home, the Alvarez home, and has been for almost forty years. She naps in the afternoon. Unfortunately, she isn't well and spends much of her time in bed, but we'll see her for dinner at six. I want you to meet her—a most extraordinary woman. The people in the government I work with, the press, and the government agencies that provide me my security believe I live next door when here in the Baja, safely behind those walls, privately attending to my mother. My movements are generally followed, but because of the threats to my life, much is also concealed—especially from the media—for security reasons. So once I come here, I'm able to move around as Señor Peña or the Condor as much as I wish. What these two estates allow me to do is 'launder' myself, so to speak, much as we do our illegal profits. You'll see how we do this when we go to dinner tonight."

Raul stood and put his hand on Alvarez's shoulder. "Pablo, I'll excuse myself and attend to the details for our meetings in the capital. Enjoy your lunch. If there's anything requiring your attention, I'll bring it to you."

"Thank you, my friend. I appreciate that."

Raul got up and went downstairs, and the two of them were alone, making Ray uncomfortable again, as all the Condor's focus would be on him. The only other time they'd been alone together had been right after Vasso's assassination attempt, when they had talked in the Condor's study and then had their private dinner. It had only been two nights before, but it seemed like so much longer to Ray, and so very much had changed since then. Despite those great changes and the important new intelligence learned of the last two days, as of this moment, his situation had just become far more dangerous. In the last two months, he barely had come to grips with the fact that he had fallen into perhaps the most powerful cartel in Mexico—a cartel his agency knew nothing about it. Now, over the last few minutes, he discovers that the principal figure in the Mexican government responsible for leading the country's fight *against* the cartels was himself a serious and powerful cartel leader. He had imagined a lot of potential scenarios when Bennie was preparing him for insertion, but he sure as hell never had imagined this.

14

The Peña estate
Baja California Sur
Wednesday

Alvarez watched his old friend go downstairs, and Ray alternated between watching him and looking out the tall windows toward the Pacific, not knowing how he was going to handle the changing dynamics. Alvarez turned back to him, a warm look on his face, and said, "You'll learn in time just what a good man Raul is. With the exception of my cousins, Raul and Francisco, before he was killed, have been my closest friends for many years. I'd be lost without Raul's friendship. Now you must have questions. Please ask them."

Ray was extremely anxious and fighting to control his emotions in the Condor's presence. *Jesus,* he thought. *Where do I begin?*

Focusing, he tried to use the fact that the Condor seemed to like him as a way to settle down and concentrate. This was a great intelligence-gathering opportunity, and he couldn't blow it. The more he discovered, and the longer he could hang in there and stay concealed, perhaps the more likely it would be that a way out would be revealed.

"I do have some questions, Jefe," he began. "Carlo and Eduardo—do they know who you really are?"

Alvarez appeared relaxed, and his entire demeanor was that of a teacher having a friendly discussion with an intelligent pupil. "Eduardo does," he said. "That's a secret he can handle and should know. Carlo? Well, you've seen how much I love my cousin, and he's my oldest friend, but you have *seen* Carlo. He has a big heart, but he has…limitations. I have to have him watched constantly—only he doesn't know this. He can't; it would hurt him if he felt I didn't trust him, and I love him like a brother."

Goddamn! Was he watching Carlo when I first got here and went into town with him? Jesus, I'm so stupid. Apparently I got lucky. I guess whoever was watching Carlo didn't see me slip out of the whorehouse. That's obvious; I'd be dead otherwise.

"In a way," Alvarez continued, "you've been watching Carlo for us, Ray, even if you were unaware of it. Except for wanting to visit his prostitutes, he isn't as wild around you; he drinks less, to be specific. We—Eduardo, Raul, and I—believe it's because he wants your respect. He's careless when he gets drunk, and he's only been drunk a couple of times since he came back with you. It was his drinking that got him caught in the United States, where you came to know him. You've been good for Carlo, another reason we admire you so much."

What? He's a mind reader too? That explains a lot. Mostly why I wasn't caught...thank God. I can't believe these guys really like me. What fucking dumb luck.

"Thank you, Jefe," Ray said. "I do respect and like Carlo. Because of him, I have a home."

Alvarez nodded his acceptance of this and appeared touched by the sentiment. "Please continue with your questions. It's important that you know everything."

"Jefe, the way you change how you look—did your father teach you that?"

Alvarez smiled wistfully. "Good question, but no. All through preparatory school and into the university, I wanted to study the theater, acting—it was my passion. I dreamed of being the next El Indio of stage and film fame, but sadly, I learned once I got to the university that I didn't have the talent necessary to make it a career. So I turned to philosophy instead and then the study of law and became a lawyer. But I did learn the art of stage makeup, and that's how I alter my appearance."

Ray was fascinated—another surprise he hadn't expected, the man wanting to be an actor. But it did explain how easily he seemed to change personas.

"Carlo told me he hadn't seen you for many years," Ray continued, "and when you buried your father, he met you here at the coast, and you were the Condor. I mean you looked like you do as the Condor. You didn't want them to know about you, even back then?"

Another astute question, the Condor thought. *This one is special. I was right to choose him. Like Raul and Eduardo, with some formal education, he could go far. I'll arrange for tutors first, as I did with the others, and then, eventually, we'll get him into college courses. I think he'll come to enjoy it.*

"That was my father's plan," Alvarez said. "And it wasn't at this house or my mother's estate where we had the funeral. It was at the first estate we passed today, two miles north, near were we landed. Our family cemetery is located near there, just into the hills overlooking the ocean—it's very beautiful. My father said it was best to never let Eduardo and Carlo know of these two estates, so I never have. He felt the more distance I kept between my various lives, the greater safety there was, much as he had done as Octavio. When Carlo visited when we were children, it was to the north estate. Some American leases it now; we haven't used it for years. It's only two miles away, but that two miles would have saved my family's life had anyone discovered we were still alive. It's remarkable that Carlo never betrayed us by accident, especially when we were still young. After my father moved us here to the coast, word got out that we'd been kidnapped and killed—few people knew of the deception. The proof of the success of my father's plan is that we're all still alive, and I am who I really am. As for Nicolas Peña, it is believed by most that he's an estranged bastard half brother of mine, the result of an indiscretion by my father many years ago. Few outside the upper class of our society know or care about such things—such behavior is sadly common among the wealthy. My Peña persona is a respected businessman but a bit of a recluse, and that also is accepted."

"Your father was a smart man to protect his family as he did," Ray said, looking for a means to keep the conversation going and hopefully draw out more intelligence.

Alvarez's expression became sad, it seemed to Ray, as he responded, "It's hard to speak of him like this, but I feel you must know my life story, which means understanding my father as I came to know him. Some men—such as Carlo, for example—can know many women in their lives. By 'know,' I mean like in the Bible, to lie with a woman. For my father, there was always just my mother. I was taught that God has a plan for us all and moves in mysterious ways, but I'll never understand the plan that put my mother with my father. I've tried to make sense of it but get no further than the fact that in all ways, I'm indeed the product of their union, and the combination of their personalities and characters has kept me alive and sane.

"Others would call my father a criminal—only to do so doesn't do him justice. It's true he went down a path of crime in an effort to save his brother from going to jail…or worse. But he wasn't vicious or ruthless in the sense that others in our business are. He was a kind, thoughtful man who used his superior intelligence rather than brute force to achieve his ends. Ultimately those ends were driven by his need to protect and provide for his family the best way he could. As the son of the angel who is my mother and the reluctant criminal who was my father, I've done some awful things that God never will forgive. There's no denying that I've sent many of the worst in our society to their deaths, but in doing so, Ray, I believe in my heart I've also saved the lives of many, many others. I'm speaking of the innocents who are being slaughtered by the thousands indiscriminately by the worst criminal elements in our society in this war for control of the trafficking. That I'll be cast into hell is something I fear I cannot avoid. I made that decision and forever determined my fate before God when I decided to join my uncle Enrique, as well as Eduardo and Carlos, and avenge the assassination of my father."

Alvarez paused, seemingly lost in his thoughts for a few seconds. "I suppose that's not entirely accurate. I was protecting my father's trafficking business for some time before that, after he confronted me with the truth of his life and explained everything to me. At that point, I chose to work with him and not betray him; that was twelve years ago. I was a young prosecutor in our federal Justice Department and had just been promoted to deputy attorney general. I was working hard to prosecute as many cartel members as I could back then. In most ways, I still am.

"At first, I didn't believe my father when he told me who and what he was. I was so shocked, angered by what he told me, but he was my father, Ray—I simply couldn't betray and arrest him. We were very wealthy because of the many businesses he had set up, and he was giving back in so many ways through the charitable trust he'd established. Despite the decisions that resulted in his becoming a trafficker, my father retained his conscience. His philanthropy was his self-imposed penance for becoming involved as he had, but even he realized his generosity didn't make up for or excuse his life.

"As I was unaware of my father's history or my true family name, I had no idea my family was involved in this madness until he told me twelve years ago. The more I learned from him, however, the more I realized that if the trafficking was run carefully, and if I helped with information, we might be able to eliminate many of the worst criminals in our country and, with that, take over most of the trafficking. Yes, my family would still be trafficking, but most of the needless brutality against innocent people would cease. If we could also eliminate the corruption in the government and seize control of it and the cartels, we could bring order to the trafficking, stop the gunrunning that threatens the stability of our democracy, perhaps even reduce the overall amount of drugs being distributed to America. I'd like that. Certainly men died based on the information I passed to my father while I was in the Justice Department—evil men, I believe. But that wasn't for me to decide, so I suppose that was when I really fell from God."

Fell from God? Do I dare ask him about that? It would build on our relationship, I think. I know he's Catholic—almost everyone is down here. He's killed people, for Christ's sake, but so have I. Go ahead. Ask it.

"You believe in God, Jefe?"

Alvarez paused for a few seconds. It struck Ray that he didn't seem surprised or offended by the question, just thoughtful as he gazed at the ocean beyond the glass wall of the great room.

"I did…for many years," he said, turning and looking at him. "Now? I don't know anymore. The path my life took twelve years ago gave me doubts, made me question my beliefs. I want to believe in God, but it no longer matters; my fate is determined one way or another. The way my mother raised us, I did believe for a long time and with all my heart, and God surely knew that. Yet my life was diverted, changed forever by what must surely be God's own hand…I've wondered why. What do you believe, Ray?"

Keep it simple. Stick with the background Bennie came up with.

Ray shrugged. "I don't know if I do. The woman who raised me after my parents were killed believed, but we didn't go to church much. She was kind and read to me at night from the Bible and told me stories of the good things believers did. She kept telling me I was saved because I believed, but I never understood what I was saved from. I always felt lost, like I didn't belong somehow, and I left her and that family when I was thirteen."

Alvarez nodded sympathetically, as if he understood Ray's feelings, then said, "Well, I must say the events of the last week have given me reason to reflect once again on my beliefs."

He leaned toward Ray and had a strange look on his face that Ray was having a tough time reading, as if he were troubled, but there was more there—pain maybe, he thought.

"God *must* have a plan for you and me," Alvarez continued, "because if you hadn't been arrested and jailed with Carlo, you wouldn't have saved his life in the prison yard, you wouldn't have become friends and escaped together, and Carlo wouldn't have brought you to me. If Carlo hadn't brought you to me, I would have selected Miguel to be Eduardo's second at the Vasso meeting instead of listening to Carlo and having you and your knife there. Had that happened, Eduardo and I certainly would be dead at the hands of Guzman and his friend, and the Gang of Four would have won."

He paused again, slowly sat back in his chair, and went on. "We can never really know in our temporal life—that's our life here on this earth, Ray—whether God exists, or, if there is in fact a God, what his plan is for us. But if you do have faith, and do believe, it seems God chose to send you to me, and you saved my life. *Res ipsa loquitur*. Do you remember that from the other night?"

Ray purposefully looked slightly puzzled and then answered, "It's the Latin, Jefe? The facts speak?"

Alvarez smiled warmly. "Almost—*the facts speak for themselves*. God *must* exist! How else can we explain the events you and I have been a part of? And he knows my sins, yet I wasn't taken. Why? Why was I saved? Is it because he does know what's in my heart? I've been deeply troubled by this and have thought a lot about it over the last several days. I was a traitor to my faith and required vengeance for my father's death, and I took it. I was blinded by hate and personally killed the man who betrayed and murdered my father, taking God's providence into my own hands. Worse, I had Carlo kill the man's sons, for they helped their father and would have become relentless enemies had I not done so and would have soon sought their own retribution. I abandoned what was left of my core beliefs to get my revenge and, as such, left my fate in God's hands. I expected God to strike me down for what I'd done; I wanted him to, for the guilt is almost too terrible to bear, yet he didn't take me, Ray. My Jesuit teachers spoke often of God's path and righteous choices rather than acting out of narrow self-interest. How can the events we've shared not mean that the actions I've taken on my path must somehow reflect God's will, what he wants me to do?"

Alvarez leaned in again to him, his voice dropping to just above a whisper even though they were the only two in the room. "I've had little trouble seeing plots and attempts on my life, as our enemies are so clumsy and predictable. But I tell you, just between us, that I didn't see the Vasso attack coming. I was so focused on my plans and the parts that Vasso and Barega were to play that I didn't see their treachery. I should be dead and Eduardo also—the result of my carelessness and my sins. Yet here we sit, my young friend, alive, together, and my plans to help my people are that much closer to being realized. For reasons that are still unclear to me, God chose to send you to me…and you bested the assassins and saved me. There must be a purpose in this; God has brought us together, Ray, and it's up to us to learn why."

Ray sat quietly, looking at Alvarez. He was blown away by the man's soliloquy and also, because of the guilt he felt over killing Guzman, deeply troubled.

Jesus Christ, he's crazy—he must be—but that's why he likes me and trusts me. It's God's will, as if I'm his protector or something. Does God exist? Am I supposed to help him succeed in whatever he's planning? Jesus, now I'm going nuts. I don't know what I believe, but all this helps me. Carlo is blinded by our friendship; maybe Alvarez is too, despite his great intellect. I don't know about God's plan, but I do know Bennie's plan. That's all I really know for sure. If I'm careful and don't screw up and give this guy a reason to suspect me, I may live to see this to the end, whatever that turns out to be.

Alvarez's placed a hand on Ray's shoulder. "Sorry," he said. "I didn't mean to get so philosophical, and I don't want this to trouble you. It's just something I've been thinking a lot about. As I was saying, after my father built this estate and the one next door, the second and third in this area, he moved us here. He did this as Octavio Peña. My mother returned to her family's name, Alvarez, at the instruction of my father. He told her it was necessary to keep her and us children safe."

Alvarez paused and stared out toward the Pacific again, as if remembering his mother in a different time or place. He sighed just perceptibly and turned back toward Ray.

"It's important we bring order to the trafficking business. That's something I've been trying to do for many years. As much as I might wish to, I can't go back and undo forty years of family history. I'm from a family that has created great wealth through the trafficking of drugs. That, I was surprised to learn in my late thirties, is what I am. But what I can do is to get control of it and the government once and for all and reduce the violence and the crime that surrounds the drug business here in Mexico."

Overwhelmed with conflicting emotions as he listened to Alvarez, Ray didn't know what to say or do next. His first intuition was that so much of what Alvarez was trying to do was good. As he sorted through his mixed-up feelings, Luis came up the stairway and walked up to Alvarez, relieving Ray of having to say anything immediately.

"Jefe, excuse me, but Raul asked me to tell you there are some messages that require your attention."

"Certainly, Luis." Alvarez looked back to Ray. "Let's go. We'll show you the lower level and where you can freshen up or nap before we go to my mother's."

They went down the spiral staircase to the lower level. There were six small bedrooms and several bathrooms, a common room with a bar that looked out over a patio to the ocean beyond, an office for Alvarez, and a security room. Geraldo and Lorenzo were in their room, facing a rack of monitors and all sorts of other expensive and sophisticated-looking electronic gear—just what you might expect the head of Mexico's combined FBI, national police, and Justice Department to have access to. Raul was in Alvarez's office next door.

Alvarez turned to Ray and said, "Relax for a couple of hours. I have some business to go over with Raul before we go to dinner. We'll leave just before six. Wear what you have on—you look fine."

Ray went into the small bedroom that Luis had pointed out was his, and Alvarez went in the office and closed the door. When Alvarez entered, Raul looked up from the papers he was reading. "How was your lunch, and how is young Ray taking all this?"

Alvarez sat down then looked at Raul. "OK, I think. Better than I expected. It was a lot to place on him so quickly, but we had no choice. We must return, and I want him with us, in truth, I need him with me."

Raul just raised an eyebrow at the admission as Alvarez went on. "I sensed some tension in him at lunch, some apprehension, something. I think he's worried he'll make a horrible mistake somehow, now that he knows who I am."

"Christ, we've all felt that, Pablo—me almost every day."

Alvarez shook his head slowly and turned more serious. "Just watch him, help him. It was nice of you to tell him of your early mistakes. I'm certain he appreciated your mentioning it. But enough of that. What do you have for me?"

"A fax from Alberto Rodriguez regarding the preliminary investigation on his brother's assassination. You can read that on the plane tomorrow if you wish. Our investigators have nothing more than the fact that it was well planned and executed. I suspect the Gang of Four used some of the same operatives we've employed from time to time; I recognize the methods. In fact, it was my intention to retain them to assist us when we deal with the other cartels, but I'll discreetly check this out once we're in Mexico City. If I find out some of the contractors we've used were involved in this, do you want me to deal with them? If the Gang of Four did use them, perhaps they're no longer reliable."

Alvarez appeared to be deep in thought. "No, Raul, not until we talk. Make no mention of it to your go-betweens—good professionals are hard to come by. As long as they don't know about our connection to the Condor, it's best we let them be so we can have access to their expertise in the future."

Alvarez looked at his old friend, but his mind was elsewhere. His dear friend and brother-in-law Emilio had come to him with information that could have led Emilio to discovering he was the Condor. When Alvarez had shared his fears about that privately with Francisco, Francisco had taken matters into his own hands and had him killed, making his beloved sister Elena a widow. Now Francisco was also dead, and he was the only one who knew the real reason Emilio had been assassinated. Far worse, he could have stopped it and should have, but he stayed silent and did nothing, knowing that Francisco would protect him. One more tragedy he now had to live with, one more soul on his conscience.

"Pablo, you OK? What's troubling you?" a concerned Raul asked.

"Sorry, sorry, old friend," Alvarez said as he returned to the moment. "I was thinking about Emilio. Forgive me. Did Alberto finally have the funeral?"

"Yes, today, a small one—family only at their beach estate. I called and also sent a note to Alberto and Elena on your behalf, explaining you were attending to your mother. Alberto understood and passed along his best wishes."

"I'll call him tomorrow and meet with him. I'll tell him at that time that I'll be resigning from my position and recommending him to the president as the secretary. Then I'll meet with former President Castillo late tomorrow afternoon and then that shit Fernandez tomorrow night. It must be in that order, Raul."

"We've gone over this before. I understand."

"Also, I want to host a small reception for Emilio's and our friends and family at the house in the city on Saturday—just cocktails and hors d'oeuvres, say at six. Would you clear that with my sister and have someone set it up?"

"I'll take care of it, Pablo. Do you have a list of whom you want invited?"

"I'll have one shortly. People need to be called so plans can be made, so let's get that done before dinner. Have a time and place been set for my meeting with that idiot Fernandez?"

"Yes, the president will meet you privately for cocktails at the penthouse on Reforma he keeps for his girlfriend and thinks no one knows about tomorrow night at eight. He'll have the address couriered to me when we get to the city—the pig, like I don't know where that whorehouse is already. I wish you would have let Eduardo kill him years ago like he should have."

Alvarez smiled. "Easy, Raul. We'll be done with him soon enough. How are your plans proceeding?"

"All will be done by Friday. You don't need to know all the details. Fernandez is scheduled to depart for Hermosillo at nine Monday morning; he'll no longer be a problem by eleven. In order for my plans to be kept in absolute secrecy, I'll need help from the circle. I'm using Luis, but you know Luis…I don't trust him to do as he's told. I plan on using Ray, now that he's joined us. Do you have any problems with this? When it's discovered that the crash was no accident, all trails that could possibly be investigated must be controlled."

Alvarez looked concerned. "You seem certain the investigators will discover the crash is no accident—is there no way to conceal this?"

Raul shook his head slowly. "It's not possible to create an explosion, however small, without there being some telltale signs. The first small explosion will occur as the jet lands, the second several seconds later. According to the man I have doing this, to any observers it will appear as if part of the landing gear failed on landing, and as the engine and wing hit the runway, the wing fuel tank exploded. Perhaps this will destroy all the evidence, but I can't be certain. The National Air Safety Board will no doubt ask for—and we should allow it—help from the Americans. It would look wrong if we refused their offers of assistance, especially since it's an American-made aircraft. I doubt our crash investigators could find any evidence, but the American investigators are very good. Even then, it will be hard for them. Our man placing the devices is very knowledgeable about all this but understandably reluctant to participate. In order to control him, I need to control his family. That's what I planned on using Luis for, but again, you know Luis—things could get out of hand. He's nothing like his father was. I'm thinking Ray could help me with him."

Alvarez, looking melancholy, shook his head. "I wish Luis's father were still with us. I never should have elevated Luis to the circle—I realize this now. You did try to warn me. I should have listened."

"That's all in the past, Pablo. I'll control him; put him out of your mind."

"I'm worried we're placing too much responsibility on Ray too quickly, especially if you draw him deeper into your plans."

Raul nodded. "Perhaps, but there's something about him, Pablo, something that tells me he can handle whatever I need him to do. He's strong, reliable, and smart."

Alvarez smiled sadly. "I agree. Do what you think is best." His look turned dark again. "What's the possibility of survivors?"

Raul understood where his friend was going with the question; it had to come up eventually. "Possible, Pablo, but not likely. The president's new aircraft is the new Boeing jet. The security protocol is to fuel his plane only from proven, tested sources that have been continually under guard. Fueling in the capital for both legs of the trip saves having to make security arrangements for fuel in Hermosillo. In other words, there'll be an abundance of fuel onboard, so the crash and subsequent fire will be catastrophic. I'm told the president's aircraft will have a landing speed of almost one hundred forty miles an hour with the added fuel it will be carrying. The crash at that speed will be significant. Think about crashing a fuel truck at that speed—that's what it will be like."

Alvarez's tone changed, becoming quieter as he went on. "Who else will be aboard? I despair at the thought of their deaths, but we need Fernandez dead, in this way and at this time. The equinox has just passed, and we're in the noted period of the Mayan calendar. So many people believe in it and its prophecies. We must use this belief to strengthen our grip on the people. As we get closer to the solstice, their interest will continue to grow. With our citizens' beliefs, in their eyes our ascent to the presidency will become that much more significant. I'll truly become one with the people."

Raul paused as he reflected on what Alvarez had said. He had to admit there were times lately when his old friend spoke about parts of his plans that made him wonder whether Alvarez hadn't been pushed beyond any reasonable emotional limits. While he could appreciate, and even admire, the timing of the assassination of President Fernandez in a purely tactical sense, he intuitively knew there was more to it for his friend. He was beginning to believe that the entire notion of becoming one with the people wasn't just talk, some abstraction, but rather that Alvarez really believed this. What bothered Raul the most was that he had no idea where that sort of thinking would lead. His friend was already over the top emotionally, what with having faced a certain death, only to have Ray—or God, perhaps—intervene. Raul was still struggling with Pablo's beliefs about all that. Now he was beginning to have private doubts about his friend's sanity and couldn't discount the fact that maybe, just maybe, everything that had happened was simply too much for one good man to bear. Although Raul was troubled, he went on with his train of thought regarding the details of the plane crash. The clock was already running and there was no turning back anyway.

"In order to have Fernandez's death appear as an accident," he said, "it will be necessary to do it this way, and most certainly others will also perish. I'm sorry, but that can't be helped. Out of security concerns in the north as a result of the attack on Rodriguez, we've told the presidential office we're limiting the passengers to the flight crew, Fernandez's immediate security detail, and two of his personal assistants. And, of course, there'll be a half dozen media representatives aboard. Altogether, sixteen to twenty people will be accompanying the president. His new plane is configured with the general seating area up front, then a conference area and social spaces in the middle cabin, and, at the rear, the presidential office and bedroom. Most of the passengers should be sitting forward I would think. If there are survivors, this is where they'll come from. As I understand it, all the fuel is stored in the wings and in the main tank between the wings, and the general seating is well forward of this area. Once the jet crashes, the center cabin and the president's private spaces will be devastated by the explosion but the front not nearly so, as it might well be blown free of the worst of it. That's the best I can offer."

Alvarez shook his head slowly again. "That's something, I guess. Thank you. I'll want the names of those who perish. I must take care of their families."

"I'll take care of all the arrangements, Pablo. Don't worry about any of this."

"Thank you. Much of my plan depends on the president being dead and in this way. The impact on the people will be tremendous and shocking. They'll be hit hard emotionally. If, on the heels of this, we can give them a great victory over some of the other cartels, one that gives them hope for the future, they'll always remember those who delivered them this future, and we'll have their loyalty and devotion. This is important if there's to be a second term." Raul nodded his agreement, but his uneasy feelings on that aspect of the plan returned.

For the rest of the afternoon, the secretary for public security for Mexico and his chief aide went over the routine business required by the cabinet secretary whose responsibility it was to coordinate the country's fight against the drug cartels. Among the subjects reviewed was the initial planning for what was to be a spectacular raid on the site used by the Gang of Four for one of their infrequent get-togethers. The local federal police commander had been tipped off as planned regarding the meeting and had alerted Alberto Rodriguez's office, which had forwarded the information on to them. Raul's call the day before had indeed made Commander Diaz of the Sinaloa office of the federal police popular with his superiors. If the raid went as planned, the government could soon celebrate a significant victory in their war against the cartels. The people of Mexico, and perhaps even the world, would believe they had dealt the traffickers a crippling blow, when in fact they would help hand over near total control of the trafficking within Mexico to one powerful, carefully concealed man.

15

La Casa de Campo del Sol Poniente
Zihuatanejo, Mexico
Monday, late afternoon

Manny looked intently out over the deep-blue Pacific, thinking about everything that had occurred over the last few days. He'd been doing that a lot lately. Dressed as he was—in khaki golf shorts, a white Tommy Bahama silk shirt, and leather open-toed sandals—his apparel was as far removed in both appearance and comfort from the typical wardrobe required of a general officer in the summer as it could be. His attire, however, perfectly suited his surroundings as he sat in a teak deck chair on the paved-stone terrace of Alberto's family vacation home. The villa was located on a bluff overlooking the expansive white sand of La Ropa beach that met the waters of the Pacific Ocean near the Bay of Zihuatanejo. La Casa de Campo del Sol Poniente (the Villa of the Setting Sun) had been in the family for more than seventy years. The large walled estate had been remodeled and upgraded over the years, most recently by Alberto and Emilio when it had become clear to the brothers that, given the professional and often personal war they were waging against the cartels, the estate needed to be completely modernized to include the latest in security systems.

As a senior general officer and base commander, Manny was required to get DOD approval to leave the United States. Given the circumstances surrounding Emilio's death, and in due consideration of Alberto's and Emilio's positions of importance in the Mexican government, the secretary of the army gave Manny quick permission to leave for whatever period of time he felt was necessary. Manny secured the use of one of the air force's C-37A executive jets from the Sixth Air Mobility Wing out of Florida to fly him and Beth; his aide, Colonel Phil Romero; and his cousin's families down to Mexico for the service.

They had arrived this morning after the flight from Fort Bliss to the small Mexican air force base in Pie de la Cuesta on the coast of Mexico, north of Acapulco. Alberto had arranged for them to then be flown by Mexican air force helicopters to the beach only a few hundred yards below the family's villa. For security reasons, today's funeral arrangements were known only to a few. In most instances, even those with a need to know some aspect of the logistics, such as the Mexican air force colonel who commanded the base at Pie de la Cuesta, were notified by phone only thirty minutes prior to their arrival on the base. The general who called from Mexico City didn't give the colonel any explanation as to why an American army general was to arrive on his base or why he also was to expect two American-made Sikorsky S-70A Black Hawk helicopters from the Mexican air force at any time.

The colonel also wasn't told who else was accompanying the general or why they were appearing so suddenly out of nowhere. He was ordered to allow it, refuel the helicopters, and clamp a security lid on everything that had taken place. Generals being generals, and colonels being colonels, the base commander was only too happy to oblige, no questions asked. The Black Hawks were hastily refueled, as requested, after landing and took off immediately after the passengers from the United States arrived and were loaded aboard.

The Black Hawks landed on the wide white-sand beach at the base of the bluff below the villa, where they were met by Alberto and troops from a special-forces platoon he controlled. The family members were then escorted up the well-beaten private path from the beach to the villa and shown to their rooms to rest briefly and freshen up before the service. With the exceptions of Manny and his aide, Colonel Romero, who with their professional eyes spotted several concealed defensive positions in the dense, jungle-like foliage on either side of the path, none of the family members were aware of the numbers of men-at-arms surrounding them.

Located on the expansive estate grounds was a small, traditional white-stucco chapel with a steeply pitched roof and a simple white timber cross projecting above the peak of the small bell tower. The service was conducted in a picturesque courtyard that fronted the chapel, with only the immediate family in attendance. Emilio's casket was then taken inside the chapel, carried by six young, solid-looking men in dark business suits, whom, from their bearing, Manny recognized as soldiers. Following the ceremony, the family was served a private buffet dinner in the villa and then once again returned to their rooms under the watchful eyes of the security details.

Manny turned away from the incredible ocean view before him and looked at Alberto, who stood at the fully stocked bar on the patio, mixing a pitcher of margaritas. He was worried about the state of mind of his close cousin. It was clear to him that Alberto wasn't himself and hadn't been since word of Emilio's assassination had been delivered to him.

What the hell kind of world are they living in down here? Manny thought, as he watched Alberto. *The organized crime seems so pervasive. They can reach out and attack and kill a man as decent as Emilio almost with impunity. Jesus Christ, it feels like Mosul in 2003—the unchecked power of tribal warlords coupled with an almost complete lack of civil structure. Only this is the western hemisphere and a country we share a border with. Something has to be done. We've ignored this problem for long enough.*

The fact that Emilio had been killed by individuals involved in the rampant and seemingly worsening illegal trafficking business hadn't yet been proved, but Alberto had no doubts as to who was responsible and had told Manny why he believed this in a private discussion before the funeral. Alberto told him in great detail about the attempt to compromise him and the threat on his family. Alberto felt sick at heart that he hadn't anticipated that his double cross of the one calling himself the Condor would lead directly to an attack on his younger brother and ultimately his death. With his years of experience fighting the cartels, he should have expected some sort of retribution but hadn't. His failure to do so weighed heavily on him.

Alberto turned from the bar and brought a tray with a pitcher of margaritas and two glasses over to where Manny was sitting. With the other family members resting upstairs and the staff having been told the cousins desired privacy, they were alone on the terrace and would remain so. Manny took the offered drink from Alberto and said, "With all the enemies you and Emilio must have made over the years, you seem very certain that this Condor killed him."

Alberto sat down in the deck chair opposite Manny, took a large drink of his cocktail, set it down and looked at him for a moment before responding. "What we say from this point on, Manny, must stay between us. Much depends on this."

"Of course, *mi amigo viejo*."

Alberto nodded. "We, meaning Mexico, are in grave danger of losing our war against the cartels; the foundations of our system are broken. The cartels are taking advantage of a perfect storm. The confluence of opportunity caused by our current weak, corrupt president; the terrible immigration situation on our northern border; the basic inhumanity of the cartel leaders—it's all overwhelming. And worst of all, the growing power from the vast amounts of money created by the trafficking is vested in the worst possible criminal elements of our society. In the border states, our local police and prosecutors have almost all been compromised to some degree. In the most active trafficking regions, we've completely lost most of them. I strongly suspect, as did Emilio, that many levels of our federal government also have been compromised, and that list is headed by our interim president."

Manny sat back in his deck chair, his eyes a little wider. "Jesus Christ, Alberto, that's a hell of an accusation."

"Nevertheless," Alberto continued, "that's the reality I'm faced with—only now I'm alone. You see, after we reorganized Emilio's federal investigation agency and my federal police to form the Federal Police Corps under my command, Emilio and I were able to do much in the way of clandestine special operations. We had an agreement—we would trust only the two of us with complete knowledge of our operations, our public ones and some private operations we also were running. Emilio suspected for a number of years that our president is in fact a pawn for a cartel—which one he never knew for sure or could prove—but he was getting close to making his case. You must remember that Emilio was one of President Fernandez's top deputies at Justice when he was the attorney general. It was in that position that he first came to suspect that Fernandez hadn't achieved his record on his own. I suspect this is the true reason for his assassination. Given how close we were as brothers, those responsible for his assassination must assume that whatever Emilio knew I also know. Therefore, I'm at greater risk than ever, as is everyone in my family. The irony is that I know what Emilio was working *on*, but he hadn't yet shared with me any more than his base suspicions. I can't yet make a case against our president or any of the others, I suspect. The truth is hard to get at without alerting those whose loyalties we question."

Manny shook his head in disbelief. "Christ, I don't know what to say. In my business, the enemy has pretty much been standing right in front of me, pointing a weapon at my face, not behind me in the shadows. But to come out and accuse your president of being a criminal—well, that's a significant and dangerous step."

"Understand, Manny, it's not an accusation but a fact. Perhaps one that Emilio couldn't yet prove in a court of law, but if you knew the president as Emilio and I have come to know him, you'd believe me. With some of the clandestine operations Emilio and I have been secretly running the last eighteen months, we've been able to capture a number of cartel members, which has greatly increased our intelligence take. With rigorous interrogation, these prisoners have provided us with actionable information regarding the cartels and other interesting matters. Emilio was building his case against the president for presentation to Secretary Alvarez based on our new—and we believe confidential—intelligence information when he was killed."

Manny raised his eyebrows a little, a questioning look forming on his face. "How confidential is confidential? In my experience, Al, if more than two people know a secret, it probably isn't much of a secret any longer, and, as you said, you folks have a bit of a security problem down here. Also, believing what you do about your president, how can you be certain he didn't have Emilio killed? He's sure as shit in the perfect position to do so."

Alberto peered over his drink and looked grimly at his younger cousin. "You and I agree about secrets, Manny. Until he was killed, the only two people who knew what was really going on since the reorganization of my federal police corps were Emilio and me. And now it'll be between just you and me. My secret is still safe, I believe—*solo entre nosotros dos*—eh, amigo, just between us two? As to your last point, while I know President Fernandez is corrupt, and he may have been involved as a pawn in Emilio's assassination, he didn't know about our secret operations with respect to the cartels. In other words, he wasn't directly threatened."

"Hold on a second, Al. I'll accept, for the moment, your premise that Fernandez wasn't responsible for Emilio's death, but why do you suspect he was just a pawn? A pawn how?"

"I spoke with Elena about that morning," Alberto said. "She and the children were supposed to be with Emilio on their way to mass. She said the president called and requested an immediate meeting with him, so she and the kids stayed behind. I haven't been able to find out what that was all about—the facts are confusing. The man rarely called Emilio directly... Why that morning? Anyway, be that as it may, I believe the man is too stupid and too great a coward to have done this. I believe he's being controlled somehow. I'm puzzled, I'll admit, as to why Emilio's family was spared, but this attack on us was made by a very different sort of man, I think."

Manny was shaking his head again. "How's it possible that your president didn't know what you and Emilio were up to?"

Alberto took another long drink, then set his glass down and looked directly at his cousin, as if trying to measure his words. "You'd be the first to agree with me that getting and keeping information on your enemies is the key to defeating them. So I came up with a plan to accomplish this, and, with Emilio's help, we put it in place. We've been running a shadow operation outside the government: a small, handpicked, private intelligence-gathering-and-strike team. They're all well paid, highly trained, and armed with the latest technologies and weaponry to attack the disease at its roots. I believe we've achieved absolute airtight security in this small group. Neither the president nor Secretary Alvarez were ever briefed about it. Our clandestine operation was—until Emilio's death—known to just the two of us. We staffed it with the most vetted of subordinates from sources outside our departments, including Spanish-speaking ex-military and law-enforcement personnel from outside the country. Using captured cartel funds—and you wouldn't believe how much we have—we pay our clandestine team extremely well.

"We call our shadow group Los Pueblos Fantasmas, the People's Ghosts, for that is who we are, who we're doing this for. As I said, it's small—about a hundred loyal men thus far—but the results we've achieved have been spectacular. For added security, each of the subsections within Los Pueblos Fantasmas is further compartmentalized. Outside of a small command group headed by me, no one section knows more than what their particular expertise is. We have intelligence, communications, logistics, and strike sections; we even have our own air support. The men we've recruited are professional, very good at what they do, and of course are attracted to the money we pay them. But they aren't just soldiers of fortune; they're much more than that. Our men are honest, moral, law-abiding citizens who believe in our cause and are willing to do what's necessary. A dozen of our leaders are retired senior noncommissioned soldiers from your US Army Special Forces or your elite Corps of Marines.

"We specifically sought and recruited Americans of Mexican heritage who had retired or left your services after a minimum of twelve to twenty years. Most wanted a better, more financially secure life and were looking at new careers. We enticed them back to what they knew best but for far more money. Their greatest assets are that they're completely unknown to the cartels and my government and that they hate the cartels and the threat they represent to your country. We have elements of our intelligence section undercover in several of the worst cartel-controlled areas. Once our intelligence section has ferreted out something actionable, we quietly move in and attack with our strike teams.

"One of the first valuable pieces of intelligence we gathered in the last eighteen months was that what we had taken for a random increase in the intercartel fighting that started in the north following all the deportations from your country wasn't random at all. There's an unknown cartel in the north, an extension, we believe, of an old crime family from Chihuahua that we thought was headed by two brothers, Eduardo and Carlo Vargas. We believed for a long time that they were no more than hired enforcers for the Mendoza family's El Puño Terrible—Terrible Fist—cartel from that same area, but we were wrong.

"During our early interrogations of captured cartel members, we confirmed that the Vargas crime family is really a more powerful cartel run by a mysterious relative of the Vargas brothers, a man known as El Condor de Muerte."

This name got Manny's attention. "The same guy you said threatened your family?"

Alberto nodded. "Precisely, and the man whom I suspect is responsible for Emilio's assassination, although I believe Emilio's assassination has nothing to do directly with our shadow operations. The Condor has made, I believe, a brazen move for reasons I can only guess. I believe Los Pueblos Fantasmas remains secure."

Manny stared at Alberto, shaking his head in amazement at everything he had heard. "Well, it sounds brilliant, Al, if you in fact have and can maintain your organizational and operational security."

"I believe we have. We initially paid for everything from family money so as not to use federal funds, which would require records. We're now completely self-sufficient, and, as I said, with the cash we've captured in our first operations, we haven't had to use one peso of accountable funds, and we've been repaid our initial expenditures."

"What kind of money are we talking about? What have you managed to lay your hands on?"

"We've taken possession of just over twenty million US dollars in the last eighteen months," Alberto told him.

"Holy shit. Twenty million?"

"Si, Manny."

"That's impressive as hell."

"What's impressive is in that same time, we've also captured and detained several former cartel leaders and members who actually have sat at the same table as this person they call the Condor and then had their organizations destroyed by him. All those we have in detention are thought to be dead—by their cartels, their families, everyone. Just this past week, we picked up several members of the Mendoza cartel we've been watching who were witness to their leaders' recent murders. This is important intelligence because it confirms that the Condor has been getting more and more bold over the last year. Our information tells us this Condor de Muerte has taken over their transshipment routes, to the great displeasure of La Pandilla de Cuatro."

"Sorry again, Al, but who the hell is this Gang of Four? I've read some briefing papers on your cartels down here, but they all start to run together."

"They're a loose alliance between what for years have been the four largest, most powerful cartels in the northwest and east. After years of internecine violence among them, their leaders formed an alliance and effectively divided up the transshipment routes among them. As a group, they've been fighting the Mendoza cartel in the north-central part of the country for refusing to join their alliance."

Manny took a sip of his margarita and then put it down, a concerned look on his face. "I'm not familiar with your constitution, Al, and the individual rights of your citizens, but can you get away with all this? I mean, how long can you detain a citizen, for example, even if he's a criminal, without charging him and putting him on trial? Surely you have some form of habeas corpus down here, don't you?"

Alberto nodded. "Not to the extent you have in your legal system, but we can't detain indefinitely, for our *recurso de amparo* is fundamental to our constitution. It's in this area, Manny, that Emilio and I were—and are—at great risk, as we've systematically violated many of the rights of those we've detained. I'll also admit we've obtained some of our best intelligence from—how should I say this?—very aggressive interrogation methods that have further violated the rights of certain detainees. It was Emilio's hope that once we replaced our corrupt president with a good one, a presidential decree codifying our creation of Los Pueblos Fantasmas could be arranged."

Alberto leaned in toward Manny and continued. "With Emilio now dead, my hopes for replacing Fernandez with my friend Secretary Alvarez are made more difficult, maybe even impossible, given the political enemies he and I share. There likely will come a time in the near future when I'll be brought forward to answer for the crimes I'm committing in the name of my country, but I'm prepared to do so. What I do know is that finally, finally, we're beginning to make some progress against this cancer on my country. It isn't a perfect solution, Manny, but given everything I face, it's all I have to work with."

Manny sat back again in his deck chair. He was amazed and couldn't hide it. "Well, in a word, I'm dumbfounded and in awe of not only your operation but also your incredible courage. But I'm also deeply troubled... and not by any potential civil rights abuses. Given the depth and breadth of this cancer on your country, I honestly don't see how you could ever make something like Los Pueblos Fantasmas public. If it were me, I'd never reveal its existence. Kill all the sons of bitches you can and then fold the tent, and nobody's the wiser." Manny paused, his look becoming more serious. "So where do you go from here?"

Alberto was gazing toward the majestic vista to the west and then looked back at his cousin. "Folding the tent, as you suggest, is something I long considered, but Emilio was against this—he being the constitutional lawyer he was. Now...well, now I'll revisit this idea. As to where we go from here, we've been eating around the edges of the cartels for years, but we're finally in a position to go after the most powerful ones. What I really want to do is take down the Gang of Four and the Condor. I'm reasonably sure he leads the strongest and most dangerous of the cartels, even though his profile appears so small. I think this is by design—not dissimilar, ironically, from Los Pueblos Fantasmas. From what we've learned recently, I believe the Condor has been taking over the trafficking business in three of our northern states for the last six or eight years, maybe longer. And remarkably, he's done so without drawing attention to himself. This is no small feat in his world or mine. If we can take down the Condor, we'll have secured a major victory in what until now has been a losing war. And if we can capture and interrogate some of his key people, we can then be very effective in our war against the other cartels and then, just maybe, get the upper hand. Another tragedy of

Emilio's death is that he told me just before he was killed that he was very close to identifying the Condor."

"Very close? What does that mean?"

"As was his way," Alberto explained, "he wished to firm up his intelligence before taking me through it. We've been running a special surveillance operation within Los Pueblos Fantasmas, attempting to track high-end aircraft trying to evade our country's radar, and there's much data to be analyzed. That was one of the tasks Emilio was working on before he was killed. Based upon his preliminary analysis, he felt he was close to identifying this Condor. I need to meet with the team that was working with Emilio on this and go through the data myself."

There was a lull in the conversation as Manny drank down some of his cocktail and then looked seriously at his cousin. "Alberto, we have an expression in my business called the 'fog of war.' You're hip deep in it right now. You have to respect the timing of the attack on Emilio. Don't underestimate this Condor. Have you given any thought to how you'll carry on with Los Pueblos Fantasmas on your own without compromising your profile in your public job? I'd say your plate is pretty full, compadre. As an old operations guy myself, I must say that with Emilio's death, the command and control of your organization has taken a terrible hit."

Alberto nodded again. "Yes, it has, and it's that command and control, to use your language, that I must reconstitute. The first step is to expose President Fernandez for the criminal I know he is and get him removed from office. Then the presidential commission responsible for such things will have to appoint an interim president to fill the office until an election can be held. If we can out maneuver our political enemies, there are few people in our government better positioned to become interim president than my friend and colleague Secretary Alvarez. Once he's the president, I can reveal the People's Ghosts to him, for I'll have an old friend and willing partner in office. But until that day comes, I need your help. I realize what I'm about to ask is a great deal, but to do what's required, I have no choice. I can't continue alone."

"What exactly do you want?"

"Manny, I need you to replace Emilio in Los Pueblos Fantasmas. I need there to be a second-in-command who fully knows what I'm doing in our organization, in case the Condor or one of the other cartel leaders gets to me before I can get to them. I can do my public job and run Los Pueblos Fantasmas, but I must have someone to share my thoughts with, someone to bounce operational ideas off. In many respects, speaking strategically and tactically, you actually would be better at it than Emilio was. You're the only one left in life I truly can trust. Until I get to a point where I can go public with Los Pueblos Fantasmas or just disband it—which means until I can destroy a significant number of the cartels or expose our president—I need a credible, respected second who knows all I know, without getting the secretary involved in my actions."

Manny was stunned by Alberto's request and the possible implications. "Jesus, Al, I don't know what to say, but my initial thought is that beyond being your friend and cousin, and giving you someone you can talk to, as we're doing now, what you're asking is impossible. I'm a US citizen and a serving general officer. Except for funerals and sightseeing trips, the laws of both our countries preclude my doing much more in Mexico."

Alberto's serious look turned grimmer as Manny spelled out the realities of his position. "Hear me out, Manny. For the time being, it would be enough if you simply were aware of those involved in Los Pueblos Fantasmas, the operations we've completed, and those that are underway. This is important should the worst happen to me. I need someone in a position to tell our government—and specifically Secretary Alvarez—what I've been doing if I no longer can. I also want my military commander in the Ghosts to know there's at least one other senior commander or leader to whom he can go. There's also the intelligence and money we've collected. I haven't completely thought this out, but what I need, and all I ask of you now, is that we set up a secure communication link so I can send you the complete picture of my operation in case something happens to me. Also, as I put more operations into play, you would be my sounding board; you have a mind for such things, Manny. Eventually, where I think and hope this would lead is to joint operations with trustworthy people in your DEA. Emilio was beginning to run such operations from our public side, but they became compromised, and he was certain they were compromised by elements within your country's DEA, not from our side—such is the level of penetration by the cartels. Given your position in your army and your responsibilities at your base, as I understand them, you have contacts with the DEA. Is this not so?"

Manny shook his head. "We *liaise* with the DEA, and I have certain operations I conduct—aerial surveillance and interdiction ops—that require I meet periodically with the DEA and other law-enforcement agencies, but we don't conduct joint operations. We secure the border; they go after the bad guys—separate operations. I don't have any contacts that I know well enough, or that I would trust enough, to tell about you and what you're running down here, especially after what you said about our DEA being compromised. But I also know the DEA is trying to square itself away. There's new leadership at the top in Washington. Recently, I met their new head of operations in El Paso, and he struck me as a good man. I'll try to get more information on the changes and the new people, but, as I said, I don't know them or their organization well. We need to tread lightly here. But having said all that, you're my family, and I'll do this much for you: I'll gladly keep a copy of any information you want me to have. I also can set you up with a secure, encrypted data-and-voice satellite link to me at Fort Bliss through our MILSATCOM system, and I'll discuss any operations you want to share with me that you feel I can help with. I can do that much and probably still keep my stars and keep myself out of prison if the shit hits the fan. I might even be able to get you someone from our DEA you can trust. As the old saying goes, I know a guy. But I require a quid pro quo, Alberto."

"Anything within my power, Manny. You know that."

Manny leaned over and squeezed his cousin's shoulder. "You can't go and get yourself killed, compadre. Promise me you'll be extra careful and stay alive."

Deeply touched, Alberto couldn't keep the emotion out of his voice as he also leaned forward, placed a hand on Manny's knee, smiled, and quietly responded to his cousin and oldest friend. "Thank you, Manny. That's a promise I'll try hard to keep. As long as only the two of us know all this, we'll be safe, and I can be effective. I have Emilio's secure, encrypted laptop here at the estate. I'll give it to you along with the required access codes. This will give you a copy of everything we've done so far with Los Pueblos Fantasmas. How will you set up a link between the two of us?"

Obviously thinking things through, Manny paused and stared off at the horizon, where the ocean met the rapidly darkening indigo sky. "My movements are well documented, given my rank, and subject to the requirements placed upon me by the army. However, my senior aide, Phil Romero, is free to travel where he wants when on leave, and I can place him on leave anytime I want. Once we get back to Bliss, I'll send Phil back down here via a commercial airline and in civvies. He'll bring you the required Satcom device and instruct you on its use. It's pretty simple. It's called a Compact Combat Tactical Terminal—CCTT. We refer to them as 'see-tees,' but it's nothing more than a powerful encrypted laptop with an integral satellite modem. I'll supply you with a personal encryption code that just the two of us will have. There's a built-in web-cam capability, so we can have secure face-to-face discussions at any time. It's an encrypted point-to-point system we use between combat commands. Our two computers will talk only to each other, nobody else's."

"Thank you. That sounds helpful, Manny, but how is it possible to keep our communications from your very capable intelligence community? Presumably we'd be using their satellites, after all."

"Not an issue, Al. We have dozens of these linkups bouncing signals off our National Security Agency birds on a regular basis as part of our training regimen. All the intelligence geeks monitoring the satellites will see are two of my devices talking, using one of my secure codes—if they even look. No one's interested in these types of low-level communications, Al. The spooks are up to their ears in real sensitive stuff from the world's hot spots. If anyone does look, or comes across our communications, all they'll see are a couple of typical registered army devices and codes, both of which will be authorized by me." Manny smiled. "Rank does indeed have its privileges from time to time."

"What will Phil think about all this? What must he know? Surely if you give me one of your see-tees, one of your laws or military protocols will have been broken."

"Phil needs to know nothing more than the fact that I'm informally assisting the head of the Mexican federal police with his war on the drug cartels and that such assistance in no way compromises the oaths we've taken to serve and protect the United States. In the multinational operations we conduct, we share these devices with our allies. Don't worry about it or Phil; he's a trusted, loyal aide. Hell, if I told him what you were doing down here, he'd try to persuade me to send you my reactivated First Armored Division I have at Bliss and shove a few M-1 Abrams tanks up some cartel ass."

Alberto smiled a small smile. "A sight I'd like to see, but, of course, impossible given the way the cartels operate. I trust you to deal with the colonel as you see best."

Manny turned and stared off again where the now dark nearly colorless sky met the black waters of the Pacific for a long moment; finally, he turned back to Alberto. "Let me think about this some more and look over what you have going, and then let's talk again. In the meantime, pour a guy another drink, will ya?"

16

The Peña estate
Baja California Sur
Wednesday, late afternoon

Ray went to the small room assigned to him but didn't nap. It didn't make sense to hang around the common room hoping to pick up whatever intelligence he could, because all the action, if there was any, was going on in Alvarez's office and the security room. He knew better than to make himself conspicuous, so he made himself scarce. He removed his shoes and then his suit, so as not to wrinkle his clothes while lying on the bed, and took the few hours he was alone to commit the day's events and information to his memory. There was so much new intelligence to retain—so much so that for the first time on this mission, he wanted to write himself notes in the worst way, but that was a passing fanciful thought. He was far too experienced for that. The intelligence revealed today was staggering, capped off by the chameleonic nature of the Condor and his true identity.

Ray gave the fact that the Condor was the secretary for public security the most thought, and the more he did, the more he knew he never would be safe again unless the Condor was killed or captured. That train of thought didn't end there, however, as eliminating the Condor wouldn't be enough; everyone in the inner circle, as well as Carlo and Eduardo, would have to be killed or jailed as well. He thought back to El Paso and the time he shared the cell with Carlo and how often Carlo had angrily talked about how he was going to get the prostitute who had turned him in to the police. If Carlo could get that worked up by a hooker, how relentless would he be if he found out Ray was an undercover cop? The shit storm would never end until he or Carlo was dead. Just putting these guys away wouldn't be enough, he thought, more troubled than ever by the uncertainty of his immediate course of action and of his future.

Prior to today, Ray's focus had been to learn what he could, eventually find a safe way to get in touch with Bennie, and then get out. Now he wondered how he would survive this mission at all. His fears were magnified with the vague implication from the Condor that in addition to getting control of the majority of the trafficking, he had to consolidate the government as well into his hands. Ray wasn't sure yet just what that meant, but it couldn't be good. The more he thought about it, as the clock slowly ticked toward five, the more he realized that whatever additional intelligence he could gather no longer mattered. Getting out alive was now his only objective, but he wouldn't be able to work on that until he reached the capital city and got a lay of the land.

He'd never set foot in Mexico City before, and his ignorance of Mexico in general was overwhelming. His intuition told him that because he was now in the inner circle, at some point in the near future, he would be alone and out of sight of the others, especially the electronic monitoring of Geraldo and Lorenzo. But if he could find a way out, he would need to disappear—and fast—until he could pass on what he knew to Bennie. Only then could Bennie pass the intelligence he'd gathered to the proper Mexican authorities so they could round up the Condor and his entire cartel.

More uncertainty crept into Ray's mind as he thought about that. How did their justice system work down here? How much of a case—and what kind of evidence—would have to be produced before the Condor could even be arrested? Who else in the government did the man control? Ray's mental list of problems went on and on. He thought back to the briefing papers Bennie had provided and was sure Alvarez's department had all the government agencies necessary to make a case against him. Their national police, their FBI—whatever the hell that was called down here—and the attorney general all worked for him. He supposed none of the department heads would be too anxious to take on their secretary, especially after he had learned that the Alvarez family name went back forty years untainted. Who the hell down here would believe him?

He needed help, he reasoned, so he needed information on who was dirty and who was clean in Alvarez's governmental sphere. He figured he would be entitled to such information as a member of the inner circle; the hard part was not asking too often or in areas in which he didn't have a need to know. "Need to know" was an operational concept any organization had to practice to keep secrets, and the organization he was in had some doozies. They might not call it "need to know," but they sure as hell practiced it.

He had to get Raul or one of the others, maybe Luis, to tell him who in the government was dirty and who was clean. Luis was young, and Ray needed to develop that relationship anyway; he'd start there. But of the three other members of the inner circle, Luis seemed to sincerely dislike him for some reason. He wasn't sure why, but if he could just get the names of a couple of certain clean officials in the government, that would be a start. Not only could this knowledge help him, but also, the Mexicans needed to know exactly who was in the Alvarez camp and who wasn't. He glanced at the new watch the tailor Dominguez had given him as part of his new ensemble; it wasn't really expensive, but it was nice, better than the one Bennie was holding for him. It was five o'clock, time to get cleaned up and dressed.

A few minutes later, he left the room and walked into the common area. Luis was alone, reading a magazine, and glanced up as he walked in.

"Hello, Luis. Where are the others?"

Luis looked up with an annoyed expression. "Upstairs, having a drink." He paused for a second and then asked, "Are you carrying your knives?"

"Just my small one. The fit is too tight in these suits to wear my big one. Should I find a way?"

Luis shook his head. "No, we all carry Glock 23s. It would look strange if the newest member of Jefe's protective detail didn't also carry one. Raul said I was to give you my backup piece. It's in my room."

Ray decided to try to make conversation with the surly Luis. "Do you carry such a weapon all the time?"

Luis stopped and looked at him with disgust. "We're the bodyguards to one of the highest-ranking officials in the government—what do you think?" he said sarcastically.

Ray didn't like the way this conversation was going. He thought about coming right out and asking the little shit what was bothering him but decided to let Luis's attitude pass; he'd find out passively in time, he told himself. Miguel was distant, but he was also older, and, as far as Ray could tell, he was quiet and reserved with everyone. Luis, on the other hand, was friendly with some of Carlo's men, just not him. After getting the weapon from his room, Luis showed Ray how the skeleton holster fit and gave him the gun. He had Ray turn around so he could check him out. "Good, your suit hangs right. No one would guess you are carrying. Of course, where we're going, everyone will know you are."

"Thank you, Luis, for everything."

Luis looked at him dismissively, then returned to the couch he'd been lounging on and went back to his magazine. Ray took another stab at making conversation. "Luis, I've never been to Mexico City. Will there be time when we get there for you to show me around?"

Luis looked at him for a second and said, "If Raul tells me to. For now, once we get to the city, Raul has put you with him, and Miguel and I will be together."

"Can I ask you another question?"

"What?"

"Do we get paid for this work?"

Luis looked at him as if he were a stupid child. "Of course. Didn't Raul go over that with you?"

"No. Since Carlo brought me here, I've had no money, but then, I haven't needed it. Carlo always pays when we go to town. Everything else has always been there—the food, I mean, and these clothes."

"You work for the government now, assigned to protect Secretary Alvarez. You'll receive twenty thousand pesos a month, which goes far in the city. Like in the north, we live at Jefe's estate, not far from downtown. There's Jefe's house and then some casitas on the grounds. Raul shared his casita with his brother, and Miguel and I share one. I don't know how Raul will arrange things now that he's in charge."

Ray didn't like the way Luis had said that. His intuition told him that for whatever reason, Luis had a problem with Raul now being in charge; it seemed that he wasn't the only one who had issues with Luis. He took another stab at friendly conversation. "I'd prefer to live with you, Luis. I don't think Miguel likes me."

Luis stared at him again, his look still unfriendly but not as severe. "Miguel likes you, as much as he can like any stranger, but he hated Guzman, the man you killed saving Jefe. Guzman and Miguel were enemies for a long time, but he wasn't allowed to kill him. Jefe wouldn't permit it. But he was glad you did. Miguel's just old and too serious. Don't worry about him."

"One last question, Luis. Who else works at Jefe's home, and do they know about him?"

"No one but us in the circle, and Geraldo and Lorenzo, knows anything. Even his wife doesn't know."

Alvarez has a wife? That's the first time anyone's mentioned that.

"That's important to remember," Luis went on. "I think she believes he has a mistress in the north, but she doesn't make trouble for Jefe. Listen, he's expecting you. You and Raul have to take dinner with Señora Alvarez—Miguel and I don't. Go upstairs and get a drink; there'll be nothing but wine at dinner. One other thing: don't get drunk, ever."

"Thank you, Luis," Ray said, smiling, but Luis already was ignoring him again. He had no idea why the guy had such a bee up his ass about him, but whatever it was, it wasn't good. Going along and getting along was almost a mantra for an undercover operative. If you wanted to live, stupid personality conflicts while undercover had to be avoided. But something seemed to be eating at Luis. Ray couldn't help feel that sooner or later, he'd have to deal with him.

He went up the wide spiral stairway and saw the others sitting in deck chairs outside. As he stepped out onto the deck, he couldn't keep from admiring the view, which helped put the dark thoughts he was having about Luis behind him for the moment. A warm breeze was blowing in from the west, and the sun was approaching the horizon as he joined the others. Raul was the first to see him coming through the glass doors and said to him as he stepped out, "Ah, Ray, did you get some rest?"

"Yes, thank you."

The Condor smiled and offered him a drink from a nearby bar cart. "Get you a quick drink, Ray? We have about fifteen minutes."

"Thank you, Jefe. Just water, please."

"Nothing to help you forget about today's flight?" the Condor said, still smiling. There were chuckles all around, even from the reticent Miguel.

"I'm fine, Jefe, but glad to be alive and on the ground."

"We all understand. I've made that flight many times and know nearly every turn, but it's still difficult." After a moment of silence, the Condor grew more serious. "Let me tell you our plans for this evening. We'll go next door, using a clever path my father devised when he first built these two estates as Octavio. He had this casita built and also built an access to a casita on the property next door. You'll see when we go. Father was never seen going into the estate next door, whereas my mother did occasionally visit this one—only she did so as an invited guest. She was often Octavio's hostess during parties or dinners when it was necessary for my father to entertain. At these functions, she was simply introduced as his close friend from next door. They carried on that polite fiction for twenty years. They were truly husband and wife only at my home next door and never outside those walls. One last thing before we go, Ray. My mother knows me as myself, but she's aware of my Peña identity. I've led her to believe that was necessary for my protection."

Ray nodded his understanding as Raul glanced at his watch and said, "It's time, Pablo."

With that, Ray, the Condor, and Raul went back downstairs to the common room. Raul opened a door Ray assumed led to a closet or storage space of some kind with a key he produced, to reveal a standard-looking stainless-steel elevator door. He pushed the only button there was in the jamb, and the door immediately opened, allowing them to enter the small space. The doors closed, and the elevator started down slowly with a metallic clunk.

Ray guessed they had gone maybe twenty or thirty feet when the elevator stopped and the doors opened. As he had expected from the Condor's description, they were in a narrow, concrete-walled tunnel, perhaps eight feet in height, with bare light bulbs in industrial-looking wire fixtures providing what little light there was. The tunnel led downhill to the south towards the adjacent Alvarez family estate. They walked several hundred feet before reaching a steel door at the end. Raul looked through a peephole, obviously checking to see whether anyone was on the other side, and then led the way through the door, emerging into a nicely finished room not unlike the common room they'd just left at the Peña casita. The first thing Ray noticed was a sliding glass door that opened out to a patio on the ocean side, from which he saw the beach. They had dropped considerably in elevation when they had come next door.

As he stepped into the room, Raul closed the door they had just passed through, and Ray noticed it was part of the wall paneling and not immediately obvious. A casual observer never would guess a door was concealed in the wall. They took a stairway to the main floor, and he realized they were in a comfortable guest cottage. After they went out the front door and followed a well-worn path that led uphill toward the main house, Ray glanced back down the slope and saw how perfect the tunnel connection to the adjacent Pena estate was as a means of secretive movements. Alvarez's mother's guest casita stood at the low bluff's edge fronting the ocean, with open grassy areas on the other three sides; nothing more than a simple-looking casita in an open clearing overlooking the beach. No one could ever guess its true purpose.

Ray returned his attention to the main house as they reached the rear patio area of the older but comfortable-looking hacienda. They entered the main living room, where a small, gray-haired woman in her seventies was standing and waiting, dressed in a simple black dress with a delicate gold cross hanging from her neck. She clasped her hands, and a look of relief came to her face when she saw the Condor. She reached out to him, saying in her soft voice, "Pablo, my son, thank God you're home and safe."

Jacques Pablo Alvarez went to his mother and hugged her gently for a long moment. He turned, looking at Ray, and said, "Mother, I'd like you to meet Francisco's nephew, Ray Ortega, who has taken our dear friend's place as one of my aides."

Teresa Alvarez Vargas turned, looked at him kindly, and said, "Señor Ortega, I was saddened to hear of Francisco's passing, but I rejoice to think that he's at peace and with God at his side. Welcome to our home."

"Thank you, señora," he said as he gently took her offered hand and nodded, thinking that she looked frail, maybe even unhealthy.

"Raul," Teresa said, reaching for his hand, "thank you once more for watching over my son."

"It's my privilege as always, señora."

She took her son's arm, and the two of them led Ray and Raul into an elegant dining room that was dominated by a large, old, wooden crucifix on one wall. They had a simple dinner served by two older women dressed in traditional-looking maid uniforms. From the looks of the two servants, it appeared to Ray they had been doing this for more years than he'd been alive. The conversation during dinner was mostly about family, but the recent violent death of Emilio Rodriguez was mentioned only briefly. It dawned on Ray that was the reason the Alvarez's mother was wearing the simple black dress; she was still in mourning over the loss of her son-in-law. The day turned into a beautiful evening, and with their dinner finished, Alvarez gently walked his mother out onto the terrace overlooking the Pacific, where they took coffee and after-dinner drinks.

Just after the sun set, as the quiet chimes of a clock in a nearby room announced the nine o'clock hour, the Condor's mother slowly stood up and said it had been a lovely evening, but it was time for her to retire. After a long, tender embrace, the Condor told her he had to return to the capital but would be back in several weeks and would be able to stay for a few days. With that, he and Raul also said their good nights, and the three of them retraced their footsteps back to the guest casita, through the tunnel, and back again to the Peña casita.

It was clear to Ray that the visit had made the Condor very pensive, even sad. Once they were in the common room, the Condor turned to him and Raul and, in a somber tone, said good night and slowly went up the stairs alone.

They watched him until he was gone, and then Raul turned to him and said quietly, "His recent visits with his mother sadden him. I think he believes she isn't long for this world, and her passing will be the end of the last real connection he has with his father. He's never gotten over his father's death or the guilt he feels for having killed those responsible." Raul sighed. "Oh, well, get some rest, Ray. We need to be up early—say at five thirty—and must leave here by six. Wear your new dark-gray suit for your first day in the capital city."

Ray nodded. Out of curiosity, but also out of a need to try to reduce his anxiety, he asked, "Raul, may I ask where we'll go tomorrow and what it will be like?"

Raul nodded and smiled a tight smile. "I'm sorry I haven't told you more. I'm sure you must have many such questions. We'll leave from next door, as if that's where we've been staying for the last week. Our national police escort stays outside the walls when we visit but will take us to the airport in La Paz; it's about fifty miles from here. Jefe has a personal jet there that will take us to the capital. It's about a ninety-minute flight, time enough to have a light breakfast en route. It's usually a pleasant flight, especially compared to what you did today, so you can relax. We should be there by eight thirty and will go directly to Jefe's estate for a brief time and then to his office in the Zocalo by ten. Jefe's children will be gone by the time we reach the estate, but you'll get to meet Salena, his wife. She knows nothing of our business, Ray, so you must be very careful when you're around her."

"Yes, Luis told me."

"Good, good. Go now. Get some rest. The next several days are important, but we'll get into that and your part in our plans on the plane and later tomorrow."

Raul paused, looking at Ray as if he had something more to say and was deciding whether he should. Then he went on in a more serious tone. "We've placed much new information on you in the last several days, some of it no doubt very confusing. But there is much more you need to know, especially about what Jefe has planned for the future. In many ways, I know it's unfair for you to be given so many surprises in so short a time. The rest of us have had years to prepare for what's coming, and we're asking a lot of you. I don't want you to be concerned—just keep doing what comes so naturally to you: listen and watch. One of us will tell you what to do when and if something else is required."

Raul placed a hand on Ray's shoulder. He smiled at him, looked down, and shook his head. Then he looked back with warm, friendly eyes and in a softer voice said, "You're a fine young man, and I realize I haven't properly thanked you for everything you've done since you joined us. The men you saved are my closest friends and, with the death of Francisco, the only true family I have left. I don't have the faith or the beliefs Pablo sometimes shows. I don't seek the answers to some of the questions I know he asks and undoubtedly has shared with you. I don't make friends easily, but I want you to know I consider you a new friend. In time, I hope you'll be able to think the same of me."

Several conflicting thoughts shot through Ray's head as Raul finished his statement. *We probably could be friends—how am I supposed to deal with that? All I can do is disappoint this man; it's my job. This is crazy, but my intuition never has failed me—he's a good man. I sense it; there's no evil in him. What Raul and Alvarez are trying to accomplish is mostly good. If Alvarez does get control of all the trafficking, reduces the amount of drugs going into the country, and stops the gunrunning and all the killings, a lot of lives will be saved. Could I have arrested Dad if he'd done to me what Alvarez's father did to him? A hard question without a good answer, if you're honest. This is getting too complicated; I need to get out and away from these people. Forget about friendships. I hope I don't have to kill them all.*

After the few moments of silence, as thoughts swirled around in his head and without really thinking about it, Ray said, "I do think of you as a friend, Raul. I hope I don't let you down."

Raul was smiling warmly at him. "You won't, Ray. It's not possible for true friends to do so. Good night, my friend."

Ray stood there for a second, watching as Raul turned and walked toward his room, his confusion about his thoughts and feelings growing. One last question had been gnawing at him since his lunch with the Condor, and he had to ask Raul while he had the chance and while the atmosphere seemed right. "One last question, Raul, if I may be allowed."

Raul stopped and turned to him. "Yes, Ray, what is it?"

Ray paused, knowing he needed to be careful. "Earlier today, during lunch with Jefe, he told me it was important to get control of our enemies and the government so all the killing of innocents could be stopped. After what we did with the Mendozas, and with what I heard you and Jefe talking about on the plane this morning, I think I understand how we'll deal with our enemies, but a government…that's such a big thing, so powerful. How can Jefe possibly control something like that?"

Raul's look became very serious, and Ray thought he maybe had misread the situation and pressed his luck with him too far. Then Raul shrugged and said, "Actually, it isn't as difficult as it sounds. All we have to do is kill the president."

17

The road to La Paz
Baja California Sur
Thursday morning

Today was day eighty-six in the cartel, and Ray's anxiety from yesterday had intensified. *All we have to do is kill the president.* It had been said so flatly, so devoid of emotion. As they drove to the airport in La Paz, he felt almost desperate and increasingly unsure of himself, and those were bad—maybe even fatal—feelings for a covert operative. Controlling your emotions and the situation you were in, even if that control was passive and subtle in nature, was everything to an undercover operative, and he was losing it.

Ray had mentally and emotionally prepared for his role in Bennie's plan, the sitting around in jail and even going south with Carlo and joining a cartel. He had imagined himself in a lot of scenarios once he was in a cartel—being a gofer, a driver, maybe even a soldier expected to kill for the leaders—and had become confident that he could handle himself in those situations and remain believable, safe. But headed to the La Paz airport, as he now was, to catch a private jet and fly into the Mexican capital posing as a bodyguard and aide to the secretary for public security—one of the most powerful and senior officials in the country, who was himself a cartel leader—was a scenario he hadn't conjured up in his imagination. If that weren't enough to deal with, Raul calmly had told him they were going to assassinate the sitting president of the country, and, given Ray's position within the inner circle, he knew he'd be expected to help somehow.

Complicating his outrageous reality further was the fact that Secretary Alvarez was the likely choice to succeed the president, and it was that thought that left him feeling desperate. The only saving grace was that any outward signs of his distress wouldn't lead immediately to suspicion from the others. As he was the new man on the Condor's detail, it was expected that he would have some trepidation as he traveled with the inner circle for the first time, ironically another example of the covert cover matching as closely as possible an agent's true makeup—Bennie's rule number one for operatives.

Raul briefly reviewed the day's schedule with Ray and the others during their morning coffee before leaving the casita and taking the tunnel back to the Alvarez compound. After arriving in Mexico City and then dropping by the Alvarez home and then the office, they would be meeting with the head of the federal police, Alberto Rodriguez, who would be told that Alvarez was resigning and recommending him for the position of interim secretary. This was to be followed by a meeting with former President Castillo, apparently Alvarez's mentor, and then they were to visit President Fernandez at a secret location where Alvarez was going to resign from his cabinet post; why he would do that was another confusing detail to Ray.

He was still trying to sort out the many complications facing him when they arrived at the small but nice La Paz airport on the outskirts of the old capital city of Baja California Sur. They drove to the end of the main terminal building and arrived at a manned gate that allowed access to an area where wealthy individuals and corporations kept and boarded or deplaned from their expensive private aircraft. An unnamed federal officer driving the lead SUV—with Alvarez, Raul, Geraldo, and Lorenzo aboard—followed a police-escort vehicle as it slowly maneuvered up to a glistening white business jet parked off to one side.

Before they got out, Luis turned to Ray and said, "From here on, everyone we'll meet will only know Jefe as Secretary Alvarez, so think before you speak."

Seems everyone wants me to think before I speak. Well, don't worry, fellas—this shit is so complicated, I'd do that anyway. "Of course, Luis."

By the time Ray retrieved his luggage from the back of the Escalade, the others were already aboard the jet. One of the pilots was standing at the foot of the steps, and he took Ray's bags and welcomed him aboard. Ray climbed up the steps, noting the type of aircraft from a door label, a Gulfstream 200. The interior was similar to the turboprop from the day before, only larger and more luxurious, if that were possible, he thought.

Beyond the first grouping of four plush seats, where the two communication techs and Miguel and Luis sat, were two more seats on the left and a three-person divan on the right, where Alvarez and Raul were sitting. Ray took the last seat across from Alvarez because it faced forward. The copilot had closed the jet's door by the time he belted himself in, knowing from the flight yesterday where his shoulder strap was. The engines of the luxury jet quickly spun up, and, within minutes, they were positioned at the end of the runway, then accelerated with incredible speed and were airborne.

As the glistening white jet climbed into the sky, Raul said to him, "Ray, if you look on the side of the seat, you can turn toward us."

Doing as he was told, he located the controls and turned his seat so it was almost facing the couch. Alvarez immediately started going through some files Raul had brought aboard.

"Ray," Raul began, "before we reach the capital, I need to tell you about some of the people and situations you'll face today. No one knows of Jefe's other identities, not even his wife, Salena. That's the most important thing to remember."

Alvarez looked up at that and said, "She's a lovely woman, Ray, not unlike my mother in character, very devout. I married late in life, so we've only been together ten years. She isn't well educated, but she's a fine mother to my two children and a wonderful hostess and escort for the many social functions my office requires I attend. I do care about her, but she must never know the details of my full life."

"No, of course not, Jefe."

Alvarez nodded and went back to his reading.

"Ray, while Jefe in his true life has political enemies," Raul said, "they aren't our concern or a real danger to him or us—more a nuisance. But the other cartels, well, that's a different story. To assassinate the secretary for public security is something they most certainly would want to do. As a business, we have our enemies deeply penetrated and know of most of their moves. This has taken years to achieve with great patience, but those are two of the important things Jefe has taught us: patience and the value of intelligence. As the secretary, it wouldn't have been possible for him to get people inside the cartels—even they are far too careful for that, but they didn't see our people coming from the criminal side. With our sources in their midst, we can keep Jefe reasonably safe and also plan our future actions against them.

"Second only to us, the man the cartels fear the most is the head of the federal police, Alberto Rodriguez. He's an uncompromising, dangerous force to the cartels, including us—a truly honest, brave, ethical man, unlike our president, who's so weak. Rodriguez is second in importance only to Jefe in Mexico's fight against the cartels. This means he's also fighting us but doesn't know it. He and his brother, Emilio, who was the country's chief prosecutor until he was killed last Sunday, were the two people we most closely watched. Emilio was married to Jefe's sister Elena. Because of this and simple moral reasons, we tried to compromise them in order to control or neutralize them, but they're courageous and clever, and we failed. However, one of our enemies, it seems, didn't fail. I don't know which one is responsible, and that's a problem and a threat we need to solve."

Out of the corner of his eye, Ray noticed Alvarez glance up momentarily at what Raul had said, then just as quickly return to his reading. He couldn't be sure at all why he had done it, but it struck him as strange somehow. Raul went on. "Even though he's one of Jefe's oldest friends, Alberto Rodriguez is the most dangerous man in the government to us until we can fully execute Jefe's plans and right all the wrongs in this country. Never forget that. He and Jefe have known each other for years, and while they aren't as close as they once were, they're still old friends. Try to stay relaxed and act normal around him. If possible, say very little if the occasion comes up. Understand?"

Ray nodded, knowing Raul had unknowingly given him an opening to get more information about the plans to kill the president. So he said, "It's hard for me to understand what you said about the president being weak. Are not presidents the strongest or most powerful of men?"

Raul shrugged. "Usually, yes, but it was by great luck that Fernandez even became president, and then he needed the help of some of our political enemies to achieve that. But it no longer matters what our enemies did—we will soon be rid of him, as he is about to suffer a tragic accident. I don't want you to think too much about this or worry, but it'll be necessary for you to assist me with the final details. We'll speak more about that once we're in the city."

Oh, shit, an accident I'm supposed to help with? How do I stop it? Do I stop it? I don't see how I can without exposing myself. Do I break cover if that's the only way? If I do, I'm dead. Jesus, another thing I have to explain to Bennie if I live through this. But at least I now know of one honest man in the government, Alberto Rodriguez. Can I get to him? Could he help me stop this and get to Bennie?

Ray popped back into the moment, realizing he'd been silent and staring as he was thinking. "May I ask another question, Raul?"

"Sure. What is it?"

"Do we have other friends in the city? I mean, others who work for Jefe, like us?"

"There are others in the government who work for the Condor, if that's what you're asking. I'll point them out to you if and when the need comes up. There aren't many, but they're in important positions for us. You also must be very careful around any of them, for they know nothing of Jefe's full life. They know Secretary Alvarez, and they know of the Condor, but they know them as two different people."

Geraldo came up to the aisle, handed Raul several items that looked like leather wallets, and then turned and returned to his seat. Raul opened each one and looked it over, then said, "Here are your official credentials: your identification, driver's license, and other papers that confirm that you're Ray Ortega of Hermosillo."

Raul handed a small leather folder and a wallet to him. He looked inside and was amazed at the quality of the forgeries. The leather folder contained his official ID identifying him as a special security agent, Office of the Secretary for Public Security; it even had a gold badge. It wasn't unlike the credentials his father carried as a division chief in the department back in Sacramento.

"These papers will be accepted, Raul?"

"Certainly. They're real, issued by the government. Now sit back and relax until we get to the city."

Of course, dummy. They're not forgeries if the government issues them, and that's what happened, apparently. I hope I get out of this assignment alive. Dad would get a kick out of this ID.

Raul and Alvarez returned to their papers and conducted routine business, by the sound of it, as Ray alternated between gazing out the window and listening to their conversations. After a short while, he heard the change in engine noise—what little there was of it—and also saw that the pilot was starting his descent into Mexico City. He had to admit that despite the ominous reason they were returning to Mexico City, a small part of him was excited. He'd never been to the Mexican capital and always had wanted to visit. Also, as his thoughts moved more and more toward getting out and away from these people, there would likely be greater opportunity to do so in the capital city. *Hell of a way to finally see the place,* he thought grimly.

Raul brought him out of his thoughts. "Ray, we're almost to the city—a couple more things before we land. While we're Jefe's personal security detail, there will be far more security around him in the city: federal police drivers and guards as well as the capital police at the estate and at the office. No one, of course, knows anything except that Jefe is what he is, the secretary for public security. We must be careful when speaking between us that no one else is within hearing distance. OK?"

"Yes, Raul."

"After landing, Jefe and I will deplane with Geraldo and Lorenzo and leave with his federal police security force. You and the others will stay back and follow separately. If there's any press, they'll leave with us—Luis knows the routine. We very much stay in the background down here. The danger is that someone from the north could recognize one of us and connect our business in the north with Secretary Alvarez. The last thing we want is to raise that question in someone's mind. That explains for you why we and Jefe actually meet so few people in the north and why Eduardo and Carlo are so important. They're the everyday face of our organization; it's enough that people know the Condor exists. In his mystery there's fear and uncertainty for those we do business with and for those who work for us. The greater the mystery, the greater the Condor's legend. This is an aura Jefe has worked hard to create. People are left to their own imaginations to wonder who Jefe is and how powerful he is. Do you understand?"

"Yes, I think so," Ray said. "I'll admit that until the night of the Vasso meeting, I was afraid of Jefe. I'm not ashamed to tell you this."

"Well, you have nothing to be ashamed about, Ray. You're well liked, and you're needed. We'll be landing soon. Make sure you're belted in."

Ray nodded and did as instructed. *Alvarez's creation of the Condor is nothing short of brilliant,* he thought. *It has to be the frustrated actor in him—he's playing the role of a lifetime. The first twelve weeks, the man unnerved me. I never could read him, and I worked for him, but I didn't know him. I think maybe only Raul and Eduardo really know him; what Raul said explains a lot. When you couple this mystery shit with the information he could provide as Alvarez, no wonder everyone's scared shitless of him. It appears as if he knows everyone, yet no one knows him…simply brilliant. But it doesn't matter how much good they're achieving killing off the other cartels if I can't stop them from killing the president, and I don't see how I stop them and live through this—not yet, anyway. Would I risk my life for President Fernandez? I don't know. I want to see Dad again—what's that make me?*

The plane made a rapid descent as Ray looked out the window, struggling with his thoughts about just surviving. He couldn't see much, however, due to a hazy layer over the city as they descended through the brown muck and landed smoothly at Benito Juarez International Airport. As had happened at the airport at La Paz, the private jet taxied away from the large public terminals toward a small terminal building across the airfield reserved for the use of private-jet fliers. The sleek jet slowly pulled into a large hangar, the rolling doors already open. Inside were two SUVs with a two-car federal-district police escort.

They quickly deplaned, and Alvarez, Raul, and the two electronic wizards climbed into one of the SUVs and immediately departed with the police escort. Ray and the others waited in the hangar for a few minutes; then he retrieved his luggage once more and joined Luis and Miguel in the second black Suburban. As with every vehicle Ray had been in since being brought into the cartel, the heavily tinted windows obscured all the passengers from view. With everything he already had on his mind, it occurred to him that as one of Alvarez's bodyguards, if one of the other cartels decided to try an assassination attempt, he might well get killed in the process protecting Alvarez yet again. *Jesus,* he thought, *if it's not one thing in this mission, it's something else.*

Try as he might, because of the haze or smog—whatever it was that was blotting out the sun—Ray had no idea which way he was headed as the SUV seemingly turned one way or another at every other intersection en route to the Alvarez compound in the city. His internal compass was completely messed up. One moment they would be on a broad boulevard, the next a narrow commercial or residential street. Crowds of people were everywhere. He seemed to remember reading that there were twenty million people living in the greater Mexico City area. From what he could see, that was probably true.

After nearly thirty minutes, the streets became hillier, and they entered some beautiful areas with lots of parks and even what looked like forests, surrounded by both modern and historic-looking commercial buildings, restaurants, high-end retail shops, and a few galleries lining many of the streets. *Kind of like San Francisco,* Ray thought. They turned off the wide treelined boulevard they'd been traveling on and onto a narrow cobblestone-paved residential street with huge old cypress trees lining each side. Most of the residences were hidden behind tall stone or stucco vine-covered walls, but from what Ray could see, they looked old and massive. The SUV turned through a decorated entry gate with an iron trellis that arched overhead and a family crest centered in the apex of the arch. The vertical spikes of the heavy wrought-iron gates looked as though they were tipped in gold as they slowly closed behind the Suburban. They pulled up in front of an opulent mansion that looked like something out of an old Hollywood movie.

The mansion was two stories high, covered in a warm off-white stucco that took on an almost light-pink hue where the morning light hit the stucco directly. There were large and small combinations of arched windows everywhere and rough-hewn beams protruding out beyond the edges of the roof. Most of the second-floor windows led to balconies with decorative wrought-iron grilles around them, and smaller windows had window boxes with colorful flowers pouring over their edges. The entire mansion was topped by a low, sloping roof covered with reddish terra-cotta tiles. A butler—*A real butler*, Ray thought—complete with a formal uniform, was waiting at the open side of the two tall ornate entry doors. Ray got out, grabbed his bags from the back of the SUV, and headed toward the main entry, but Luis stopped him before he could get there.

"Come with me," Luis said in his typically edgy way. "I talked with Raul, and he has us living together. I'm supposed to take you to our casita first so you can drop off your bags."

Ray nodded and followed the ever-unfriendly Luis, wondering how he was supposed to do his job in this new, unknown environment with the pressures he was facing while having to live with man like Luis, who seemed to hate him. They walked around the house on the cobblestone walks, completely surrounded by trees overhead and shrubbery and flowers everywhere. They turned the corner of the mansion into the rear yard, which featured a large pool and lush, manicured lawns, all surrounded by a perimeter of old large trees and flowering shrubs near the actual stone wall surrounding the estate.

Ray could see that Luis was leading them to a small casita in a corner of the estate, two outside walls of which were part of the surrounding compound wall. The casita was of the same architectural style as the mansion, just smaller. Luis walked up and opened the unlocked door and went in, and Ray followed. *Comfortable* was the first thought that came to mind as he stepped inside. They were standing in a furnished living room and dining area, with a kitchen counter along one wall. On either side of the main room were doors that led to the two bedroom suites, each with its own private bathroom.

God, what a shame I'm traveling in the company of traffickers, Ray thought. *I could get used to this lifestyle. Jets, chauffeured SUVs, chefs, servants, and now this. Wow.*

Luis pointed out Ray's bedroom and told him to dump his bags for now; he could unpack later. Despite Luis's attitude, he said, "Luis, before we join the others, where are we?"

Luis's typically harsh look softened somewhat, as if he didn't think his question was stupid. "We're north of the Centro, the city center where Jefe has his office, in an area called Lomas de Chapultepec. It's perhaps the nicest part of the city in which to live. The estate is known as La Casa Rosada."

The Pink House—how appropriate, Ray thought before he refocused on Luis and said, "I've always been poor, Luis. This place is like nothing I've ever seen."

"You'll get use to it," Luis said dismissively, returning to form. "We spend more time here than we do in the north. We can cook here, but that would be stupid. Like I told you yesterday, we always take our meals at the main house. We have our own private dining room, and the chef is good. There are servants who do everything for us so we can concentrate on protecting Jefe. Raul told me to tell you to allow the other servants to do their jobs; the staff here is very proud. Jefe's father bought this place for him years ago, after he finished law school. It's been his home since then, and much of the staff has been here as long as Jefe has owned it. Come on—you need to meet Jefe's wife. And remember, be careful what you say around her, El Cuchillo."

Ray started to say something to Luis about calling him that, but he knew from the sarcastic way Luis had said it that he was mocking him, as if he didn't think the nickname that so many of the others used with respect was deserved. Luis was looking at him hard, his hands on his hips. "Forget I called you that. That's a name we'll leave in the north. Let's go."

Ray followed Luis back to the mansion, thinking that Luis was nothing more than a punk. They entered through a back door into a service area and laundry room, then passed into a service hallway that skirted a large commercial-quality kitchen where classically attired cooks were busy working. Luis paused at a door and pointed out their private dining room. *Very nice, just like everything else,* thought Ray. The service hall intersected a wide, elegant main hall that led to the entry foyer, where Raul stood with a tall, shapely, beautifully dressed woman. Her shoulder-length blond hair was elegantly styled, and she was smiling warmly at Ray as they walked up. She extended her hand, which Ray took in his.

"Señora Alvarez," Raul said, "allow me to introduce you to Ray Ortega, nephew to my dear brother Francisco and me. Ray, Salena Olivia Delarosa Alvarez, the secretary's wife."

"Welcome, Señor Ortega. I was so saddened to hear about Francisco being taken so suddenly. Please accept my condolences."

Ray was a bit dazzled by the beauty of Alvarez's wife and her soft, kind voice but quickly gathered himself. "Thank you, Señora Alvarez."

"Your car is waiting, Salena," Raul said. "Let me walk you out."

Ray looked at Luis, who was admiring Alvarez's wife as she and Raul walked out the door. Luis then looked at him, his typically surly look returning, and said quietly, "Let's go. Raul told me to show you the house so you'll at least know where to take a piss when the time comes."

Several of the important rooms off the grand entry foyer were Alvarez's private offices and the security room where Geraldo and Lorenzo worked—only here, two additional staff members were with them. Alvarez waved them in as they passed by his partially open office door, and he motioned that they should wait until he was finished with a phone call. When he finally hung up, he smiled at Ray and asked, "Did Luis show you your quarters?"

"Yes, Señor Alvarez. They're very nice."

Alvarez smiled and nodded, acknowledging the correct use of his name. "Good, very good. Remember, until you get more comfortable, think for a moment before speaking—you did well. You'll accompany Raul and me to the Centro. For the next few days, it'll be necessary for you to meet others I work with and give them the chance to meet you and offer their condolences regarding Francisco. By now, almost everyone in my departments who knew Francisco know of his passing. They'll be courteous and their good wishes mostly genuine. Just try to keep the conversations short until you become more comfortable with your new responsibilities."

"Certainly, Señor Alvarez."

Alvarez nodded to him then turned to Luis. "We leave at nine fifteen. Finish your tour and have Ray at the front drive on time, and then you're free to leave and carry out your duties…and Luis, keep your head and be careful."

Luis acknowledged the order with a nod and led Ray out. They continued with the tour of the mansion, but Ray wasn't paying close attention. All he could think about was the pending assassination attempt and the unknown part he would have to play in it, as well as the cryptic reference Alvarez had made to Luis's duties. The only small ray of hope, if there was any, into his otherwise dangerous, dark future was that he would be meeting the one man in the city he knew for certain was good. If he could get to Alberto Rodriquez without compromising himself, maybe he could put a stop to the developing madness and somehow live.

18

La Casa Rosada
Lomas de Chapultepec, Mexico City
Thursday morning

At 9:15 a.m., more tense and uncomfortable than he'd ever felt in an undercover situation, Ray was waiting outside near the vehicles and their police escort when Raul and Alvarez came out the front doors. They left the estate in their motorcade and arrived thirty minutes later at the Zocalo, Mexico City's huge central square. He had read about the Zocalo, the vast plaza surrounded by historic buildings that housed not only government offices but also museums, businesses, and, at one end, the architecturally impressive national cathedral. The motorcade pulled into a secure basement garage, its entry built to look similar to the historic architecture of the adjacent Department of Public Security and Justice building. After they exited the vehicles, a private elevator took them up to the fifth-floor office suite of Secretary Alvarez.

In addition to Alvarez's large private office, with its view of the square, there were a half dozen smaller offices for undersecretaries and assistants of one kind or another, as well as a central area where dozens of secretaries were working away at their computers and phones. After Alvarez stopped to warmly greet his older, matronly-looking private secretary, at her impressive desk just outside his office, they entered and Raul closed the door behind them. Alvarez took off his suit coat, sat down at his desk with its neatly piled folders, and seemed immediately focused as he started looking over the papers. Raul pointed Ray to a formal but comfortable-looking seating area at the far end of the office. The two walls adjacent to the sitting area were covered with shelves and volumes of what appeared to be legal books.

As Alvarez conducted the business of the secretary for public security, a never-ending stream of aides came and went; calls were taken and placed; and he and Raul remained at their corner seating area. After they first sat down and made themselves comfortable, Raul placed a folder and some pencils on the coffee table in front of Ray and told him to read the information and do what was asked. Ray did so and quickly realized that what he had in his hands was the Mexican equivalent of a standardized test. The cover page of the slim booklet before him read, "*Examen de Eqivelency Estándar*" (Standard Equivalency Examination). Confused, he leaned over and quietly said to Raul, "I don't understand. An examination?"

Raul looked at him warmly. "Yes, Ray. One way we'll pass the time in the city is that you'll begin to take classes to expand your education. This test will let us know where you are with your education and what we need to help you with. Jefe told me you were a good student when you were younger, correct?"

Reciting the relevant portion of the identity Bennie had created for him, he said, "I had to go to school when I was in jail, but that was five years ago."

"But you enjoyed it, no?"

Ray nodded. "Yes, I did like learning."

"Then you'll enjoy this, I'm sure. Jefe did the same for me. Carlo and the others…well, they're very useful and loyal, but except for Eduardo, who's quite clever, they aren't inclined to learn much. This will benefit you in so many ways, Ray. Pablo has great plans for you. Don't worry about how you do on this exam—just do the best you can. All this will show us is where to begin with your education."

Ray nodded his understanding but was thinking, *Shit, how much do I show? Junior-high-school level? High-school level? Be careful here.*

The test took several hours, and he manipulated the results as best as he could. He showed aptitude in basic math, reading, and reasoning—stuff he thought would appear as common sense—and appeared ignorant about almost everything about Mexico, including its history and geography, which, unfortunately, was far too close to the truth. Around the time he finished, an aide rolled in a cart with their lunch. Ray gave his completed test to Raul as Alvarez came over and joined them around the coffee table.

As they started eating, Alvarez put his sandwich down and said, "Ray, right after lunch, the director of the federal police will be meeting me here. He'll want to meet you and express his condolences regarding Francisco because he knew him almost as long as I did. Say as little as possible, but if asked, you know your Ortega family history, correct?"

"Yes, Señor Alvarez. I have it all up here," Ray said, tapping his temple.

"Good. Of all our adversaries, Alberto Rodriguez is our most dangerous. As Raul already may have mentioned to you, at this meeting I'll be telling him that I'm resigning from my office and making him the acting secretary until President Fernandez can make his appointment permanent, so don't be surprised about this. It's all part of a greater plan."

Although Ray nodded as if he understood, he was puzzled by what Alvarez had just told him but also excited to meet the head of the federal police. They finished up their lunch, and the remnants were removed. At precisely two o'clock, Alvarez's personal secretary knocked on the door, entered a few steps, as was her custom, and announced, "Mr. Secretary, Señor Director Rodriguez."

"Thank you, Dolores. Show him in, please," Alvarez said, looking up from the work he was doing at his desk. Dolores stepped aside, and a tall, intelligent-looking man of about fifty walked in. Alvarez came out from behind his desk and accepted Alberto Rodriguez's extended hand, then turned the handshake into an embrace.

"Alberto, I'm devastated at the loss of Emilio. I'm so sorry my duties have kept me from telling you in person until now."

"Thank you, Pablo. We live in dangerous times with a determined enemy—of course I understand. The less we're actually together, the better. Our enemies would like nothing more than to also get the two of us."

Alberto turned to Raul and said, "I was deeply saddened to hear of your brother's passing, Raul. I feel as if I've known him my entire life. Please accept my sincere sympathies."

Raul looked genuinely moved, Ray thought. "Thank you, Mr. Director. I appreciate your kindness and thoughts at what must be a very difficult time for you as well. I was shocked and angered to hear about your brother."

"Thank you, Raul," a sincere Alberto said.

Alvarez watched the warm exchange and then said, "Alberto, allow me to introduce you to Ray Ortega, Francisco and Raul's nephew, who has taken Francisco's place on my detail. Ray, Señor Alberto Rodriguez, the brilliant leader of our federal police and my great, dear friend."

Alberto turned to him, and Ray saw kindness in his eyes. "Señor Ortega, my condolences about your uncle," Alberto said. "He was a good man. I was much younger than you are when I first met him."

"Thank you, sir," Ray said as they shook hands.

Alberto turned back to Raul. "I was unaware he was ill, Raul."

Raul shrugged. "No one knew, Mr. Director. His death was sudden and unexpected. His heart just stopped."

Right, just after the slug hit it, Ray thought, concealing the spike in his emotions the memory of that afternoon still inflicted on him. Rodriguez never had taken his eyes off him, he noticed, during their brief exchange. In addition to the kindness he saw there, his eyes were penetrating and focused. *This is the guy to use to get to Bennie, but how? Not a conversation—hell, we'd never be alone; maybe a message drop? Possible, but still dangerous. I need to think about this—he may not even believe me.*

"Please sit, Alberto. We have much to discuss," Alvarez said, gesturing to the corner seating area.

They all sat down, Alvarez at one end of the fine leather couch and Alberto in the matching chair nearest him, while Raul and Ray sat at the other end. For the next hour, Alvarez and Alberto reviewed the status of the investigation into Emilio's death and Alberto's preliminary plans for a raid on the Gang of Four in the coming weeks.

At one point in the discussion, Alvarez said, "I don't need to know your details, Alberto. I know you'll conduct the raid brilliantly. Just be careful it isn't a trap like the earlier business with the Mendozas."

"I'm of course planning for that possibility, Pablo," Alberto said somberly.

Ray watched and listened with feigned nonchalance but inside he was amazed. From his association with Carlo he knew the truth about the government's failed Mendoza operation, for it had been Eduardo who had planned the surprise attack on the government forces raiding one of the Mendoza's minor compounds based upon confidential information supplied by Alvarez himself. All for the purpose of repairing what had become a frayed relationship with the Mendoza's so they could ultimately be suckered to the high level meeting that saw them murdered. Ray knew innocent lives had been lost because of what Alvarez orchestrated, but as with all of his actions, the end result was that one of the more ruthless major players in Mexico's war with the cartels had been eliminated. The moral contradictions of Alvarez's actions were driving Ray crazy.

Alvarez and Alberto touched upon several smaller issues. Then, following a lull in the conversation, Alvarez said, "Alberto, there's one last issue we must discuss, and for reasons that will become obvious, it must remain between just us for now. I don't know exactly what Emilio shared with you regarding certain activities of our president, but it appears the president has been stealing revenues from the people and trying to hide this from us all. Are you aware of this?"

Alberto, who was sipping coffee, placed his cup down and said, "Yes, Pablo, but only to a small extent. Emilio shared his suspicions with me, but he said he didn't have all the evidence confirmed and could not yet make his case in court. He also said there was no way for me to help without potentially alerting the president somehow to the investigation. He was keeping a tight security lid on his actions, and, sadly, it seems his caution was warranted but not sufficient."

Alvarez nodded then went on. "The principal reason I wanted to meet with you is to tell you I'm meeting President Fernandez this evening, and at that time, I intend to resign from my position."

The shock was obvious on Alberto's face. He quickly sat forward. "No, Pablo, you can't! Why?"

"I must, my friend. I cannot in good conscience continue to serve in the administration of this man. His delay of the elections started me down this path, and now, with the evidence of his probable wrongdoing, I must resign."

Alvarez opened a folder he had picked up from the coffee table and handed Alberto a piece of paper. "Here, by law, I can name a temporary secretary until the president names my replacement. I've named you as acting secretary, with all rights and powers, effective noon on Monday."

"No, Pablo, please don't do this," an exasperated Alberto said.

"It's already done, my friend. I'm meeting later today with Castillo to tell him this to his face and also to tell him that his handpicked protégé—and husband to his beloved sister—is likely a criminal. Then I intend to confront Fernandez this evening."

Alberto looked grief stricken to Ray. "This is a mistake. Why not just present the evidence Emilio was able to collect before his death and force Fernandez to resign? It's likely the presidential commission would then pick you as interim president until elections can be held. Why do this?"

Alvarez shook his head. "What you suggest is something I considered, but the reality is the evidence is not yet conclusive—that, and I don't wish to be the president, Alberto. I love my country as you do, but after what happened to Emilio, I wish to return to a private, quiet life and care for my mother and watch my children grow up. I realize this must look like cowardice to one who has served our country for so long and so courageously as you have done in such a dangerous position, but that's my wish. As interim secretary, you'll be in a better position to ascend to the presidency, if and when Fernandez can be forced from office. I intend to make Castillo aware of this fact as well later today. It's you who should be president, Alberto, not me."

Alberto was shocked at the thought of himself as president. Not once had he ever considered it. While technically a member of Castillo's party, he wasn't a politician. He was a police officer, nothing more, and never had aspired to the office. He'd never even thought of holding the secretary's position—that was for politicians or lawyers too. This was crazy, and he had to talk his friend out of it.

"Pablo, please don't do this. I would refuse the presidency if offered. I shouldn't even be the secretary. You must reconsider."

"My mind is made up," Alvarez said. "My letter of resignation will be effective noon on Monday, but I'm planning to hold off on announcing my intentions until Monday morning. This will give us the weekend to quietly transfer the responsibilities of this office to you. If you decide you don't want the position, that's your prerogative in the future. But in the near term, this is for the best, my friend. I realize I'm interfering with whatever you had planned for tomorrow and this weekend, and I apologize, but I must do this and in this way. Can we plan to meet here tomorrow, say at nine, and begin the transition?"

Alberto looked at Alvarez for a long few seconds with a stricken expression and then said quietly, "Of course. I'm at your orders, Mr. Secretary."

Alvarez patted him on the arm. "Thank you, old friend, for understanding. One last personal item: I wish to host a small reception Saturday night in Emilio's honor, just a few of our close friends and family. Would this be acceptable to you?"

Alberto's look had turned to one of resignation; he clearly wasn't happy with everything his old friend had told him. Sadly he said, "I would be honored to attend."

Ray witnessed the entire exchange in silence, and it took all his professionalism to keep his face neutral. *He's one smart son of a bitch. Feed Rodriguez that line of shit about wanting out and then kill the president. Alvarez probably will become the president and have Rodriguez believing he really wanted out. He's probably going to feed the old president the same bullshit story later today. I need to warn Rodriguez about the assassination, but how? I don't even know how Raul plans to do it, except it'll look like an accident. I just don't see yet how I can stop this.*

Alvarez walked Alberto out of the office and shook his hand once more. He stopped at his personal secretary's desk and said, "Dolores, no calls please, unless it's the president."

"Of course, Mr. Secretary."

He returned to the office, closing the door behind him, and rejoined Ray and Raul in the seating area. Raul, a serious look on his face, said, "That was brilliant, Pablo, and well played. Have you thought of taking Rodriguez to your meeting with Castillo? To repeat the story with both there together would better establish your position, would it not?"

Alvarez sat looking at Raul, his lips pursed as if he were thinking about it. "That thought crossed my mind also. Perhaps you're right. Call Alberto and ask him to meet us at Castillo's home at five. He won't like it, but tell him I insist." Alvarez turned back to Ray. "You've heard a lot here this afternoon, Ray. Do you have any questions?"

"No, Señor Alvarez. I understand what you're doing, I think."

Alvarez stared intently at him, an emotional look on his face. "Do you, Ray? Do you really?" Slowly he leaned into Ray, and, in a softer voice, he went on. "There is madness in our country, and it must end. If I can gain control of the government and also eliminate the Gang of Four and Barega, we'll control almost everything. By controlling policy and most of the significant trafficking, I can eliminate a great deal of the drug-related violence in our country. In time, with all the resources I can bring to bear on this national shame, we can deal with the many smaller gangs and groups that want into that business, and I can put an end to the chaos that has plagued us for so long. That has long been my dream, ever since I chose to become a lawyer and go to work in the Justice Department."

Alvarez sat back in his seat and looked off into the distance, as if recalling an earlier time. He appeared so troubled to Ray. Then he looked back at him and continued.

"For many years, this country has been a partner with the worst of the cartels. Did you know that, Ray? Choosing to deal with the devil instead of fighting him—even at this, the government failed. The devil they chose continues to wage terrible violence on the people as they try to monopolize the trafficking from their safe haven in Sinaloa, and our government stands by and does nothing. Sadly, the Americans will still want their drugs—I can't help that; I wish I could. But human weakness is such that there will always be a market for drugs and therefore ruthless people who want to take advantage of such weakness and provide them what they crave; the money is simply too great to ignore. If we don't control it, the drugs will continue to be provided by others, but these others are without principles or virtue or a personal philosophy based on doing good for others. They're criminals of the worst kind, with little regard for human life. At least in my way, as we go on providing the Americans the means to escape, or their recreation, we also do a service to our country. And, like my father before me, I can help many others with the revenue. And we will, Ray, for I swore this on my father's grave. It isn't a perfect solution to the problem, but it's what I can do with the life my father left me."

Alvarez leaned forward again. "When I studied philosophy in college…" He paused. "Do you know what I mean when I say 'philosophy,' Ray?"

Ray had been staring at him, amazed at the outpouring of emotion, and he had to quickly regroup. "I'm sorry, Jefe. I've heard the word but don't know its meaning," he lied.

"Don't worry about that. In time you will, and you'll also study philosophy, I think," Alvarez said, a small smile coming to his face. "Simply said, it's the study of basic concepts such as truth, our existence, reality, justice, and beauty. I studied philosophy so I could better understand my life. I then studied the law in order to join the government and help rid our country of the vicious, dangerous criminals who traffic in drugs and kill and intimidate so many of our fellow citizens, only to find out late in life that my father, my family, was part of that criminal life. *How could this be?* I asked myself. *Why did this happen to me?* I loved my father without reservation my entire life and thought him to be the most brilliant, kind, caring of men. And then he tells me of his secret life, my true life. My study of philosophy helped me cope with this awful reality. If not for philosophy, I couldn't have survived."

Alvarez looked at Ray for a moment, the naked honesty of his admission filling the room. Softly, he went on. "I had to choose, Ray—a terrible, terrible choice no son should have to make. And after I chose to help my father, instead of arresting him and putting him behind bars for the rest of his life, forever staining our family name, I became part of his criminal conspiracy. To uphold my oath to the government and to send my father to prison would have accomplished very little, for the other cartels would have simply kept on with the madness. I couldn't do that, so I chose to help my father, my own personal devil's bargain. When he was betrayed and murdered, I found and killed those responsible for his violent death…to satisfy my personal desire for revenge. I realized soon after that a part of me died that day as well. I was lost. But salvation is a wonderful thing, and my initial salvation came when, with my lifelong friend Raul's help, I began to fully understand the type of organization my father had built and saw that perhaps it would be possible to finish what I had started as a young man in the Justice Department but with methods—and in ways—I never could have imagined. The night my father told me of my family's history, I thought my life was over. I've come to believe that may not be the case." Alvarez slowly sat back in his chair with what Ray could see was a very sad look. "I want my life back, Ray. Can you understand this?"

Ray stared at him, amazed and, in a strange personal way, moved by Alvarez's emotional outpouring. *God, he is—or thinks he is—what's the word? Altruistic. Thinks he can be the benevolent dictator, do whatever he wants, however he wants, but all for the good of the people. The funny part is I think it could work for his country, but it does little for mine. He's right about the hopheads—they want their drugs, and they don't give a goddamn who's supplying it. Jesus, a philosopher cartel leader—who knew? But he's crazy if he thinks he can get away with this and get his life back. For all his intelligence, that seems a delusional thought, but his goals are so sincere. Then again, he's planning to murder a sitting president. Whatever good he accomplishes will be wiped out with that single act, even if Fernandez has been corrupted wouldn't it? Who knows how Alvarez and Eduardo have controlled him. I can only image the kind of threats someone like Eduardo has probably used.*

He was looking at Alvarez while thinking about what the man had been telling him and the question he had asked, becoming more and more uncertain of his feelings, but then he reverted to character, quickly trying to think of what to say next. "I…think I understand, Jefe, some of it. I know that it's good if others like Barega are dead. He wanted you dead."

"Yes, Ray, he did, and you prevented it. Is that cause enough to kill him? Does his action justify any action we take?"

Jesus, what does he want here? Philosophy 101? Be careful.

Ray put a quizzical look on his face. "Yes, Jefe. If you don't kill him, he'll try to kill you again. I didn't like killing Guzman, but it had to be done. Better Guzman than you or me. Is that philosophy, Jefe?"

"Yes, Ray, that is *a* philosophy and an important one that we'll talk about again soon."

Raul had rejoined them on the couch after making his call to Rodriguez and had been following Pablo's philosophy lesson. He felt sorry for Ray. His friend Pablo was obviously deeply troubled by the events about to unfold. Alvarez felt great remorse about the lives of the innocent people who would unfortunately perish along with the fool Fernandez. Alvarez always got this way, philosophical, before big events, always concerned about the killing of innocents. His personal guilt at having avenged his father's murder hung over him like a dark, suffocating cloud—a cloud Raul believed never would go away, however successful his plans were. Raul remembered well when his friend had walked him down the same philosophical road he was now walking Ray.

Pablo so badly wants acceptance from Ray, Raul thought as he listened to the conversation. *This is curious. He and Carlo are much alike in this. It must have to do with Ray saving their lives. I suppose one sees great virtue in someone who saves him from certain death, then seeks acknowledgment from the virtuous one in return. Pablo sees God's hand in all this, so there's no changing him, even if I wanted to. He gets so depressed, just as his father did. I still hate what his father did to him. Pablo should have been a philosopher or the lawyer he is or even a priest. He would have been a good priest, I think. But not this, not the leader of this business. Killing his father's assassins took so much out of him; it's so obvious. I should've saved him from himself and killed the bastards when I had the chance and deprived him of his personal revenge. He might never have forgiven me, but he would have his soul, and the guilt wouldn't be eating him up. I only hope he forgives me for what I must do to protect him from Alberto. Perhaps when I've helped Pablo with what has to be done, he'll be at peace somehow, when he's in a position to save more people from the other cartels. Maybe there can be redemption for him. For all our sakes, I hope so.*

Several seconds of silence passed, and then Alvarez leaned closer to Ray again and said, "I see you finished your examination. Let me see your pencil and that paper. I want to write two thoughts down for you to read and keep. I want you to think about them, and then we'll talk more about them later. And don't look so worried, young friend. This isn't another test. I just want you to think about what I write."

Ray did as told, and Alvarez quickly and neatly wrote out the two thoughts. When he was done, he handed them to Ray and asked him to read them out loud, which he did. The first thought was short, and he got through it quickly: "Any man may easily do harm, but not every man can do good to another."

The second thought was longer, and Ray read it in a slow, halting way, with Alvarez helping with certain words he pretended he didn't know. After several tries, he finally recited it to Alvarez's satisfaction: "There will be no end to the troubles of states, or of humanity itself, till philosophers become kings in this world, or till those we now call kings and rulers really and truly become philosophers, and political power and philosophy thus come into the same hands....For it isn't easy to see that there is no other road to happiness, either for society or the individual."

When Ray was finished, Alvarez said almost reverently, "These words were written by a great philosopher named Plato, more than two thousand years ago. The first thought was a philosophy I believed in when I graduated from law school and went to work in the Justice Department. I wanted to be one of the men who could do good for others, and prosecuting those involved in trafficking seemed so noble a pursuit to me. And with the life my father had provided me, I felt it was my destiny."

Alvarez paused and sat back in his chair, the look on his face becoming sad once more. "Then came father's revelations of his own past, my family's past. I felt God had abandoned me that night, and I lost all faith. I ask you, Ray, what is a man without his faith? Without faith, where is divine guidance, absolution, or redemption? It was only after I began to fully understand my father's life, and after I became aware of the intelligence and power his organization possessed, that I realized that not only was it possible for my earlier convictions and beliefs to still be fulfilled, but also that there might be a path to forgiveness…and maybe even salvation. Only the means to make it happen required that I bridge the two very different worlds that I was now a part of. It was then that I thought of the philosopher kings of Plato's works… Plato's words saved me, Ray. These words are what drive my life, what I live by. Once you understand what Plato was saying, you'll understand me." Alvarez smiled a melancholy smile, got up, and went to his desk.

Ray watched him walk away and was deeply troubled, feeling more trapped than ever by his conflicting emotions. As he watched him, he thought, *You're not an enigma; you're insane. You must be. I feel sorry for you, for what your father did to you, for the way your life turned out, but you're dangerous and irrational. You had choices, no matter how hard they were. Maybe I'd have done the same thing if it had been my father. I honestly don't know. What's right here? I also took some philosophy, but Machiavelli, not Plato. How about "the ends justify the means"? If a man's methods are illegal, even evil, but his intentions are good and the result is that thousands of innocent lives are saved, does that justify the evil? Shit, man has used that rationale forever in defending war. Is this any different? I believe you mean well, but Machiavelli cuts both ways. I'm a cop, and I don't know if the president is a criminal or not; my job is to stop you, no matter how much I may admire you for what you're trying to do. In any case, I can't just sit by and condone more murder. Anything I can do to stop you has to be good if it keeps you from murdering and acquiring more power and exposes you and your entire family for what they are. The real bitch is that I'm not sure what you are—that's not that clear to me anymore. Except for the business with the president, I can't help but feel that you and Raul are good and that you're actually doing good. Who am I to judge? Hell, maybe Fernandez is just another fucking criminal and the world would be a better place without him. Christ, I need help. If I take you down, surely someone worse will take your place, probably someone we don't know about, and we'll start all over with this garbage. Taking you down might actually make things worse. This is all too complicated. Where does good end and evil begin?*

19

Department of Public Security
The Zocalo, Mexico City
Thursday morning

With all the contradictions of his present circumstances swirling through his head, Ray was as confused and lost as he'd ever felt after the emotional soliloquy from Alvarez. While the retelling of parts of his life story filled in some gaps on what Ray already knew, the history seemed an incongruity with the man's plans for the future. He couldn't shake the reality that so much of what Alvarez was trying to do was in fact good, but how could that matter if he murdered the president and the man wasn't a criminal? Raul touched Ray's arm as he was trying to sort through his conflicting thoughts and emotions and raised his eyebrows as if to say, "Come with me," and then he got up and headed for the door.

"We're getting coffee, Pablo," Raul said. "Can I bring you something?"

Alvarez, who appeared to be in deep thought, looked up from his desk, smiled faintly, and said, "No, thank you."

"We'll be just a few minutes."

As Ray and Raul started to leave the office, Ray realized that his mixed feelings and confusion over right and wrong were exacerbated by his growing sense of friendship with Raul. He just knew there was no evil in the man. Yet, over the next several days, he was supposed to help him kill the sitting president. Given the conversation between Alvarez and Alberto Rodriguez, President Fernandez could in fact be more than just a pawn in the Condor's organization but also a criminal. Ray couldn't know for sure, but he was aware that in the back of his mind, one small but important part of the puzzle was resolving itself—when push came to shove, he'd save himself before saving the president. The notion went against everything he thought he knew and believed about himself, and it was maddening.

Raul led him down the main hall and then a secondary one and out a door at the end that opened onto a small balcony that overlooked the Zocalo. Ray closed the door behind them and turned toward the square. The view was magnificent, the day a fine one as the sun was beginning to show through holes in the overcast; long rays of bright light shone on the national cathedral and a portion of the great square. The historic buildings and cathedral surrounding the world's second-largest public square were incredible to see spread out before them.

Raul turned to him. "Sorry you had to go through that, Ray. I also have had that conversation with Jefe, and I've known him for almost forty years. Since the day his father told him of his true life, and with his involvement in the killing of the men who killed his father Armando, he's never been the same man. He wasn't meant to be a criminal, and it has hurt him deeply. We all have our demons, but his are so much worse. Can you understand this?"

Ray was wondering why Raul had brought him out here and was still struggling to maintain his game face due to his situation and his own demons. "I think so," he finally managed, then added, "He seems troubled by so much for such a powerful man."

Ray paused while looking out over the Zocalo. He was disturbed by his intuition, which kept telling him Alvarez was indeed a good man and one who had a deep, sincere connection with God. He realized that what troubled him as much as the planned assassination attempt was the growing connection he felt with Alvarez as he wrestled with his own dormant religious beliefs in some unexplained way, most likely a result of the guilt he felt over killing Guzman. He'd never really considered how killing someone in the line of duty might affect him, and he was surprised at how deeply affected he was. He knew what his job was, but on a very personal level, he still felt a need for some answers. He thought maybe Raul, as wise as he believed the man was, could help him, even if Raul didn't know the truth about him or why he was asking.

"Can I ask you about something Jefe talked to me about when we were alone? Is that permitted?"

Raul gave him a curious look. "Of course, but with me only. What is it?"

"Yesterday, at lunch, he spoke to me of God and God's plans for all of us, and I was confused. I'm not sure I believe in God, but how can it matter? We're criminals, are we not? But Jefe seems to think a lot about God."

Raul looked at him and shook his head slowly. "Yes, we're criminals, Ray. We traffic in drugs, and that's a fact, but we're nothing like the miserable bastards we're trying to defeat. We've tried to protect and defend the innocent, not kill them. We've dealt harshly with some of those in our business, especially those who kill with so little regard for life. And on our orders, many more of the worst that plague our country will be killed, and soon. But we've never harmed the innocent, Ray. That's what separates us from the others; that's what makes us different. The Fernandezes of the world who made their accommodations with our enemies in order to enrich themselves or advance their careers, or those in the police we have used, already had made their pacts with the others. We simply eliminated their bosses, and they became our whores instead.

"The only way I can explain it—the only way it makes any sense—is to say we're in a just war, and there are casualties in wars. God forgives the soldiers who fight for good, does he not? Well, we also are soldiers, and we also fight the good fight. With the death of his father at the hands of those associated with the Gang of Four, Pablo, in his heart, declared war on them. He would willingly sacrifice himself to rid us of these men and their evil ways. I realize what I say may not matter to men like Alberto Rodriguez or his brother, Emilio, and the police or the courts, but it matters to me. Any man who would sacrifice himself for the good of his country and the people isn't a criminal in my eyes."

Raul paused and looked out over the Zocalo for a full minute. Ray stayed silent and watched him, knowing in his gut he agreed with everything Raul had just said. Raul turned back to him, the emotion of the moment clear on his face. "The philosopher Plato, whom Jefe knows so well, also once said, 'Is it not better to be ruled by a good tyrant rather than a bad democracy?'

"Our elected officials have done nothing for years but sleep with Luis Arellano and Ramon Fuentes, the leaders of the largest, most ruthless of the cartels involved in the Gang of Four. The blood of tens of thousands of innocent citizens is on their hands while the government allows them to do what they please in exchange for information on the others and for their own selfish safety. It's Jefe's wish to end all that. If he must use the realities of the life his father left him and be thought a criminal to accomplish this, then that's something he accepts and something we should help him with. The politics of our country—and therefore the real power—are largely controlled by jealous and lesser men. The leaders all wish to be president but lack the courage to face the worst of the cartels and take them on directly. These cowards always will oppose Pablo's ascension to the presidency unless...unless there's a crisis, an overt, direct threat against the government. Only then, when their personal cowardice may be used against them, can we gain the presidency."

Raul gazed again out across the Zocalo, his pained look turning hard and grim for a moment; then it slowly turned sad, it seemed to Ray. Raul turned back to him and went on but more slowly now, his tone softer. "I was a nobody when Armando picked me to befriend and watch over his son. I was about your age, reliable, and loyal to Armando for the help he had given my family over the years back in our old neighborhood after some of our enemies killed my father. I wasn't smart like you are; I'd never attended much school. Ironically, I also wasn't a criminal. Until Pablo's father revealed his family business to us and we became involved, I'd never done anything illegal.

"As I grew up with Pablo, however, I changed, and it was all for the better. I may be older than he is, but he was like another big brother to me and helped make me the man I am. He taught me the value of education and the wisdom to use it wisely. He showed me what character really is, and, through his example, he showed me integrity. I don't feel like a criminal, Ray. I guess that's what I'm trying to say. Yes, we're involved in trafficking, and we're killing our enemies. I wish that weren't the case, but it's the business we inherited from our fathers. Pablo has no choice but to continue in this business, for if he stops, the Gang of Four and those like them will only expand; others like them will get in; and they'll all continue the slaughter, much of it with the assistance of the weak men in our government. The others who traffic lack principles and a philosophy of life founded on right and virtue, and if they're allowed to live, the killing will go on and on and on. That, on his father's grave, Pablo swore not to allow."

Raul paused and sighed, once again looking out over the majesty of the Zocalo, his gaze fixed on the great national cathedral. "The cathedral," he said, "is it not the most beautiful thing you've ever seen? I stand in awe of men who could conceive and build such a place of worship."

He turned back to Ray, and, as a father would talk to a son, said, "As to God and your questions, I'm afraid I have no answers for you. I wish I did, but any understanding of God is beyond me. Pablo speaks often of his relationship with God, and while he says he no longer believes, or he's no longer sure, that's not true. He believes most devoutly, I think, but as he said, past events have filled him with doubt. He was devout for many years and misses it…not taking the sacraments."

Raul placed a hand on Ray's shoulder and said slowly, "Our Jefe, in his heart, is a good and decent man who was unexpectedly shown a different road, a terrible road, and out of love for his father and his country, he passed down it. To do so cost him much of what he was, or is, and forever changed his life for the worse. That's as simple as I can explain it. I've come to believe if we can eliminate the other cartels and set the government right, it will give him some small measure of peace. These are complicated subjects, Ray, and you're new to our circle. I just wanted to help you understand and make sure you were all right."

As they stood on the balcony, Ray realized he was beginning to understand Raul at least as well as Alvarez, and his intuition about him from the night before wasn't wrong. Raul was a decent man; there was *no* evil in him, despite the plans that were in the works, as contradictory as that seemed.

He pulled himself together for the moment. "Thank you, but I'm fine. I like Jefe," he said, realizing that was a partially true statement. "I want nothing bad to come to him."

I have to help stop this, but it feels so wrong. I need to get out of here and away from these men while I still understand the small difference between them and me.

Raul patted him on the back. "I think you'll become a very good friend of his in time. Come. Let's get that coffee."

Over coffee, Raul explained how Pablo had helped him receive not only a high-school education but also eventually a college one and told him that Pablo intended to do the same for him. They returned to their work in Alvarez's office until four fifteen, when Dolores came in and announced it was time they left for their meeting with Castillo, the former president.

They left the office, went back down the elevator, and were met in the basement garage by their police escort and the SUVs. It had rained hard in the late afternoon, leaving the city cleansed a bit, but there was no rain as they left the Zocalo. The monsoons had come, Raul casually remarked, and the air was clear and fresh. For the first time as they drove through the city, Ray actually could see in the distance. It didn't help, really, except now that he could somewhat see the sun, he had a vague idea of which direction they were heading—not that it mattered, because he recognized nothing.

They ended up in another affluent residential area not unlike Alvarez's, at the guarded gate of another mansion. They were passed through, and the three of them were met by a security type who answered the door and, after nodding in recognition to Alvarez, allowed them inside. Alberto Rodriguez was waiting for them in the foyer, obviously unhappy to be there. The guard led them toward the rear of the mansion to an enclosed greenhouse off the kitchen, where the former president of Mexico was, by the look of it, sunning himself in his wheelchair.

Castillo was a short, stout man in his late sixties, and what little hair he had left was white as snow. Although he'd been confined to a wheelchair since the stroke that had necessitated his resignation from the presidency, he still had a politician's smile and a firm handshake as he greeted them.

The stroke had left Castillo with limited use of his left side, but his mind was clear and sharp once again, and with patience, he could say what was on his mind slowly but clearly out of the right corner of his mouth. Over a lemonade-like drink from a pitcher the old president kept nearby, Alvarez told Castillo of his intentions to resign and why. Castillo was saddened by the news that his former protégé and sister's husband was potentially a thief and stealing from the people, but he also said he recently had suspected it as well. Alvarez told Castillo he was going to make Alberto Rodriguez the interim secretary and suggested that despite Alberto's reservations, the party should support Rodriguez for the presidency once they could get their indictments and force Fernandez to resign.

The old man turned to Alberto and asked him slowly, "Do you want to be president, Alberto?"

"No, Mr. President," Alberto said firmly. "With all respect to Secretary Alvarez, I do not. It's an office I have never aspired to and am ill prepared for. I would reluctantly serve as the secretary for public security, but that's where I should remain. I'm a police officer and an investigator. That's what I am and how I wish to serve my country."

Castillo patted Alberto on the knee and smiled softly, then said slowly in his now-typical manner, "You were always so honest, Alberto, so direct, and despite your reluctance, you would be a good president. I'd hoped to see Emilio as president one day. He would have made a very fine one. My heart is broken at your family's loss."

Castillo turned to Alvarez, reached out with a shaky hand, and took him gently by the arm. "Jacques, come closer, please." Alvarez did as requested and leaned in toward the old president. "I understand your need to go back to a quiet life. Your children are young, and now is a good time to be with them. Life's circumstances have forced me to my own quiet life. Even if I were my old self, I think I would miss sitting here in my greenhouse, tending to my flowers. But my time is in the past, Pablo, and I'm afraid your time is the present. Our country needs you at this critical moment in our history. You have accomplished much and at a great cost. But whatever your wishes, if Fernandez can be removed from office, I'll push the party to support you. I would hope you would agree to serve. If you decline, there's nothing I can do, but I intend to recommend you."

Alvarez shook his head. "With all respect, Mr. President, my decision is made, but I've told Alberto I won't announce it until Monday morning, effective at noon. I'm meeting with President Fernandez this evening and will tell him of my intentions at that time. What he chooses to do with the information is his business. He may elect to tell the press tomorrow, for all I know, but tonight, I'll tell him."

"Fernandez will go north on Monday to see the camps for himself, something he should have done months ago," Alberto interjected. "Your resignation will look bad in the press. He'll want some time to consider this. He'll wait until then to mention this to the press that travels with him; nothing will be gained by announcing this tomorrow or over the weekend."

Alvarez looked hard at Alberto and said flatly, "He will do what he will do, Alberto." After some additional small talk, they left—Alberto in his motorcade and Alvarez, Raul, and Ray in theirs.

As they drove off, Ray thought, *I can't believe I'm going to meet the president of Mexico. Bennie said there were a lot of good men down here who had to cooperate with the cartels in order to survive and accomplish anything. Does that make President Fernandez corrupt if he's one of them? Or is that just the price a good man has to pay down in this shithole to survive? Whatever he may be, I can't stand by while he and others are murdered. What's the plan? An accident, Raul said. The plane, maybe? Possibly, but he said the accident would occur in Hermosillo. How's he getting to the border camps from Hermosillo? Maybe they'll hit his motorcade, but the camps are too far north to drive to. Will they attack his chopper?*

Their conversation with Castillo had taken less than an hour, and it took them forty-five minutes to get back to the Polanco area of Mexico City and to the luxury high-rise apartment building where Fernandez secretly kept his girlfriend. They pulled up to the awning at the front of the building, and the three of them quickly got out and entered the lobby. Raul recognized the three well-dressed men standing near the security desk as presidential bodyguards from the Estado Mayor Presidencial (EMP).

Escorted by two of the president's guards, they went directly to an elevator. The doors closed behind them, and a third guard inserted a key card into the slot that indicated the penthouse. The elevator ascended quickly, and when they reached the penthouse level, the doors opened to what looked like the foyer of a luxury residence, not a typical lobby or hallway as all three had expected. Standing in casual attire alone to greet them, a cigar in one hand and a smile on his face, was the current president of Mexico.

Ray had seen photos and news videos of Fernandez because of the mess at the border with the new immigration law that was forcing so many Mexican illegals in the United States to return, but to see a country's president up close for the first time was still an event to him. The man appeared relaxed, but there was something about his eyes Ray didn't like—as with Guzman's before he had attacked Alvarez, they seemed to dart about, as if he were wary. He wasn't unlike Alvarez in height and appearance, and, even dressed as casually as he was, Ray thought the man looked presidential.

Alvarez stepped toward him. "Mr. President," he said flatly.

Fernandez nodded to Alvarez and then turned to Raul, his smile disappearing. "Raul, I was sorry to hear about your brother, Francisco. I didn't know him well, but I know he was a good and loyal aide to the secretary here for many years. My condolences."

"Thank you, Mr. President. Your thoughts are appreciated."

"A sudden heart attack, I hear? You had no warning of his condition?"

"No, Mr. President," Raul said. "He was always a bull, always the strongest. It was quite sudden and unexpected."

"I see. Well, I'm sorry. Who's your young friend?"

"Mr. President, allow me to present Ray Ortega, my nephew. He's our sister's son and was a fine young police officer in his own right. The secretary was kind enough to select him to take Francisco's place in the security detail."

Fernandez turned to him, a small smile on his face, and extended his hand. "Señor Ortega, I'm pleased to meet you. You have my condolences regarding your uncle."

"A great honor, Mr. President. Thank you," Ray said, as Raul had instructed him on the drive over.

Fernandez turned back to Alvarez, the pleasantries almost concluded. "Pablo, can I get you and your people a drink? We have almost anything you may desire."

"No, thank you, Mr. President. What I have to say won't take long. I respectfully ask that we meet alone, sir."

Fernandez noted the formal tone and the seriousness of Alvarez's demeanor. He had hated Alvarez for many years but concealed it. "As you wish, Mr. Secretary," he said, just as formally. Fernandez led them into the living room and poured a drink for himself, then turned to Raul and the others. "Raul, please help yourself to whatever you want. The secretary and I will be in the study."

The study was through a pair of doors to one side of the foyer. Fernandez hardly ever used the room, so it was spotless and uncluttered. He closed the doors behind Alvarez, walked to the plain desk, and sat down, indicating to Alvarez to do the same.

"So, Mr. Secretary, what's so important that we need to meet like this?"

"Mr. President," Alvarez said as he opened his briefcase and removed a slim folder, "certain information has come to me regarding your private affairs that leads me to believe you're stealing from the people of this country."

The president stared at him for a long moment, a dark look coming to his face, and then he said slowly, "How dare you, Alvarez!" But inside he was thinking, *The bastard. How could he know? What has he learned? My God!*

"Save it for the cameras, Mr. President. The Department of Justice has an auditor report that indicates you're transferring oil revenues out of the country. The evidence is adding up and will be presented soon. I'd get a good lawyer if I were you. It's only a matter of time before the case goes to the courts and the legislature. Six months from now, you'll be expressing your indignation from a jail cell in the federal district penitentiary."

President Fernandez drummed his fingers nervously on his desk. "So, Mr. Secretary, you reveal your ambitions. You see yourself in Los Pinos—is that it? Well, I have nothing to hide, and I won't resign, no matter what you threaten here tonight."

"You misunderstand, Mr. President," Alvarez said coolly as he opened the folder and slid a letter across the table. "I'm the one resigning. I no longer wish to be associated with your administration, effective noon on Monday. I've named Alberto Rodriguez as the acting secretary for public security, as I may under the law, also effective noon on Monday. I'm here only to tell you of my decision and to say that if you should consider not permanently naming Alberto as secretary in the days following my resignation—but should instead attempt to place into that important position one of your political lapdogs—I'll go to your wife and provide her with a detailed account of your relationship with Dijanna Moreno. You're an embarrassment, Mr. President, as a man and a president. However, I won't humiliate you any further than you already will be. For the sake of our country, I just want you out as president. Honor Alberto Rodriguez, and your *little princess*, as I believe you refer to her, won't be revealed by me."

Good God, Fernandez thought, *how does he know? How does he fucking know? Has he had me under surveillance? That has to be it. I hate this man. Does he know of my plans next week? I don't see how. We didn't discuss them here, and I've kept the details from Dijanna. What she doesn't know she can't tell.*

Although Fernandez was fighting as hard as he could to keep his face impassive, he was roiling inside. "I see you've been your usual thorough self, Pablo—my compliments. I tell you now that next week I'm lifting my decree, and we'll have elections within two months. Furthermore, I tell you between us two that I intend to resign from the presidency so a new president may be elected at that time. So you win. If it won't be you in the presidency, then who will it be? Alberto Rodriguez?"

You pompous peacock, Fernandez thought, *this time next week I'll be safely hidden away in my new estate in Montevideo with the money and Dijanna and no extradition treaty. Tuesday night we're gone. It's all set, and there's nothing you can do about it.*

"You surprise me, Mr. President, and I don't believe you regarding the decree or your intentions. But rest assured that with the evidence in my and Alberto Rodriguez's possession, you'll be in jail."

What's he up to? Alvarez thought, a sudden sense of unease coming over him. *Run—he'll try to run. Maybe he'll try to get the Condor to hide him? No luck there. I have to tell Raul to watch him closely this weekend. He has to be on that plane Monday morning.*

"I seriously doubt anything I do surprises you, Mr. Secretary. Rodriguez will get your cabinet position and the presidency in time, if that's your wish. Now…is there anything else?"

"No, Mr. President."

"Then I bid you good night. You'll excuse me if I don't see you out," Fernandez said flatly.

Alvarez stood and looked contemptuously at the man. He utterly loathed him. The Condor part of him had found it necessary to use him for a while, but that time had passed, and the weak, corrupt man had served his purpose. Without another word, Alvarez turned and left the study. The guards for both sides had hardly moved in the five minutes he and Fernandez had been alone.

Alvarez walked up to Raul and Ray. "We can go. My business is finished."

Five minutes later they were back in the SUV, heading to the estate. Not a word was said due to the presence of their capital police driver. Once they were back at La Casa Rosada, Alvarez asked Raul and Ray to come into his office. With a concerned expression, he removed his suit coat, slid it over the back of his chair, and sat down, motioning to them to do likewise.

"He told me he's lifting his decree and holding elections within two months, Raul, and he'll resign so a new president can be elected. He's up to something—I sense it. He's a coward, so I suspect he plans to run, but where could he go that we couldn't find him? Watch him closely until Monday."

"Of course, Pablo."

As Ray listened to the conversation, he knew he didn't know these men well enough to draw any conclusions, but it was clear that Raul was also bothered about something; he had a strange look to him. As he was thinking about this, Raul proved him right.

"Pablo, if Fernandez really intends to do as he says, should we not reconsider our plans? You might well get nominated by the party, especially if Castillo backs you. If that happens, you'll get the presidency without the need for further bloodshed."

Alvarez slumped in his chair and looked depressed as Raul asked his question, and then he slowly shook his head. "You know I can't take that chance, Raul, and one term won't be enough to right the republic. Fernandez has almost four years remaining in his term. I need the shock of his death after what just happened to Emilio to frighten the cowards in the party who oppose me. No one will want the presidency in the face of outright attacks on the government, which is how Fernandez's accident will appear, despite your planning. I know how you feel, and no one's more sickened by what has to be done than I am, but for the sake of the country, it must be done, and some lives must be sacrificed."

Raul was as solemn looking as Alvarez had become, and then he said, "I understand. All will proceed as planned. Will there be anything else?"

Alvarez shook his head and said softly, "No, old friend. It's been a long day."

Raul stood, so Ray did as well. "Ray and I have business to attend to. Get some rest, Pablo."

Alvarez nodded and still appeared depressed as they left the office. Raul stopped by the security room and had a quick, quiet word with one of Geraldo's men. Then he turned to Ray and said, "Let's go."

Ray had no idea where they were going or why, but he knew it had something to do with the assassination plans, and the desperation he had felt on the road to La Paz returned. They didn't go out the front doors but took the rear service hall that Luis had shown him earlier and went out the door at the end. Raul led them to a paved courtyard on the side of the mansion that fronted a four-car garage. Several of the typical black SUVs and a number of sedans were parked there. Raul walked up to a dark-colored sedan and motioned with his head for Ray to get in the front passenger side. Instead of going toward the main entry, Raul pulled around the side of the garage, following a narrow drive Ray hadn't noticed before, and drove toward the rear wall of the estate. A solid but otherwise nondescript gate opened automatically as they slowly approached. With his cop's eye, Ray spotted several security men in the deep shadows to one side. They pulled out onto the residential side street and headed toward what he was beginning to understand was the more commercial area of Lomas de Chapultepec and, east of that, the city center.

Not fully understanding everything that had been said over the past couple of hours, he decided there was no harm in saying, "Raul, may I ask a question?"

Without taking his eyes from the road, Raul said, "Go ahead."

"I didn't understand when Jefe said the president has four more years, and he needed more time."

"Presidents get elected to one six-year term, Ray. Fernandez, however, was appointed by the presidential commission, which had the authority to fill President Castillo's term after his stroke. Under the law, Fernandez can then run for his own term and effectively serve almost ten years. If he dies in office, the commission must fill the vacancy again, and the same law applies. If he simply resigns, we'll have early elections, and a new six-year term will begin for whoever wins the election. Jefe must be the new president, and he must have the time he needs to clean up and heal our country. However wrong it appears, it's the only chance we'll have to break up the cartels and return the country to the rule of law."

Ray nodded in thanks and wondered at the rationalization. He had been taught that two wrongs never make a right, but he also was beginning to think that whoever made that up never had seen the dangerous cesspool Mexico had become. The doubts and questions that had been tormenting him all day only worsened with the thought.

20

Near Benito Juarez International Airport
Mexico City
Thursday night

A soft rain had returned to the city, making the dark night appear even darker as they drove into the heart of the capital. If history proved anything, Ray thought, presidential assassins killed for all kinds of reasons, most of them just plain crazy. Alvarez and Raul were many things, but crazy wasn't one of them, he decided, at least in Raul's case. The more he was around him, the more he liked him, which was a conflict he was having great difficulty resolving. As Raul silently drove them through the night, it occurred to him that the men he was with—and helping, he reminded himself, until he could figure out a way to extricate himself and live—were really fomenting a coup d'etat. Alvarez also was showing himself capable of doing whatever was necessary to achieve his goals, which made staying covert that much more important. Ray had no doubt, despite the close personal feelings Alvarez and Raul had shown toward him, that if he became a threat to their plans, he'd be a dead man. It didn't help much, and only confused him more, that he honestly believed both men would feel bad about having to kill him.

What was more troubling and kept going around and around in his head was that Alvarez's goals for the country actually seemed noble, and the actions they were plotting were perhaps even justifiable if President Fernandez really was a criminal, and not just corrupted by the Condor. From his mission briefings, Ray knew that many good Mexican officials had cooperated at one time or another with local cartels simply to keep themselves and their families alive, yet they still managed to do some good work. Such was the lawless pit that Mexico had become at the hands of the cartels. For Alvarez to change his life as he had and devote himself to the elimination of the vicious cartels could hardly be thought of as anything but noble. How in the hell was he, as an undercover American law-enforcement officer, raised and trained as he was, supposed to deal with that? Nothing in America's history, he thought, could compare to the culture of unchecked crime and the near-total collapse of the government and the rule of law that existed in Mexico. Civilized solutions, sane solutions, whatever they looked like, seemed impossible. Was Alvarez's solution the only way? Ray wondered.

His thinking over the last twenty-four hours kept returning full circle to where he had started. Was what Alvarez was attempting actually bad? From the little he had overheard regarding the sitting president, he was corrupt, maybe even an actual criminal, but the pragmatic cop in him told him assassination wasn't the answer. Yet he trusted his intuition, and in his current predicament, it kept telling him that stopping Alvarez didn't feel right, despite the innocent lives that surely would be lost along with the president. Was there a point, he thought, where doing the right thing was actually bad? He recalled how many revolutions the United States had supported in other countries where it had been difficult to see the difference between the good guys and the bad. Yet his country's leaders had done just that—picked one side and helped them make war against the other, all for perfectly rationalized reasons that came closest to aligning with a national view of right. He couldn't help feel he was a country of one at the moment, forced into making a similar judgment yet ill equipped to do so.

He and Raul drove through the city in silence, negotiating mostly residential streets, until they came to the one boulevard Ray had come to recognize, Paseo del Reforma. As Raul turned onto the boulevard, he said unexpectedly, "I need you to know I'm a man of honor."

Ray was baffled by the statement and had no idea where it had come from or why. The despair in Raul's voice was palpable, and Ray replied truthfully, "I know you are honorable. Why do you say such a thing?"

Raul gave him a quick glance and then returned his gaze to the boulevard in front of him. "I need to show you something," he said, "and then explain your part in helping Jefe and me. You've shown yourself to be a loyal friend, and I know you'll do as I ask, but sometimes, for the greater good, we're asked to do awful—even despicable—things. It's just such a thing I'll be asking of you, but more important, I ask you to understand."

Ray had no idea what Raul was talking about, but he had no choice but to continue to go along. "I'll do whatever you ask me to do, Raul. No questions asked."

Raul nodded and continued down the boulevard. By nature Ray was more of a listener than a talker and as such was comfortable with long periods of silence, but as they drove on for another thirty minutes, he grew increasingly uncomfortable with the silence between them. He realized they were more or less retracing the route they'd taken this morning and heading in the general direction of the city's airport. This was confirmed a short time later when he saw the flashing landing lights of a commercial airliner as it dropped out of the overcast and passed overhead in front of them in its descent to the airport. The rain had stopped by the time they turned off the grand boulevard onto a street marked REVOLUCION, which paralleled the barbed-wire-crowned perimeter fencing that surrounded the airport. Given Ray's situation, he was struck by the irony of the street name as he stared out at the slum like neighborhoods that surrounded the country's international airport and wondered what Raul was going to ask him to do.

Raul slowed down and turned down a street that led to what was clearly a more upscale residential development. The street morphed into a wide, long parking lot ringed by brightly colored blocks of two- and three-story apartment buildings. Unlike the very upscale part of the city where La Casa Rosada was located, this neighborhood wasn't affluent, but neither was it as poor as the other neighborhoods they had passed through. From his briefings with Bennie, Ray recalled that Mexico was largely a country of two classes, either very rich or very poor, and that unlike America, there wasn't much of a middle class. He guessed they were likely in what passed for a planned middle-class neighborhood down here. The street and parking areas had curbs and gutters common to American residential streets and were paved, and the small apartment blocks appeared neat and clean, as far as he could tell under the harsh yellow glow of the many streetlights that lined the parking area. Raul maneuvered until he found a space that faced a turquoise-colored building in front of them and then turned off the ignition.

Without taking his eyes off the apartment he seemed to be watching, Raul finally said, "Building six, Ray, the front corner apartment. The man who lives there is the key to our plans for the president. His name is Roberto Nieves. He lives there with his wife and three daughters." Raul glanced at his watch. "Soon he'll come out and walk to the end of the block where we just entered, just as he has for the last twelve years. He'll then walk the half kilometer down Revolucion to the east security gate of the airport and be granted entry."

The undercover cop in Ray was intrigued and curious how such a man could be key to something that involved the magnitude of the assassination of Mexico's president. Deciding his relationship with Raul was solid, he asked, "How is it possible that such a simple man can be so important?"

Raul turned, looked at him for a second, and said, "He's a civilian maintenance supervisor working for our country's air force, and while his trade and station in life may not appear all that special, it's where he plies his trade that is. He's one of the shift supervisors for the country's presidential air-transport unit. He has full clearance to our president's jet at all times."

This revelation surprised Ray, and possible scenarios flashed through his mind regarding how such a man could help facilitate Raul's planned accident for President Fernandez.

"Nieves is from a large family in the north," Raul continued, "and had the character and desire to make a better life for himself and his family. He moved south, entered technical school, and studied hard, making top grades. He's very good at what he does, and he's also a good man. Regrettably for him, the same can't be said for some in his family. Nieves has an older brother, Raphael, who, like Roberto, started out trying to make a better life for himself by joining our military. He did well for many years, rising to become a senior sergeant and a valued specialist within our army's counterterrorist unit. But somewhere along the line, Raphael let his greed overtake his good sense. He and several other members of his unit deserted a few years ago and sold their services to the Mendoza brothers, whom Eduardo believes specifically recruited them. You see, Raphael's specialty is electronics and explosives, and he was therefore in high demand. Eduardo was aware of him from the beginning and traced all his movements and actions since he joined the Mendozas. After we eliminated them, Eduardo placed Raphael Nieves and his family under lock and key near Hermosillo, in a safe house he maintains there for intelligence purposes.

"Several weeks ago, the last time we were here in the capital, just before you joined our circle, Francisco contacted Roberto Nieves and told him we had his brother, Raphael, and his brother's family, and they would be eliminated unless he did as instructed. Out of love for his brother, and fear, no doubt, he agreed. Tomorrow you and Luis will be flown by private aircraft to Hermosillo, where Eduardo will meet you. Raphael has made several sophisticated but small explosive devices that you'll bring back to the city, along with him. Tomorrow night we'll meet with Roberto, who'll then see that two of the devices Raphael has built are placed on Fernandez's aircraft tomorrow night during the course of his normal maintenance duties. After he finishes his shift on Saturday morning, Roberto will be flown to Hermosillo while we hold Raphael here with Roberto's wife and daughters. Monday the president will fly to Hermosillo on the first leg of his inspection trip of the border mess; Roberto will be there to watch his arrival, and, as instructed by his bomb-making brother, he'll trigger the devices at the exact time required to make the destruction of the president's aircraft appear to be an accident. Only a man like Roberto Nieves, with his understanding of how the president's aircraft works, can do this. Francisco was to be responsible for sitting on Raphael and watching over Roberto's family, assisted by Luis, but with his death, I must now ask you to oversee this distasteful but necessary duty."

Ray was stunned by Raul's revelations of the plot's details and his part in it, but he kept his act together enough to look unfazed and then asked the obvious question. "Why isn't Luis in charge of doing this?"

Raul looked at him for some time and then answered slowly, as if searching for the right words. "I wish you could have known Luis's father. You would have become friends, I'm sure. As a young man, he was much like you. As he grew older, he was very much like Eduardo, only more outgoing in personality, a good man and a good friend. When he was killed six years ago, Jefe was distraught with the loss and, out of sentimental reasons, picked Luis to take his father's place. Even with your short time with us, I know I don't have to tell you that Luis has no business being in such a sensitive position as our circle. He can be irrational, and he doesn't have your intelligence or patience. He's immature and has some very bad personal habits I don't think you're aware of yet. I've seen the way he treats you; he's terribly jealous that Jefe has taken such a deep interest in you, whereas Jefe has kept him at a distance, especially over the last several years. Incidentally, I spoke privately this morning with Luis about this. I can only hope he changes his attitude toward you accordingly, but I doubt he will. He's not the type of man to recognize his limitations and accept them."

Ray thought he saw a potential opening to extricate himself from this mess, so he took a shot and interjected, "I'm sorry that my being here has caused such feelings, Raul. Perhaps it's better if I leave and return to Carlo in the north."

Raul smiled and patted him on the shoulder. "No, no, Ray. That's not possible. Even if you weren't needed as much as you are with our plans, Jefe never would allow it, nor would I—you're a true friend. No, I'm afraid something must be done about Luis, but that will have to wait until our plans are complete. We're too far along to deal with him right now. I need you to watch over Luis and make sure he does as I say."

Ray wondered exactly what Raul was talking about when he said he was probably unaware of Luis's bad habits. *Drugs, maybe?* he thought. Raul's sentiments about him being a true friend only made him feel worse, but he stayed in character and asked, "What exactly do you want me to do?"

"You and Luis must watch over Raphael, as well as Roberto's family, until Roberto does in Hermosillo what we require. Then you'll fly Raphael back to Eduardo and pick up Roberto and reunite him with his family. Nothing more is required."

Ray was glad to hear that, aside from the bombing itself, no other lives would be taken, but in the interest of maintaining his cover, he asked, "Nothing more, Raul? But the family will know about us."

Raul looked very sad. "Roberto has said nothing to his wife or children. I suppose it's possible his wife could associate his absence with the president's accident, given his job, but it doesn't matter. They'll have the threat of a death sentence hanging over them, or, more precisely, that's what we'll make them believe. Roberto's involvement as the one who places the bomb and the threat alone will buy their silence. Neither Jefe nor I want the family harmed further—that, and they know nothing of who we really are or that we're in any way involved with Jefe."

Ray nodded and resumed watching the apartment in silence, trying to digest everything he'd learned. A few minutes later, Roberto Nieves emerged from his apartment building, a small backpack over one shoulder, and headed quickly to the corner and turned south down Revolucion. The street lighting wasn't the best, but to Ray, Roberto looked so typical—a simple man quietly going off to do his important work and support his family. He hated the thought of the man carrying a death sentence to work with him.

Raul and Ray left the neighborhood and returned to La Casa Rosada, passing Roberto on their way. That night Ray didn't get any sleep knowing what he now knew about Raul's scheme and, worse, his part in it. Having to share a casita with Luis didn't help either, especially after what Raul had told him about the man. While he was grateful that neither Nieves nor his family would be harmed, it didn't mitigate the fact that unless he could stop the assassination attempt entirely, those aboard the presidential jet also would lose their lives. As had happened on too many nights on this mission, Ray found himself staring up in the darkness at the slowly revolving ceiling fan, his thoughts also going around and around.

Friday morning came far too soon for him, and he was up early and went into the office with Raul and Alvarez, as scheduled. After lunch, once again held in Alvarez's office around his coffee table, Raul returned him to the mansion. Miguel drove Ray and Luis forty-five minutes west of the capital city to the town of Toluca de Lerdo and the small airport located there, where a King Air twin-engine plane was waiting for them. Luis climbed aboard first and immediately went to one of the backseats of the nicely appointed cabin and started to sack out, leaning his seat back and putting his feet up on the seat facing him.

Ray followed Luis up the steps, and the lone pilot closed the cabin door behind him. After securing it, the pilot noticed Luis arranging himself for a nap, so he turned to Ray and invited him to sit up front with him. Raul had briefed him on the pilot and his checkered past as a smuggler, thinking this would reassure him regarding the pilot's discretion and dependability, but it had the opposite result, and Ray wasn't the least bit comfortable with the man or the situation but accepted his offer to sit up front. He hated small planes, even fancy, expensive ones such as the King Air, and knew he'd be more comfortable being able to see forward.

The thousand-mile flight to the small northern city of Hermosillo took three hours, and if not for the mission and the company Ray was in, it would have been almost enjoyable given the nice day and how calm the air was. They landed at the airport on the western outskirts of Hermosillo and taxied past a small modern passenger terminal to one of the many hangars near the general aviation terminal. The large sliding doors were already open, and the pilot slowly taxied the King Air into the metal building. Off to one side, Ray recognized two of the Condor's black Cadillac SUVs. As the pilot shut down the engines, Eduardo and several members of his guard entourage stepped out of the vehicles, two of them holding Roberto Nieves's handcuffed, unhappy-looking brother, Raphael, between them.

Luis woke up when they thumped onto the runway and was the first out as soon as the pilot taxied them to a stop and opened the door. Smiling, Eduardo approached them and embraced Luis and then Ray. Another of Eduardo's men walked up—gingerly, it seemed to Ray—with an old leather satchel that had to be carrying the explosive devices and handed them to Eduardo.

Eduardo turned to Ray and said, "I'm told, El Cuchillo, that these special packages are safe to carry and won't work without their electrical parts, which you'll find in a separate package."

During his early police training, Ray had been exposed to some explosives and wasn't the least bit comforted by Eduardo's explanation but nonetheless took the satchel from him with a nod. Luis and Eduardo's men escorted the bomb maker onto the plane while Ray and Eduardo were transferring the package.

Eduardo went on. "We just gave the bomb maker something to knock him out, so you should have no problem with him on your return flight or until you get him to wherever you'll be keeping him. Once he has recovered and told his brother how to make these devices work, his usefulness will end."

Eduardo's tone and look couldn't have been clearer—*Eliminate the bomb maker as soon as possible*—which seemed contrary to what Raul had told him. Ray nodded to Eduardo his understanding and walked back to the plane. Luis and the other guard had Raphael belted into the rearmost bench seat when Ray entered. The pilot stood near the door, watching, a questioning look on his face, clearly wondering who the semiconscious man was. Ray placed the satchel in the nearest seat as Luis glanced at him and then turned to the pilot, saying, "Get us back to Toluca now."

The pilot nodded to Luis, then turned to Ray and said, "Will you be joining me up front for the return flight?"

Ray shook his head. "Not this time. I'll sit here."

The return flight wasn't nearly as comfortable as the flight to Hermosillo had been. The weather hadn't changed, and the air wasn't any bumpier, but Ray couldn't get his mind off the bomb-filled satchel at his feet. It was nearly dark by the time they made their approach in Toluca and taxied to the hangar they'd left earlier in the day. As the pilot slowly pulled into the hangar, out his window Ray saw the quiet, hulking presence of Miguel standing beside one of the mansion's SUVs, waiting for them. The pilot shut down the plane, stepped into the cabin, and opened the door. Miguel ducked in through the cabin door and helped Luis with the now mostly conscious Raphael. Ray followed, carrying the satchel and glad to be back on the ground in one piece. He had placed the leather case between his feet on the flight back, and on their approach through the overcast that seemed to perpetually shroud the area near the capital, they had hit some turbulence rough enough to make him wonder whether his mission would end spectacularly in a midair fireball.

He climbed into the backseat of the SUV beside the still-manacled Raphael Nieves, who looked at him with a combination of fear and hatred, as Miguel and Luis climbed into the front seats. After traveling for only a few minutes down the highway that led back to Mexico City, Ray was surprised when Miguel turned off on a rural gravel road. He'd noticed from the right-hand cockpit seat on their takeoff earlier this afternoon that the airport was on the northeastern edge of the small city of Toluca, and east of that were what appeared to be lots of small farms dotting the landscape. It was to one of these small farms that Miguel drove them.

They turned off the rural road down a long, rutted dirt driveway and pulled up to a small stucco farmhouse. Miguel and Luis got out, so Ray did too, still clutching the satchel. Miguel opened Raphael's door, dragged the bomb maker out, and, with Luis's help, took him inside. Ray followed, not knowing what to expect. The small home was basic inside but clean, and there were packages on the kitchen table with some provisions. Miguel shoved Raphael into one of the kitchen chairs as Luis stood next to him, then went to and opened what turned out to be a bedroom door, where Roberto Nieves was handcuffed to the bed. Miguel produced a key and brought in a terrified looking Roberto, who seemed to tear up upon seeing his older brother. He also was pushed into a chair, and then Miguel slowly sat down with the brothers.

Miguel turned to Ray and said. "Give me the case."

Ray did as instructed, and then Miguel turned to the bomb maker and said quietly but with great menace, "Show your brother what must be done."

Ray watched in fascination as Raphael showed Roberto how to hook up, place, and then activate the two small bombs. The devices were surprisingly small, as were the electronic packages that controlled them, but it became clear to Ray from the discussion at the table that, given where they were to be placed, they were more than powerful enough to destroy the presidential aircraft. One device was to be attached to the locking mechanism of one of the landing gear, and the second was to be placed in the wheel well but against the exposed side of the main fuel tank. When President Fernandez's jet landed in Hermosillo on Monday, Roberto would be nearby, where he could watch. And then, at a precise moment, he'd send a signal via a cell phone that would trigger the devices in an exact order. If Roberto pushed the initiation key at the right time as the jet landed, it would appear that the landing gear had failed and that the jet had exploded upon contact with the runway.

Ray's palms were sweating as he listened and watched; he knew instinctively that if he couldn't find a way to stop this before the bombs were placed or activated, there was no doubt that the president's jet would be destroyed, killing all aboard. The trick seemed to be not getting himself killed in the process. He wondered whether that was even possible or if it was an either-or scenario.

Once Miguel was satisfied that Roberto knew what he was supposed to do, he looked at Luis then Ray and motioned with his head for them to follow him to the living room. Once out of ear shot of the brothers he said quietly, "Take the mechanic back to his home Luis. He'll tell his family they're to go with you. Bring them back here." Miguel then turned to Ray. "Raul wants you to go with him and Jefe tomorrow. Luis will drop you at La Casa Rosada on the way. Report to Raul and tell him everything that has happened and give him the remaining bomb and detonator. This is very important."

Ray nodded at Miguel's order, trying to stifle his surprise at the mention of a third device and wondering what it was to be used for. He and Luis left with Roberto and the bombs but not before Miguel blindfolded Roberto. Luis drove as Ray rode in the back with the handcuffed, blindfolded airline mechanic lying near his feet on the floor. Neither Ray nor Luis said a word for the rest of the trip. When they arrived at the mansion, Luis activated the front gate but didn't turn in. Ray got out, closed the car door, and walked through the gates as they closed behind him. He walked up the driveway toward the front doors, still holding the satchel with the third bomb and the electronic detonator. He dreaded the idea that Roberto Nieves's family was about to have their innocence shattered and perhaps their lives forever changed once it became clear to them they were to be prisoners or hostages of sorts, but those feelings were overwhelmed by the presence of the third device. What was it for? Who else was to be murdered?

As Ray approached the front doors, they opened, and an unsmiling Raul stepped out to greet him, obviously having been alerted by the security room about Ray's arrival. Ray approached Raul, wondering how he was going to stop what were clearly two bombings without getting killed. A sickening feeling overcame him, and a shiver shot up his spine as he walked up to the man he couldn't help like, realizing that in order to stop a presidential assassination and also save himself, he may well have to kill.

21

Headquarters building
Fort Bliss, Texas
Friday afternoon

After returning from his cousin Emilio's funeral, Manny spent Thursday and most of Friday dealing with the many issues that fell under his responsibility as commanding general of a major US Army base. By lunch on Friday, he was pretty much caught up with everything he had missed while in Mexico. He hadn't slept much, as he'd spent his evenings going through the files on Emilio's computer. Alberto wasn't kidding when he'd said Emilio had been keeping thorough records of all the intelligence gathered, the money and drugs confiscated, the interrogations, and the details regarding all the actions conducted by the various teams of Los Pueblos Fantasmas.

After reading the reports on some of the paramilitary actions and the interrogations that had taken place, Manny knew it was likely that under Mexican law, Alberto would be left open to prosecution for everything he had done in the interest of freeing his country from the ever-present violence of the cartels. The basic rights of a number of Mexican citizens obviously had been denied. One captured cartel lieutenant, a man in his midsixties, had died during his interrogation, the bearer, it turned out, of undiagnosed heart disease. If a prosecution were to happen, the government would have little difficulty making their case based on Emilio's documentation. It was amazingly complete, including videos, transcripts, and detailed after-action reports of every operation, right down to exact body counts—everything a prosecutor would need to convict Alberto, provided by one of the best constitutional lawyers in Mexico, his brother Emilio. *Better than a confession*, Manny thought. He was determined to talk Alberto into burying Los Pueblos Fantasmas when the time came and would easily be able to look himself in the mirror afterward. As far as he was concerned, any legal debt Alberto owed his country had been paid, and then some, with Emilio's death.

One of the more interesting operations Manny read up on late Thursday night was the recon operation Emilio had been running to track cartel aircraft. According to Alberto, buried within the data was the possible identity of the Condor. In all his years in the military, with all the deadly action he'd seen, the idea of retribution or revenge had never once entered Manny's mind. He was a professional warrior; that was it—executing the national will and foreign policy of the elected civilian authorities who commanded him on behalf of his country's citizens. But as he read through Emilio's reports, finding and identifying the Condor became increasingly personal for him, and he was surprised at the emotion he felt. *I'll help Alberto nail that son of a bitch if it's the last thing I do,* he thought before hitting the rack.

Manny's senior aide, Colonel Phil Romero, had caught a late flight to Mexico City the day they got back from the funeral and was due back anytime. With the equipment and codes Manny had sent down with him, he would have his secure link to Alberto.

His sergeant major, Jeff Green, entered the office and stood before his desk. "Sir, would you like to go over your trip arrangements for tomorrow?"

Manny looked up from his reading at his old friend and top soldier. "What trip, Jeff?"

"The general may recall that he agreed to meet with Senator Martinez tomorrow at his ranch in Arizona."

Manny leaned back in his chair, rolled his eyes, and exhaled deeply. "Oh, shit, I forgot about that. Any way to get out of it? I enjoy seeing Pete, and there are things we need to discuss, but my plate is a little full at the moment."

"With respect, sir, no fucking way. The colonel said I was to make sure you attend. Says there's a shit storm brewing over all the deportation camps down south, and the senator is up to his ass in alligators. It'd be a good idea, sir, to see what the man needs and help him out, but that's only if you like him…sir."

Manny stared pensively at his sergeant major. "Yeah, Jeff, I like Pete, and you know it, ever since the Point. Can't leave one of my roommates hanging in the fucking wind, I guess." He paused, thinking, and then said, "Get the G-2 on the horn. I want a complete and thorough briefing on everything we know that's happening at the border—up to and including today—put on paper, and I want it in as few pages as possible. I also want to see updated force projections and options for our contingency plans if any blowback to Mexican authority moves north through our wire. Tell the G-2 to have the G-3 and the G-5 help on that. And Jeff, please tell the colonel to be brief, and I want it done yesterday."

"Yes, sir. His concise and to-the-fucking-point intelligence briefing with the G-3 and G-5 supplements are on my desk whenever you want to read them, General."

Manny, an amused look on his face, chuckled. "Jeff, you son of a bitch, when did you get them going on that?"

"The day you left for your cousin's funeral, sir. Figured you'd want Senator Martinez to know what you know. Shot the shit out of the G-3's regular Thursday-afternoon golf game, sir. I 'spect I'm on his shit list for that."

Manny smiled. "Jeff, sometimes I think *you* should be sitting behind this desk, not me."

Sergeant Major Green's face never changed as he stoically replied, "With respect, General, we can't have that. You do a passable job as a general officer, but the troops would go to shit if you were the sar major, sir."

"Jesus, Jeff," Manny said with another chuckle, "I'd bust you to PFC if what you said wasn't so damn close to the truth. Get the hell out of my office and get me that report, and don't worry about the colonel. I'll have a word with him."

The sergeant major came to attention and said, "There ain't a colonel in this man's army that worries me, General, but thank you for the thought just the same, sir." He executed a precise about-face and left the office.

Manny had spent an hour reviewing his G-2's summary when the sergeant major knocked at his door and entered. "Sir, Colonel Romero to see you, sir."

Manny looked up, nodded, and said loudly toward the partially open door, "Colonel Romero, get in here!"

Colonel Phil Romero, in civilian clothes, strode into the office and came to attention at precisely the required distance in front of Manny's desk. "Excuse my appearance, sir, but I came right from the airport. Thought you'd want a report as soon as I got in."

Manny smiled warmly at his chief of staff and longtime friend. "Thanks, Romey, and thanks for running the errand. Helluva thing for a full-bull colonel to be doing, sneaking around Mexico City in civvies. I'm grateful." He looked at his sergeant major. "Jeff, close the door and stay. I want you both in on this. Please take a seat, gentlemen."

After the sergeant major did as ordered, he and the colonel gave Manny their complete attention.

"Gentlemen, what I say from this point on must stay between the three of us, but first, I have an order. As commanding general of this base, I've been informally asked to assist certain officials within the lawful government of Mexico with their war on the criminal cartels responsible for the shipment of untold quantities of drugs into our country and weapons into theirs. Due to the sensitivity of the information provided to me by a reliable, competent senior Mexican authority, and the informal and covert nature of his request for assistance, in the interest of operational security, I've determined to handle this personally, with minimal staff assistance. Furthermore, I've decided I won't bother briefing FORSCOM with this operation. I make that decision with due consideration of the very sensitive nature of the Mexican intelligence provided to me, as well as the knowledge that the legality of my actions could come into question by higher authority. You'll note for the record, Colonel Romero, suitably safeguarded in your secure file, that I've informed you and the sergeant major of my intentions, that you both registered the proper protest of my actions, and that having had your protest noted for the record, Colonel, you carried out the orders I assigned to you. Is that clear?"

Colonel Romero looked at Sergeant Major Green, who nodded, and the colonel responded for both of them. "General, Jeff and I have discussed the recent events and concur with what you're doing and why, and we want to help. You don't have to do this."

Manny nodded gratefully. "Thanks, Phil, and you too, Jeff. I appreciate your loyalty and friendship, but it has to be done this way. The likelihood of this getting out and the shit hitting the fan is pretty good, and I don't want your careers busted because of what I've chosen to do. Write up the order, and let me see it. Then put it in the file, Phil. No one's going down with me if my involvement with my cousin becomes deeper or becomes known."

"Yes, sir," Colonel Romero said. Manny looked to his sergeant major for acknowledgment of his order as well.

Sergeant Major Green had a pissed-off look on his face. "Sir, I've got my thirty years in and know where a bunch of other general officers have bodies in closets, including that four-star asshole at FORSCOM, so with respect, General, fuck the order—I'm in. Ain't nobody in this man's army going to be raining any shit down on my head. I've got some family that has gone down that drug road, and anything we can do to help stop it, I'm for."

Although Manny wasn't surprised, he was moved by the feelings of his old friend. For many years, he had known about the kind of life Jeff had left behind in his hometown of Detroit, as well as the choice a benevolent judge had given a troubled young black kid from the inner city to join the army instead of going to jail for some long-forgotten petty crime he had committed. He was aware that Jeff had found a new family in the army and excelled at everything he'd ever tried. Jeff's motivations were honest and noble, and anything he could do to see a few druggies killed was something he'd take great pleasure in, knowing the only thing better would be having them in his own gunsights.

"You have my gratitude as always, Sar Major, and thanks, but the order goes in the file. Colonel, please see to it at your earliest convenience."

"Yes, sir," Colonel Romero said formally.

Manny spent the next hour giving Colonel Romero and Sergeant Major Green a concise report regarding everything Alberto had told him, specifically about Los Pueblos Fantasmas. This violated Alberto's two-man rule, but unlike his cousin, Manny had people he could trust, and he couldn't do what was required to help Alberto alone. Colonel Romero and Sergeant Major Green were impressed with what the general's cousin had set up and was trying to do. This made them more determined than ever to help in any way they could.

After Manny finished his briefing, he leaned back in his chair and looked at Colonel Romero. "Phil, you have an intelligence background. I put on disk a report about a recon operation my cousin Emilio was running. The day before he was assassinated, Emilio told Alberto he was very close to identifying this Condor character, and it was based on information in that operation. I looked at it but so far have come up empty. I'd like you to take a look, then get it to Jeff. After you've both had a chance to review it, maybe between the three of us, we can help Alberto find the Condor. This is personal with me. I admit it—I want to get this bastard before he can get to my cousin. But if, as Alberto believes, the Condor is a bigger player in all the crap down there than people realize, and he's trying to consolidate his position in the cartels, we'd also be doing Mexico some good if we can help nail this son of a bitch."

"How about I take a look at it now, General?" Colonel Romero offered. "That way, we can talk about it on our flight to Prescott tomorrow." The colonel glanced at his watch. "In the meantime, sir, we're coming up on sixteen hundred. I told your cousin we'd test our hookup about that time."

"OK," Manny said, "but fill me in on tomorrow's trip first."

The colonel nodded. "It's a simple in-out, General. We have one of the Airdale's C-20Bs out of Florida and are scheduled for wheels up at eleven hundred to the Prescott Municipal Airport, with a scheduled landing at twelve hundred. Senator Martinez has arranged for ground transport, and we should be at his ranch by twelve thirty. You and the senator will have the afternoon to talk. There'll be cocktails and a barbecue at seventeen hundred hours. All told, we could be on the ground for upward of eight hours—plenty of time, I think, to see what's on the senator's mind. We'll get back here ninety minutes after you wish to leave. I suggest departing around twenty-one hundred, which would have us back here no later than twenty-three hundred hours."

"Sounds fine, Phil. Business aside, it'll just be good to see Pete again. Just he and myself and Hank, I suppose?"

"As far as I know, that's it, General."

"Excellent. Unless anything comes up, Phil, take what's left of the day off, finish that file, and let's get together for breakfast at my quarters at eight tomorrow. Jeff, you're stuck here with me the rest of the day, but I'd like your thoughts on that file as well for tomorrow's flight. Phil, see if you can get Alberto on the line. Then you can take off."

"Yes, sir." Colonel Romero went to the credenza behind the general, opened the oversize laptop that was the general's CCTT, flipped the screen up, and turned on the device. A camera was built into the edge of the screen to capture anything and anyone that was in front of or near the computer. The colonel typed a few commands, and an instant-message window appeared. He then typed, "Safety One for Ghost One," followed by the twelve-digit password the general had given him to communicate with Alberto, and waited.

Manny was watching him and couldn't help smile when the colonel typed the code names. "Safety? Ghost?" he asked.

"I needed some code words for you two in case the whiz kids at the NSA tapped into your see-tees, and that's what I came up with, sir. It'll make it harder for them to figure anything out if they ever look into this. I had no idea about your cousin's private army when I thought of 'Ghost.' It's just a pleasant coincidence."

Manny smiled; being an all-American safety on the West Point football team had been one of the highlights of his life; it was a nice touch by Phil. The respondent portion of the message box suddenly said, "Ghost One here."

When Phil clicked the camera icon, Alberto's live image filled the screen, and his voice came over the built-in speakers. "Hola, Manny, Colonel. I can see you perfectly—an extraordinary technology."

"Nice to see you, Al. I want you to meet my command sergeant major, Jefferson Green."

Sergeant Major Green was standing at parade rest in front of Manny's desk and was visible to Alberto in the background. "Hola, Sergeant Major. I've heard much about you, all good."

"Hello, sir. With respect, the general probably lied."

"Well, I'm glad to finally meet you. I'm sorry it's under these circumstances."

"May I say, sir, how sorry I was to hear about your brother? I'd like nothing better than to help you kill some of the bastards responsible for that, sir."

Alberto smiled at the senior sergeant's directness; he liked such men. "Your sympathies are most appreciated, Sergeant Major. Thank you very much."

Manny spoke up. "Alberto, the colonel and Jeff have work to do, so they won't be part of this discussion."

"It was a pleasure to see you again, Colonel, and to meet you, Sergeant Major Green," Alberto said.

"Yes, sir," the sergeant major said. "Watch your six, sir."

Jeff and Phil left the office, and Manny and his cousin were alone, even if some thousand miles apart.

"What did your *sargento* mean, Manny, by 'watch my six'?"

"Old fighter-pilot term, Al. Your six o'clock position is your ass."

Alberto shook his head and smiled. "I like your sergeant, Manny. He seems very competent."

Manny nodded. "He's the best and has saved my sorry ass under fire more times than I care to remember. He has half the medals for valor he should have, and he has a couple of everything we award except our Medal of Honor, our top one, and you mostly get dead getting that one." Manny paused for a second and then leaned in toward the camera, the look on his face growing more serious. "Listen, I've been reading up on your operations, especially the synopsis on the special recon Emilio had going. I'd like to hear your thoughts on that first."

"OK," Alberto began. "We've had several basic problems in fighting the cartels, their exact whereabouts for one. You can't arrest or attack what you can't find. One of the other big problems we've had is the freedom of movement the cartels have enjoyed, especially by air. If a flight originates from a non-towered airstrip, stays below one hundred sixty meters, and doesn't fly over one of General Oberon's airbases or a towered civilian airport, then as far as we can tell, the flight never existed…we never saw it. Emilio had the idea that if we could start tracking flights of the more sophisticated aircraft attempting to avoid detection, we might be able to follow the flight paths to destinations and identify major cartel figures, including where they live and work. His logic was that only the top cartel leaders would have access to sophisticated, very expensive aircraft and also be able to fly in such a manner. In an effort to close the gaps in our air-traffic control system, Emilio and I bought a half dozen Russian-surplus mobile-radar platforms in complete secrecy through a shell company we set up offshore. You'll find the details in Operation Eyes On in Emilio's computer."

"I saw that. You boys have been busy," Manny interjected. "Six Russian MRPs had to set you back a few million bucks apiece, and the fact that you paid for them, and presumably the start-up training that goes along with them, from your—how shall I put this?—private fund is damn impressive."

"Thank you," Alberto said. "With the help of Russian technicians we managed to get into the country quietly; we trained a small group of our men in the operation of these radars and located these units in gaps between established radar sites, once we determined where the biggest gaps were. We established secure communications between them, and we started looking for black flights, meaning low-altitude, high-speed, no transponder flights. In the last six months, we've tracked—or more accurately, partially tracked—dozens of such flights."

"Jesus Christ, Al. That many?"

"Yes, but regrettably, only pieces of flights. Usually one of our platforms will acquire a target, but once it passes out of range, it fails to be picked up by one of our others, having changed course or landed. But occasionally we get lucky, and two or more stations will pick up a flight at different times but with identical characteristics in flight profile, which allows us to say it's the same aircraft, and we can now draw a line on its course. From that line, we're then able to start projecting highly probable courses to origination points and to likely destinations by eliminating any heading that takes the flight near a known radar site. The net results of this are that we've successfully, we think, identified a half dozen previously unknown airfields or sections of highway being used as airstrips and are now watching several of the more promising of these locations. One of them is an area south and west of Hermosillo that appears to be a fairly regular origination point, and another is near Chihuahua. What's significant about these two locations is that the same aircraft, or possibly the same aircraft type, is using these areas on a fairly regular basis, weekly or biweekly. It was the type of aircraft that caught the interest of one of our bright young operators."

"The type of aircraft, you say? Like what? What are these characteristics?" Manny asked, extremely interested.

"It was the speed that attracted the operator's attention," Alberto explained. "To our knowledge, most of the cartel aircraft are simple prop planes or, in the case of several serious cartels, turboprops such as your American King Air. What this young operator detected and passed on to his seniors was that he, from time to time, had what he was sure was a hit, a contact, on a turboprop aircraft that was flying in excess of three hundred fifty miles an hour at a very low altitude—very fast for a turboprop. We've run down the possible aircraft types and have concluded there's only one that meets our criteria of being a turboprop and having a top speed in excess of three hundred fifty miles an hour at such low altitudes. It's an Italian-made aircraft, very expensive, and there aren't that many sold around the world. We contacted the manufacturer, but they only cooperated to the extent that they confirmed they haven't sold any of their aircraft to Mexican citizens—just a few companies, all of which checked out as being legitimate. This was helpful information because we know for certain that such a craft exists and is owned somewhere in Mexico by an individual. The fact that there's no record of anyone owning one here all but confirms that whoever has it doesn't wish us to know this. Given the cost of this type of aircraft, we believe there's no doubt it's cartel owned. We've run thousands of private-aircraft ownership records for all planes registered in the country and matched them up with wealthy individuals and corporations. This unidentified plane exists. Therefore, we believe it's being used regularly by a cartel leader.

"Emilio spent hours going over the data," Alberto continued, "and told me he was sure where the flights by this aircraft were headed when going west, but he wanted to firm up his analysis before bringing it to me for action. He told me this the night before he was killed. Manny, he was animated, excited. I'm certain he had discovered an answer, but he was killed before he could tell me more."

Manny had a troubled look on his face. "Listen, Al. I'll go through it all again and again until I can make sense of the data. You take care of your other business, and I'll take care of this. OK, compadre?"

"OK, and thank you. One last item of interest came in this morning. I mentioned the Gang of Four to you, yes?"

"Yeah, the four cartels that allied themselves."

"Well, one of my district commanders in the north forwarded me an anonymous tip he received directly from an informant who occasionally has supplied him with reliable information. The informant told Commander Diaz that this Gang of Four is going to have a summit of sorts in a couple of weeks and has provided the location."

"Does Commander Diaz know the identity of this informant?"

"No. The man simply identifies himself as a friend and says what he has to say. He doesn't call back, and he always uses a one-time cell phone."

Manny leaned back and shrugged. "Plausible enough, I suppose. You know far more about such things than I do, but it begs the question: is this a setup like the Mendoza operation you told me about?"

"Possible, Manny. We will, of course, base our planning on that premise. I'll sketch out a plan to deal with this opportunity and get it to you for a review."

"I'll look it over, but I have to ask, given what you told me about the Condor and his methods, isn't it likely he or someone at his direction is Commander Diaz's source? I mean, if he's really trying to take over things down there, getting you to kill four of his most dangerous competitors seems a no-brainer."

Alberto sighed in resignation. "I acknowledge that's a real possibility, but to that I must answer, so what? I would strike a Devil's bargain to reduce the major cartels from six to two. As long as we get the bastards, I don't care who's helping me at this stage in the game."

Manny nodded. "I understand, of course, but watch your step."

"Thank you, Manny."

"*De nada*, cousin. Listen, I've got to go. Like Jeff said, watch your six, and I'll contact you on Sunday at sixteen hundred hours, if for no other reason than to check in."

Manny signed off, closed up his see-tee, and mulled over everything Alberto had said. He turned back to his desk and realized how beat he was from the last several days. He needed dinner and some decent sleep, something that had eluded him since the day he'd received the news of Emilio's death. He grabbed a few files and his personal laptop, stuffed them in his briefcase, and left his office. He passed through the open office area where his staff worked and barked, "As you were" to the few soldiers who had arrived to work the off shift before they had a chance to jump to attention in his presence.

He strode out to the parking lot in front, where his official car with its three-starred license plate was parked. The dayroom orderly, as was his duty, had given his driver a heads-up, so his driver already was standing at attention beside the open rear door. Manny would have preferred a Humvee and to drive himself, but his rank and position had taken him up and over such simple pleasures. Jeff more than once had reminded him that the troops and NCOs who busted their butts in what may appear to be menial or unimportant jobs did so to earn the privilege that went with being something so simple as the general's orderly or driver. The staff sergeant who drove for

Manny was extremely proud of his responsibility. Manny returned the sergeant's crisp salute and said, "Home, Harry. It's been a helluva week."

"As quickly and safely as I can, General," the sergeant responded as he closed Manny's door.

As Sergeant Morehead drove them toward the main boulevard of the base, Manny thought, *Shit, no rest for the weary, not even on a Saturday. But I can't leave Pete hanging in the wind. Too old and close a friend for that, so…I guess I'm having ribs in Prescott tomorrow.*

22

La Casa Rosada
Lomas de Chapultepec, Mexico City
Friday night

It was late. After spending Friday flying all over Mexico with Luis and then giving Raul a detailed report on the day, Ray finally was able to return to his casita. With Luis out in Toluca watching Roberto Nieves's family and brother, he found himself alone for the first time since coming to the capital city. Given his situation and state of mind, there was no way he could enjoy it. His rising anxiety about the assassination plot and his part in it was further intensified when Raul told him what the third explosive device was for.

Over Alvarez's instructions to the contrary, Raul told Ray that in order to protect Alvarez from himself, it would be necessary to also eliminate Alberto Rodriguez on Monday. Not only would the assassination remove from the scene the one brilliant mind who might be able to figure everything out and expose the Condor and his cartel, but also two assassinations on the same day of such high government officials would reinforce the notion that the cartels were indeed taking the fight with the government to the capital. Despite the great care Raul was taking to make the attack on the president's plane appear to be an accident, in time he believed the investigation would discover the true cause. When that discovery also was linked with Alberto's assassination—a link Raul intended to pin on the Gang of Four—Mexico would be united in its rage for revenge on the cartels, and the new President

Alvarez could deliver with the attack on the Gang of Four they already were planning.

Before Ray had left Raul and returned to his casita, Raul told him they would be taking turns watching over Roberto Nieves's family out in Toluca until after the planned air disaster on Monday. Raul wanted Ray to remain with him through the party on Saturday night, saying he needed his help placing the last bomb package on or in Alberto's official car. With that added thought now hanging over his head, sleep was more impossible than ever. He had to be up at seven to meet Raul for breakfast and should have gone straight to bed, knowing that more than ever he needed to be sharp, but he had things to do.

Despite how it made him feel, he knew when he returned from Toluca and reported back to Raul, he wasn't going to expose himself to save the Mexican president. It was a selfish thought, maybe even a cowardly one, but he couldn't help it—he wanted very much to live. With the news that Alberto also was to be targeted, he now found himself back in a deep emotional limbo. Alberto was the one man he knew he could trust down here and, given the way Raul had spoken about him, the one man who probably could take Alvarez on if he indeed pulled off the assassination of Fernandez and rose to the presidency. Ray was back to wondering how he would survive any of this, but he knew with certainty he had to save Alberto, whatever the cost.

In the casita, he rummaged around the small kitchen, searching for the few items he felt he needed to prepare for a possible message drop to Alberto Rodriguez. It wasn't much of an idea, but it was the best he could come up with, and he had to try something. He took the Scotch tape he found, a pen, and the small square of paper he had taken from a pad next to the telephone on the kitchen counter and laid them on the desk in the living room. He then took the two fifty-peso coins he'd found on Luis's nightstand and placed them beside the other materials. He knew he was no spy—he'd never been trained in the tradecraft he had read about in books—so he was winging it. He took the four-inch square of paper and carefully wrote in small but clear block letters:

ALVAREZ IS CONDOR DE MUERTE
OF CHIHUAHUA, ALSO NICOLAS PEÑA
OF BAJA SUR. PRESIDENT FERNANDEZ TO
BE KILLED MONDAY IN HERMOSILLO
"ACCIDENT." YOU TO BE ASSASSINATED
MONDAY BY A BOMB IN YOUR CAR.
ALVAREZ WANTS THE PRESIDENCY.
CONTACT BENNIE SANTIAGO, US DEA
ONLY. REPEAT: ONLY. CONDOR SPIES ARE
EVERYWHERE. TRUST NO ONE.
SIGNED, TROJAN HORSE

It was as concise as he could make his message so that it would fit on the small square of paper yet get all the key intelligence in. He placed the two fifty-peso coins precisely in the middle of the message and wrapped the message tightly around the coins. Satisfied, he then scotch-taped the entire assembly. He left one portion of the paper uncovered with tape and carefully wrote, "ALBERTO."

He looked at the finish product and was satisfied. He could carry the message around unnoticed, feeling the combined weight of the coins in his pocket. Sometime tomorrow, either at the office or at the party that night, he intended to try to slip it into Alberto Rodriguez's suit pocket. Surely he would feel the weight of the coins and check the pocket. The risky part was the transfer. Ray wasn't a pickpocket or anything; he knew if he slipped the message into his pocket and Rodriguez immediately knew it, he'd act strangely, perhaps causing a scene of some kind and blowing everything. He had to be careful, not get seen making the transfer, and do it delicately enough so Rodriguez was none the wiser. Rodriguez had to find the message after he left Alvarez's presence—that was crucial—ideally just before he left Alvarez's office or as he was leaving the party. *If I can't do it, I can't do it, but at least I'm prepared, and I tried*, Ray thought as he got undressed for bed.

Saturday was tense. After breakfast with Raul, they joined Alvarez in the foyer at eight fifteen and made the drive to the office. Raul was carrying the small explosive device in his briefcase, and Ray had no idea how the device was to be placed on Rodriguez's limo or when; nor could he see any plausible way to stop Raul without exposing himself. Alberto Rodriguez joined Alvarez in his office at nine, and the two of them went through file after file, reviewing projects, personnel, budgets, long-term plans, and many other subjects and areas the powerful secretary for public security was responsible for. Rodriguez made note after note on one of several legal pads he had brought with him in his briefcase.

Ray was given several books, tutorials really, to read on the history of Mexico, and another on the country's geography. Raul told him he easily had passed the math and reading portions of the equivalency exam, meaning he had at least a high-school proficiency in those two subjects. As he was reading—or more accurately, pretending to read—he tried hard to follow the discussions at the other end of the large office. Most of it was bureaucratic mumbo jumbo, but at several points, the developing details of the upcoming raid on the Gang of Four as well as Fernandez's Monday travel plans were discussed. Ray listened carefully and got it all.

"The president," Alberto began, "will arrive at the presidential hangar at eight forty-five. The rest of his party has been instructed to be there by eight thirty."

"Who all is going, Alberto?" Alvarez asked. "For the obvious security reasons, I advised the president to keep his party as small as possible…only those he feels he really needs, in addition to his presidential-security team."

Alberto shuffled through some papers. "I have the approved manifest here. In addition to the flight crew, the two pilots, and three flight attendants, there'll only be his personal aide, his military aide, several members of the media he favors, and his four personal guards—sixteen to eighteen people total. Upon arriving at General Garcia Airport in Hermosillo, the presidential party will be transported by car a short distance across the field, where General Oberon will be waiting with four of his transport helicopters for the flight to the army's staging area in Magdalena, and then they'll fly to the camps at Nogales and Agua Prieta. The army will meet the president at all three locations and provide ground transportation and added security."

Alvarez nodded his acceptance but looked depressed, it seemed to Ray. The meeting carried on through lunch and into the afternoon. At four, the two senior officials called it a day.

"We'll see you at La Casa Rosada at six, Alberto?" Alvarez asked.

It was clear to Ray that Alberto wasn't the least bit happy about the planned party, but he responded politely, "Yes, I'll be there."

Ray looked for an opportunity all day to slip his message to Rodriguez, but it never came, and doing so seemed far too risky anyway. The day's business finished, Alberto stood and looked down at the great accumulation of files he needed to take with him. Raul glanced at Ray and said, "Allow us to help you with those files, Mr. Director."

Raul handled the opportunity so deftly that the distracted Alberto simply nodded and thanked him. After Alberto and Alvarez shook hands, Ray and Raul followed Alberto to the elevator carrying the two boxes of files. When they reached the secure garage and the elevator doors opened, Alberto's driver saw them coming and opened the trunk, then quickly stepped toward Alberto to open his door for him. As they placed the boxes of files in the trunk, Raul quickly removed the small but powerful explosive device from his inside jacket pocket, leaned in, and attached the magnetized package to the underside of the trunk space, near the frame for the backseat, where it couldn't be seen. If Ray could have stopped him he would have, but in that brief instant, he saw no way to do so without revealing himself. Every instinct he had told him to stay covert and get to Alberto Rodriguez.

Raul closed the trunk, and they stepped to the open car door, where Alberto nodded his thanks to them before his driver closed it. Each alone with his own thoughts, the two of them stood silently watching the armored limousine drive up the ramp. All Ray could think was that Alberto's car was now a ticking time bomb, and he had until around noon on Monday, if he understood the plan, to make Alberto aware of this.

Several minutes later, Alvarez arrived in the garage, and Ray and Raul joined him in his motorcade for the drive to the mansion. With so many parts of Alvarez's and Raul's plans now in motion, very little was said on the drive home. As they got out of the vehicles in the front drive, Raul told Ray to relax for a bit, clean up, and be back at the mansion at five thirty.

Luis was hanging out in the small living room of the casita when Ray arrived and he looked up as Ray walked in but said nothing. Ray was glad Miguel was watching their hostages this evening. The idea of Luis alone with the family bothered him greatly after Raul's vague reference to his habits, whatever they were. Ray just nodded to Luis and went to his room. He didn't know what he would do if he couldn't successfully pass his message to Alberto, but he did know that before he ever allowed the device to be triggered, he would somehow warn Alberto, even if it meant exposing himself. He sat on the edge of the bed, trying to see a way out of the situation until it was time to rejoin Raul at the mansion, but he couldn't think of anything that could save Alberto, the president, and him.

He was feeling lousy when he and Luis met Raul in their dining room at five thirty. Raul was having coffee as they walked in. After asking a server to get them each one, Raul outlined what was coming up.

"We're expecting about sixty people, including the wives," he said. "There'll be important people here from the government and also a few close friends of Rodriguez and Pablo from the business community. The capital police are in charge of everything out front, including traffic control on the streets and parking. They have roadblocks set up in a one-block perimeter, as well as antiterrorist teams on all four walls. They've thoroughly checked the grounds and will be conducting roving patrols during the party, which is expected to last until nine at the latest. The police also have the guest list and have officers who know everyone by sight. The caterers are using the car park for their truck, and the capital police will have four men there and two in the kitchen. The police have vetted all the servers, so we just have to concern ourselves with the party. I'll take the front, near where the guests will come and go. Luis, you and Ray will take the rear corners near the buffet and bar. We'll circulate occasionally during the party. When we do, we'll do it casually and slowly. Ray, some guests, when they realize you're Francisco's and my nephew and taking his place, may seek you out to express their condolences. This is to be expected; try to keep your conversations as short as possible, but be cordial, OK?"

"Yes, Raul," Ray said grimly.

"OK, use the toilet now if you have to. Then we'll meet in the great room and take up our places. We should have a room of friends, but let's be watchful still."

How am I going to slip Rodriguez my message if I'm standing in a corner all night? Ray wondered. *It has to be tonight or never.*

The great room of La Casa Rosada was exactly that, a great room. Ray's dad's home in Sacramento had a so-called great room, but it was a dreary closet compared to this. The large formal space stretched across the front of the mansion and was accessed through a wide, richly decorated opening from the foyer. The entry foyer itself was bigger than the great room at his dad's place. Large, arched windows on one side looked out over the front drive and lawn. The two-story-high space was crowned by immense timbers marching down the room every eight or ten feet, from which magnificent crystal chandeliers were hanging. The tall walls were trimmed at the top and bottom with decorative wood moldings, and the richly plastered walls were covered with fine-looking paintings depicting scenes from Mexico's history.

Ray's assigned spot turned out to be in the back corner of the room near a large polished mahogany bar. The door from the butler pantry was off to his side, so he could watch the comings and goings of the servers. *I need some luck,* he thought. *Unless Rodriguez hangs around the bar, especially near the time he decides to leave, I'll have almost no chance of slipping him the note unseen. At least the room is so big that I don't have to worry about Raul or Luis seeing me if and when I do it. I just need to keep an eye on Alvarez and make sure he's not close by.*

Alberto was the first guest to arrive, walking in alone a few minutes before six. From what Ray had heard, all the other guests would arrive fashionably late, closer to six thirty. Raul took Alberto directly to Alvarez's office, where they could wait for the other guests in private. Beginning a little after six, well-dressed, affluent-looking couples began to arrive, a few at a time and at a steady pace. By six thirty, the room was only half full, but, according to Ray's rough count, it looked as if most of the guests were present. The only guest he recognized was old President Castillo, who was rolled in by an aide and accompanied by a pleasant-looking older woman Ray assumed was his wife. The guests apparently knew one another, for there were lots of smiles and handshakes and knots of men and women around the room engaged in quiet but animated chatter. The caterers, in their formal livery, were busy offering delectable-looking hors d'oeuvres in addition to what had been set up at a buffet table to one side. The older, formal-looking bartender Ray was stationed near was doing a bang-up business, and several classy-looking waiters were wandering around the room with champagne in tall crystal flutes. All in all, quite the cocktail party, Ray thought—an uptick nicer than the keg of beer and pizza parties he was accustomed to.

Alvarez and Rodriguez, accompanied by Salena, Alvarez's knockout wife, made their entry right at six thirty, drawing everyone's attention. They walked to the center of the room shaking hands and hugging well-wishers along the way. Once they were in the center of the room, each with a glass of champagne in hand, Alvarez's formally attired old butler tinkled a little bell in an obviously prearranged ceremony and, in a dignified manner, asked for everyone's attention. The room grew quiet, and Alvarez proceeded to thank everyone for coming to honor the memory of Emilio Rodriguez, friend and brother. He made several minutes of what Ray thought were heartfelt remarks about Emilio and then led the assembly in several toasts. Alvarez and Alberto shared a quick embrace, and then Alberto thanked everyone for coming as well. It was clear to Ray—and he suspected to everyone in the room—that Rodriguez got pretty choked up during his brief remarks. Once the formalities were complete, the somber atmosphere rapidly dissipated, and everyone appeared to be having a good time. Raul had said that with his knowledge of this particular group of people, he suspected most would party until nine o'clock, and then they would start to leave—some to go home, most to head out to luxurious spots in the city for dinner.

From six thirty to eight thirty, Ray rotated to every corner of the room, slowly and without drawing attention, taking his cues from Raul. He'd been worried about drawing attention, but that was a fool's concern with this group, accustomed as they were to servants; they paid no more attention to him than they did the lamp tables.

Several times in the first hour, Raul brought over male guests who had known or knew of Francisco and introduced them to Ray, and they expressed their condolences. By eight thirty, Ray began to despair of having a chance to pass Rodriguez the note. He knew the evening was drawing to a close, and for the last half hour, he'd been thinking of possible ways to get near the man, but that would require leaving his post and drawing attention to himself from Raul or that pissant Luis. He decided he would do nothing that might endanger his cover just yet.

As Ray mulled these thoughts over in his head, Rodriguez joined a group of four gentlemen gathered at the end of the bar nearest to him. Ray's heart jumped, for this was as close to him as Rodriguez had come all night. He was barely six feet away, standing almost with his back to him. Ray slowly moved a little closer. He was eavesdropping on the conversation, which, by its subject matter, not only looked as if it would continue for several minutes but also identified one of the older gentlemen as the chief justice of Mexico's Supreme Court. He knew this was it; he had only these few minutes to try to save some lives.

Ray removed the coins and note from his pocket and palmed them in his right hand, which he kept casually clasped with his other hand in front of him. And then providence smiled on him. One of the gentlemen standing to Rodriguez's left was very expressive with his hands as he made a point, gesturing just as a waiter with a tray of empty champagne glasses was passing by. The waiter flinched, and several of the glasses tipped and fell off with a crash to the parquet floor, delicate crystal fragments and champagne spraying the immediate area. Rodriguez bore the brunt of the mini carnage as the glasses exploded at his feet.

The din in the room was such that only a few of the nearby guests were even aware that several glasses had been broken, and they paid little attention. Luis, in the corner nearest to Ray, glanced over and just as quickly looked elsewhere. Seeing the momentary opportunity, Ray moved quickly. The gracious Rodriguez had his back to him as he told the mortified waiter not to worry; he was fine. Ray quickly moved over to him, brushing by Rodriguez and dropping the note into the outer left pocket of his suit coat as he did so. He excused himself to Alberto for the minor jostling and bent down to help the waiter with cleaning up the mess. Alvarez's old butler arrived at that time and adroitly mentioned to Ray that he'd take care of this, so he needn't bother. Ray stepped back to his post near the bar and nervously glanced at Rodriguez, who ignored the housekeeping going on near him and resumed his discussion with the chief justice, apparently oblivious to the drop and unfazed by the waiter's accident. For the first time in several minutes, Ray started to breathe normally again.

As Raul had predicted, around nine o'clock the guests slowly drifted out of the great room. Alvarez and Rodriguez positioned themselves in the foyer and bid good night to their guests. By nine thirty all were gone, and Rodriguez, with one more embrace from Alvarez, said his good nights and left. Ray was ecstatic but masked his joy as he and Luis gathered around Raul. Alvarez came over and personally thanked everyone, and, with Salena on his arm, he headed up the grand stairway to their private apartment. Raul, Luis, and Ray made a quick tour of the kitchen areas and coordinated with the capital police the departure of the caterers and the other staff. Raul and the police commander then went off to check out the streets, allowing Ray and Luis to call it a night.

Back in his room, as Ray closed his door, he was pumped; he had done it. He wondered when Rodriguez would discover the note. Surely when he got home and undressed, he'd feel the extra weight in his pocket, maybe even during the drive home. How fast would he react? In fact, Ray paused and wondered for the first time *how* he would react. Rodriguez wouldn't simply show up the next morning and arrest Alvarez; he'd need proof. As Ray lay in bed, he thought about the possible repercussions of his action, realizing that in his desperation to warn Rodriguez, he hadn't thought out all the possible consequences, intended or unintended. As he stared up in the darkness at his one constant companion, the ceiling fan with its quiet rhythmic beating the one antidote to his growing insomnia, he thought, *Dumb—I never actually thought of what Rodriguez's response might be. Surely he'll try to locate Bennie first; that's the most logical play. Probably nothing will happen tomorrow, except maybe the president's trip will be canceled. But if that's not done right, it could tip off Alvarez. Jesus, I should have thought this through more…No, that's crap—whatever the fallout, I had to take this shot. For sure I'll know on Monday. If the presidential flight is canceled, I'll know. At least I tried to stop some killings for a change.*

23

Fort Bliss, Texas
Saturday morning

After Manny's trying week, Saturday morning came earlier than he would have liked. Colonel Romero joined him at his quarters for breakfast as planned, and as they finished up and headed out the back door, Manny stopped to kiss Beth and let her know he would be off post all day and would not be back until midnight. Beth had grown accustomed to her husband's unique workdays. Being off post could mean riding around in a Humvee in the middle of the Texas desert with his troops, or it could mean a day at the Pentagon in DC or at FORSCOM headquarters in Atlanta. She seldom asked anymore; if Manny felt she needed to know more, he would tell her.

Manny had ordered his driver to take the weekend off, so the colonel drove them to his office. Sergeant Major Green was already in, and the skeleton staff with the Saturday-morning duty had fresh coffee ready for him. Manny attempted to take care of the stack of papers Jeff had organized for him in his in basket, but his mind was on his upcoming meeting with Senator Martinez, his old academy roommate. Manny's G-2 had done a superb job on his intel update, and it painted a lousy picture of the situation south of the border. Manny's first order as the incoming commanding general of the base and the commander of the newly established US Army Border Corps was to increase the number of patrols that drove up and down the nearly two thousand miles of wall and fencing he was responsible for that separated Mexico from the United States. His six thousand troops assigned to this duty—a reinforced brigade-size force commanded by one of the half dozen brigadiers who worked under him—had immediately worked out the logistics to carry out his order.

The second day he was CG of Bliss, in addition to their primary task of watching the fence line from overhead, Manny ordered the Predators of his aerial reconnaissance company to keep an eye on the developing deportation camps south of the border. As more and more illegal immigrants were being deported under the new immigration law, a great many of those returning to their native country were staying near the border in makeshift camps with the hope of being among the first to be allowed to return to the US under the new law. Their presence was wreaking havoc on the Mexican government's relief and policing agencies.

The Predators didn't violate Mexican airspace, although if they had done so, no one would have been the wiser, as stealthy as they were. The small, complex flying machines stayed right over the border in US airspace and trained their many cameras on the camps undetected. Manny had his G-2 staff put together some videos and photos for his old academy roommate that normally would have had restricted access. These security restrictions were necessary so as not to reveal to potential enemies the capabilities of the new generation of Predators, which were truly astounding. As a member of the Senate Intelligence Committee, Senator Martinez had the necessary clearances to view the material.

Jeff knocked on the general's door and entered, breaking Manny's train of thought, and announced it was time to get to the airfield. When they arrived at what was thought of as "the general's hangar" at Biggs Field, Colonel Romero was waiting at the foot of the steps of the air force business jet with a nattily dressed flight sergeant in a dark-blue skirt and light-blue short-sleeved shirt and tie. The colonel, like Manny and Sergeant Major Green, was in his woodland-colored army-combat uniform with its digitized camouflage pattern. Their everyday uniforms were comfortable and wrinkle free, making them perfect for trips when a more formal uniform wasn't required. Manny would have preferred not to have an orderly on so short a flight, but the air force had its rules also, and one of them was that when you fly a three-star around, he or she gets the service.

Manny walked up, with Jeff trailing behind. "'Morning, Phil. Ready to get this show on the road?"

"They're ready, sir. This is Senior Airman Mallory Anderson. She'll pass the canapés if need be."

"'Morning, Senior. Nice to see you again," Manny said, casually returning her salute.

"Good morning, sir, and welcome aboard," the beaming young woman said, flattered she'd been recognized from previous trips.

Manny entered the C-20B, the air force's designation for the Gulfstream III business jet assigned to him. He poked his head through the flight-deck door and greeted the pilots—a major in command and a captain copilot. "Good morning, gentlemen. As you were," he said, returning their salutes. "How's the weather this morning?"

"Nothing but a few light clouds, General," the major responded. "Should be a quick, smooth flight."

"Thanks, men. Carry on." Manny turned and walked down the main aisle, removing his black beret as he did so. The one major difference between the military version of the G-III and its civilian counterpart was the communications area opposite the galley, which was manned full-time by a senior airman sitting at an array of equipment. As a senior commander, Manny always had secure communications hookups to the DOD, FORSCOM, and his base; that was a requirement of his position. When they were in Mexico, Colonel Romero had assumed the communications role with the see-tee that never seemed to be out of his reach and that he checked regularly. Onboard the air force business jet, the communications sergeant had this responsibility. Manny passed through an opening that separated the airman's part of the cabin from the comfortable passenger area. There were two groupings of four seats in the Gulfstream, and he headed to the right, rear, forward-facing seat, as was his custom when flying on this type of craft. Colonel Romero took the seat next to him across the aisle, and Sergeant Major Green sat in the seat facing his general.

The senior airman came back to see if they required anything. "Other than a cup of coffee, if you have one, we're fine," Manny said. "We need some privacy during the flight. Could you see to that?"

"Of course, General," the perky airman said. "Coffee is on the way while we taxi. Once we're airborne, pick up that phone if you need anything, and I'll be right back. You know the drill, sir. If we get any communication traffic for you, I'll call first."

"Sounds fine, Senior, and thanks."

Senior Airman Anderson delivered the coffee and then closed the cabin door behind her. The C-20B took five minutes to taxi out to the end of the main runway and then accelerated quickly and smoothly, lifting off and making a big right-hand turn in the climb out to the west over the Franklin Mountains.

Manny got right to business. "Make anything out of that recon operation data, Romey?"

"Yes, sir, and it's pretty interesting. I think I figured out what your cousin twigged to that got him all excited." With that, Colonel Romero gave a concise report of what he'd discovered. The long and short of it was that by plotting the few course segments that the general's cousin's reconnaissance efforts had tracked and overlaying them on a map of northern Mexico that showed all known radar installations, he had been able to easily identify a half dozen gaps in the radar coverage. When linked together, the segments started to reveal undetectable flight routes across the country. The track segments that Operation Eyes On had captured fit consistently with several routes that wound their way around the radar sites.

"What I did, General," the colonel explained, "was borrow a decent relief map of northern Mexico from the G-2's office last night, and then, using some info on Mexican airports I retrieved from several air traffic control databases, I located all the civilian and military radar sites. From the available information, I figured out likely radar-coverage zones and dead zones, based on the topography. Given where your cousins were locating their MRPs, it's clear they figured this out also. The known radar-coverage zones don't leave much land area open. The guys in G-2 could do a far more accurate job, but what I did gives us a start. Your cousin Emilio had bits of several different headings from the Chihuahua and Hermosillo areas and another from a point farther east, probably the state of Nuevo Leon or Tamaulipas. But if you'll notice, here at the west coast, things start to come together. The flight paths converge over the Sea of Cortez about here and then head straight for Baja. Emilio saw this and sent a couple of his mobile radars out to Baja. Sure as hell, his data indicates that a couple of weeks ago, they picked up a flight coming off the main coast in the weeds, crossing over Baja and going straight west at a point about halfway between here and here—the airports and radars at Loreto and La Paz—and then turning south over the Pacific. The profile and speed characteristics are for a uniquely fast turbo-prop. Their west-coast radar lost track as the aircraft rounded Point Hughes to the south, but it did manage to catch the plane decreasing in speed, as if it were executing an approach, and turning back toward the coast before it was over the horizon. If you look at the map, sir, there just isn't a hell of a lot of anything if you project the course back to the coast."

"Jesus, Romey," Manny said with admiration as he looked at the map and all the information the colonel had provided. "How much sleep did you get last night?"

"I'll admit, sir, not much, but I got real caught up in this, and time just got away from me. My old intel juices were flowing there for a bit."

Manny smiled. "Superb job. What's your analysis?"

"Well, what we know with pretty reliable certainty," the colonel said, "is the general area this craft flew to in Baja. What we don't know—but what Emilio probably did—is what's so special about this area. He and Alberto know their country—we don't. I'd guess that given the general area where the plane must have landed, Emilio either figured out who owns this flight or, at the very least, narrowed it down to a few suspects."

Manny turned to Sergeant Major Green. "Anything to add, Jeff?"

"No, sir," he said, shaking his head. "The colonel's done fine. Looked like a lot of lines to nowhere to me."

"Me too," Manny said. "Thanks, Romey. Like Jeff said, you done good. We'll run your summary by Alberto tomorrow when we make contact at sixteen hundred. Maybe he knows what Emilio knew about that stretch of the Baja."

"Thank you, sir."

Colonel Romero's review of the data took the full hour of the flight. As soon as they'd finished, the phone next to Manny buzzed, and the major up front advised him that they were making their final descent into Prescott. None of the three even noticed they had been dropping and slowing for the last fifteen minutes. Ten minutes later, they touched down at Love Field, eight miles north of Prescott. The G-III taxied to the transient-aircraft tarmac, where a black, late-model Suburban was waiting. Standing beside the open driver's door was Senator Martinez's rumpled, curmudgeonly chief of staff, Henry "Hank" McDonald. Sergeant Major Green followed Senior Airman Anderson off the plane, followed by Colonel Romero and then Manny. After thanking the airman, they headed to the Suburban and greeted Hank.

"General, nice to see you again. Welcome to Arizona," Hank said, extending his hand.

"Hi, Hank. Nice to be here. Pete at the ranch?"

"Yes, sir. He is. Romey, good to see you…and you too, Sergeant Major."

There were handshakes all around, and then they loaded up, and, with Hank at the wheel and the general in the front seat beside him, they made the fifteen-mile trip to the Martinez family ranch. Senator Martinez's father had been a successful restaurateur in Arizona and had bought the four-hundred-acre ranch west of Prescott some fifty years earlier; the senator had inherited it after his father's death. The simple but attractive ranch-style house was rugged looking on the outside, with its mix of split-log siding and old stonework, but it was very comfortable inside. The rear areas of the house, including the large flagstone patio, faced the east, overlooking the valley that most of the ranch acreage comprised. In the distance, downhill to the east, Prescott was clearly visible.

Hank led them from the front drive around the south side of the house on a well-worn path to the patio in back. Manny could smell meat roasting the moment they turned the corner. Senator Pete Martinez was standing within a seating area of Adirondack chairs arranged to catch the view down the valley, with a well-stocked bar cart nearby. A large stone barbecue stood off to one side, where the senator's cook was grilling their lunch, the source of the pleasant smells wafting in the air.

Manny walked up, smiling at his old roommate. "Pete, you're looking good. You seem no worse for the wear, swimming with all those beltway sharks."

Like his former West Point roommate, the junior senator from Arizona was a tall, handsome ex-athlete with a bright political future in his party. He smiled as they shook hands and replied, "I'll show you the scars some other time, all-star. You look fit, as usual." The senator's warm countenance suddenly changed, becoming very serious as he reached out and grabbed Manny's shoulder. "Let me say right off that I was sorry as hell to hear about Emilio. I know how close you two were."

Manny's smile also turned to a grim look. "Thanks, Pete. Damn miserable business down south."

"And getting more miserable by the minute, it seems," Pete said. "Thanks for taking the time to meet with me. I need to get as clear a picture as I can regarding the situation down there, which means getting your views on the entire border mess."

Manny shrugged. "I'll tell you what I know, Pete, but we're mostly ground pounders, and then that's even limited to our side of the fence line. But I do have some aerial photos and video of the camps that my G-2 put together, plus his assessment of the situation and our force structure to deal with any civilian unrest, if it comes to that."

"I appreciate that, Manny."

As Manny and Pete were talking, Hank, Colonel Romero, and Sergeant Major Green quietly joined them. "Why don't we eat while we talk?" the senator said, pointing to where the cook was finishing up their lunch.

After they dished up the ribs and beans that Pete's longtime family cook had prepared from an old family recipe, they sat down at a heavy wooden picnic table on the corner of the patio to eat. Manny inquired about Pete's mother and the rest of the family and brought Pete up to date on the careers of some of their old friends and West Point classmates. After finishing their lunch and cleaning up, they gathered the deck chairs into a quasi circle to review Manny's intelligence report. During the flight in, Manny had told Colonel Romero and

Jeff that, for the time being, he wanted no mention made to Pete of his conversations with Alberto, the communications hookup that was in place, or any of Alberto's clandestine activities. Manny trusted Pete, and even Hank, but for the time being, he wanted Alberto's operations to be kept under wraps. For the most part, the conversations for the next three hours stayed centered on Manny's detailed report, the conditions in the camps, crime increases in the American southwest, and possible changes to government policies.

Finally there was a brief lull in the conversation, and Pete said, "Thanks, Manny. I greatly appreciate the update." He took a quick glance at Hank before continuing. "Let me go off on a tangent for a minute. As a member of the Senate Intelligence Committee, I'm privy to information that you may or may not know, and my hands are tied on what I can share with you without it first sifting down through channels. In an effort to get as much information as possible on the border mess, Hank has been doing some quiet digging on his own, using knowledgeable sources he has at Langley and the DEA. He's discovered some intelligence we feel needs to be shared with you that you may otherwise not get access to and, in my view, is better than what the committee has anyway. Because this intel isn't coming from the committee, my legal aide has determined we can share it with you and not get me booted out of Washington…or jailed."

Manny smiled. "Well, naturally, Pete, I want to help keep your sorry ass out of jail, but I also subscribe to the adage that a field commander can never have too much intelligence, so anything you can pass on is appreciated."

Manny's comment made Pete smile as well, but his look grew serious again as he said, "Manny, with all due—and certainly deserved—respect to Romey and Sergeant Major Green, I'm not sure exactly what you'd want them to hear. Some of this gets pretty wild."

"That's an easy one, Pete. They hear whatever I hear unless superior command specifically makes it 'need to know' for me only. I can't do my job effectively without their being in the know. Does that take care of that?"

"Yes, and thanks. No offense at all, I hope, Romey and Sar Major?" the senator asked as he turned and looked at them.

"None whatsoever, Senator," Romey said.

"Hooah," echoed Jeff with a nod.

"Thanks, fellas," the senator said, nodding his thanks. He turned to his chief of staff. "Hank, how do you want to handle this part?"

Hank cleared his throat and then said, "General, what we'd like to pass on to you would be far clearer if you got the dope right from the horse's mouth. I have two of my sources cooling their heels in a motel in town. I can have them up here in fifteen or twenty minutes. They're both DEA guys—the best DEA guys, I should have said. May I have your permission to get them up here?"

Manny's look turned to one of concern. "Hank, I have it on reliable authority that the DEA in my neighborhood is compromised. How well do you know these guys, and why do you believe they can be trusted?"

Hank sat back in his chair, his eyes expressing his surprise. "I'd love to know how or why you think the DEA in your area is compromised, General, but maybe we can set that aside till later. Sadly, you're right; there are certain DEA offices in Texas and New Mexico that for sure have been compromised by the cartels. In an effort to get on top of this problem, the top managers at the DEA have all been replaced in the last twelve months. The new intelligence director, Charley Willis, is an old friend of the senator's and mine. He's as squeaky clean as they come, but in the end, I guess you'll have to let me vouch for him."

"Me too, Manny," Pete interjected. "I've known Charley for years. He's one of the good guys and was brought in principally because there are moles in the agency. One of his missions is to root them out."

Hank nodded his agreement with what his boss was saying. "With him, General, is a longtime DEA field agent by the name of Bennie Santiago. When the rubber meets the road in DEA, Bennie is usually driving the truck. The new DEA director, Theodore Mills, and our friend Charley brought him in as a special agent in charge to run whatever it is they're doing to clean up their agency. Bennie's the sharp end of the stick on their counterespionage or covert shit, whatever they call it. I really think you need to hear what they have to say, sir."

Manny glanced at Colonel Romero and said, "Sure, Hank, OK. I met a Bennie Santiago from the DEA a couple of months back. Same man, I assume?"

"Yes, sir, he told me. He works some of the time out of the El Paso office, said he made his manners, but no one in El Paso has a clue what he's really doing. He's key to everything with respect to decent intelligence, simply because he's the one who seems to be generating it all."

"Romey?" Manny said, turning back to the colonel.

"I liked him, General. I say we trust Hank and the senator and get them up here."

Manny turned back Hank. "Get 'em up here, Hank."

Hank took out his cell phone and punched in a number. He knew he had coverage because Charley had called him at eleven thirty to tell him they were checked in at the hotel and awaiting his call.

At the Prescott Resort and Conference Center, Charley and Bennie were sacked out on the two queen beds in their room, watching television, when Charley's cell phone went off. He swung his legs off the bed and glanced at the screen, noting that it was Hank. "Right on time, Bennie," he said.

Hank told Charley the coast was clear, and he should come on up, then added, "Charley, the general has his aide, Colonel Phil Romero, with him, as well as his sergeant major. He wants them involved in this, so talk with Bennie, OK? You know he won't like that."

"Right, Hank," Charley said. "I will. We'll be there in twenty."

Bennie was putting on his shoes as Charley was talking to Hank. He hated waiting around and had been antsy all afternoon.

"Let's go," Charley said. "We have the general's attention."

"'Bout fucking time," Bennie mumbled. "I'm going nuts just sitting here."

Hank's directions were simple and clear, and the seven- or eight-mile drive to the ranch in their rental car was mostly behind them. Charley decided not to tell Bennie about the colonel and sergeant major until they were almost there. As they turned off the highway onto the ranch road, he knew he had to give Bennie a heads-up.

"Before we get there," Charley said, "I know how you feel about 'need to know,' but the general has his aide, Colonel Romero, and his sergeant major with him. They're to be a part of this, I gather, at the general's insistence."

Bennie looked at his friend and smiled, then chuckled. "Didn't want to tell me back at the room, eh, old pal? Get me on the road first—balls of steel. I knew it."

Charley had known Bennie so long that he realized that instead of being mad at him, Bennie was pulling his chain for some reason. "You're not mad at me?"

Bennie shook his head. "Naw, I met them both when I met the general right after he assumed command; they were always around. I knew this would be no different. If I were in his shoes, I'd do the same damn thing. Have to have trusted subordinates like that when you shoulder the kind of responsibilities he does. Kind of why you keep *me* around, right?"

Charley smiled back warmly. "Thanks for letting me off the hook. I want to get you the support you need to find Ray, and I'd do just about any underhanded thing I can think of to get it."

Bennie had his arm on the back of Charley's seat and patted him on the shoulder. "I know that, and I appreciate it. How do you want to handle the discussion with these jokers?"

"We'll play it by ear, but this is your show, Bennie. Tell them everything you feel you can. We can trust these guys, and this is the only way I can think of to locate Ray."

24

The Martinez ranch
Prescott, Arizona
Late Saturday afternoon

Bennie hated politicians and wasn't looking forward to this meeting as Charley pulled the car to a stop in front of the senator's simple ranch home. He'd been on the streets for thirty-five years, fighting the menace that was drug trafficking, and more often than not, down through the years, politicians at every level and of every stripe had used that same menace as a sort of prop to further their careers. Bennie didn't trust any of them, including Senator Martinez. But he was also a pragmatist; Ray was in deep shit down in Mexico, and he had put him there and then lost control of the situation. That was a bitter pill for a veteran control agent to swallow, and there wasn't anything he wouldn't do or try to get Ray back safely. He did, however, instinctively trust the new commanding general of Fort Bliss, who, in their short meeting a couple of months before, seemed to understand the issues at the border—that, and the man's cousin was the top cop in a country where the life expectancy of an individual in that position often was measured in months. The recent assassination of General Rodriguez's other cousin, Emilio, was proof of that. He was going along with Charley's plan because it was the only lifeline he saw, and in his gut, he knew getting to the general's surviving cousin, Alberto, was also an avenue that needed to be exploited if he was going to help Ray.

As they got out of the car, Hank was waiting for them. Greetings and handshakes were exchanged, and then Hank took them around to the patio.

When they came around the corner, it was clear to Bennie that the cocktail hour had been declared, even though it was barely four o'clock, as the others were gathered around the bar cart, and each man had a fresh drink in his hand. Hank made the introductions and made sure he and Charley also had drinks. Then, with a look to the senator, he kicked off the conversation.

"Please have a seat, fellas," Hank said, pointing to two empty Adirondack chairs. "Let me start by bringing the general, Romey, and Sergeant Major Green up to speed with what the three of us have been doing, and then I'll turn the discussion over to you, Bennie. OK?"

"Fine, Hank," Bennie said tersely.

"General, because of the problems at the border that have arisen as a result of the new immigration bill," Hank began, "and because Pete is a border-state senator and was the bill's principal author, in an effort to stay on top of the Mexican situation, I reached out to some friends I consider experts on all things in the south. In addition to these two guys, I have a contact at Langley who's the top man on the Mexican desk over there. At first I met with each independently because I thought their individual areas of expertise made that logical. Also, it seemed the best way to keep a low profile, keep everyone's secrets safe, and keep our meetings off the political radar. We met informally—socially, really—with the intent to keep our conversations private, just between friends. To my surprise, the more I learned separately, the more I came to realize that the slew of problems they have in Mexico are all connected, and the principal source of the problems isn't our immigration policy—Lord knows that has exacerbated things down there—but rather, it continues to be drug trafficking."

Hank paused and took a couple of sips of his drink and then glanced at each of the men sitting around him before going on.

"The more I learned, the more I realized I needed to get my friends to come together if I wanted to be able to do my job, which is to help the senator formulate policy. I needed Charley here to get a detailed intelligence estimate from my CIA contact directly and not from me or some worthless agency executive summary, which, given the competition and rivalries between the agencies, is what he'd get. Together, I hoped, they would then be able to shed the kind of light I needed to help Pete make policy. Charley brought in Bennie because, as you apparently know, the DEA has been compromised down here, and it's his job to find out who the traitors are. He's in charge of the covert side of things for the DEA, and his operatives are developing some amazing intelligence at great personal risk. Before I go any further, I don't suppose, General, you'd like to share with us how you know or suspect that the DEA in your area of command has been compromised?"

Manny looked at Hank for a few seconds, thinking, and then said, "Let's hear from Bennie first." He shifted his steely look to Bennie. "How about you take us through what you know, and then I'll tell you what I know?"

The focus from everyone present was intense and now shifted to Bennie. He nodded to the general and then looked at each of the men around him before continuing. "Jesus, where to start? I don't think you fellas want or need a complete history of the last forty years of the drug trafficking trade from South America through Mexico into this country, so let me see if I can summarize the more recent history to give us some context so we can get to the real business of what we're here to discuss." Bennie paused and took a healthy drink of the old Scotch Hank had poured him, gathering his thoughts before going on.

"Over the last twenty-four months or so," Bennie began, "a number of significant events have occurred in Mexico. At first glance, these events seem unrelated, having only the fact that they're all occurring in the same country as the common denominator. But we've been developing intelligence—and when I say 'we,' I mean Hank's guy at the CIA, Charley and me at DEA, and Hank and Senator Martinez in their jobs—that starts to tie together what we thought up until now were random events. First there was the stroke suffered by President Castillo, a good man by every account, that forced him to give up the presidency—nothing sinister here, just bad luck. This resulted in the legislative appointment of the interim president, Fernandez, elevating him from his position as federal attorney general all the way to the top job. He was a popular pick at the time. He serves out the last four years of the Castillo term and becomes a shoo-in for his own six-year term because of the pull Castillo has within the party. Young, good-looking, good speaker, and thought at the time to be very clean, with a great record as a prosecutor. Being the former president's brother-in-law didn't hurt either.

"A year into Fernandez's term, however, folks were seeing a guy who looked nothing like the ballsy, street-smart prosecutor they all thought they knew and were getting. The man just doesn't appear to be that competent, even with the simple stuff. Then comes your immigration bill, Senator, and, as Hank explained it to us, you and others from Congress and the State Department met with Fernandez and gave him a heads-up on what was coming in the way of deportations, and he still fucked it up on their side. Now everyone is seeing what looks like incompetence, but Hank's guy at the CIA sees far worse, and frankly, so do I.

"Hank's CIA source has studied every move Fernandez has made since his days as the city attorney of Hermosillo. His analysis is that the man has been owned by someone, a cartel probably, from the time he was the AG of the state of Sonora and likely earlier than that—that's, like, ten years at a minimum. The basis for his reasoning is that during the worst of the cartel violence back then, the one thing the warring factions were very good at was killing government officials, especially at the local and state levels. With our contacts in your cousin's national police, General, we know that more than five thousand local officials were murdered—or kidnapped and presumed murdered—in the northern states during the five years Fernandez spent as the AG of Sonora, and he miraculously lives through this? Not likely. This fact becomes even more suspect when you couple his tenure as state AG and his significant prosecutorial record with what we saw on our side of the border: no drop in the smuggling. After all of Fernandez's busts, our informed estimate is that the quantities of drugs coming out of Sonora actually went up, not down! Unfortunately, we didn't make this correlation until recently. What was believed at the time—and was in a way true but clouding other possible explanations—was that other cartels simply were slipping into the vacuum created by the busts and taking over the abandoned transshipment routes. This turnover made our job harder as the faces and methods changed.

"We now know it was more likely just one cartel moving in on the others, a previously unknown cartel that I now know for a fact exists, and they were likely the ones taking out the competition and using Fernandez as a front man to help them. Now, as the only evidence Hank's CIA source has that supports his professional intuition that Fernandez is dirty is that he wasn't killed during this period of increased violence, this means the bosses on the seventh floor at Langley don't buy it or support it. But Charley and I agree—the Mexican president is a cartel flunky. I then was surprised to discover Hank also believes this, and, in talking with him, it sounds like you agree too, Senator."

Senator Martinez was sitting forward in his chair, his lips pursed, his expression serious. "Yes…I guess I do, Bennie. I hadn't really thought about it much, but I met and talked with the man for several hours, and he's not what his reputation suggests. After our conversations, it's impossible for me to imagine he had the guts or wits to stay alive. To be brutally frank, he struck me as shallow and slick."

Bennie turned to Manny. "General, you're probably a very good poker player, because our collective assertion is that the president of Mexico is a cartel-connected crook, and if this astonishes you, you hide it well."

Manny slowly shook his head. "I'm not surprised, Bennie…and I'll tell you why, but please finish first. I have a number of observations, but it's best I make them known after you're done."

Bennie nodded and went on. "Because we had so many operations on our side of the border going bad, likely due to classified information being leaked, some months back Charley and our director, Ted Mills, asked me to set up a special operations unit outside all our existing intelligence and operational divisions, the purpose of which would be to try to ferret out traitors inside the DEA in the southwest. To this end, I recruited sharp people from outside the DEA to staff this special unit, and until this past week, only the director, Charley, and I knew about it. We currently have complete operational security on this project, and now you five gentlemen, plus Hank's guy at the CIA, know about it. That's nine guys; I can't stress how important it is that it remains just us nine.

"Five months ago, I put into play an operation with the goal of trying to slip agents into cartels, in a dangerous and rather unorthodox way. You don't need to know the specifics, but the plan was risky, and it worked. Not only were we able to get a man into a cartel, but it also turned out to be the one I referred to earlier as being previously unknown to us. My agent was able to make contact with me twice when he was inside, and the intelligence he's provided so far has been outstanding and actionable. General, the cartel my man is in goes by the name of its leader, El Condor de Muerte, the Condor of Death, and its leader is simply called the Condor." Bennie paused. "I see this name means something to you, General."

Manny smiled a small smile. "It does, Bennie. Obviously I'm not the poker player I thought I was. You're talking about the same guy who tried to get to my cousin Alberto and could be the one who killed Emilio. Is that right?"

"Yes, sir, same group. Ted Mills told Charley, and then he told me, about the coercion attempt on your cousin and how we helped get his family to safety up on your base. I just learned of this last Monday and was dumbstruck. General, I don't believe in coincidences. An action like the one attempted by the Condor against your cousin Alberto—the co-opting of the most senior federal police official by a heretofore previously unknown cartel leader—and then two days later the murder of your cousin Emilio, after Alberto defeated the attempted coercion, are in my opinion connected. Alberto defeated the Condor's attempt on him, and the Condor hit back. That's how I see it.

"When Charley and I talked earlier this week and he made me aware of some of the other possible connections, the old street cop in me asked, Why would a low-profile, successful operator who seems to have things going his way make such a big, dramatic play? Especially if our assumptions are correct, and he already has the president of the fucking country in his pocket? I mean, if it ain't broke, don't fix it. But then, my pal Charley here, who's always been the brains of our outfit, said something so simple, so obvious, that I was embarrassed I hadn't thought of it myself. He said, 'Maybe the Condor made this play because he was scared.' Say, of something like being discovered by the Rodriguez brothers. Maybe your cousins got too close to something, General.

"Fellas, Charley's question got me really thinking because that possibility never crossed my mind, not once. Granting the point that we can hardly rely on criminals to act logically, with this one I think we can. This Condor has earned it—by staying off our radar for so long and, if my read of the data from the last several years is correct, by waging successful, organized, systematic attacks on the other cartels. If the Condor is as smart as I think he is, there are only two possible reasons for breaking cover and making such a big play as he did against your cousins, General. Either he was looking to protect himself from something the Rodriguez brothers had discovered in their roles as head of the federal police and as the attorney general, or—and this is scary in my mind—he has a plan, and the next step is a big play leading to…what? Something more dramatic, perhaps, but certainly not to just raise his profile. That would be dumb, and this guy ain't dumb."

Colonel Romero cleared his throat before saying, "Bennie, excuse me, but maybe taking both brothers out was the big play. They're important figures in the government, and the government has been cracking down on the cartels, largely, as I understand it, because of the general's cousins."

Bennie leaned forward in his chair and shook his head. "Sorry, Colonel, I don't buy that. Think about it for a sec. This Condor could have tried to murder either of them at any time, without making contact and revealing himself or his operational prowess. He made contact with the general's cousin for a reason. It's not knowing why he did that's confusing, and frankly, it scares the bejesus out of me."

"I agree with Bennie, Romey," Manny said, looking at Colonel Romero. "The Condor had or has a greater objective, and just killing my cousins wasn't it. I also think he's right about Emilio's assassination. It was a message for sure, and if Charley here is guessing right, maybe a threat was eliminated. Go on, Bennie."

"General, let me see if I can further summarize with some kind of clarity what's a real murky, dangerous situation and pull all this shit together," Bennie said. "I think there are big things brewing down there—of an undetermined nature as of yet, but big. We have intelligence that there's a rogue cartel, led by this asshole calling himself the Condor, which our best information tells us is an evolution of a small cartel from Chihuahua run by two brothers named Vargas. Until the last twelve weeks, we didn't know much about them, and what we did know led us to believe these brothers were merely enforcers for the Mendoza brothers' cartel, which I'm assuming everyone here knows is one of the six big players in this mess, along with the Gang of Four. Have you been briefed on the Gang of Four, General?"

Manny glanced at Colonel Romero and said, "Yes, I have, Bennie, in general terms."

Bennie nodded again and went on. "OK, fine. Now, in the last week, our sources tell us the Mendozas have come up dead. That's unconfirmed at this point, but my sources are reliable. Also, it's possible even Ramon Vasso, another player from the central-northern states, might have been eliminated recently. We're hearing quite a bit of low-key chatter about his having gone missing. But the Vargas brothers and the Condor apparently are still around and very active. That makes them the number-one suspects for those possible murders. At about this same time, the Condor reaches out to your cousin down in the capital and demonstrates a lot of balls and operational sophistication, if he is indeed responsible for your cousin's assassination. All in all, that's a lot of really bad shit. The only good news is that I seem to have a man who somehow has gotten close to these people, confirming their existence and some of their actions." Bennie paused and glanced around the group letting what he said sink in before going on.

"I've spent the last couple of days going back through eight years' worth of operational reports and the little intelligence that the Mexican government has shared with us, and I think what we have here is a careful, smart, well-organized cartel leader who's managed to keep an extremely low profile all that time. I also believe he's been systematically targeting other cartels in the central-northern states: Sonora, Chihuahua, and Nuevo Leon, for sure—for at least eight years, maybe longer. Couple all this with the fact that President Fernandez made his bones in Sonora, and I make the Condor suspect number one as being the guy pulling the president's strings.

"Fernandez, for his part, fucks up his country's response to our deportations, and a mess ensues that finally requires a large movement of their army, the one force that's been the most effective against their criminal insurgency, away from the hot spots where they were bivouacked up to the refugee camps in the north. A giant diversion of the army, gentlemen, in the CIA's and my opinion, with horrific human consequences—all seemingly controlled by the Condor, if my guesses are right. This makes the Condor—if you'll pardon my vulgarity, General—one dangerous motherfucker. Now the problem, and the reason Hank got us together..." Bennie again looked slowly from man to man. "My agent has been inside twelve weeks now, but I haven't heard from him in the last eight."

Bennie stopped and raised his hands as the general and Colonel Romero leaned forward in their chairs to interrupt.

"Now before you jump in and say anything, guys, let me finish," Bennie went on. "In his first contact report with me, in addition to detailing his infiltration and confirming the Condor's existence, my agent said the Condor has an entourage that travels with him, and that includes personnel who monitor all forms of communications anywhere around him. Trojan, the code name for my operative, said communicating would be difficult at best because of this—another indication of the sophistication of the man we're dealing with here. My agent managed another contact a couple of weeks later in which he was able to confirm that the Condor, when he's in the northern states, moves around between three estates, each located outside one of the state capitals. From his detailed descriptions of the estates and their relative locations to the capitals, I think I've identified the areas where they're located. We also know the Condor spends about half or two-thirds of his time elsewhere—where, we have no clue, but when he bugs out to points unknown, we know he's using a very slick Italian-made twin turboprop to move him around, a Piaggio 180 Avanti, to be exact."

"Bennie, excuse me, but I have to ask..." Colonel Romero interjected with a glance at his general. "Is there anything special about this aircraft?"

Bennie paused, curiosity showing on his face. "Well, yeah, it looks different, for starters. The props face backward, and it has little wings on its nose. Oh, and it's apparently the fastest turboprop made. That the kind of stuff you're asking about?"

"Yes, exactly," Colonel Romero said with another quick glance to Manny.

"What gives, Colonel? Why do you want to know this?" Bennie asked, leaning forward while glancing from the colonel to the general, sensing they weren't telling him something.

The colonel looked at Manny, who responded, "Before we answer that, the obvious question is why you believe your man is alive. If I understand what you just told us, in addition to the possibility of your agent having been discovered and killed after his second communication with you, the Condor has been taking out his competition, presumably in armed actions. Isn't it possible—even likely, given your agent's newness to the cartel—that he was a foot soldier, a new enforcer, to use your nomenclature, and got killed in some action? In battle, it's always the common soldier who's at greatest risk. Why do you believe he's still alive?"

Bennie's look became very serious again. "General, when we sat down together this afternoon, what went unsaid is that all of us here just flat have to trust each other. This, in my view, not only means with the sensitive information we all possess but also with each other's areas of expertise and with each other's instincts. General, you'd have to know my guy like I know my guy. He's the best, and by that I mean he's got smarts and guts. That being said, because of circumstances I can't begin to fathom, he's somehow fallen into a situation where I think he has to use an abundance of caution to keep from revealing himself because to do so would mean risking his life. What I'm saying is that when he feels he can contact me without compromising his life, he will. You just have to go with my gut on this one."

Manny nodded. "Well, Bennie, I'm no stranger to gut calls—we go with your instincts—but that begs the question, what in the hell do we do now?"

"General, from my perspective," Bennie said, "finding a way to get in touch with my agent and getting him the hell out of Dodge is task one. Assuming he's alive—and like I said, I believe he is, given the excellent actionable intelligence he provided after four weeks inside—my guess is he has plenty to tell me, so I need to find him and make contact with him."

"You're not suggesting," Colonel Romero said, "that you or someone who works for you is going to go down there and nose around these estates covertly somehow and try to make contact? I certainly don't know your business, but I do know infiltration and recon operations, and that doesn't sound like a wise tactic."

"General, Colonel, if I may," Charley spoke up. He turned and looked at Romero. "No, Colonel, that would indeed be a careless way to proceed, for all the obvious reasons. From the data we have so far, the Condor is far too careful not to be aware of his immediate surroundings and anyone who should enter them. I suspect he has a well-schooled, loyal group of enforcers. How else can we explain the position he seems to have attained as one of the big six, now that the Mendozas are dead, yet go unknown for all these years? The fact that Bennie's agent seems to have gained acceptance is a remarkable achievement, considering the Condor's caution. I would add that I agree with Bennie's gut feeling on the current status of our operative. He was alive and accepted for at least the first four weeks leading up to his second report. I think he still is, and he's being careful for the obvious reasons Bennie has articulated. But we also don't necessarily have to go with Bennie's gut feeling on his agent's situation either and patiently wait for him to call—although I need to add that I've trusted Bennie's gut feelings for more than thirty years, and I don't remember a time in the field when he's been wrong."

Charley looked at his old friend, smiled, and then returned his gaze to Manny. "General, what we came for here today, in addition to sharing information, is to solicit your help as commander of the Army Border Corps in a DEA reconnaissance mission we'd like to mount. We have a classified plan for finding and contacting our agent, but we don't have all the assets we require, and you happen to have what we need."

Charley wore a slight smile on his face. As he looked at Manny, awaiting a response, he and everyone else saw the general's expression go from his normal, interested look to a knowing smile. "What do you and Bennie have in mind, Charley?"

"Your Predators, General. We'd like to borrow some of them and have them nail down the exact estates in the areas Bennie has determined the

Condor operates out of and then watch them and see if we can spot our man."

Manny's smile disappeared, and he took on what Colonel Romero thought of as his "general look." "Well, to use the poker metaphor again, Charley, I call," he said. "There has to be more to it than that. That's not that wild a request."

Charley glanced at Bennie and then answered for the two of them. "The thing is, General, we'd like to keep this just between us."

Manny, who'd been leaning slightly forward in his chair, sat back, realization slowly dawning on his face. He folded his hands together and rested them in his lap. "I think I understand. You want me to order a military penetration of Mexican airspace—technically an act of war, incidentally—and not discuss it with the Mexican government or my superior headquarters. Is that it?"

Charley nodded. "Yes, sir, it is, only I think I've come up with a way to do this and keep you out of trouble if the shit should hit the fan, as my great friend and colleague here would say." He reached over and gently grabbed Bennie's shoulder.

"Well, I'm all ears," Manny said. "How do you propose to keep me out of Leavenworth? That's what we're talking about if I agreed and this came out, you know."

"I realize that, General, which is why I came up with this idea. Your cousin Alberto, while not the president, is a responsible senior government official down there, the head of the federal police, for Christ's sake. What if we got you to ask him…to ask us…to help him with a very sensitive joint interdiction effort that required certain assets that could be temporarily placed under DEA control?"

"General," Bennie interrupted, "when I visited you a couple of months back, and you showed me your recon stuff, you explained how the shift commanders planned all the flight plans and the surveillance take. What Charley and I are suggesting, sir, is that you do nothing more than assign one of these units, preferably the one with the most junior commander, to us and tell him he's to take his orders from me. Then I'll make the calls on the flight plans. Your guy will just be following his orders, and I'll be the one who'll be ordering your assets into Mexican airspace—only I'll be doing it in a joint exercise and with the invitation of the Mexican federal police, if your cousin plays ball with us. If we're found out, and this thing goes tits up, well, Charley and I will get wrist slaps from our director for not being more forthcoming with our activities or some such shit. If ever I had to go before a congressional committee and testify regarding my actions, I'd simply stand by the necessity to maintain security in an environment rife with traitors. Plus, I'd bet your cousin would graciously send up testimony on my behalf. I won't get in much trouble, General…if this ever sees the light of day, that is."

Manny looked at Colonel Romero. "Romey, what do you think?"

Colonel Romero slowly shook his head. "Hell, General, this thing goes tits up, I think anyone investigating would see right through it. Who'd believe that you and your cousin didn't discuss it? Having said that, it could work. The Predators are hard to see, and no one's going to know they're there anyway. Worst case…one suffers a mechanical, and it crashes. They have self-destructs onboard, so there wouldn't be much left but little pieces. We could explain a self-destruct over Mexican airspace…bad navigation chip, whatever. All things considered, sir, I say let's help these guys."

"Jeff?"

The hulking sergeant major had barely said a word all afternoon. He removed the cigar he'd been slowly smoking during the conversation and said curtly, "I say do what you generals do best, sir—fucking delegate this. Order me to hold the DEA's hand, and render whatever assistance we can offer. I'll tell the eggheads controlling the toys what to do. They believe I speak for you, so no pissant captain or major will question any order I give. And as you personally know, General, I've never had a problem with pissant young captains, sir, not even hot-shit hero types. If the shit hits the fan, I'll tell folks I let these smooth-talking, paper-pushing sons of bitches from Washington talk me into it. Ain't no one going to fucking Leavenworth, sir. Like I told you before, I got my thirty in, and I know where the fucking bodies are buried."

Manny turned to Senator Martinez. "Well, Pete, you seem to have a few boys sitting on your patio, drinking your watered-down booze, and talking about committing a technical act of war against a sovereign nation. How do you feel about that?"

Hank jumped in before Pete could. "General, I'm sorry. The senator isn't here. Something I can help you with?"

Manny was nodding at the obvious play, but the senator spoke up. "No, Hank, not like that." The senator slowly looked at each man in the group, his gaze stopping on his old West Point roommate, and then he went on. "I'm no beltway insider, fellas, at least not yet. I realize most citizens think members of Congress are self-important windbags, but some are patriots, and I'd like to think I'm one of them. If we do this, I'm in. If we're discovered and I'm asked, I'll tell the truth." The senator turned and looked directly at Sergeant Major Green. "Sergeant Major, I could never look myself in the mirror again if I let you take the fall for something I knew about and could stop if I wanted to…but I *don't want* to stop it."

Senator Martinez shifted his look back to Manny. "Manny, I think the president of Mexico is a cartel-connected criminal, and their country is quickly going to hell. According to these guys here, we have an opportunity to access an intelligence source that not only could provide us excellent information regarding the drug trafficking into our country but also perhaps shed light on corruption at the highest levels in Mexico. If the head of the federal police asks our DEA for help, I think we should render it."

Manny nodded to Pete, as if to say, "You are a patriot, and I expected no less," then turned to the others and slowly leaned forward. "Men, I spent a couple of tough days this week in Mexico burying my cousin…a brother, really. While I was down there, Alberto told me a lot about the problems he's facing and what he and Emilio were trying to do about it. Talk about not being able to look yourself in the mirror. Alberto has twice the guts I'll ever have. Bennie, I don't know if this is corroborating intel regarding your speculations, but Alberto told me Wednesday night that Emilio was close to making a corruption case against President Fernandez. He also confirmed, from sensitive intelligence sources he controls, that there does indeed exist a low-profile but powerful cartel run by this Condor and that it's systematically eliminating other cartels and gangs in the north-central states. His sources have recovered the remains of the Mendozas, Bennie, and also have eyewitnesses to their murders. So your speculation is speculation no more. Alberto already has asked me for help, and I intend to provide it, so I'm now officially passing on his request for assistance. Now, what the hell are we going to do about this?"

Bennie smiled. "Thanks, General. It's good to know some of my guesses weren't full of shit. To start, I'd like to come down to Bliss as soon as you'll let me."

"How about after supper, Bennie? The air jockeys are real nice to me and gave me my own G-III for the day. Want a ride?"

"Sure thing, General, and thanks. I have a bag in the car."

"Good. That's settled." Manny slowly looked at each of the men around him. "Three more items, gentlemen, also not for dissemination. I have it on good authority that sometime in the next several weeks, there's going to be a gathering of this Gang of Four. The responsible authorities in Mexico are aware of this and are planning a rude crashing of that event. If the information about this meeting is correct, Alberto and his federal police may be in a position to reduce the number of major cartels from six to two."

"Jesus, General," Bennie exclaimed, "how reliable does your cousin believe this information is?"

"I never said I got this from Alberto," Manny responded, but he was smiling. "My intelligence source said they've previously used this snitch, and the information is reliable. Second—again to be kept between us, as Alberto's life is riding on our honors here—Emilio told Alberto the night before he was killed that he was close to identifying the Condor."

"Hot damn, General. I knew it!" Bennie exclaimed. "Who is—"

"Hold on, Bennie. Hold on," Manny interrupted. "Alberto doesn't know who he is yet. But he has all of Emilio's records that led him to wherever he was headed. He asked me to help him, and maybe together we can find out who this prick is. Romey has looked over the data and figured out a few things that may be what got Emilio all excited. I'll keep you fellows posted on our analysis, but I'll confirm this: a big part of the trail involves an aircraft of unusual flight characteristics. I think we have flight plans for the aircraft, Bennie, that your man says the Condor uses. And with Alberto's input, these flight plans may lead us to a short list of suspects. Other than that, I don't know anything else.

"Lastly, Bennie, Alberto told me about a joint operation he was running with you guys a couple of months ago against the now-dead Mendoza brothers that went bad. I can't tell you how Alberto knows this, but he knows for certain that the Mendozas—which probably really means the Condor—were tipped off regarding the raid from our side, specifically your El Paso headquarters. If I can get you more information on this, I will, but that's all I know for now. What I'm saying is this all fits with your scenario."

Bennie smiled and nodded at Charley, who subtly tipped his glass in salute.

"In the meantime," Manny told Bennie, "let's get your ass to El Paso and crank up a few of my birds tomorrow and find your man."

Everyone broke into smiles at the pact they'd made with one another. Manny turned to the senator. "Pete, what the hell does a guy have to do to get some decent food and some of the good booze around this joint?"

Pete smiled broadly. "Like I told you at the Point, roomie, if you need something, just ask, asshole, just ask," the distinguished gentleman from Arizona replied.

25

La Casa Rosada
Lomas de Chapultepec, Mexico City
Sunday morning

Day eighty-eight in the cartel—today was the day; Ray was sure of it. Today Miguel had the duty of babysitting Roberto Nieves's family and his bomb-making brother. Roberto was now in the Hermosillo area under Eduardo's control. Sunday was typically everyone's day off, and what activity there was at the estate centered on family and church. Raul had told Ray last night there was nothing on the schedule that required him to be up early, so they could sleep in. Luis did, but after tossing and turning all night, Ray was fully awake at five; the president of the country and the only honest man he knew who might be able help him would be killed tomorrow unless he could find a way to stop it, and there was no sleeping with that thought in his head. He lay in bed until seven, trying to see a way through the next twenty-four hours, but he still couldn't figure out a way to save the president, Alberto, and himself. In every scenario he thought of, at least one of them would die.

Frustrated and increasingly upset, Ray got up, dressed, and walked up to the mansion. He entered the kitchen to find two of the on-site capital policemen having coffee with the one of the chef's assistants, who apparently had drawn the short straw and had kitchen duty on a Sunday. There was a staff dining area off the kitchen, where two of the younger maids were sitting, one reading the morning paper and the other doing her nails. Even the ever-present Geraldo and Lorenzo weren't to be found, their duties having been taken by the two other men who worked for them in the communications office.

Waiting around for Alberto to discover the note and do something was killing Ray, and he was growing increasingly worried about possible unintended consequences as a result of his desperate play last night. How Alberto responded—the actions he took—might well end up exposing Ray as a traitor, which inevitably would lead to his death, but he also knew he was right to have tried. There was a small gym on the first floor that he'd been told he could use whenever Alvarez or Salena wasn't using it. At seven on a Sunday morning, he had it to himself. He lifted some weights to burn off some tension, staying away from the more sophisticated apparatus so as to avoid any appearance that he'd seen such equipment before, much less knew how to use it. After working out, he returned to his casita, showered, and changed into the more casual clothes the detail wore around the northern estates.

Alvarez, Salena, and their children went to mass, escorted by four capital policemen in two chase cars. When they returned, Raul, at Alvarez's direction, invited Ray to have lunch with the family, so he met the Alvarez children for the first time. Meeting them disturbed him further. Seeing Alvarez's wife laughing and watching as the children splashed in the pool made him think of Alvarez as a husband and father, which only confused things more. He got to thinking about the kids and how radically their lives would change when it became known their father was one of the biggest drug traffickers in the country and an assassin. Even worse was the thought of the impact on their innocent lives if Ray had to kill their father to save himself—a real possibility. He had to get out of there.

He excused himself as soon as he thought he could and not draw undue attention from anyone. As he walked back to his casita, thinking about everything but mostly about Alvarez, he realized that if he were truly honest with himself, there was much he admired about him. The parts of his plans he was aware of would go a long way toward cleaning up Mexico. If not for the planned assassinations, there was no denying that Alvarez was very different from the typical cartel thug. The man had a conscience, and Ray sensed good in him. That was what troubled him the most. Alvarez's motives were such that Ray actually respected and admired him for them, and that was a place he didn't want to go, not with what was planned.

An hour after he returned to his casita with his confusing and desperate thoughts, the phone rang, and Raul asked him to come back up to the mansion and meet him in Alvarez's study. When Ray got there, Raul was alone, sitting at Alvarez's large antique desk, going through some official-looking papers. He looked up as Ray walked in. "Ah, Ray, have a seat. I must accompany Jefe into the city to help him continue the transition of his office to Alberto. Before I go, though, I wanted to know how you were feeling."

Ray was stumped and instantly nervous. *Why that question now?* he wondered.

"I'm fine, Raul."

"Come, Ray. You seemed upset at lunch. What is it?"

Jesus Christ, he's intuitive! Think—keep it simple. He paused for only a second, knowing any delay would make the wise, intelligent Raul more curious than he already was.

"I'm sorry, Raul, if my actions have caused you any concern. I know you have a lot to deal with. I was thinking about tonight with Luis and also thinking about what you told me about him. I hope I don't let you down. That was what was bothering me."

Raul smiled, tossed the papers he'd been looking at onto the desk, stood, and came around to him. "I suspected that's what it was."

He took Ray by the shoulder, as he often did when showing friendship, and gently squeezed it. "After everything you've done—your courage, your anticipation—how can you doubt yourself? Trust me when I say you'll do fine. Luis is no match for you in any way. Just remember the plan and sit on the family until noon tomorrow, and all this will be behind us. One change for tomorrow: I'll come out and get you, and we'll have Luis escort the bomb maker back to Eduardo in Hermosillo alone. He can then pick up Roberto, return him here, and reunite him with his family. I want you nearby tomorrow, and I know Jefe feels the same. It'll be an historic day, and you've earned the right to be a part of it. I have to leave and go into the city with Jefe, but we'll return by six to take you and Luis to Toluca and pick up Miguel. Get some rest while I'm gone—it's liable to be a long night."

Ray was relieved; Bennie's axiom to keep your undercover persona close to your own had again served him well and covered his obvious loss of concentration and control at lunch. He wondered what it was Raul had seen that had betrayed him, but he wasn't going to dwell on it, as he'd managed to get away with it. Raul started to turn to lead them out of the study, but Ray stopped him. "Excuse me, Raul, but Jefe spoke to me about a book—*The Republic,* I think it's called. He told me a man he admires wrote it a long time ago, and if I was ever to understand him, I needed to understand what this man wrote. He said he had a copy here in the library, and someday, after some help with my education, I would enjoy reading it. I wondered if I could look at it now."

Raul smiled. "Of course, Ray. Plato's work is here somewhere; Jefe looks at it all the time. But I should tell you, El Cuchillo, no one, except possibly Pablo, really enjoys reading Plato."

Raul squeezed his shoulder affectionately again, shook his head, and chuckled at the thought of Ray sitting around trying to read a work by the great philosopher, then turned and walked out. Ray watched Raul until he turned the corner, heading for the motorcade out front. With everything else he had weighing down on him, another thought had come while he was at the casita, trying to sort through this whole chaotic mess. It was clear that Raul was deeply conflicted about the planned killing of Alberto Rodriguez. Ray could see it in him as easily as Raul had seen through him at lunch. Despite his high and important position in the cartel, Raul wasn't a killer. From everything he had observed in the north, Ray knew that while Raul had organized and ordered actions against their enemies in other cartels that surely had resulted in many deaths, he never personally had killed anyone, just as Ray hadn't killed anyone until Guzman. Ray found himself wanting to save Alberto even more, if only to save Raul from himself.

He shook off the chill that came over him at the thought of the small, sophisticated explosive in the trunk of Alberto's car and perused the well-organized book-filled shelves of Alvarez's private library. After a few minutes, he found a copy of *The Republic* in a section devoted to books on philosophy, but it appeared untouched, with not a mark or frayed page, as if the volume never had been read. As he walked by Alvarez's credenza, with the intent of returning to his casita to read in private, to his surprise he noticed an older copy on the corner. He picked it up and carefully flipped through it. He knew immediately this had to be Alvarez's personal copy, as the pages were worn, some dog-eared, and, in what would have been blasphemy to any librarian, there were personal notations in the margins throughout the volume, clearly written by Alvarez.

He'd been giving a great deal of thought to the private conversations he'd shared with Alvarez. It struck him that Alvarez, at his core, was in many ways as pious as his mother had seemed in the short time Ray had spent with her at their recent dinner in Baja. Clearly the schism created twelve years ago by the revelation of his father's hidden criminal life, when compared to the life of privilege and responsibility he had known for thirty years, had torn him in two emotionally.

Without thinking, Ray sat down in one of the side chairs in front of Alvarez's desk and spent the next hour reading through the pages of Plato's seminal work. He had taken two philosophy classes in college. The first he chose to take for good reasons; it dealt with ethics, and he thought an aspiring police officer would benefit from such a discourse. The second class, on the roots of existentialism, he took only because of an incredibly beautiful girl and philosophy major he'd met and started to get to know in his first philosophy class. Being nineteen, he thought his chances of getting laid would be enhanced if he had another class with her, which turned out to be an interesting but failed personal philosophy, he thought later. In the short time he spent with her, she was always talking about Nietzsche and Heidegger and the meaning of "being" and spouting other existential bullshit, none of which Ray understood. In the end, he lost interest in her, thinking that getting next to her wasn't worth having to listen to the crap that the professor kept droning on about in the class and that she repeated when they were alone. He figured any philosopher dumb enough to support national socialism and Hitler in Germany in the 1930s and '40s had little to say that he'd be interested in, so he dropped the girl and the class after a month.

Ray didn't have to read much to get a better understanding of Alvarez, however, nor did he have to read any of what Plato had written. For the hour he sat in Alvarez's study, he did nothing but read and reread the notations and questions raised by a young Alvarez in some instances, and, later on, clearly after Alvarez's father's revelations, notes by a more dark and questioning Alvarez that had been written in the margins. Even the handwriting had changed over the years. The young man had written in pencil—politely, it seemed to Ray, as if recognizing that writing in the great philosopher's book was somehow an intrusion. His notes were small, clearly printed questions—a scholar probing intellectually. The older Alvarez had used a pen at times, expressing thoughts of a more permanent nature, and the questions were far more personal, with more references to God as well as philosophy. Ray was struck by several themes that appeared throughout the book more than once, in several different forms, but always asking the same questions:

If my goals are virtuous, am I?

Can the cardinal virtues of wisdom, courage, moderation, and justice truly exist in the world in which I live with the evil I face? Does believing I hold them in my being actually make me unvirtuous and vain?

How does good overcome evil without becoming evil in kind?

If, in the search for justice, I must hurt some to save many others, am I nothing more than a tyrant?

If one seeks justice and honor over wealth and injustice, is his path righteous, no matter the cost?

If I'm truly honorable, can I then be a true philosopher king? Is it hubris to think such a person can truly exist?

Where does the philosopher king end and the tyrant begin?

In avenging my father and doing what I must against these evil men, am I to be saved by Exodus—an eye for an eye—or am I to be condemned by Leviticus for not resisting the evil?

Can equitable retaliation exist in a just, moral world?

Ray thought he'd discovered what must have been the most recent scribbling in the margins, for these thoughts were clearly penned after the unsuccessful attempt against his life and seemed to reveal his most-guarded inner doubts about his plans.

If I eliminate the others and stop the insanity, does that justify what I've done and what I'm doing?

Even if the outcome is good and my intentions just, have my methods lost me my immortal soul?

Will sacrificing my life in the pursuit of a greater good be enough? What of my immortal soul? Is redemption even possible?

Is Kierkegaard right? Is it my responsibility to understand myself, to understand what God truly wishes me to do? Is it to find my truth, to find the one idea for which I can live and die? Is my truth on this path?

A stranger arrived and protected me where no other could. How can this be if not by your hand? This stranger also saved those I love most dearly. How can these disparate occurrences be chance?

Knowing everything I've done, you allowed me to live. Why, if not to do your will?

The people cry out for your help against the evil, and I answer for them. Am I your instrument? Are my choices my own or by your divine guidance? How am I to know?

Why have you not struck me down if I'm not doing your will?

Are my actions free will? Am I to be granted your redemption by grace?

What is your plan for me? Tell me! Show me! Am I doing your will?

Ray slowly sat back in his chair as he read the last few anguished scribbles. There was much more, but he'd read enough. He knew he was a reasonably intelligent cop. He had no illusions about having all the answers; so many of the great philosophical arguments were lost on him. What he did know—what his father had tried to instill in him as he had grown up, the son of a cop—was that you had to understand simple right and wrong. Without that, real decency didn't exist. Life wasn't always black and white, his father had further warned. There would be gray areas, and when faced with them, he would have to trust in his wisdom and intuition to show him what was right and what was wrong. The last thing his father had told him when they were discussing this was that he had no doubts about him. But Ray was now facing the black and white his father had warned him of, and the gray emotional fog he found himself immersed in made him doubt himself.

He thought about the deep anguish evident in Alvarez's writing and what Alvarez had told him about his father, and then he thought of his own father. *What would I have done if Dad had revealed the same thing to me? Would I have turned him in? Probably not...shit. Thank God I haven't been given that choice. What does that make me if I really don't know? Am I any different from Alvarez? Any better? If someone killed Dad, and I found him, would I bring him to justice or kill him myself, as Alvarez did? How often after a shift with my friends have we bullshitted over beers about how we'd kill the fuckers ourselves? Save the taxpayers the expense of a trial. How many times have I said that in my life? Was that the beers talking, or would I have done it? Maybe in the end, the only difference between Alvarez and me is that I'll never have to find out. Is he insane? If not, what is he? Good? Just? Maybe he is, deep down, but only someone insane would think he could be a philosopher king, and good men don't kill their country's president. But what if the president is bad? I mean a real criminal and not just a cartel flunky trying to save his neck. Can such vigilantism be justified? What was the American Revolution if not the act of vigilantes? Is the only difference that we made our intentions known? Can the difference be that simple? God, this is confusing, I hope I'm doing the right thing.*

Before this mission, Ray had thought he knew right from wrong, but now he was unsure what right really was. Helping the deeply conflicted, compromised Alvarez would accomplish a lot of good—he was sure of it. What would happen if he exposed him or, worse, killed him? He honestly didn't know, and that was the problem eating at him. For sure the planned raid against the other big cartels wouldn't come off, and he knew that was an opportunity that shouldn't be missed. No doubt the other established cartels would expand—something Alvarez as the Condor had been preventing them from doing. A big part of him told him to help Alvarez and Raul until they could kill off a bunch of the really nasty bastards, but that required time—time he didn't have. A president whose character and innocence he was unsure of would be dead, and probably all the others traveling with him. And so too would be the clearly good Alberto Rodriguez, who was maybe the best hope Mexico had, given what Ray had overheard old President Castillo saying. He'd forgotten almost everything he'd learned in the two philosophy classes he had signed up for in college, but one poignant thought came to him from Nietzsche: *He who fights with monsters should look to it that he himself doesn't become a monster. And when you gaze long into an abyss, the abyss also gazes into you.*

Ray was beginning to realize how deadly true that quotation was, for he was in such an abyss and felt it boring holes through him, yet he couldn't see a way out of his situation. Despite his best intentions, the enveloping darkness and resulting desperation were closing in on him. He returned to his casita and avoided Luis, instead spending time on his bed in the privacy of his room, again staring up at the ceiling and his one constant companion as it slowly and rhythmically went around and around and around.

Raul and Alvarez returned by six, as planned, and he and Luis were waiting for Raul at the front door of the mansion. None of his conflicting, deeply troubling thoughts had been resolved, and his tension and anxiety were as high as ever. His head was pounding, and with each passing day, he had been experiencing more frequent and increasingly worse headaches. The current pain was no doubt a result of what he knew was coming, as well as his required part in the plot. But there was more; as far as he could tell, Alberto Rodriguez hadn't taken any action on the note. Either aspect of his situation would be enough to send him into a tailspin, but together, they were almost unbearable.

Alvarez was deeply preoccupied, it appeared, and simply nodded to Raul, Luis, and Ray as he passed them and went inside. Raul didn't go in; instead, he silently motioned to Luis and Ray to follow and then led them around the end of the mansion to the car park. They climbed into the sedan Raul preferred and set out for Toluca. Luis shared the front seat with Raul, and Ray sat in the back; oddly, very little was said on the forty-five-minute drive. The long periods of silence were all the evidence Ray needed to surmise that the significant events about to take place were weighing on everyone, even the surly and dangerous Luis. As they pulled up to the small farm house, Miguel was on the covered front porch, sitting in an old chair that was entirely too small for him smoking a cigar. He stood as they parked and came off the porch.

Luis started to open his door, but Raul stopped him, fixed him with a hard, serious expression, and said, "Keep the family safe, Luis, and the bomb maker contained. I'll be back around noon tomorrow. You and Miguel will then take him to Eduardo. Ray and I will return the family to their home. Any questions?"

Luis shook his head and got out. Ray started to open his door, but Raul turned in his seat and stopped him too, taking his arm but saying nothing until Luis was near the house. Raul's look was still serious as he said quietly, "Watch him closely, Ray. Among Luis's many flaws, he has a…thing for young women. It's disgusting, and I don't want the mother or her daughters harmed any more than they already have been. Also, it's very important to my plans that the brother is returned to Hermosillo. Eduardo doesn't yet know this, but when I come get you tomorrow, Miguel will be carrying new instructions for him. Despite my best efforts, any decent investigation of tomorrow's event will reveal the president's accident was deliberate. It's important that we lay a trail that leads to Raphael Nieves as the bomber and the Gang of Four, and I've devised such a path. Once Eduardo learns of it, he'll see the necessity also and keep him alive until we can use him. Understand?"

The investigator in Ray understood perfectly, and, given the growing respect he had for Raul's intelligence, he should have guessed Raul would have planned a diversion such as this.

"Of, course, Raul. I'll do as you wish."

Raul patted him on his arm. "Trust your instincts, Ray, and you'll do fine. See you tomorrow."

Ray got out as Miguel waited for him; they nodded to each other then Miguel got in with Raul, and they drove off. As he watched them, Ray thought about Raul's casual comment to him, not knowing at that moment where his instincts would in fact lead him. All he could do was shake his head at that disturbing reality. He looked around, wondering where the big black SUV Miguel had driven out here from the estate was, and decided it must be out of sight in back. Luis had gone inside, so he quickly went in as well, thinking about Raul's warnings about the man.

Luis had made himself comfortable on the couch in the living room and found a TV station showing a Mexican football game, his favorite pastime. Ray went to the smaller of the two bedrooms and looked in; Raphael Nieves was lying on the bed, stripped of his clothes, his left wrist handcuffed to the metal frame, the look he gave Ray a mixture of hatred and fear. Ray closed the door and went to the larger bedroom, where Roberto's wife and daughters were being held. He partially opened the door and peeked in. The mother and all three girls were on the bed, clutching one another, terrified looks on their faces.

Ray instantly felt awful and stepped fully into the room. "Is there anything you or your daughters need, Señora Nieves? Food or something to drink?" he asked softly, kindly.

The mother shook her head as the girls all seemed to squeeze in closer to her, their terrified gazes becoming worse as he stepped closer.

"I'll bring you something anyway. Then I'll check back every couple of hours. Just knock on the door if you need to use the bathroom."

The youngest girl—she couldn't have been more than nine or ten—said in a weak voice, "I want to go home. I want my papa."

Ray tried to keep his face impassive but kind. "You'll see your papa tomorrow," he said. "I promise." Then he got out of the room as quickly as possible.

Luis was paying him no attention; he merely glanced at him for a second as Ray went to the kitchen and looked for some food and something to drink that he could take to the family. The best he could come up with was half a bag of what passed for potato chips down here, a jar of a spicy cheese spread, and some bottled water. He took the items into the family's bedroom, set them on the nightstand, and left without saying a word.

He returned to the kitchen and sat down at the rough wooden dining table; time was running out. He wasn't sure exactly when President Fernandez would get to Hermosillo tomorrow, but from what he'd overheard during the meeting between Alvarez and Alberto, it would be about 11:00 a.m. Raul wouldn't take action against Alberto until sometime after that, he reasoned. Everything seemed to come down to his note and what Alberto might do with it. The ball was in Alberto's court, and only he could take the necessary action to save the president and himself and still allow Ray to keep his identity secret from Raul and Alvarez. Surely Alberto would cancel the president's trip, which was the key event that had to take place. Once Alberto acted, Ray would improvise on his evolving plan from there. His next step would be to somehow slip away from Alvarez and Raul and get to Alberto and reveal himself as the source of the note. That would be tricky, especially once Alvarez and Raul became aware he was missing. He didn't even know where Alberto lived, which likely meant he had to get to the Zocalo and Alberto's office.

There were still so many unknowns, even if Alberto did cancel the president's flight. Alvarez and Raul were nothing short of brilliant, as far as Ray was concerned; they'd certainly start looking for answers as to why the flight was canceled. Alberto was no doubt a cautious and clever man but it was likely Alvarez and Raul had their own operatives in Alberto's sphere that might catch wind about some information coming into Alberto's hands warning him of the assassination attempt. That would lead to nothing but trouble and danger because a logical possibility for them to investigate would be a leak from within the conspiracy. How long would it take Raul to eliminate the possibilities and figure out Ray was likely the traitor in their very small group?

Raul would be devastated to find out he was a traitor to their circle and an undercover agent to boot—of that Ray was certain. Since arriving in Mexico City three days ago, he had felt the friendship between them growing. Despite his best efforts, Ray's undercover persona was merging with his true identity. He couldn't help it; the building pressures were just too great on him. The lines between black and white were blurring further, the gray area his dad had said he would have to navigate becoming harder and harder to see through. He knew it was foolish and naïve to think this situation wasn't going to turn out very badly for one of them. Raul would take no pleasure in killing Ray—in fact, he knew Raul would dread it—but he would do what he had to do to protect Alvarez; they were just too close, and Alvarez's life dream was in sight. Could he get to safety before Raul got to him? He had serious doubts about that.

Earlier, Raul and Alvarez had looked normal, Ray thought—or as normal as they could look, given that they were perpetrating a coup d'état—when they'd returned from today's meeting with Alberto. Clearly if Alberto had found the note, he was being careful with his actions; that was to be expected. But why on earth didn't he cancel the president's flight? Why hadn't there been some kind of action today—something, anything? There was no way Alberto could have missed the note, no way.

26

Department of Public Security
The Zocalo, Mexico City
Monday morning

Point of fact, unknown to Ray, that was exactly what had happened. Whether it was the champagne, the events of the last week, or the revelation that his friend Alvarez was resigning, Alberto was so distracted and unfocused after leaving the party at the Alvarez mansion that he hadn't noticed the message. But Alejandro, his longtime personal servant and valet, had.

When Alberto returned home Saturday night, as he undressed, he was casually aware that the waiter's accident most likely had splashed champagne and even crystal fragments onto his suit, so he tossed it onto a chair in the corner of his bedroom, an indication to Alejandro that he needed it to be laundered. For most domestic servants, especially long-tenured ones such as Alejandro, who had served Alberto's father before serving him, Sunday was a day off. So the suit and Ray's ominous message had lain on the chair until this morning.

After Alberto dressed and left his estate in Colonia Polanco Chapultepec for his office off the Zocalo, Alejandro entered his employer's bedroom and, seeing the suit, picked it up to tend to the cleaning. As was his practice, he went through the pockets to make sure Alberto hadn't misplaced or forgotten anything important. He found the peculiar object, coins wrapped in paper, and noticed it was specifically intended for his employer. *Such an odd thing*, he thought. It was clear to Alejandro that the paper wrapping the coins hadn't been removed or tampered with in any way because the careful tape job was still intact. At first, he set the package on Alberto's nightstand next to his bed, thinking to leave it for him to discover. After turning over the suit to one of his assistants to take care of, however, he went back to the bedroom, sat down, and examined the package carefully for a long time. The oddity of the object unsettled him to the point that he decided, however silly it may end up appearing, to take it to his employer.

When Alejandro had first been retained by Alberto's father as a valet, despite being raised in a protected, affluent environment where domestic servants were the norm, the young Alberto was always respectful and courteous to him. After Alberto's father died, Alberto was even more considerate as his employer, and, as a result, Alejandro's personal feelings for Alberto ran deep. He pocketed the strange object and went downstairs to the servants' locker room off the kitchen. He told the housekeeper he had personal business to attend to, slipped into his formal coat and hat, took the car in the car park reserved for the use of the senior staff, and drove to El Centro. After arriving, he parked in a reserved visitor's space in the garage, took the public elevator to the main lobby, and identified himself to the security officers at the desk. After a telephone call to the director's office, Alejandro was met by an administrative assistant who came down to the lobby, and, along with a young capital guard, he was escorted to Alberto's fifth-floor office and shown right in.

Alberto was alerted to his valet's presence by his senior administrative assistant and was immediately curious. In the entire time Alejandro had worked for him, Alberto couldn't recall one instance when he had come to the office without being summoned. He was at his desk, looking over his prepared remarks for the noon press conference announcing him as the new secretary for public security, when Alejandro was shown in. He immediately stopped what he was doing, thanked the escorts, asked to be left in private, and gave his valet his full attention.

"Alejandro, this is unexpected. Is something wrong?" Alberto asked in a kind voice.

Alejandro cleared his throat and in his rich baritone said, "I'm sorry to disturb you, señor, but I found this object in your suit coat as I was preparing to send it out and thought it might be important. I felt uncomfortable, given its uniqueness, to leave it in your room."

Alejandro handed the wrapped coins to Alberto and then stepped back and stood almost at attention. Alberto looked the package over, noticing that it appeared to be what its shape suggested: a couple of paper-wrapped coins, addressed to him. He looked up at Alejandro and asked, "Where did you say you found this?"

"The jacket of your suit, señor, the dark-gray pinstripe you wore on Saturday, in the left outside jacket pocket."

What the hell? Alberto thought. He put on his reading glasses and carefully pulled off a small piece of tape, placed it on his desk, then peeled off another, until he could unwrap the package, which held nothing more than two fifty-peso coins. He slowly and carefully laid out the small piece of paper on his desk and then, out of habit, covered the note with a blank sheet of stationery so as to preserve any potential prints or other evidence and smoothed it with his hand. He removed the stationery and stared at his name centered on the paper. *Who did this and why?* he wondered.

He carefully took the piece of paper by a corner and turned it over, realizing there was writing on it, and read Ray's clear but very small printed message:

ALVAREZ IS CONDOR DE MUERTE
OF CHIHUAHUA, ALSO NICOLAS PEÑA
OF BAJA SUR. PRESIDENT FERNANDEZ TO
BE KILLED MONDAY IN HERMOSILLO
"ACCIDENT." YOU TO BE ASSASSINATED
MONDAY BY A BOMB IN YOUR CAR.
ALVAREZ WANTS THE PRESIDENCY.
CONTACT BENNIE SANTIAGO, US DEA
ONLY. REPEAT: ONLY. CONDOR SPIES ARE
EVERYWHERE. TRUST NO ONE.
SIGNED, TROJAN HORSE

As was his custom when reading, Alberto subconsciously took in the entire message at a glance, with certain word combinations jumping out at him. He sucked in a rapid breath as "Fernandez to be killed" registered in his consciousness a nanosecond before "Alvarez is Condor" and "bomb in your car" did. He carefully read the note a second time, his hands beginning to tremble.

"Alejandro, did you read this?"

Alejandro had worked for Alberto for a long time and knew his employer as a father knows a son. The shock on Alberto's face couldn't be hidden. Whatever the note said—and that was what it had to be, a note of some kind—had struck Alberto like a thunderclap.

"Of course not, señor. I thought it odd, so I brought it directly to you. Was this the correct thing to do?"

"Yes, it was," Alberto said quickly as he grabbed his phone and punched a button that immediately summoned his senior administrative assistant.

The young man stepped into the office and said, "Yes, Mr. Director?"

"Please take Alejandro to the executive dining area and see that he's made comfortable." Alberto turned back to his valet and said quietly. "Alejandro, it's important that you remain here until we can talk further, but there's a serious matter requiring my immediate attention, so I ask that you wait for me in the dining room. And please say nothing to anyone about this—no one."

"Of course, señor," Alejandro said soberly.

Alberto's assistant led Alejandro from the office and closed the door behind them. Alberto sat stunned, reading the note over and over.

My God, Pablo is the Condor? How can this be? I've known him and his family since prep school; it simply isn't possible. How did this note come to me? Where was I Saturday? Think...I was only in three places: home, with Pablo at his office, and at the party at his home. It had to be at the party. I knew everyone there; they're all important people in the government and in business. Most are friends; they would have told me something like this, not slip me a note. There were some strangers, though, the waiters and other servants. Which ones work for Pablo? I need a list. It has to be someone who works for Pablo, doesn't it? Think, Alberto, think. Who else could it be? Who's Bennie Santiago, and what's this reference to

'Trojan Horse'? Is that literal? Has a DEA operative gotten close to Pablo? Is this note even real? If it is real and Pablo is the Condor, that means the Americans do have someone covertly in with him. If that's the case, why haven't they warned me before now, especially about an assassination attempt? They would; they'd have to, unless...Do they suspect me as being unreliable? That can't be! They would know of Manny, and he would answer for me. Alberto glanced quickly at his watch. *Good God, the president is almost to Hermosillo! There's no time!*

All these questions and thoughts shot through Alberto's mind like sunlight through a child's kaleidoscope: flashes but with no real shape or organization. Alberto was flustered and panicked and needed to get control of himself. He grabbed the encrypted cell phone issued to all members of the cabinet and the military, as well as their top subordinates, and thumbed down through his directory until he found the name of his federal police commander in Hermosillo. He punched in the three-digit speed-dial number, and almost immediately Colonel Juan Munoz answered the phone. "Yes, Mr. Director?"

Alberto glanced at his watch; it read ten after ten. "Munoz, are you at the airport?"

"Yes, Mr. Director, I am."

"Listen, carefully," Alberto told him. "We've received a credible threat to President Fernandez's life. He's ahead of schedule and will land within thirty minutes. The moment he does, I want him taken to a secure place, a hangar, somewhere at the airport—you select it—and I want a massive force placed around him. No one gets near him, you understand me? I'm contacting the presidential guard and General Oberon. Coordinate with them. General Lopez and his presidential guard have jurisdiction once the president arrives. Call me as soon as you have the president secured. And Munoz, do this as quickly and quietly as you can."

"Of course, Mr. Director. Can you tell me the nature of the threat?"

"No, Munoz. I'm not sure. I just know an attempt will be made in Hermosillo. Quickly, Munoz!"

Alberto next dialed General Oberon, the chief of the air force, whom Alberto knew was in Hermosillo to personally escort President Fernandez on his tour of the squatter camps near the border in the American-made helicopters he was so proud of. He gave him the same message and then called General Javier Lopez, the man in charge of the presidential guard, who didn't answer. *He must be with the president*, thought Alberto. He dialed General Lopez's office next, identified himself, and asked to speak to the most senior officer present.

"This is Colonel de Herrera, Mr. Director, General Lopez's chief of staff. How may I help you?"

"Colonel, my office has received a threat against the president that will take place in Hermosillo. I believe the threat is credible, and immediate action is required. Where is General Lopez?"

"He's with the president, Mr. Director. Can you tell me the nature of this alleged threat?" the colonel asked casually.

Alberto rarely lost his temper, but given the dire situation and the colonel's condescending attitude, he lost his stoic composure and nearly shouted into the phone, "Colonel, you listen to me, you ass! This threat is *real*. You contact your people in Hermosillo immediately, or by all the saints and the Virgin Mary, I'll have your balls. Do you understand me?"

"Of course, Mr. Director…immediately," the shocked, flustered colonel stammered.

"Now, Colonel!" Alberto screamed.

"Mr. Director, have you tried calling the general directly on…on the president's aircraft?"

Alberto sat back in his chair, realizing he had almost come to his feet while yelling at the colonel, and tried to regain control. "No, I wasn't briefed that the in-flight communications systems were operational. Give me the number quickly!"

The thoroughly panicked colonel gave him the special number known only to a very few. Alberto quickly punched in the number on his secure desk phone. He heard a variety of electronic clicks and what sounded like static but no ringing and no answer. The colonel was still on hold on Alberto's cell phone; Alberto told him the system wasn't working and then ordered him to get a hold of General Lopez as soon as the plane landed.

What do I do about Alvarez? he thought. *I have to call him. What if the note is some sort of elaborate hoax? How can I know for sure? Goddamn it! I need time to think this through. Why aren't the communications on the new jet working?*

The communication systems on the new presidential jet didn't work because Raul Ortega didn't want them to work. The vetted, though thoroughly compromised Roberto Nieves, after placing the explosive devices in the landing gear, also had discreetly disabled the cabin's communications equipment. The only way to know this prior to takeoff would have been to test them as the plane sat on the tarmac. Raul had counted on no one thinking of doing such a test.

Alberto dialed the number of Secretary Alvarez; the time was now ten twenty. He was quickly routed to Dolores, who put him straight through.

"Good morning, Alberto," Alvarez said pleasantly. "Are you on your way over?"

"Mr. Secretary," Alberto said sternly, "my office has received a credible threat against the president to take place in Hermosillo."

Alvarez was stunned. "Say that again. What?"

Pablo sounded surprised, maybe even shocked, as he should be, but for what reason? Alberto wondered. *Is it because I informed him of the threat or because I discovered his intentions?*

"I just received information from an unidentified caller who said the president is to be killed in Hermosillo. That's all I have."

There was a significant pause in the conversation before Alvarez said, "Surely there's the possibility this was a hoax call, Alberto. This happens all the time, doesn't it, my friend? Why lend credence to this one in particular?"

"My instincts say no, Pablo. This threat is real. Something about the caller made me believe him. I've alerted my people and General Oberon. General Lopez is on the plane with the president, so I relayed word through his chief of staff."

Alberto thought he heard Alvarez sigh. "Very well, Alberto. Perhaps you should come over directly. We'll deal with this further when you get here."

"Yes, on my way," Alberto said, wondering what in the world he was going to do next.

Across the Zocalo, Alvarez slowly set the phone down in its cradle. Raul was watching him closely, having heard only half the conversation, but he could tell something was very wrong. Alvarez got up, slowly walked over, and sat on the couch next to him, his expression tense and grim.

"That was Alberto. Someone just called him and told him the president is to be killed in Hermosillo. Someone has found us out, Raul."

"That's not possible!" an exasperated Raul responded. "Only we in the circle knew—unless Roberto Nieves somehow risked the lives of his family, but he's not the type. We've controlled him completely."

Alvarez shrugged. "Perhaps he has more courage than you suspect. But he's not the only one outside the circle who knows. Eduardo also knows, and therefore some of his people must know as well."

"Damn few," Raul said tersely. "Eduardo is *always* careful, and he'd never reveal all of what he knows to any others. But I'll check this out personally. This makes no sense; his men are loyal professionals and have worked for him for years. They can be relied on to do as instructed."

"Do what you can to find out who talked, but do it carefully, my friend. We're now in very dangerous waters, for it seems reasonable to assume that whoever learned of our plan also knows we're behind it. Don't draw additional attention to yourself."

"Of course I'll be careful, but I must disagree with what you just said," Raul told Alvarez. "It seems more plausible that while this person, whoever he is, has picked up on the plot, there's no way he knows of us. Eduardo's people don't know about the connection between the Condor and us, and if it was Nieves, same thing—he has no idea who's behind the plot, and those are the only possibilities I see."

Alvarez, his look becoming more ashen, said, "Alberto is on his way over. I will learn what I can."

Raul just nodded and then got up and quickly left the office; with Alberto on his way over, he knew what he had to do and was dreading it. He had almost told Alvarez about the contingencies he had in place to deal with possibilities like this but had stopped. Pablo never would agree to the killing of Alberto, even under the threat of exposure. His conscience was overloaded already with all the collateral damage of the plan; Raul would have to do this on his own.

He went to the balcony that overlooked the Zocalo and took out his cell phone; the number that would initiate the electronic charge to the explosive package in Alberto's trunk was on speed dial: 666. He wasn't religious at all; in fact, if pressed, he would have admitted to being an atheist. The religious connotation of the number 666—the symbolism for the Antichrist—was something he was aware of when he had programmed the cell phone; it just seemed sickly appropriate given what the device was to be used for. He'd give Alberto a few more minutes until his intuition told him it was likely he was en route. He had the number on his screen; all he had to do was hit Send, and the most serious threat to Pablo and him would be eliminated.

Back across the square, Alberto was still sitting at his desk, trying to decide what to do next as he stared at the note and the warning about a bomb being in his limousine. Who had access to his car? Not many, but any list would contain a dozen names. He wasn't even sure how secure his car was if he wasn't near it. Maybe dozens more had access to it as it sat in the garage beneath his building or when it was parked at his estate. He sat up and palmed what he still believed was his secure cell phone and dialed the number of Colonel Phillip Montoya of the capital police, the head of his personal security.

The colonel answered immediately. "Yes, Mr. Director? Montoya here."

Alberto started to respond and give the orders that he was formulating in his head when the line "Condor spies are everywhere" from the note jumped out at him. He paused for a second, wondering whom he could really trust, and then decided he had no choice but to go on. "Colonel," he said, "I'm urgently required in the office of the secretary for public security across the Zocalo. Please meet me in the garage."

Colonel Montoya was surprised, as the director never had asked him to do this before, but he quickly answered, "Of course, Mr. Director. I can be there within five minutes."

Alberto ignored the files on his desk that he'd been reviewing in preparation for his meetings with Alvarez and this afternoon's press conference and went briskly into his outer office. The two members of his security team who were always nearby when he was at work—young, sharp-looking police officers in nice suits—stood as he entered the large open office space. He continued down the hallway toward his executive dining room, where he had sent Alejandro, with the two young officers closely following him.

As Alberto entered, Alejandro was sitting at a table alone, having tea, and started to stand when he saw his employer. "No, no, Alejandro. Sit," Alberto said, waving him back into his seat. Alejandro did as requested, and Alberto joined him after first telling his guards he required some privacy. As they moved to the dining-room door, Alberto looked at his valet and said quietly, the tension in his voice evident, "Alejandro, the note you discovered was of grave importance. I can't reveal the contents, but I want to tell you how grateful I am that you did what you did. I must leave and deal with the information you brought me. Please don't be alarmed, but I'm putting extra security on you until I can get to the bottom of the problem. There's no threat to you directly, but for reasons I can't share with you at this time, it's important that you be kept secure and that you speak with no one about this situation. The head of my security will personally take you to the estate and stay with you. I'll explain everything when I can. Understood?"

Alejandro leaned forward and, in a rare show of emotion, patted Alberto on the arm. "Yes, I understand. Please don't concern yourself further with me. Take care of yourself."

Alberto slowly nodded. "I will, old friend, and thank you."

Alberto stood and headed for his private elevator, his perplexed but alert guards trailing. When the elevator opened at the garage level, a nervous-looking Colonel Montoya was there waiting.

"Mr. Director, good morning. I am at your service and have ordered up your car."

Alberto turned to his two guards. "Please give me and Colonel Montoya some privacy."

The two men nodded and moved away again but were watching their charge with increased interest and concern. Alberto turned to Colonel Montoya, stepped closer, and said, sotto voce, "Colonel, I've received what I believe to be credible information indicating that someone has placed an explosive device in or on my car."

The colonel's shocked expression turned to horror as Alberto's driver pulled up at that moment with his armored limousine. The colonel instinctively stepped back. "My God, Mr. Director, we need to get you away from here now!"

Alberto's police driver got out and was walking around the car to open the rear door when Alberto ordered him to stop and stay where he was. He turned back to Montoya. "Here's what I want you to do. First, call the bomb-disposal team leader of my federal police. Make sure he knows you're acting for me, and order him here as quickly as possible, with as small a team as possible. And, Montoya, this is most important—make sure the disposal people arrive discreetly without drawing any attention. We must keep this threat contained—speak with no one else. Second, once you've made the call—again, without raising attention—have my car moved to a remote area of the garage and put a security net around it until the disposal team gets here. Whoever has planned this must be watching and waiting for my departure, when they're certain I'm in my car, so we have the advantage. Then have them find that device and preserve any and all evidence—that's crucial. Lastly, my valet, Alejandro, is upstairs in my dining room. Select three or four of your best men and escort him back to my estate and stay with him until I order you relieved. Understood?"

"Yes…yes, Mr. Director," the nervous colonel said.

"Make your call, and for God's sake, make sure the disposal team knows this threat is real."

Alberto summoned his driver over to him. He was a senior sergeant in the capital police and had been driving him for the last five years; Alberto believed he could trust him. "Tomas, do you have a personal vehicle here?"

The puzzled sergeant looked at him and said, "Yes, Mr. Director, but it's in the employee garage next door."

"Please, Tomas, take me there. I'll explain why on the way."

27

General Ignacio Pesqueira Garcia International Airport
Hermosillo, Mexico
Monday, 10:30 a.m.

Lilly Vasconsuelos hated assignments like this, but there were dues to be paid in television journalism, and one of the first was that the newest—and therefore least experienced—reporter got all the shit assignments. Such as standing in the rain on the observation deck at the airport, waiting for the president to land, and then doing a puff piece on the new presidential jet instead of being at the president's press conference and asking the head of state hard questions, such as what was he was doing about the mess at the border. *Who really cares about the president's new jet anyway?* Lilly asked herself when the assignment editor at her station had summoned her to his office. This was a chance, he'd told her, for her to show him something.

Some chance, Lilly thought as she sat in the station's van and attempted to repair the damage to her hair caused by the rain slicker she was forced to wear so her hair and on-camera clothes wouldn't get soaked. As she checked herself in the hand mirror she carried, she thought she looked like something the cat had just dragged in. One of the station's more senior reporters would be at the news conference to be held in a hangar next to the airfield, out of the rain, and get the chance to ask the really important questions. Lilly was reduced to maybe meeting the chief pilot and getting all sorts of wonderful information about a new jet no one wanted to know anything about anyway.

"Shit," she said out loud for the tenth time to no one in particular. The cameraman, who had been setting up outside, stuck his head in the side door of the van and said, "Looks like the flights have stopped, Felix."

"Come on, Lilly," her producer said. "That's our cue. Time to set up. The president is due anytime now. And quit looking so angry. The rain has stopped. You'll look fine on camera."

Lilly looked at him crossly. "Yeah, sure, Felix. The only thing good about this assignment is that it's live."

Lilly's station, TelHerm Channel 10, was independent and usually ran third in its market, but it featured a popular host who had a top-rated midmorning local news and entertainment talk program. A presidential visit was always news, so they would be doing his landing live and then recap his airport news conference and run Lilly's presidential jet piece at noon. As far as Felix could tell, they were the only station covering the arrival. All the other local channels and regional networks were at the hangar for the news conference. Lilly would get to do the arrival from her perch and provide a lead-in for her jet piece. Felix figured she would get a good minute live, which would be nice exposure for the very good-looking young reporter, and then do a two- to three-minute piece on the new presidential jet at noon, depending on whom she talked to and how interesting the material she collected was—all great exposure for her. Focus groups had indicated to the station manager and the producer that Lilly was likeable across the board and especially liked by males in all age groups. This was good for the station, and for her, even if she hadn't been told about it. She already thought she was pretty special, so it was best not to inflate her ego more.

Felix and Lilly joined the cameraman by the railing of the observation platform, from which they could see the entire airport.

"Lilly, you'll stand here," Felix said, marking her spot with a chalk *X*. "We were told that once all air traffic has been halted, we'll have ten minutes until President Fernandez's plane lands. We'll see it there in the north on approach. Once it's a minute out, that'll be our cue to Adolpho in the studio, who'll then send it to you live. Remember, do your introduction, then say, 'Here at General etcetera, etcetera airport…' Then say the president's flight is on approach and give me about ten seconds or more about his new jet. Make it interesting, please—how much it cost and anything else you found in your research. The better it is, the more will be included in the noon recap. We'll go tight on the plane, and you'll then be out of the shot. The president's plane will land from the northwest as usual, there," he said, pointing in the general direction of the airstrip, "and then go from right to left in the frame. We'll watch the rollout and then pull back to you in the frame, and you'll say more about the president's visit to Hermosillo at noon, and then we'll send it back to the studio. Got it?"

"Yeah, yeah, I got it," Lilly said testily. "Can I just say, 'General Garcia Airport'? Do I have to say the entire name? I mean, most people don't know who General Ignacio Pesqueira Garcia was anyway."

"The entire name, Lilly—more professional that way."

"Felix," the camera operator interrupted, "I think I see the president's jet. Look—out to the north. It's the only one there."

Felix turned and looked to where the cameraman was pointing. "Good, and it's on time. Studio, get ready," he said into his headset. "Quit messing with your hair, Lilly, and get on your mark. You look fine."

Out to the north, the only jet in the sky was still distant, perhaps five minutes out. If not for the bright landing lights, it would have been difficult to see against the high gray clouds that only twenty minutes earlier had been dumping the rain that had so irritated Felix's young on-air talent. *They're all alike*, he thought. *Far more interested in their appearance than the subject they're reporting on.*

As they watched the 787 Dreamliner draw closer, Felix was concentrating on the timing. "OK, studio, have Adolpho send it to us. Get ready, Lilly. On my mark…"

In their headsets, Felix and his cameraman heard the discussion in the studio that was going out live to several hundred thousand homes in the northern states. Adolpho Perez, the popular host of the program, had developed a reasonably wide following. They heard him smoothly wrap up the subject he was discussing and then segue into an introduction about the president's visit before sending it to "Lilly Vasconsuelos, our reporter live at the airport."

Felix was doing a silent countdown for Lilly, who wore a carefully concealed earpiece and heard the pompous Adolpho do his lead-in. When the moment was perfect, Felix pointed to Lilly. She had given considerable thought to her opening. Although she'd been warned to focus just on the arrival and the jet and not to mention all the other issues that were in the news and making the president's visit necessary, she decided to add a little something anyway. A number of state officials she'd been talking with, as part of a story she was developing on the immigration problems, had vented their frustrations and disgust about the job the president was doing. An admirer in marketing who was working up the nerve to ask her out had shared with her some of the focus-group results, which told her she wouldn't get fired anytime soon, so, armed with that reassurance, she launched into her intro.

"Thank you, Adolpho. This is Lilly Vasconsuelos, coming to you live from General Ignacio Pesqueira Garcia International Airport, where President Fernandez's new American-made Boeing jet, *Mexico One*, is making its final approach into Hermosillo on his much-anticipated—and what many local officials believe is his long-overdue—first visit to the north to see firsthand the immigration camps in Nogales and Agua Prieta. Following a brief arrival ceremony and news conference, the president will continue on to the border area in one of several air force helicopters flown in especially for the event. President Fernandez will be accompanied by General Oberon of the air force and General Omar Pasqual, the army commander in this district."

Lilly glanced toward the runway and the approaching aircraft. "As you can see over my shoulder, the president's new jet will be touching down in just a few seconds."

As the camera operator slowly swung the camera to Lilly's left and tightened the focus, she knew she was out of the shot. She glanced at Felix, who was looking at her with a tight grimace and would have unloaded on her if they weren't live. *Well, the hell with you Felix. I said it*, she thought, *and it was good. Fernandez should have visited the camps long before now.*

Lilly turned to watch the landing and the rollout of the president's jet before she got ready for her next shot and the send back to Adolpho in the studio. The 787, painted mostly white but trimmed with the green and red of the national flag, flared smoothly as it approached the ground. The senior air force colonel at the controls of Boeing's most sophisticated new design pulled the nose up slightly to flare the aircraft into perfect position for a typical landing. It was at that moment—just as the landing gear gave off that brief bit of blue smoke, when the motionless tires first met the concrete of the runway and were immediately accelerated to 140 miles per hour—that everything seemed to move in slow motion.

As the main landing gear softly touched down, the nose gear still hanging in the air, the jet suddenly tilted to the right as the landing gear on that side collapsed and disappeared. The right engine and wing, hidden from view from the observation-deck vantage point by the body of the jet, gouged into the pavement as the commercial aircraft lurched severely, farther to the right. Sparks flew as the right wing and center portion of the main body violently exploded into flames. The front third of the main fuselage broke free from a point just forward of the wings and continued down the runway in a cockeyed sideways slide. The rear portion of the aircraft was instantly gone, consumed in a rolling fireball of orange-and-yellow flames and a dense cloud of roiling black smoke. The front third of the aircraft skidded sideways off the runway and rolled into the adjacent weed-covered field, changing shape from an identifiable aircraft fuselage into a crumpled pile of torn metal and carbon-fiber composites, the vibrant colors of the Mexican flag still evident. The camera operator had done his job magnificently. He managed to keep the entire event in frame and in focus, his days as a camera operator for Mexican-league football games having honed those skills.

The farmhouse
Near Toluca, Mexico
Monday, 10:00 a.m.

Ray glanced at his watch for the umpteenth time since dawn. Forget maintaining a covert persona—just keeping his breathing something close to normal was becoming increasingly difficult with each passing minute. Not sleeping well had become the norm for him during this assignment, and, as events continued to unfold, the problem was getting worse. Last night had been no exception. As Luis slept soundly on the couch, Ray had spent the night slumped in a ratty overstuffed chair, staring at Luis or up into the darkness, another night spent listening to the soft, rhythmic sounds emanating from a cheap ceiling fan, his head pounding from another of his headaches. More and more while at the estates in the north, late at night his thoughts had drifted to contingency plans for disappearing, just slipping away when everyone else was asleep. Once he'd been told about the move to the south, he'd looked forward to getting to the capital city, where the opportunities for doing so seemed more possible.

Since his arrival in Mexico City, he had depressingly dismissed any such notions. After becoming familiar with the estate and the routines and really thinking about it, just getting out of the estate posed insurmountable problems. If he walked out the main gate, he would be questioned by the guards but not stopped. He was part of the inner circle, and everyone knew this. He could talk his way past them; if he wanted to take a walk to clear his mind, who could stop him? But he knew the guard commander reported everything of even a remotely unusual nature to Raul. As Raul was the leader of the inner circle, nothing happened in the immediate vicinity of Alvarez without his knowledge. Ray might make it out of the gate, but how soon would it be before Raul was called and told of this unusual happenstance? Just taking a midnight stroll, however innocent, likely would be reported. To his knowledge, no one had ever done such a thing, and once he walked off, then what?

Ray knew if he walked away there was no going back; he would turn a bright spotlight on himself. If he walked away, it would have to be for good, and it would be dangerous. Where could he go? The US embassy was always his first thought, but he had no American identification, no passport, nothing. He'd have to talk his way in, past the marine guards, and then convince someone to let him see the security officer, who could turn out to be an asshole and not believe him or, worse, not allow him to remain on the grounds. He needed to get to an official who would be willing to call and verify his claims—no small task, all things considered. Bennie had said there was a DEA liaison at the embassy from time to time, as joint operations were conducted, but given Alvarez's penetration of DEA, that would be the last person he would seek out—if there even was an agent present at this time.

He had money, a little more than two thousand pesos. It might be enough to get him back north to the border area. He could lie low, take buses or trains, and make his way to Las Palomas and retrace his footsteps back through the tunnel. He had his Glock and his knives; the crazy old man at the house wouldn't be a problem if he could surprise him. Despite his nature and everything he had once believed about himself, Ray was no longer a stranger to murder and could do what was required if it came to that.

There was always the possibility that Alvarez could react strongly to his walking away and place the worst interpretation on it—that he was a traitor—and reinforce escape avenues Ray knew about, such as the tunnel. More likely, knowing Alvarez and his personal feelings for those close to him, he would suspect some kind of foul play by one of their enemies against one of his close friends. He would know it wasn't the government, and Alvarez would stop at nothing to get a trusted friend back safely. And the power he could bring to such a search as the president of Mexico was nearly limitless.

That was how Alvarez might think, Ray thought, but not Raul. Raul was almost as smart as Alvarez and not nearly as affected by the strong, distracting emotions that guided Alvarez. Raul didn't worry about what God thought or whether every action held some deep-seated philosophical meaning. If Ray walked off, especially if Alvarez and Raul learned about the contents of his note, Raul would assume the worst—that Ray was the traitor—and govern his actions accordingly. Ray would have to become invisible or die. If Alvarez did become president and ordered all law-enforcement agencies to find and detain him for questioning, especially if they tied him to Fernandez's assassination, how long would it be before he was caught?

Then there was Alberto Rodriguez. Ray still believed he was his one ally in all this. He knew he lived near the Alvarez mansion but didn't know exactly where. If he could get to the Rodriquez home and get the security people there to take him to Alberto, he would listen, especially if he indeed had the note. But could Alberto protect him? Was that even possible if the president of the country declared you a public enemy? He had his doubts.

Ray sadly had concluded that such thinking—walking away and somehow surviving—was bullshit, pure and simple. Even if he made it back to the United States and into some kind of protective custody, as long as Alvarez or any part of the senior leadership of his organization existed, what kind of life could he expect to have? He would be hunted until they day they got him or until he got them. And from where he sat right now, that looked like a pretty one-sided fight. He decided he had no choice but to live by the mantra "Keep your friends close but your enemies closer." He'd read that when he was in school; he wished he could remember where. Some ancient Chinese warrior, he vaguely recalled. As dawn approached and his thinking returned to the here and now, he thought, *Perfect, just fucking perfect. My principal enemy, if that's what Alvarez is, lives by the words of a two-thousand-year-old Greek, and now I'm being guided by an almost equally old Chinese philosopher.*

Ray's greatest problem, however, the one really eating at him, was that he didn't think of Alvarez as the enemy. Whatever Alvarez was, he was as close to him as anyone could hope to be. His proximity was a prison, but in a way, it was also his sanctuary. The only thing he had going for him in his present hell was the personal friendships that Alvarez and Raul deeply desired to cultivate with him. One only had to see the long-term friendships Alvarez had with Miguel and Raul and the recently departed Francisco to appreciate how important these friendships were to him. As perverse a thought as it was, under different circumstances Ray and Alvarez would have been friends. These kinds of thoughts made him realize he had to get out. His time and sanity were running out.

How could Rodriguez have missed the note? This question replaced his thoughts of escape and perverse friendships and circled around and around in his head. Unlike when he was at the estate, he could have easily walked away last night, as soundly as Luis slept. But he couldn't do it and leave Roberto Nieves's family alone with Luis, not after what Raul had told him.

He was just as trapped as if he were at the estate—probably more so, as a conscience could be far more enveloping than any wall.

He desperately needed information. With Luis still sacked out on the couch this morning, he had no choice but to disturb him and potentially alert him as to how he was feeling when he turned on the television and found the national news channel. To his shock, there was a story from the Mexico City airport reporting on the president's departure to Hermosillo. He stood up and went to the kitchen thinking, *Jesus Christ! Why wasn't the flight canceled? What is Alberto doing and why?*

He went back to the living room, where the now-wide-awake Luis was watching him with a mixture of curiosity and annoyance. He picked up the remote, turned the television off, and turned to Luis. "Sorry to wake you. I was bored and wanted to watch some news."

Luis looked at him for a second and then said tersely, "Give that to me."

He handed him the remote. Luis started looking for a sports program of any kind, so Ray went back to the kitchen table to try to think. He was unsure of the exact timing of the attack in Hermosillo but thought it was to be around eleven. He had no more than an hour to do something, if he was going to do anything at all. All night long, he had struggled with the possibility that Raul would deal with Alberto first. That would be a disaster for him, whether or not Alberto got the note, because Ray knew of no one else in the government he could trust, and he could see no way out of the dark hole he was in except through Alberto Rodriguez. He couldn't just sit by and let Raul assassinate him, but how on earth could he stop it, stuck outside the city having to watch over the Nieves family? As the minutes dragged on, Ray sank deeper and deeper into an emotional pit as he thought about those who would perish with the president if Alberto didn't stop the attempt. What was Alberto up to? He had seen it just now on the television: a replay of the president boarding his jet earlier this morning and taking off for Hermosillo. Had Alberto somehow discovered the explosives and removed them? He could only hope that was the answer.

It took all the strength and experience he could muster to remain seated in the kitchen, appearing to read a magazine, instead of pacing around. The tension was killing him, and the pounding in his head was now constant. He looked at his watch again—10:40 a.m.—less than thirty minutes until the attack if Alberto didn't act on the note. If that happened, many innocent people were going to die along with the president because he hadn't done more. The naked truth was that he had saved himself at the expense of others; that was a hard truth to discover about oneself, and the feeling made him sick to his stomach. He should have done more, he now realized, and decided right then and there that he would. If Alberto was still alive, he would do anything necessary to warn him of the pending attack on him, even if it meant exposing himself to Alvarez and Raul. He had no choice; that was the price he had to pay to keep a shred of his honor. The looming problem was how could he do more than he already had, stuck in Toluca as he was.

He heard Luis get off the couch and looked up and saw him looking at his watch, then unholstering his Glock. Ray's anxiety was spiking as he got up and cautiously walked into the living room. His intuition told him he was in danger, and the hairs on the back of his neck suddenly stood up. He wanted to draw his Glock or his knife, but instead he stepped closer, where he could get at Luis before Luis could bring his weapon to bear on him, and asked, "Luis, what are you doing?"

Luis looked contemptuously at him and sneered, "I'm doing what Eduardo said to do and what you and Raul don't have the balls for."

Luis brushed by him and went to the bedroom where Raphael Nieves was being held, opened the door, and stepped in. Ray was momentarily frozen in fear and confusion. The bomb maker was still lying on the bed, handcuffed to the frame. Before the man could fully sit up, Luis quickly aimed and shot the startled man in the head, instantly fouling the wall beyond him.

Ray flinched at the loud shot but was shocked out of his state and stammered, "Luis, wh-what have you done? Raul needed him back in Hermosillo!"

Luis ignored him, took another couple of steps in, and shot the bomb maker twice more. Ray heard muffled screams from the other room as Luis casually turned, holstering his gun, came out of the room, and got right in Ray's face. "Eduardo was going to kill him anyway. He told me so. I just saved us the fucking useless trip, didn't I?"

Luis started to walk past him, reaching for the door of the second bedroom. Ray was lucid but still in a state of shock, his ears ringing from the loud reports in such a small area. He'd been feeling ill while sitting in the kitchen, trying to see a way out and also save Alberto, and now he felt worse with the odor of burnt sulfur permeating the living room.

He reached out and grabbed Luis by the arm as he was turning past him. "Stop, Luis. What do you think you're doing now?"

Luis jerked his arm free; the look on his face was pure hatred. "Get your fucking hand off me. What do you think? You really believe we can just let them go? They have seen us and heard us. You not only have no balls—you're stupid as well. But I'm not about to let such beauty go to waste before we have to deal with them. I get the oldest one; you can have the mother and the others. I don't give a shit, but I get the room. Just get the others the fuck out of there until we deal with them, before I kick your ass all over this room."

Luis quickly turned and opened the door, and, without thinking, Ray reacted. He flexed his forearm, and his H-K sprang from the sheath strapped to his arm into his hand. In a smooth, continuous motion, he pressed the button on the side, and the four-inch serrated blade locked into place as he struck at Luis in a flash. Luis never saw the attack coming, his arrogance, stupidity, and appetites overriding any semblance of caution or common sense. Roberto Nieves's wife and daughters, alerted by the gunshots and the loud conversation between Ray and Luis, were terrified and cringing in a tight heap on the bed. The two youngest were crying loudly as Ray savagely plunged his knife between Luis's ribs, extracted it, and rapidly stabbed him several more times. Luis made a loud guttural sound and, bleeding severely, collapsed in a heap at the foot of the bed. Somehow, probably because of the ordeal with Guzman several weeks earlier, Ray could tell Luis was done for. He reached down and took Luis's gun, stood, and stuck it in the rear waistband of his slacks. All the daughters were hysterical now, having witnessed the brutal killing. Realizing he was still holding the bloody knife,

Ray quickly leaned down and wiped it clean on Luis's pant leg, folded it up, and put it in his pocket. He turned to the mother and, in a shaky but gentle voice, said, "Come on. Get your girls. I need to get you out of here and to safety."

Roberto's wife was on the verge of hysteria but now was also confused at Ray's kind tone and didn't know what to think or say. Frozen with fear, she stared at him as the girls continued to cry.

"What's your name?" he softly asked the woman.

She continued to stare at him, but he saw in her eyes that she was trying to see a way out. Finally, meekly, she said, "Maria."

"Please, Maria..." Ray said. "We don't have much time. I won't harm you. We have to go."

Ray could tell she had reached a conclusion. She slowly nodded and told her daughters to do as the man had said. Ray turned and went to the living room, then stopped in his tracks as he tuned into what was coming over the television. The local station had interrupted its programming for a news bulletin, and now some studio talking head was reporting that the president's plane had crashed upon landing in Hermosillo minutes before, and they were switching to an on-site live feed from the airport, courtesy of a sister channel of their network. Ray was stunned for the second time in minutes and could do nothing more than sit down on the couch and watch as a replay of the president's jet landing, crashing, and suddenly bursting into flames was broadcast. As Maria came into the room, clutching her girls, she saw a despondent Ray staring at the floor, shaking his head, and mumbling, "What have I done? What have I done?"

General Ignacio Pesqueira Garcia International Airport
Hermosillo, Mexico
Monday, 10:50 a.m.

Lilly, to her credit, was the first to come to her professional senses, saying into her microphone, even though she was out of the shot, "It's crashed! My God, the president's plane has crashed and is burning in a great fire about halfway down the runway. The president's jet looked to have made a perfect landing before suddenly swerving violently off the runway. As you may be able to hear from the sirens in the background, the emergency equipment located here at the airport is responding. I can see some equipment moving now—two fire engines as well as several police cars from the station building across the field. President Fernandez's jet broke into at least two large sections as the middle portion violently exploded. The front part of the jet continued farther down the runway, and, as you can see, it's been badly damaged, but there's no fire there that we can see from here."

Lilly heard the studio's executive producer screaming at her in her earpiece to go to senior reporter Jorge Vera, who was outside the hangar and nearer the actual crash site. Lilly—smoothly, she thought—said, "Let's go to Jorge Vera, who's on the ground near the crash site. Jorge?"

Felix grabbed Lilly the moment he knew they were off camera, his face a mixture of shock and something else. He turned to the cameraman, who was still training his camera on the chaotic scene. "Did you get it, Ramon? All of it?"

"I think so, center frame the entire time. We were just the right distance away to keep it there and in focus."

"My God, Lilly, my God," Felix said, turning to her. "No one could have survived that, no one. But you did great, just great. I forgive you for your comment about the camps."

Lilly was rattled, but for whatever reason, she was in the moment. "Let's get moving, Felix. We need to get closer, a different shot. Where can we go?"

"Nowhere, I'm afraid," Felix said, shaking his head. "The president's security is very tight. We'll do no better than where we are if we move, but no one else will be allowed in here to our position, so we should stay. We have an exclusive view from here. Ramon, your camera is still live. Stay on the fire and the rescue equipment. I'll get the tripod. We're going to be here for a long time. Lilly, what research do you have on the jet? You did do research for your piece, right? Tell me you did."

"Of course I did, Felix, you ass."

"OK, OK. I'll get the studio to come back to you, and you tell us everything you can about the president's new jet. Improvise if you have to…

stretch it out—just don't say anything too outrageous...Studio! If you haven't done so already, get me everything you know on that jet and now!"

No more stupid stories for me. This is the break of a lifetime, Lilly thought as she turned and watched what was left of the president's jet burn up on the runway. And she was probably right.

The farmhouse
Near Toluca, Mexico
Monday, 11:00 a.m.

Ray was shell-shocked. How could Alberto have missed the note or not acted on it? *So many people now dead,* he thought, *all because I didn't have the guts to do more and stop this.* When he looked up, Maria was staring at him, as were the daughters, with frightened eyes. Before he could do anything about it, he knew he was going to be sick and quickly turned away and vomited what little breakfast he had eaten earlier into the corner at the end of the couch. He was embarrassed, afraid, and suddenly full of guilt. He turned and sat back on the couch, wiping his face with his shirt sleeve, wondering what to do next. He looked up at the mother and knew the one thing he could do right was to get her and her family to safety, but where? He stood, unsteadily walked past her, and squatted over Luis's body. He went through Luis's pockets until he found his wallet and the keys to Miguel's SUV. He removed the considerable cash he found and went to Maria, who was trying to keep her girls safely tucked behind her, and said, "Let's go...please."

He went through the kitchen and out the back door to where the black estate Escalade was parked and opened the front passenger door and the rear door behind it. Maria was staring at him through the kitchen screen door, not sure what to believe but starting to think that maybe the young killer wasn't evil somehow.

"Please," Ray implored, motioning for her and her daughters to join him. "Others will be coming, and soon. I have to get you out of here!"

Maria came slowly out the door, her daughters tightly bunched behind her and clinging to her skirt. "You in front with me, Maria. Put the girls in the back."

Ray walked to the other side and got in the driver's door. Maria just stood there. The stranger wasn't forcing her at all; his weapons were out of sight; and he just sat in the big luxury SUV looking at her as she stood there and looked back at him. She finally decided she had no choice but to trust him and got the girls into the backseat, and then she climbed into the front with Ray, jamming herself as tightly against the closed passenger side door as she could.

Ray looked at her. "The only thing I can think of is to get you to the bus station in Toluca, where you can buy tickets to wherever you think you can stay hidden for a while. Do you have such a place?"

After a moment, in a weak, frightened voice, Maria said, "Yes, yes, there's my aunt. She lives alone, near Acapulco."

Ray nodded, started the SUV, and quickly drove them off. It took him only a few minutes to get back to Toluca and then only five or ten minutes to find the bus station after asking a passing pedestrian at a crosswalk where it was. He parked in the half-empty lot in front of the run-down station, quickly got Maria and her girls rounded up, and headed for the main door. Once inside the noisy waiting area, he turned to her. "Here, take this," he said, handing her what had to be several thousand pesos, which he had taken from Luis. He glanced up at the electronic display and saw a bus to Acapulco would be leaving in less than an hour.

He turned back to the family. "Listen, Maria…get your tickets and get to where you're going. Stay out of sight and say nothing to anyone about what just happened. This is for your own safety. Draw attention to yourselves, and others like the man who killed your brother-in-law and wanted to harm you will come for you. If I can, I'll try to save your husband. He's deeply involved in all this but against his will. He's a good man."

Suddenly she grabbed him by the arm and started to cry. "I can see you aren't the Devil. Thank you. Thank you. Please save my husband, please!"

Ray knew he looked rattled—there was no concealing it—but he patted her hand and said in his most reassuring voice, "I'll try my best."

Maria held his arm as she stared at him with her large brown eyes. "When will we be safe?"

All he could think to say was, "You'll know."

He quickly turned away and started walking out, thinking she and her daughters might never be safe again. He saw several small shops and restaurants along one side of the waiting area, and he had a sudden thought and veered toward a gift shop. He walked to the counter, purchased a prepaid cell phone, returned to the parking lot, and climbed into the Escalade. He just sat there, quietly looking at the phone. How long had he wished for such a moment? He had lost count as the days had run together, one into another.

He wanted to call Alberto in the worst way and try to warn him directly of the plot against him, but he knew that would be a fool's errand. With the president's plane burning up on a runway in Hermosillo, the federal police headquarters would be a cluster fuck; there would be no way to even get to Alberto. He decided to try anyway and punched in 066, the Mexican equivalent to 911. More quickly than he thought it would take, a female voice came on the line. "Emergency services. Please state your name and emergency."

He paused and then said, "Connect me with the federal police headquarters in Mexico City."

There was a brief pause, and then the same impatient voice repeated the request. "Please state your name and emergency."

He could tell this was going nowhere and disconnected. It hit him hard that there was nothing he could do for Alberto, exiled in Toluca as he was. He slumped down in his seat, feeling lost and sinking deeper into despair. After a minute, with all his dark thoughts and the devastating events of the past twenty-four hours crushing down on him, he did the thing he knew he had to do. He slowly tapped out the message-drop number Bennie had him commit to memory months before, hoping Bennie wouldn't actually answer. His mission was over—that much was certain—but far worse, he knew in that instant that his life as he knew it was over. What he didn't know was how to tell Bennie or how to live with it.

28

Department of Public Security
Mexico City
Monday, 10:30 a.m.

Alberto's driver, Tomas, felt embarrassed as they walked up to his banged-up, rusted-out VW Lupo parked in his spot in the employees' garage. It was a privilege to be a member of the capital police and to be as trusted and respected as he was, but the job didn't pay that much, and his vehicle reflected his financial situation. He hadn't expected to be giving the director of the federal police a ride anywhere, and the front passenger seat was cluttered with this morning's newspaper and the remnants of yesterday's lunch. He opened the passenger door, muttered an apology, quickly cleaned the seat, and then stood at attention to one side as the clearly distracted and disturbed director got in.

As Tomas pulled out of the garage and merged into the heavy lanes of traffic snaking slowly around the Zocalo, Alberto's two security escorts in their chase car moved in behind them. Without looking at Tomas, Alberto said, "For your ears only: someone placed an explosive device in my car. That's why I've asked you to take me to the secretary's office."

Tomas was shocked and then relieved. A close friend of his from the police academy had been the driver and body guard to the director's brother and had been killed in the RPG attack that had killed Emilio Rodriguez. "My God, Mr. Director, is it the same bastards who attacked your brother?"

Alberto turned and looked at him. "I don't know for sure, but my guess is yes. Please do what you can to get us across the square as quickly as possible—and, Tomas, not a word to anyone about the events this morning. Also, once we get to Secretary Alvarez's office, remain with your car. Make sure no one has access to it while I meet with the secretary. For our safety, we may need it again."

Tomas had a wife and five children he loved deeply; he merely nodded, wondering whether having achieved his position as the director's driver was really the great accomplishment he once had thought.

The drive from Alberto's office in the federal police headquarters on the south side of the Zocalo to the Department of Public Security on the north side would take only ten minutes even in the heavy traffic and Alberto knew he needed to use the time wisely, but he was overcome with conflicting emotions and unfocused as a result. He didn't know what to think. He and Pablo Alvarez had drifted apart over the years and weren't as close as they once had been, but that was more a result of the great but different responsibilities they each carried as they climbed up through the government. Before this morning, if asked, he would have said Alvarez was his oldest and closest friend and the one man besides his dead brother he could always trust and count on in the fight against the cartels. That belief, however, had just been shattered, destroyed by the contents of a note from an unknown undercover operative out of the United States, if the note was to be believed.

The most important and immediate decision he had to make was how to tell Alvarez how the information had come to him. He decided he would make no mention of a note or when he had received the information. Telephone logs were kept of all calls to his offices, and they wouldn't show a call coming in when he might say it did, but he would deal with that later; logs could be altered. Also, if Alvarez was the Condor, it was likely he had informers in his office who could report on Alejandro's arrival. That was an unusual, although perhaps innocent-looking, event. Alberto decided that if pressed, he would say a second call had come to his house, and Alejandro had relayed the information to him. Alberto needed to talk with Alejandro alone again to get their story straight; Alejandro he could trust. All these thoughts raced through his mind as Tomas's car crawled through the Zocalo traffic. Alberto pulled out his personal, unencrypted cell phone and tapped in Manny's personal number.

Manny's recorded voice came over the line. "Sorry, but I'm away from my phone. Please leave a message."

"Shit!" Alberto cursed under his breath. He had to be careful; he thought Tomas was reliable, but now wasn't the time to make a mistake. He would operate on the premise that everyone was a traitor unless he knew without question where that person's loyalties lay.

"This is Alberto," he said. "Let's talk at noon my time. If not then, I'll try every two hours if I can. By then, you'll understand why."

He disconnected and glanced at Tomas, who seemed distracted by this morning's events and oblivious to the short, quiet, cryptic call. *Hopefully I can make the noon call. If this information is real, Manny will understand if I can't.*

Tomas drove straight to the guarded VIP area in the basement parking structure of the Department of Public Security building. As soon as Tomas stopped, Alberto bolted from the car before the chase car carrying his two personal security officers could come to a stop. They joined up with him as he was impatiently punching the elevator call button for the third time in front of a nervous-looking young security officer guarding the elevator. Once the elevator arrived, Alberto and his bodyguards rode in silence to the top floor of the building, where they were expected, and Alberto was shown straight to Alvarez's office.

Alvarez looked up from his desk as Alberto walked briskly in. "Ah, Alberto, you made quick time. Now, what's the nature of this threat that you think is so different from the other hoaxes you've received and moved you to alert everyone?"

Alberto had long trusted his intuition when it came to people and situations, and he felt Alvarez's air of normalcy was forced. Perhaps it was just a heightened sense of paranoia, but he couldn't take that chance. Pablo Alvarez was no fool, and he was smart. If the note Alberto had received was true, and Alvarez learned the information had come to him at the party, Alvarez would do what he already had started to do, which was put together a list of everyone who had been at the house Saturday night. Whoever had written the note had to be someone who was at least allowed physically close to Alvarez, if not actually someone in his entourage. He could be a servant or police guard perhaps, someone who had overheard a secure conversation and was a patriot or, more darkly, someone working for Alvarez who was loyal to the corrupt president. The possibilities were endless, but the individual must have been at the party. Once a list of everyone who was there Saturday night was compiled, somewhere on there would be the source of the note. And that someone was an informant working for the DEA or perhaps even a covert agent. That was the truly remarkable part, Alberto thought—the possibility that someone from the DEA actually had infiltrated that close to Alvarez.

Alberto glanced around the room as he entered; Alvarez wasn't alone. His old friend and longtime security man, Miguel, was sitting at the far end of the office, watching him closely—maybe even too closely, he thought, or was that his paranoia again? He couldn't be sure. Alberto nodded to him and then looked at the secretary, who gestured for him to speak. "Feel free to say whatever is on your mind, Alberto. You know Miguel is a trusted friend."

Alberto cleared his throat and put on his most professional front to try to keep his emotions in check and conceal what he now knew and was feeling. "Mr. Secretary, the caller first spoke with my receptionist, who then had him speak to my administrative assistant. The caller indicated that he had sensitive information regarding Emilio's assassination that could only be given to me personally. My assistant made the correct judgment that I should take the call. The caller, without preamble, told me President Fernandez was going to be killed in Hermosillo, and an attempt also would be made on my life today. He said my official car had been compromised with an explosive device that would be detonated upon my departure from my office. I have my bomb-disposal team conducting a search as we speak. If a device is found, we'll have confirmation that this isn't a hoax. In the meantime, while the search is conducted, it's my judgment that we should treat this as a real threat against the president. Call it my police intuition if you wish."

Alvarez solemnly nodded, but inside he was reeling with apprehension as he thought, *My God, a bomb in Alberto's car? Is this a coincidence of some kind? Has one of the Gang of Four decided to move against him? Perhaps even me? If so, how do they know about the president? Have we been penetrated? Is there a traitor among us?*

With those thoughts in his head, Alvarez was now also disturbed but tried to remain impassive. "That's enough for me, Alberto. We'll proceed on the premise that the threat is genuine. What have you done to this point?"

Alberto glanced at his watch; it read 10:45 a.m., the president's scheduled arrival time. "I've notified my people in Hermosillo, General Oberon directly, and the office of General Lopez through his chief of staff. I also attempted to call the president directly on the aircraft but was unsuccessful. I instructed my commander in Hermosillo to coordinate with General Lopez and the presidential guard upon their arrival and get the president to a secure location at the airport until we can coordinate his actions from there."

"Do you recommend canceling his tour of the camps?" Alvarez asked.

"Yes, yes, I would, but of course that will be up to the president and political considerations, which I realize are complex. Also we must consider how secure General Oberon feels his helicopters are. The ground transportation in the north is as secure as we can make it. I, of course, have escort forces to back up the presidential guard, and the local army commander has his forces as well. My greatest concern is the shoulder-fired surface-to-air missiles we know the cartels have acquired and also the RPGs…like they used against Emilio."

Alberto's encrypted cell phone rang. The caller ID let him know it was Commander Munoz. "Excuse me, Pablo. This is Munoz, my commander in Hermosillo." Alberto took the call. "Yes, Munoz?"

"Mr. Secretary!" an agitated Munoz said. "The president's plane just crashed on landing. It's almost completely destroyed and on fire. We're making our way to the scene, but the wreckage and fire are…are…catastrophic!"

"Slow down, Munoz. Take a breath. Was there an attack of some kind—a missile, perhaps?"

"No…no, I saw nothing of the sort. We are on the opposite side of the airport and not near the terminal where the president's plane was to taxi, but we were very near the runway. The plane touched down, and then it veered sharply toward us. Several people thought one of the landing gear collapsed suddenly, and then the wing and the engine struck the ground. I saw sparks, and then the plane exploded into flames. It all happened within a few seconds of landing. One of the press people here at the hangar says their station had a crew on the terminal observation deck across the way and has it all on video."

"Which station, Munoz?"

"Local Channel 10, I think he said. I have to go help. We're at the forward part of the president's aircraft. It broke free and crashed down the runway. There was no fire in that part of the plane, so we're checking for survivors. I'll get back to you when I know more."

"As soon as you can, Munoz, every fifteen minutes."

"Yes, Mr. Director."

During Alberto's call, when it had become clear to Alvarez that the plane had crashed as planned, he got on his intercom and summoned his senior administrative assistant and Dolores into the office. They'd heard only the last part of Alberto's conversation.

Alberto was ashen faced and tense when he ended the call and said solemnly, "As you probably overheard, Pablo, the president's plane crashed on landing. I'm told the crash was catastrophic."

Alvarez turned to his to senior assistants. "Keep what the director just said secure for the time being, until we know more about this tragedy in Hermosillo."

Dolores gasped and put her hand to her mouth, tears forming in her eyes as Alvarez's senior aide just stood there, his mouth agape.

Alvarez went on. "We don't know if this was a deliberate act or simply a tragic accident. I want only senior staff to be notified, as well as the directors at the AFI and the National Air Traffic Investigation Board. Have them organize an investigation team and get them moving to Hermosillo. Have them coordinate with General Oberon for transport and security; we'll alert his office from here to expect them. No one is to speak with any media; all information is to come out of this office. All calls from anyone are to be referred here for me or Director Rodriguez. Make sure all the other directors are made aware of my order. Get the situation center up and manned. Any questions?"

Dolores and the senior aide shook their heads, obviously still stunned at the news, and hurried out of the office. Alberto stood and went to the other end of the room, where Miguel was sitting, just watching him. The old bodyguard had yet to say a word or even acknowledge Alberto's presence beyond a look. Alberto turned on the television and scanned the cable listings, looking for the Hermosillo independent station. When he found it, a clearly flustered studio personality was giving a report and then said they were cutting to a reporter on the scene. A very pretty young woman appeared onscreen and gave a recap of the events from her perch on the main-terminal observation deck as the camera slowly zoomed in on the still-burning wreckage. As the reporter spoke, the camera panned to the left, and the forward part of the wrecked jet was visible, identifiable only by its general shape and the cockpit and nose areas, which were intact. Rescuers were carrying bodies out of this part of the wreckage, and Alberto thought he recognized Munoz among those assisting the injured.

Alvarez joined Alberto in front of the television. After some live shots, they cut back to the studio and showed a replay of the plane's approach and landing. Alvarez grabbed a remote and apparently was recording the broadcast. The station showed the replay in real time and then in slow motion, with the program's pretty-boy talking head speculating that it appeared clear that one of the landing gear on the president's new billion-peso jet had failed on landing.

Alvarez turned to Alberto. "Your thoughts…an accident or a deliberate act?"

Alberto looked devastated. "Given the threat call, Pablo, it surely was a deliberate act, likely made to appear as an accident. Without the call, I would have said what I've just seen was an accident. But we can't ignore the warning, if that's what it was."

Alberto's phone rang again. "It's Munoz, Pablo," he said as he saw the incoming number. "Report, Munoz," he ordered brusquely.

"We have some survivors from the forward part of the aircraft, sir. At least ten or twelve, maybe more. We've removed eight so far and have them headed for the hospital. The fire-rescue people are cutting the more severely injured out of the wreckage, where they're pinned and—"

"The president, Munoz...Do you have the president!" Alberto interrupted angrily.

"No, Mr. Director, I'm afraid the president has perished, sir. Both pilots were conscious when we reached the scene and were attending to some of the others. They and the two flight attendants seated nearest the front mercifully were spared any severe injuries. The chief pilot, Colonel Delgado from the air force, said President Fernandez was in his office in the rear of the aircraft on approach, with his aides and General Lopez of his presidential guard. Only those seated in the forward part of the cabin—the part that broke free and didn't burn, Mr. Director—only those poor souls have any chance of surviving. There's nothing left of the others."

Alberto sighed and took a moment, fighting to get his emotions under control. "Good report, Munoz. Seal off the area. No one gets in or out except for doctors and ambulances. Have some of our men in each vehicle that leaves the site. I want guards on the survivors' rooms at the hospitals. No one is to talk to any survivor."

"With apologies, Mr. Director," Munoz said, "I didn't think of this, and several ambulances already have left."

"Send cars and men now, Munoz!" Alberto nearly shouted. "I want all information on this disaster held tight. No one talks to anyone without my express approval. I want federal police with every survivor. Understand?"

"Of course, Mr. Director, of course. Immediately."

Alberto hung up and looked at Alvarez. "My apologies for my outburst, Pablo. Any further instructions?"

Alvarez appeared contemplative, but inside he was as devastated as his old friend but for very different reasons. The information Alberto had received couldn't be coincidental; someone had found him and Raul out, but who? He was so close to achieving his dreams—how had this happened? He could only hope Raul would be able to find out and soon, and end the threat.

"No, no, Alberto. Well done. Let's have all calls forwarded to my office and coordinate the investigation from here and the situation center down the hall—senior staff only. Have your deputy coordinate events at your office and relay all information here."

"Yes, Mr. Secretary," Alberto said sadly as he hung his head and stared at the floor.

Alberto didn't have the opportunity to make his noon call with Manny. By then it was confirmed from the crash site that there were a total of twelve survivors, all from the forward section of the jet. President Fernandez was dead; Alvarez called the senior members of the legislature and former President Castillo and told them the news as soon as Alberto's investigators had confirmed it on the scene. The president's remains hadn't yet been recovered or identified, but all the survivors had, and the president and General Lopez weren't among them.

At noon, when Alberto wanted to speak with Manny, he was instead at Alvarez's side as Alvarez conducted a formal live announcement to the country from the press room in the basement of the Department of Public Security building. The entire country was told that the investigation into the crash of the president's jet, which had resulted in his death and the deaths of six others accompanying him, was just beginning, but there was no initial evidence to suggest the crash was anything more than a tragic accident.

Alvarez wrote the release himself and delivered it smoothly, firmly, and calmly as the stunned crowd of reporters watched and listened. Many observers thought he appeared "presidential." Alberto was at Secretary Alvarez's side, but his gaze was no longer one of shock or sadness. Rather, his look, to anyone who knew him well, was one of pure hatred and anger, for he had no doubt in his mind he was looking at his brother's killer.

29

Predator Control
Fort Bliss, Texas
Monday morning

Bennie was optimistic for the first time in weeks. He and Manny had arrived at the base Saturday night near midnight, and Sergeant Major Green personally had driven him to the VIP quarters and set him up there in a comfortable room. He spent Sunday getting introduced to the Predator team Manny had assigned to him and then planning the logistics for pinpointing the Condor's three estates from the air. After weeks of sleepless nights, worrying and wondering about Ray, last night Bennie couldn't sleep either, excited as he was at the prospect of actually doing something that might help his covert operative. At 0700, Sergeant Major Green delivered Bennie to the general's quarters for breakfast. After they finished, the sergeant major took him to the secure drone control center, where Bennie continued planning his operation.

Several hours later, as Bennie was working out details of the drone surveillance with the young captain whose team was assigned to help him, one of the NCOs told him the general was on the line for him. Bennie took the telephone and said excitedly, "Good news, general. Your people are top-shelf. This is going to be easier than I ever would've imagined."

It was as if Manny hadn't heard a word he'd said. "Bennie, have one of the men drive you over here ASAP," he said brusquely. "Something's come up."

From the general's tone, Bennie immediately knew something was very wrong. "What is it, General?"

"Not over the phone, Bennie. Get moving."

"Yes, sir." *Shit,* Bennie thought. *I knew things were going too well. What the hell has happened now?*

The staff sergeant who had taken the general's call drove Bennie the eight blocks to the headquarters building and Manny's office. Colonel Romero was standing in the orderly room outside the office and waved him in. The general and the sergeant major were already in the office as Bennie passed through the door, and Colonel Romero closed it behind him.

Bennie shot a quick glance at the colonel and then at the others in the room and saw the tension in their faces. "OK, General, tell me. What the hell's happened?"

Manny was sitting at his desk, his look grim, his hands clenched. "We just got word that President Fernandez's plane crashed about fifteen minutes ago as it was landing in Hermosillo. From the NSA flash message, it sounds as if the crash was catastrophic."

Bennie stared at Manny and then slowly sat down in the chair next to him and said, "Oh…shit."

"The NSA has some video they're sending me that they picked off a Mex-Tel communications satellite," Manny said. "I wanted you here when we got it. Looks like you might be right—big things may in fact be happening, if this wasn't an accident."

Bennie jumped to his feet and paced in front of Manny's desk as he ran a hand through his hair. "Jesus Christ, General, this was no fucking accident! I wasn't expecting this. But like I told you Saturday night, I don't believe in coincidence. A cartel—and my money's on the Condor—just knocked off the president." He stopped pacing, took a deep breath, and looked at Manny. "The million-dollar question is why? This move makes no sense from a cartel point of view. The logical presidential replacement is the secretary for public security, and his record and character are superb compared to Fernandez. My gut feeling is that things just got harder—not easier—for the cartels with Fernandez out of the way, so why do it?"

"Sit down, Bennie, please," Manny said, forcing a small, tight smile. "As to your question, I don't have a goddamned clue. But you said some interesting things the other night. Like maybe the Condor was afraid of something, which is why he's striking out at the Mexican government's leadership, if he in fact did this. Or he has a plan, and the next step was a big play, leading to something more dramatic, you said. Well, this is about as goddamned dramatic as you can get. Maybe it's as simple as the fact that Fernandez was indeed working for the Condor, or some other cartel, and they knew the heat was on with the skimming operation Alberto mentioned. Maybe Fernandez was going to come clean and perhaps divulge other information. We can speculate all we want, but it won't get us anywhere.

"Alberto might be able to shed some light on this. He's no doubt up to his ass in alligators, but he messaged me over a nonsecure line a little while ago and said he'd try to make contact at noon and every two hours after that, his schedule permitting, and I would know why. He had to be referring to the crash, but his initial call came in before it occurred—that's what's really bothering me. I'll want you here for that, Bennie; I need to introduce you two anyway. For now, maybe you and Romey can kick the intelligence around and see if you can make sense of this. Romey, take Bennie to your office, and I'll call you when I get the video feed."

They all nodded and filed out of Manny's office. Bennie and the colonel weren't getting much accomplished when Manny buzzed them about fifteen minutes later. They walked back to his office, gathered around the general's see-tee, and watched the NSA replay of the crash as recorded by one of the Mexican television stations a couple of times before they had seen enough.

Manny's phone buzzed, and Sergeant Major Green answered it and handed it to Manny. "The G-2, General."

"Yes, Colonel?" Manny listened for a minute and then hung up, a solemn look on his face. "That was Scott. It's just been confirmed. Fernandez is dead."

"General," Bennie said as the others sat quietly in shock, "everyone will call this an accident. I think we all agree it looks like the right gear collapsed on landing, and then the wing tank blew when it hit the runway, but this was an assassination...and a goddamn near-perfect one. Someone with resources and access compromised that plane and blew that gear as sure as shit as I'm sitting here. No way was this a coincidence. Anyone disagree?"

The others nodded in silent agreement. After some more discussion that got them nowhere, Bennie hung around Colonel Romero's office until a few minutes before noon, and then the team gathered again in Manny's office. By twelve thirty, it was clear that Alberto was tied up and wouldn't be calling. This was confirmed when Manny's G-2 called to alert them that there was a news conference from Mexico taking place right then that CNN was carrying. They tuned in and saw Alberto at Secretary Alvarez's side as the news was delivered to the people of Mexico and the world regarding the death of President Rafael Fernandez.

After the news conference, it made little sense to sit around the general's office waiting for more news or for Alberto's next call, so Bennie went back to the recon unit to check up on the Chihuahua-estate surveillance that the young captain and his team were putting into play and also to call Charley in DC. He silently cursed himself as he pulled out his cell phone and saw that he'd killed the battery, as he was prone to do when immersed in a project and distracted. He'd been so excited to get to Fort Bliss and start the search for Ray that he'd forgotten to charge it last night. He switched it off, knowing Charley would be following the events in Mexico in his capacity as director of intelligence, and if he wanted to contact Bennie and couldn't reach him on his cell, he'd know to call Manny's office.

Later in the afternoon, Alberto contacted Manny on his personal cell and, in a very short conversation, said he would contact him at 1600 via the see-tee, so Bennie remained at Predator Control until then. When he returned to the general's office, Colonel Romero was setting up the see-tee and getting ready to initiate contact when Alberto beat him to it from his see-tee at his home in Mexico City.

"Ghost One for Safety One" appeared in a pop-up dialogue box on Manny's screen. Romey clicked on the video-stream icon, and Alberto's tense, drawn face filled the screen. "Hola, Colonel, Manny."

"Hi, Al," Manny responded. "Tough day. We've been following events here and saw the crash video. How're you holding up?"

"Not good, Manny. Not good. Before we go on, I need a favor."

"Anything, Al. Name it."

"I need you to track down an American DEA official by the name of Bennie Santiago for me, and I need you to do this in the strictest of confidence. I'll explain later."

All heads in the room turned and looked at Bennie, who was sitting off to the side of the general's desk. Bennie looked back at the others in amazement. Alberto saw the astonished looks on the faces of Manny and Colonel Romero at what he believed was a simple request and was puzzled. He couldn't see the others in the room through his limited camera view.

"For God's sake, what is it, Manny?" Alberto said nervously. "Why the odd reaction?"

Manny, eyebrows raised, said, "Alberto, I'd like to introduce you to Bennie Santiago. He's here in my office."

It was now Alberto's turn to be astonished. "Not that I'm not pleased to meet Mr. Santiago, Manny, but how on earth is it possible that he's with you and obviously privileged to this secure communication?"

"We'll get into all that, but first you guys need to see each other, and Alberto, you need to explain why you wanted Bennie and exactly how you came by his name."

Bennie exchanged seats with Colonel Romero, and Alberto could now see him.

"Of course, Manny." Alberto's on-screen gaze shifted from his cousin to Bennie. "I'm dumbfounded, Señor Santiago, as you no doubt must realize, but I'm very pleased to meet you."

"Please, Señor Rodriguez, call me Bennie. It's an honor to meet you, sir. First let me say how sorry I am about your brother. Now what can I do for you?"

Alberto nodded, acknowledging Bennie's thoughtful comment. "Does the name Trojan Horse mean anything to you?"

Bennie snapped back in his seat at the mention of the code name of his operation. After a pause of several seconds to collect himself, he leaned toward the monitor and said, "Yes, it does, Señor Rodriguez. It's the code name for a covert DEA operation I've been running in Mexico for three months. I managed to slip one of our best operatives in with a suspected high-level Mexican drug trafficker in a prison up here. And after an escape I orchestrated, my operative was taken into a little-known cartel down there that we suspect is involved in much more than their profile would indicate. But he's been silent for almost nine weeks, and out of desperation, I solicited the support of General Rodriguez to help me find him, which is why I'm here. Please sir, how did you find out about this? Has my man become compromised? Is he all right? Don't tell me he's involved with President Fernandez's death somehow."

Alberto looked amazed at what Bennie told him. "Well, Bennie," he said, "he's silent no longer, and as far as I know, he hasn't been discovered. I still don't know who he is, as a matter of fact, and I presume he's still relatively safe. As to his involvement with the president's assassination—and gentlemen, the crash was an assassination—I have no idea how he's involved, only that he made an attempt to warn me about it. This past Saturday night, at a party in my brother's honor, hosted by Secretary Jacques Alvarez, I was unknowingly the recipient of a note addressed to me from someone who signed it Trojan Horse. I have no idea who slipped it to me, Bennie, but it said to contact you and only you."

Bennie was overjoyed, and his face showed it. "Sir, you've made my day. To know that my agent is alive has lifted a great weight off my shoulders."

"I'm happy for you, of course," Alberto said, "but I also have dire news, I'm afraid."

"I thought you said he was all right, sir?"

"I'm afraid none of us is all right. Let me read your agent's note, and you'll begin to see my problem." Alberto slowly read the note.

ALVAREZ IS CONDOR DE MUERTE
OF CHIHUAHUA, ALSO NICOLAS PEÑA
OF BAJA SUR. PRESIDENT FERNANDEZ TO
BE KILLED MONDAY IN HERMOSILLO
"ACCIDENT." YOU TO BE ASSASSINATED
MONDAY BY A BOMB IN YOUR CAR.
ALVAREZ WANTS THE PRESIDENCY.

CONTACT BENNIE SANTIAGO, US DEA
ONLY. REPEAT: ONLY. CONDOR SPIES ARE
EVERYWHERE. TRUST NO ONE.
SIGNED, TROJAN HORSE

"Jesus…fucking…Christ," Bennie said softly, breaking the stunned silence in the room. "You're talking about Secretary Alvarez, as in your boss, Señor Rodriguez?"

"I'm afraid so, Bennie. I wish it were otherwise."

"Now the plane crash makes perfect sense," Bennie said quietly.

"Yes, it does," Alberto replied, "and I have the sad duty to report that by eight o'clock this evening my time, the Permanent Presidential Commission will overwhelmingly approve a motion to name Alvarez the interim president. It seems, gentlemen, if the information in this note is genuine, my country is to be led by perhaps our most notorious cartel leader."

"Jesus, Alberto," Bennie nearly shouted, "can't you arrest him?"

Alberto moved closer to his monitor, his face almost completely filling the screen. He was clearly very emotional, certainly because of the horrific events of the day but also because of the uncertainty of the immediate future, and his tone conveyed this.

"On what evidence, Bennie? Perhaps in time, but I have to assemble irrefutable proof. Right now, there's what? The four or five of us who know the truth? And what do we really know? What do we have? A note from an American covert agent operating illegally in my country, accusing a man whom many in the upper levels of the government have known for thirty years. A man, I must point out, from a successful, wealthy, generous family that hasn't had one scintilla of scandal ever. My God, until today, the one man after my brother I had no doubt I could trust and rely upon in our government was Secretary Alvarez. And to make matters worse, if my planned raid on the Gang of Four comes off successfully in the next few weeks—a highly probable outcome based on the intelligence we have—it'll be as a result of our new president's initial plans and orders. So when I confront him,

I'll be accusing a veritable national hero of being a charlatan, a murderer, and a cartel leader."

Manny was also visibly agitated. "Goddamn it, Alberto, forget all that shit. What about the bomb in your car? Was that true?"

Alberto sat back in his chair, trying to compose himself. There was a brief lull in the conversation, and when he spoke, his voice was quieter, more reflective. "Yes, yes, it was, I'm sorry to say. After I received the note, I quietly had one of my explosives teams go through my car, and they found the device. It was very professionally constructed—small but sophisticated—and definitely would have done the job. My belated thanks and gratitude to your agent, Bennie. He no doubt saved my life. I hope to meet him personally in the near future under far better circumstances to tell him myself."

Bennie shook his head, still in a state of disbelief. "I hope we all have a chance to see that, sir."

Alberto sighed. "Manny, it's clear to me now that all the intelligence of any significance that Emilio and I received from confidential sources against the cartels in the last few years likely has come from Alvarez. He has access to everything—all our intelligence resources, in addition to everything he must know about the cartels themselves. It's also clear, given the information we have regarding the upcoming cartel summit, that my old friend Pablo Alvarez must have some of the other cartels as deeply penetrated as he does the government. To make matters worse, as of eight o'clock this evening, he'll have total access to—and control of—all our government apparatus. I doubt I could access a file in any sort of investigation against him that wouldn't immediately become known to him. Yes, we must act and act quickly, but we need proof, and I'm at a loss as to how to assemble it. I need help, gentlemen."

"It's almost as if that goddamned Mayan-calendar prophecy crap was true," Bennie said, shaking his head.

Alberto raised an eyebrow and almost smiled. "That's odd you should say that, Bennie. I had the same thought earlier today, just after the true nature of our new president was revealed and Fernandez's plane crashed. Until today, I'd never given end-of-world interpretations a moment's thought."

"Whoa, Al," Manny said, leaning in toward the see-tee. "I'm sorry, but you and Bennie lost me there. Calendars, end-of-world prophecies—what the hell are you guys talking about?"

Alberto actually smiled a small smile. "I'm sorry, Manny, but don't despair—a depressing but purely coincidental aside with my new friend Bennie here. He was referring to two of the Mayan calendars and the end-of-days prophecy. The Long Count calendar, which covers a period of more than five thousand years, and the far shorter Tzolkin calendar have been much discussed throughout our history but more so recently. Both make reference to the winter solstice of this year as being not only the end of the Long Count Calendar but also the end of days in some interpretations; in others, it marks the descent of a deity. Various scholars and others—such as conspiracy theorists looking to capitalize on the interest in the Mayan calendar—have written much about this subject over the years. As we've gotten closer to the solstice, the interest has grown. A more learned interpretation of the calendar's glyphs states something to the effect that there will be events, whether apocalyptic or not, beginning with the summer equinox and ending with the winter solstice, from June twenty-first of this year until December twenty-first. In other words, they don't literally mean the end of the world or an apocalypse at all but rather revelations of knowledge, perhaps positive, perhaps negative, perhaps both, that have before now been hidden from view—a descending deity, for example. The coincidence I was referring to is that the equinox has just passed, and we're in the noted period.

"If one believed in such nonsense, one could take a collective view of the recent events in Mexico—the crush of human misery at our northern border, the dramatic increase in murders associated with drug trafficking, the crash of the presidential plane, and now the revelation, so to speak, that our new president is in fact evil—and conclude that the end-of-days prophecy is indeed happening and will culminate on the solstice with something...what, we don't know, maybe worse, maybe better...and then the Long Calendar will begin anew. As I believe none of this—like Bennie, I'm sure—I was simply telling him that in a moment of deep despair earlier today, he wasn't the only one to think of the prophecy on this awful day."

Manny leaned back in his chair with a look of total exasperation. "Thanks a bunch for enlightening me, Al. I probably could've gone all day without knowing that crazy shit. I'd say we have our hands full with the here and now, so what do we do about that?"

"My apologies, Manny. I agree," Alberto said. "Let's deal with what we know or think we know. First, may I have the name of your agent, Bennie, and what he looks like, so I can discover the one ally I have in the disaster my life has become?"

Bennie didn't hesitate. "Yes, sir. His name is Ray Cruz. He's twenty-six, but he went undercover as a twenty-year-old. About five ten, athletic, trim, handsome to the ladies."

"My God," Alberto said softly, looking away and thinking. "Alvarez came back to the city last week from his home in Baja. He's always surrounded by his four personal bodyguards—close friends, really—who go everywhere he does. One of these, an older man named Francisco Ortega, who'd been with Alvarez since we were boys, died unexpectedly in the last several weeks and was replaced by his nephew, a nephew I'd never met nor heard of before, not that I necessarily would have. This young man meets your description and was introduced to me as Ray Ortega. He's the new member of Alvarez's personal security and is with him almost every hour of the day. I congratulate you, Benny, on the success of your agent's penetration. It's most impressive—and in only three months, you said?"

Bennie looked very unhappy, even with the compliment. "Yeah, thanks, but while I take comfort in knowing my man is alive, I'd be a liar if I didn't say I'm troubled by his apparent success in getting so close to Alvarez so quickly. We'd hoped Ray would wind up a trusted flunky of some kind, a soldier or driver, that sort of thing, but a personal aide and that close? That's not only unusual but also incredibly dangerous for him. And to do so in three months…well, it's me who's dumbfounded now."

"That would explain why you haven't heard from him, Bennie, being as close to the throne as he is," Manny said.

"Did I understand you to say, Bennie, that your man has been out of communication for a couple of months?" Alberto asked.

"That's correct, sir…about nine weeks. Ray was able to contact me twice early on, but he was quick to mention that the cartel leader was a real cautious, intelligent sort. He had all communications around him monitored twenty-four seven. Ray was only able to slip out and make contact when he was acting as a bodyguard to the Condor's cousin, who, it seems, isn't nearly as careful as the Condor."

Alberto slowly rubbed his chin and nodded as if he were in deep thought. He looked up and said, "Then the circumstances would seem to support the conclusion that your man was likely just what you wanted him to be—a lower-echelon member, perhaps a simple guard to this cousin, as you said. As such, he was able to contact you. Something apparently happened that resulted in his being included in a very select group. He therefore had to be extremely careful, and as a result, he no longer was able to contact you. My God, what he must know? I remember him now, from the party. A waiter spilled some glasses, and this young man was standing nearby and helped the waiter. There was some minor jostling as this occurred. That's when he must have passed me the note. But why me? How did he know to contact me?"

"All I can imagine," Bennie said softly, "is that you were somehow identified to him as someone this Alvarez couldn't compromise, an enemy to Alvarez, perhaps. That's the only logical explanation, so he found his messenger. Any enemy to Alvarez would be a friend to Ray. Frankly, I'm surprised that he tried what he did. Had he been seen, or had you caught him doing it…well, I'd hate to think of the consequences."

"It's clear," Alberto said, "that your agent took such a great risk in order to try to save Fernandez and me. Only I failed him—and Fernandez—in this. I simply didn't notice the note. It wasn't until this morning, when my valet was going through my suit from Saturday night before sending it to be cleaned, that he discovered it and brought it to me. By then it was too late. The president's jet was within minutes of landing."

Manny leaned in toward the monitor again. "What about the car bomb, Alberto? Have you gotten to the bottom of that?"

Alberto nodded. "I believe so. The device was attached to the underside of the trunk. I suspect I even know how it was placed. Alvarez's closest aide is a man named Raul Ortega, the younger brother of the man Ray replaced. He and Ray assisted me the other day with some files as I was leaving Alvarez's office. There were several boxes, and they offered to carry them to the car for me and then placed them in the trunk. My guess is that Raul planted the device then, and there was nothing Bennie's agent could do to stop him without revealing himself. He then obviously conceived of the message drop and managed to pass me the note surreptitiously, to warn me and also to maintain his cover. A very sharp operative indeed, Bennie."

The others had listened in amazed silence to the exchanges among Alberto, Manny, and Bennie. It was the general officer in Manny that began to bring focus to the situation. "Alberto, we have a hell of a problem here. You're the expert—you and Bennie—on matters of police work. We need a plan to get the evidence you require. Obviously Bennie's agent would make a hell of a witness, so securing him would seem to be the priority, would it not?"

"Of course," Alberto said. "That's our first consideration, but to do so and not tip off Alvarez and also expose Bennie's agent is the more difficult problem."

"Alberto?"

"Yes, Bennie?"

"Ray sent us some great intelligence in the first four weeks he was inside. I agree with you—I can't imagine everything he's learned in the last nine weeks, especially after getting as close to Alvarez as he has. Not only is he our best witness, but he's also our best source for more evidence. Is there any way you can snatch him and hide him and not have Alvarez know who did it? I mean, there are thousands of kidnappings each year in Mexico City, right?"

Alberto looked depressed. "Regrettably, yes, there are, but what you suggest isn't possible, especially now. At this moment, there's no man in my country more protected than Alvarez, by all the legitimate services of our country, in addition to his own men. Because of my office and relationship with our new president, I can gain access to Alvarez and therefore his residence, where his retinue and therefore your agent resides—but not with any amount of force. If I show up with force anywhere, I'll be considered the criminal. Given your operative's proximity to Alvarez, he's as protected as our new president is. I would suggest, as a first step, that we try to devise a way to contact your agent and let him know that he's succeeded in warning us and that he's believed."

"That was my first thought too, Al," Manny interjected.

"Mr. Rodriguez," Colonel Romero said, speaking up for the first time, "excuse me, but who is this Nicolas Peña that the note mentions? Does he exist? And if so, how does he figure into all this?"

Alberto was silent and contemplative for a moment and also looked very unhappy. "Yes, Colonel, he does exist—or until this morning, I thought he did. He's one of our country's wealthiest, most successful businessmen, with no known ties to the cartels. He's always been a bit of a recluse but very philanthropic, just like his father before him. Peña has interests all over the country and in the United States, but he's a private man, seldom seen in public. He lives primarily in Baja Sur." Alberto paused again and began rubbing his chin, as if a thought had just occurred to him. He looked up, a bit wide-eyed, as if surprised. "My God…it's so obvious to me now. The Peña estate and that of the Alvarez family are adjacent to each other in Baja. That's how he's done this. How could I have been so blind and stupid!"

"Done what, Al?" Manny asked. "What the hell are you talking about now?"

Alberto shook his head in disbelief. "How Alvarez has successfully moved about Mexico for so long, in secrecy, with his other identities. You realize we're talking about at least three known identities, obviously with altered appearances: his real one, Peña, and, of course, the Condor. The Alvarez estate and the Peña estate are next to each other on the west coast of Baja Sur. Not really close, but adjacent. Alvarez goes to his family home, and then, somehow, unseen and unknown to others, he moves to the Peña estate and leaves from there, free to move about the country—the world, really—as Nicolas Peña. Once he's left the careful scrutiny that surrounds him as the secretary and has the relative anonymity of the businessman Peña, he becomes the Condor de Muerte. It's ingenious and so simple."

"Señor Rodriguez," Colonel Romero interrupted, "these estates in Baja Sur...where exactly are they?"

"On the west coast, Colonel, in the south, near Todos Santos."

Colonel Romero nodded. "I think I know why your brother was killed, sir."

Alberto clearly had an emotional reaction to this statement, as he sat back in his chair, a surprised and hurt expression forming on his face. He said slowly, "Tell me, please, Colonel, what do you think you know?"

"It was your aircraft surveillance, sir. The data from your surveillance troops revealed black flights coming and going from an area just north of Todos Santos. I didn't know what was down there until now, but certainly your brother knew, and he knew who lived in the area. I'm not saying he had it all figured out. Maybe he did, maybe not, but he now had a lightly populated area and likely a short list of suspects, including, apparently, Secretary Alvarez and this Peña character. How many people live in that area?"

"Not many," Alberto said pensively. "The night before he was killed, Emilio met privately with Alvarez, at which time, because of their close friendship, he probably told him where he was in his thinking." Alberto shifted his focus back to Bennie. "Motive, Bennie. There's always a motive in murder, as you well know."

Bennie nodded as Colonel Romero went on. "I'm sorry if I appear to be pressing you, sir, but how the hell can something like the travels of two such high-profile individuals in your society go unnoticed? I mean, we're talking your top cabinet official and also one of your country's wealthiest citizens. These estates must have household staffs, workers—and what about the people who travel with Alvarez? What about the press? With what Bennie has told us about the Condor, he's been around for at least ten years. I mean, Alvarez is a public figure, and this guy Peña, the rich one—you said he's well-known also. Surely someone must notice when these people are on the move or missing for some time."

Alberto's lips were pursed, his face tense and drawn, as he nervously drummed his fingers on his desk. "Colonel, let me try to explain. My God... as I think about it, it's all so clever. Alvarez has used our own culture to help him in his deceptions. As secretary for public security, he's the second-most powerful person in government after the president the cartels would like to kill. His movements in his capacity as secretary therefore aren't always made known; to announce his travel schedule surely would invite attacks. No one questions that Alvarez moves around often and in secrecy; in fact, it's quite expected. And when he goes to his Baja estate, my national police and our other security services secure the perimeter outside the walls, but only Alvarez's personal guards and closest aides—we're talking about as few as six to eight men—accompany him into his home.

"Emilio used to say, 'If you have a secret that truly must be kept, tell no one. But if you have to tell someone, make it your brother.' What I'm suggesting, Colonel, is that very few people must be aware of the truth, and they are likely close family or old friends of Alvarez. I know that until Bennie's agent became part of the group, the four personal guards around Alvarez had been with him for many years. Several of them were protecting him when he entered Saint Matthew's prep school, where we first met. I've known some of these men for almost forty years without *really* knowing them. I'm ashamed to admit it, but in my country there exists a real separation in the classes. People of means—those who have domestic staffs and personal security, for example—while typically not unkind to their servants, come to view them as part of the furniture, so to speak. In our time at Saint Matthew's, and then at the university, where my brother and Alvarez joined me, the guards were always just in the background, available to fetch a drink or provide some other service. That's what I mean by my not really knowing them. The youngest member of Alvarez's inner guard, before Ray, is the son of an old friend of Alvarez's."

Colonel Romero just sat there shaking his head slowly in disbelief as Alberto went on. "Don't you see? These people have been a part of his conspiracy for decades, perhaps, and the secrecy of their small group has been passed down from father to son, for the most part, until now. The reality, Colonel, is that in Mexico, because of the culture of the cartels and crime in general, especially the kidnappings, those with wealth must take great precautions. So moving around unannounced and having personal security forces is common. No one ever questions when Alvarez goes home to Baja and isn't seen for a week or two. In that time, after somehow assuming the persona of his neighbor Señor Peña, he no doubt quietly leaves by the front door of the adjacent estate, goes to La Paz or one of the other Baja airports, and flies to anywhere he wishes, unnoticed by all except perhaps for the very few in the financial or business world who would be interested in and are aware of where the successful yet private businessman Peña is. I mean, think about it—unless you happen to have an interest in business, or actually do business with Señor Peña, who else really knows him or cares where and when he travels?

"Now that I see the pieces, it isn't difficult for me to see how Alvarez has accomplished this. As long as the very few who know his secret keep it, he is—or was—secure. His mistake was letting Ray get so close so fast. That's the puzzling part in all this. Why, as careful and methodical as Alvarez apparently has been over these many years while creating his deception, has he made such a mistake? Your man must be very good, Bennie."

Bennie shook his head. "He is, sir, but not *that* good. What I mean is that something extraordinary had to have happened. The last thing an undercover guy wants is a high profile. Rather, he wants to blend into the furniture, as you described. No, something changed the dynamic, probably something out of Ray's control. Excuse me for the bluntness of this, but I had one thought as you were talking. Is Alvarez gay or something? I mean, Ray is a good-looking guy. Does he maybe like the kid romantically? Romantic attachments can be a real game changer in undercover work."

Alberto smiled again. "No, no, Bennie. That's an interesting thought, but I've known Alvarez for forty years. He and Emilio were roommates at Saint Matthew's and then at the university. Emilio would've known if his sexual predilections ran that way. Alvarez enjoys the company of his wife, and there were assorted others before her. He didn't marry until later in life, but it has to be something else. Manny's right; I need to find a way to contact Ray, and obviously I have to do so in a manner that doesn't betray him."

"What if I came down there," Bennie said, "to coordinate, say, on what we could be doing with the Gang of Four operations up here, for example, to complement your upcoming actions?"

Alberto was clearly interested in this idea. "Do you have some information in this regard? Can we in fact actually coordinate some actions on such short notice? I'm embarrassed to say, given the leaks we've had regarding our joint operations, on both our sides, that we've been keeping all information on our upcoming raid very tight."

Bennie nodded. "I certainly don't blame you, sir. As for the Gang of Four operations up here, we don't have much intelligence on their distribution network at all, but the cartels don't know that. We bust up the occasional operation that ends up being one of theirs, but we find that out after the fact. My thinking is that perhaps if you could arrange for me to be seen by Ray somehow, he would at least know his message was received. If he sees me with you, that'll be even better—he'll know you and I are working together and he's not alone. That's kind of what I was trying to do with the general's help, actually."

"That sounds like a good start to me, Al," Manny said. "What do you think?"

Alberto quickly agreed. "I see no harm in trying it. You're most welcome to come here, Bennie. Just contact me when you arrive. Manny has my private number, but it's best that nothing important is discussed over the phone. You'll be a guest in my home. I'll let my chief of staff know that I'm expecting you regarding matters of coordination, but I won't say anything further. As of tomorrow, despite my objections, I'm to be made the interim secretary for public security. I'll be moving to my new office, Alvarez's old one, this week. In the meantime, I'll give a great deal of thought as to how to best contact Ray. We need face-to-face contact, in private, and soon. We need to know what he knows. That's our challenge, gentlemen. Perhaps by the time you get down here, Bennie, I'll have thought of something more."

"Thanks, Señor Rodriguez. I'll catch the first plane out," Bennie said.

"Congratulations on the promotion, Al, and good luck," Manny said.

"Thank you, cousin. I'll definitely need it."

The see-tee went blank as Alberto signed off. Manny, Bennie, Colonel Romero, and Sergeant Major Green looked at one another in amazed silence, each mulling over the titanic revelations Alberto had shared.

Bennie was the first to say anything. "General, I need to update my boss on all this, and I'm extremely reluctant to do it even over a secure communications setup. I need to get to DC, and then I'll head to Mexico City out of Dulles. There are more flights out of there anyway."

"Whatever you think is best, Bennie," Manny replied.

"Sir?" Colonel Romero said. "Brigadier General Austin from the army's Management Staff College has been on post all day in connection with his duties at the Command Sergeant Major School and is scheduled to leave in a couple of hours, back to DC. He, of course, has one of the air force's small executive jets. He left word that he'd like to stop by here around eighteen hundred hours to make his manners before heading back. I suggest we get Bennie a seat on his plane, even if it means bumping someone from his staff."

Manny nodded. "Good idea, Romey. Bennie, go with Sergeant Major Green to your quarters and pack. I'll have a word with the brigadier and get you a seat on his plane. That'll get you into DC late tonight. I also suggest you call your boss and give him a heads-up that you're coming, so he can work on a flight for you for first thing in the morning. With any luck, you could be in Mexico City by tomorrow afternoon."

Bennie nodded. "Thanks, General. I'll do that. Could I borrow a phone? Like a dumb shit, I let my cell go dead."

"Sure," Manny said as he spun his desk phone toward Bennie. "Hit any outside line and dial nine." Bennie stood as Manny looked hard at him and asked. "I hate to be so blunt, but any ideas as to how you'll extricate your agent from under the nose of Mexico's corrupt new president without getting him, you, and my other cousin killed?"

Bennie was about to dial but stopped and looked at him for a few seconds. Then he shrugged and said, "General, I don't have a fucking clue, but I have to try."

30

The farmhouse
Near Toluca, Mexico
Monday, late morning

Ray sat in the Escalade, staring at the cell phone as it rang on the other end. After several seconds, he put it to his ear. He heard the usual clicking from the encryption system, and then a computerized voice indicated he should leave a message. He knew he was being recorded but sat silently, not knowing what to say. What *could* he say that would make any sense or explain his failures and the deaths he felt responsible for? How could he tell Bennie that he'd known about the impending assassination of a president but had done virtually nothing to stop it? If anyone could understand what it had been like during the past three months, Bennie could, but there was still no excuse in his mind for what he hadn't done. He wasn't in some third-world backwater. The president of a major country in the Western Hemisphere was dead; he had known about the plot, and except for his amateurish attempt to pass intelligence to Alberto Rodriguez, he'd done nothing more to stop it. To Bennie or anyone else investigating his actions, it would be abundantly clear that he had looked to save himself instead of saving the president and all the others who had died in the crash. He was ashamed and deeply depressed at the thought.

The tragedy was that Ray *had* decided this morning to do whatever it would take, even if it meant sacrificing himself to stop the attempts, especially the one on Alberto. But, like almost everything else about this mission, he controlled nothing and was stuck in Toluca, alone and without the means to act. Now President Fernandez and probably Alberto as well were dead, along with untold others, and he was responsible. He glanced at his watch; if Raul was on schedule, he was on his way out to return him and Roberto Nieves's family to Mexico City. Only there was no family at the farmhouse, just two dead bodies, one of them a longtime member of the inner circle. How would Raul react to that?

Ray realized he was being recorded yet had said nothing. After a few more seconds, he started talking, the words uneven and choppy, his tone reflecting his deep despair.

"Bennie, it's me. Listen…I don't have much time. President Fernandez is dead—you probably know that already. I got sucked into the assassination conspiracy last Thursday when the Condor—I mean Secretary Alvarez—moved us from the north to Baja and then down here…Shit, you probably don't know, do you? Alvarez is also the Condor de Muerte and the leader of the cartel I'm a part of. I tried passing a note to their top federal cop, Alberto Rodriguez, warning him about all this after we arrived in Mexico City. But since Rodriguez didn't stop the president's flight, I'm guessing he didn't get it, or I misjudged him and he's a part of this shit show somehow. Probably doesn't matter; by now he's also dead. I know because I was with Raul Ortega, Alvarez's closest friend and head of his security, when he placed the explosive in Rodriguez's car. If I could have stopped him then and somehow survived, I would have, but there was just no way…no way. I thought my note would be enough, and Rodriguez would act, and I'd still have cover, but somehow I was wrong. They're all dead, Bennie…because I didn't do more."

Ray was silent for a few moments, overcome with emotion and the cold realization that his inability—or more accurately, he thought, his reluctance—to act had resulted in so much death.

"I'm fucked, Bennie. I've let you down in so many ways. I'm ashamed… because I wanted to live…to see my dad again, but how can I face him after what I've done?"

He paused, looked out the windshield, and shook his head. "It's funny…I hadn't thought about this until now, but Alvarez did what he's doing because of his dad. Shit, I'm rambling. There's been a lot of talk about dads down here. Jesus, that must sound ridiculous to you."

He paused again and took a deep breath, trying to keep it together. "Look, I'm in Toluca, doing my part in the plot. There's no time to tell you what that is or why. Raul will be here any second. I even failed him—that also probably makes no sense to you. How can I fail someone I'm supposed to be taking down, right?"

Ray got choked up; he was losing it and knew it. The accumulated stress of his twelve weeks inside the cartel was finally too much, compounded as it was by his guilt. He sat there, taking slow, deep, breaths, trying to get control. His voice barely above a whisper, he went on. "I killed a man today, Bennie—the second time since I've been here. I had no choice. Both were total shits, murderers, but I feel…Jesus, what do I feel? Bad…it makes me feel bad. Sorry, Bennie, but I guess I wasn't built to kill…hell of a way to find out."

Again he fell silent for a long few seconds, the images of the two kills fresh in his mind's eye. He sat up a little straighter in his seat, took another deep breath, and exhaled slowly. "Look, Bennie…I'm lost to you. I can't see how I can ever come back and face you…or my dad…not with what I did. I don't want to end up in jail for what I've done—I saw what that was like three months ago. I'm not sure what's going to happen when Raul gets here. I may have to kill him if I want to live…and Bennie, he's a good man. Despite everything that's gone on down here, he's a good man."

Ray put his free hand to his face and shook his head and then looked out the window again. "Christ, I just told you I don't want to kill ever again, and now I'm saying I might have to kill him. How fucked up is that? This whole goddamned mission is fucked up, and I'm tired of it," he said, his voice rising at first and then trailing off. "Alvarez is probably the president by now. He's corrupt, but…he's also good, Bennie. His motives are, anyway. Because of the cartels, this country…this country is a shithole. I'm not sure there's any other way to end the insanity down here except to do what Alvarez is trying to do. He's a philosopher. Did I tell you that? Doesn't matter. Look…I know I'm wandering again…and this probably won't make any sense to you, but it's kinda like what the philosopher Nietzsche said about fighting monsters, only down here you have to be one to get them—there's no other way. Listen, Bennie, I'm out of time—and out of options. I realize now that I can't come home, not after what I've done…or didn't do. I only have two choices left, I think: kill Alvarez…or join him. If I kill him, it means I'll probably die too. After today, the cops are probably all on edge. I know I'd be.

"But Alvarez likes me and trusts me; so does Raul. If I join them, I can maybe help them kill more of the motherfuckers who are wrecking this country. That's what Alvarez lives for; it's what drives him. It also would buy me time—time for what, I'm not sure, but I'd go on living for a while, and that's all I have left to hang on to. Maybe sometime in the future if or when the truth of down here becomes known, and if I'm still alive, you'll have me back. I know a lot."

Ray fell silent again, thinking of what else to say. When he did speak, his voice was softer, the resignation in his tone obvious. "I'm sorry, Bennie…for failing you like I have. I did try, but one thing led to another and I couldn't stop it, or control it. Listen, whatever happens, could you get word to my dad? Tell him I tried to see right from wrong…but the gray…the gray just got too hard to see through. Tell him, Bennie. He'll understand what I'm trying to say…and tell him I…love him."

Ray ended the call and leaned forward, his hands on the steering wheel, his head on his hands, and he stifled a sob. He snapped up and yelled, as he slammed the steering wheel repeatedly, "Shit, shit, shit!"

He grabbed the steering wheel and sat for a few minutes until his heart stopped pounding in his chest and his breathing became more normal. He wiped his face with the back of his sleeve and then sat up, tossed the cell phone out the window, and started the SUV. He pulled out of the parking lot and drove slowly in the general direction of the farmhouse. He wasn't sure what he was going to do, but any action had to begin by facing Raul, who was undoubtedly on his way to Toluca and might even be at the farm already. He also had to face Alvarez one way or another—to kill him—or join him. With Alberto dead too, and his not having acted on the note, it was possible that no one down here was aware of its contents. Maybe Alvarez's secrets were still safe, and only those in the circle ever would know the entire truth.

Since the assassination attempt on Alvarez, Ray had been tormented by his growing friendship with Raul, as well as his growing respect and admiration for Alvarez. And he wondered how he ever would resolve the deep personal conflicts he was feeling. If he joined them however, those feelings no longer would be a problem. As he slowly drove back to the farmhouse, he thought maybe he was finally seeing some clarity, the gray veil between right and wrong his dad spoke of slowly evaporating, but it would require him to start his life over. He wasn't sure that was even possible.

The one remaining problem with his thinking was that he couldn't justify the murder of Alberto Rodriquez unless…unless it was proved that he also was corrupt. If, however, Alberto was truly good and simply had missed his note somehow, how could he just look the other way and join up with Raul and Alvarez? How then would he be any different from them? Maybe he wasn't; that thought sadly had occurred to him before. He knew that if he asked, Raul would arrange a private meeting, even if Alvarez was the president by the time they got back to the estate. He could be alone with just the two of them. They both liked him; they'd never expect an attack from him if it came to that. But one immutable fact still nagged him: Alberto hadn't acted on his note. What did that mean?

Another thought came to Ray as he approached the farmhouse—could he tell them the truth about himself and live? That certainly would simplify his life some, maybe even relieve most of the paralyzing stress. Could Raul and Alvarez possibly understand and accept that after he had seen the reality Mexico had become, he had changed? Could they understand that he realized it was possible to do more good by truly becoming a part of their circle? Could they forgive him for his initial mission and the information he had passed to Bennie if he decided to tell them the truth? If Alberto was dead, and it became clear that he hadn't passed on the note's contents, Alvarez's secrets were still safe. Who would even believe what he had told Bennie when it became known he wasn't only a failed agent but now a rogue one too?

Whatever the case, if Ray sensed they couldn't or wouldn't forgive him, he'd have no choice; he'd have to kill them both. He'd have to kill Raul first; he'd be armed. But Alvarez surely would try to protect his old friend. The security Alvarez would have around him now that he was president would go crazy, maybe kill him on the spot. But if by some miracle he was taken into custody, he might survive if he could get someone to listen to him. If he could get someone clean to contact Bennie, maybe there was even a way out of Mexico, but a way out to what? Dismissal and disgrace? Likely even jail? He no longer had a future back home; his failures had seen to that.

Ray's future—his life, he decided—depended completely on how Raul and Alvarez reacted. With the exception of today's attack on the president and Alberto, everything Alvarez and Raul were doing was good, even noble. But what if the president *was* a criminal, as Raul had intimated? Was murder ever a justification, even if that was true? Certainly not in a country where the rule of law really meant something, but down here? Down here, that was another story, another reality.

Raul wasn't there yet when Ray pulled up in front of the farmhouse. He parked and went inside; the television was still on, the news of the horrific day still being reported. He stood in the living room for a minute, staring at Luis's body, and then returned to the porch and sat down in a chair. The day was growing warm; the house reeked of puke and death, and he couldn't stomach it for very long. He couldn't recall ever feeling as low as he felt now. He slumped over, putting his head in his hands. He didn't know how long he sat there, but when he heard Raul approach, he looked up. He remained in the chair, his Glock holstered, but he had Luis's handgun in his rear waistband, out of sight. And then there was his H-K, concealed in the sheath on his forearm. The thought of having to kill Raul to save himself was unacceptable to him—even more so when he thought about his knife. But as bad as he felt, he also wanted to survive; there seemed to be no answer to that conundrum.

As Raul slowly pulled to a stop beside the Escalade and got out, Ray realized for the first time in his life that he was really scared, but scared of what? Raul or himself? He realized now how frightening it was to face your inner self and discover just what you were capable of. He had no idea what he would say or do or how Raul would react. His desperation made it impossible to conceal what he was feeling, and his covert veil was all but shattered. Raul wore a neutral, preoccupied expression, but he was also highly intuitive, and his look changed the moment he walked toward the porch. There was no doubt in Ray's mind that Raul sensed that something wasn't right just by looking at him.

"Ray? Why are you sitting there? You look awful. What is it? Where's Luis?"

He stood up as Raul stepped up on the porch. "Luis is dead, Raul, and so is Raphael Nieves. They're in there," he said, glancing and pointing at the front door.

Raul just stood there, shock evident on his face, and he looked past Ray through the open door, where Luis's body lay in a twisted shape on the floor. Raul looked back at him. "Jesus Christ, what happened here, Ray?"

He shook his head slowly. "*Everything* happened. We were watching the news; it was before the crash was announced. Luis was Luis. Then he just got up, never said a thing to me and went in and shot the bomber. His body is still cuffed to the bed. Then he started for the family…I tried to stop him, Raul, but he just…wouldn't… stop. I had no choice, so I killed him."

Ray wasn't aware of it, but Raul saw the tears in his eyes. Then Ray went on, his voice a little stronger, more matter-of-fact. "He was going to rape them, Raul…I couldn't allow that."

Raul, listening closely, stood with his hands on his hips. He glanced again at Luis's body through the open front door, and then he reached out and took Ray firmly by the shoulder. "Of course you couldn't. You did what you had to do. You did what was right—I expected no less of you. Where's the family?"

Ray was relieved but in a strange way not surprised. There would be no confrontation over what he had done; how intense his relief was did surprise him.

His shakiness seemed to be ebbing; he felt stronger. "I took them to town and put them on a bus. I told Maria—that's the mother's name—to stay lost and talk to no one. And Raul? I promised her I'd try to return her husband to her."

Raul nodded. "OK, Ray. OK. I'll even help you, but we must act quickly. Go out back and find a shovel, anything we can use to dig. We need to bury the bodies and leave this place. We're too exposed here, and we're expected back in the city. Now go."

Raul patted him on the back and went inside. Ray watched him for a second and then walked around the house to the back, still amazed at what had just transpired. Raul was a true friend—of that he was certain. But to find such friendship in such an awful place and under such horrible circumstances astounded him. He knew their friendship would be tested further if and when he told Raul and Alvarez the truth, but he wasn't sure he was going to do that. It was what he wanted to do, but the way forward was a dangerous maze, and he was slowly feeling his way along.

Ray located a shovel in a crude shed out back and went in the back door to help Raul with the bodies. Raul was standing in the living room, looking at the TV; Luis's body hadn't been touched. Curious, Ray walked over and stood beside him. Alvarez was on the news, holding a press conference announcing the confirmed death of President Fernandez. To Ray, the huge surprise was that he was doing so with an alive and healthy Alberto Rodriguez standing solemnly off to one side.

Ray looked at Raul. "Rodriguez…he's still alive?"

Raul turned to him, sadness on his face. Softly he said, "I couldn't do it, Ray. I stood on our balcony waiting, giving him time to get to his car and come to the office, but when the timing seemed right, I just couldn't do it." He returned his look to the television for a second and then turned back to Ray, shaking his head. "He'll figure it out in time. He's just too smart, too good. I've doomed us all, especially Pablo, but I couldn't kill him."

For the first time during his mission, Ray fell completely out of character in front of Raul. He couldn't help himself; it just happened. He looked at Raul as Ray Cruz and said, "You're not a killer, Raul. You're a good man, and Alvarez didn't want his friend dead. I wouldn't have done it either, and I *have* killed today."

Raul looked at him quizzically, clearly detecting the change in him—the tenor of his voice, the casual reference to Alvarez by name. Probably due to the circumstances, however, he dismissed the feeling and said, "Yes, but you also saved innocents—that's what we do if any of this is supposed to make sense. Come on. Let's get these bodies buried and get out of here."

In that moment, Ray knew there was no way he could ever harm Raul. As remarkable as it seemed, when compared to the reality he had thought he knew and understood just a few months ago, this man, in this broken and corrupt country, *was* a friend. Ray didn't know where that friendship would lead him, but if he could never go home again, if he stayed and helped Raul and Alvarez, their friendship could be the start of his new life.

They buried the bodies in shallow graves inside the shed where Ray had found the shovel. Although they didn't clean up the house, they did go through it carefully and remove any evidence that could link them to the obvious murders that had taken place there. Raul drove his car, and Ray followed him back to the estate in Miguel's Escalade. When they arrived at the car park, Raul walked up to him and asked him if he had the weapon Luis had used to kill Raphael. Ray nodded and handed it over. Raul then told him to go to his casita and clean up and rest until dinner; he said it would be after eight before Alvarez would return to the estate. He did as he was told and, after showering, sat on the couch in the small living room of what was now his casita and watched one of the news channels as it presented story after story relating to the president's plane crash.

A little after seven, every news channel announced that the presidential commission had unanimously voted, and Jacques Pablo Alvarez had become Mexico's new interim president. A televised news conference followed his brief swearing in, during which a sad-looking, stoic Alberto Rodriguez was announced as the new secretary for public security. Ray just sat watching, shaking his head, as Alberto was sworn in as well. Why didn't Alberto stop it? How could he have missed the note, or was it something more sinister? Was he involved somehow, perhaps as part of a different cartel? Nothing made any sense to him, and, despite the ray of clarity he had had earlier about staying and helping Raul and Alvarez carry on with the fight, all the unanswered questions pressed down hard on him.

It was after eight before the official motorcade carrying Alvarez and Miguel was finally en route to the mansion. Ray was still in his casita, trying to sort out Alberto Rodriguez's part in all this, when Raul called him and told him that Alvarez was on the way and that they were to dine with the new president. By the time the heavily guarded presidential motorcade arrived, Ray was dressed and in the entry hall, with Raul ready to greet him. The presidential guard, led by a strutting colonel who was the acting commander due to the sudden demise of General Lopez, had descended upon the estate in force several hours earlier. For the most part, they confined their activities to the grounds and the streets surrounding La Casa Rosada. Someone already had passed word to the colonel that inside the estate walls, Raul and his associates retained authority over Alvarez's security.

The newly sworn-in President Alvarez came in, followed by Miguel and several new members of the presidential guard. He looked tired, Ray thought, but his spirit was buoyant, his eyes clearly reflecting a happiness or joy he'd never seen there before. He remembered what Raul had told him on the balcony, about Alvarez perhaps finding some peace somehow through all this, and thought that was maybe the case.

"Raul, Ray, I'm sorry I haven't been able to see and talk with you before now. Where is Luis?" Alvarez asked as he warmly shook their hands and gave each of them a light embrace.

Raul turned to the colonel, who was still standing in the foyer with the other guards, said thank you, and then dismissed them. He then took Alvarez by the arm, pulled him aside, and quickly and quietly explained what had happened in Toluca. Alvarez's countenance changed from buoyant to sad as he heard the news and glanced in Ray's direction. Finally, nodding slowly, as if he were in agreement with Raul, he turned and walked up to him. Ray wasn't sure what would happen next, and he was suddenly very aware of the H-K up his sleeve and the reticent but powerful Miguel standing nearby but too far away to take down. To his surprise, Alvarez embraced him, as a father would embrace a son, and slowly Ray relaxed. He felt somehow everything would be all right, at least for the moment.

Alvarez stepped back. "I'm so sorry, Ray, that you had to go through what you did today. It's my fault for elevating such a man to such an important position years ago. I feel I owe you so much more than my life. How will I ever make it up to you?"

Given all the distressing, confusing, and even dangerous thoughts that had gone through his head earlier in the day as he'd imagined this first encounter with the new president, Ray was dumbfounded at the kindness and concern being shown. Because of his surprise and also the great emotions he was trying hard to contain, he couldn't help himself—he was deeply moved, and it showed. The day had been a horrible one, and his emotions were raw, some even exposed. As a result, his covert mask was paper thin, and he knew it. What remained of his covert persona simply said, "You owe me nothing, Jefe. It is I who owes you, for trusting in me as you do and giving me a new home."

Now it was Alvarez who appeared deeply moved, and Ray was surprised yet again. *How can someone as smart as he is not see through me?* he wondered. It had to be because of the genuine affection the new president of Mexico had for him, he decided.

"Please join me for a drink before dinner," Alvarez said as he put his arm around Ray's shoulders and led him, Raul, and Miguel into the great room.

They went to the bar, and Alvarez himself made the drinks and passed them around. Ray and the always-silent Miguel settled into one of the comfortable seating areas as Raul went through the butler's pantry and locked the door, preventing anyone from accidentally intruding upon their privacy, before taking a seat next to Ray. Alvarez stood watching his old friend, a warm expression on his face, and then said, "My friends, allow me a few thoughts and then a toast."

He paused, looking down, with one hand on his drink and the other on his chin. Then he slowly looked up and glanced at each of them individually and spoke softly, with a deep emotion Ray had witnessed only at Francisco's funeral.

"It seems remarkable to me, but twenty-four years ago, I stood in this very room and celebrated my appointment to the Justice Department with Raul and Miguel. My father and Francisco were here then, and also Luis's father. I dreamed of a just world for our people and had the hubris to believe that with my appointment I could make a difference in the fight against those causing so much suffering in our country. Years later, when my father revealed to me that he and our family were also deeply involved in trafficking and I made the decision to help him—well, I'm not ashamed to admit to you all that I was at the lowest point in my life."

Alvarez paused and took a long drink, the emotions of the moment and the stark admission clearly affecting him. With a look and a nod to Raul, he went on.

"But with Raul's help, I began to see how different my father's organization truly was and what good could be accomplished. It was then that my disillusionment and disappointment at the turns my life had taken were replaced with very different thoughts. My friends, for the last twelve years, I've had a dream, one that would mean a just and better Mexico for our fellow citizens, free of the crime and the violence of the cartels. Within the next few months, we'll see much of that dream realized. The fact that I had to replace my father in his business—a life so different from the one I'd imagined I would lead—and continue down his path is the price I've willingly paid to achieve this end."

Alvarez paused. To Ray, he appeared choked up and struggling to maintain his composure. Alvarez coughed to clear his throat and then went on, his voice becoming even softer. "More innocent people died today...because of what I had to do. Thanks to Raul and to a merciful God, many others were spared, but in what remains of my immortal soul, I swear before you all, I truly believe I've done God's will."

He paused once more and took a drink of the fine whiskey he was holding, as if fortifying himself, then looked again at each man in the room, and, with his voice changing again, more firm now, more in control and sure of himself, he continued.

"With the summit we know the Gang of Four will be holding soon, if all goes well, we'll effectively eliminate them as viable cartels. Our dear friends in those evil organizations who did my bidding years ago and have patiently and courageously risen to positions of importance will be able to take over whatever remains or be part of the leadership that survives. From those positions, they'll continue to report to us, and we'll be able to control these broken groups and take more action in the future. In time, we'll fully eliminate them. I intend to stand for election when the election is held in four years, and with the backing of the party, I'll win easily. So, my friends, we'll have ten years to set our country right. To do so would be a legacy in which we can all take pride." Alvarez stood almost at attention and raised his glass. "Gentlemen, I thank you and drink to you and all that you've done to help me in this journey."

Led by Raul, the group stood with their glasses raised. A chorus of "Salute!" resounded, and they drank their drinks.

Alvarez nodded, smiled, and said, "Gentlemen, be seated. Raul, please share with our friends what's planned for the immediate future."

Raul nodded to him and then solemnly looked at Ray and Miguel and said, "With the exception of the ongoing investigation into the crash and the state funeral for Fernandez, business should settle down to something more normal over the next several weeks. As it does, we'll continue to establish our new routines here in the city. We'll move Jefe's office to Los Pinos tomorrow, but we'll continue to live here. By morning, we'll all have new credentials; Geraldo is seeing to this. We're all now special agents of the presidential guard, and no one can question anything we do. All questions regarding us are to be directed to the guard commander, and the new commander will answer to the president and also—conveniently, it seems—to the Condor."

Raul's serious look turned to a small, wry smile. "Acting Guard Commander Colonel Ramos, that peacock of a man whom you all met earlier, will soon be appointed general in command. Eduardo co-opted him a number of years ago, and he's been one of our sources watching over the late president. He'll get instructions from the Condor to do nothing but his job and to continue to make meaningless periodic reports on the president's actions—all of which, of course, we'll already know."

Raul turned more serious again. "Our one remaining concern is Alberto Rodriguez. We all know the kind of man he is, but, thanks to our new president, Alberto's two principal subordinates—the new director of the federal police, Ricardo Quito-Perez, and the new director at the AFI, Hector Garcia Ramirez—also were co-opted some years ago and work for us. Or, I should say, the Condor. So, my friends, we'll have several windows into any action Alberto might take that starts down paths that could be dangerous for us. Any questions?"

Ray was confused about Raul's reference to Alberto, about knowing what kind of man he was. Given the fact that Alberto hadn't acted on his note, Ray had no idea at all what kind of man Alberto was or what he was up to. It didn't seem reasonable to assume he simply hadn't discovered the note, so there had to be something else, something dark, he reasoned. He slowly raised his hand, curious about another thing he'd heard; it was trivial by comparison, but there was no harm in asking.

"Yes, Ray," Raul said.

"What is Los Pinos?"

Alvarez smiled warmly at him and answered before Raul could. "Los Pinos is the official presidential residence and office. It's also a public museum and sits in the middle of the beautiful Bosque de Chapultepec. I've made it known that while I'll be using the office there starting tomorrow, I'll continue to reside here at my estate. It's but a short drive, and we have all of Geraldo's special security in place here. Until such time that Geraldo can quietly make our move to the presidential residence, it's best we stay here."

Ray nodded his understanding. The group finished their drinks, then moved to the formal dining room and sat down to a sumptuous private dinner, with just the four of them, served solemnly by Alvarez's longtime butler. Ray kept stealing glances around the table; the atmosphere was relaxed, congenial. Everyone was showing great friendship and camaraderie. But he was the outsider, far more than it appeared, or more than they realized. They had taken him in, embraced him, and, in the case of Alvarez and Raul, and Carlo in the north, befriended him.

Ray was beginning to see that in a strange and coincidental way, his life was now paralleling Alvarez's. They each had led one kind of life, an honorable life, and then unbelievable circumstances beyond their control had shattered it and diverted them to a different, unimaginable course. Alvarez had embraced the great changes and adapted, and now he was the country's president and prepared to wage an all-out war against the cartels. To Ray, it looked as if maybe, finally, Mexico had a chance under Alvarez's leadership, however compromised his new path had been or tarnished his new life may have made him. He knew now there was a price to pay in any life; the deaths he was responsible for and must now live with were all the evidence of this he would ever require. Alvarez had told him in Baja that he had bridged his two very different lives to accomplish his original dreams and goals; maybe in his parallel life, he could too. In many ways, it struck him that Alvarez had indeed found redemption down his hard path; he hoped it could exist for him as well.

He glanced around the elegant table as he took a drink of the fine wine served with dinner. *I hate that I like these men,* he thought as he listened to stories from their shared pasts, his free hand clenched in a fist beneath the table. Raul looked over at him, a genuine smile on his face, great warmth in his eyes, and raised his glass slightly in a silent salute between two friends. Ray couldn't help himself; he smiled back and saluted Raul as well, despite the deep conflicting emotions he was struggling with inside.

All Raul saw on Ray's face, or thought he saw, was a shy smile from his new young friend, perhaps an understandable look in his eye saying, "I don't really belong yet." What Ray had been thinking at that instant, as they shared that look of friendship, was, *Is it really possible to keep my true life hidden from you? Can I avoid that confrontation? In time, can I tell you my truth and live? What if Alberto did get the note? Then he knows. But if he knows, why didn't he stop the president's flight? How is he a part of all this? If he doesn't know,*

I can stay silent. At least I'll be helping to get the real bastards. I could live with that and someday explain it to Dad; he could understand that.

The fact that the Condor could help Mexico was clear to Ray now, but he wondered if it was doing enough for his own country; he knew only time would tell.

Alvarez's old butler brought in coffee and a serving cart with a variety of after-dinner drinks and then, just as quietly, left them alone again. Alvarez did the honors once more and made sure everyone had something to drink and also produced cigars for himself and Miguel. After lighting his and enjoying the smoke for a second, Alvarez said, "My friends, there's once last piece of business we must discuss tonight. For personal reasons that I ask you simply to accept, we must return one last time to the north to personally deal with Barega, no matter the dangers. Once we've done this, the Condor de Muerte no longer will exist, except as the myth or legend he always was. Raul has made his concerns about this last trip known to me, but we won't discuss them tonight. It's something I must do, my friends. I owe Francisco that," he said while looking at Raul. "Raul?"

Ray had been watching Raul, and there had been a visible change in his look from happy to concerned and deeply troubled as Alvarez explained what he had to do. Raul slowly started to speak. "I've told Pablo he doesn't owe Francisco or me a thing, and I have tried to talk him out of this trip, but he insists. So we'll make it happen as risk free as we can, given the great attention Pablo now attracts. It'll be announced next Sunday that the president needs to return to Baja to visit his ailing mother. We'll be accompanied to Baja by a large contingent of the presidential guard, the national police, and, of course, the media. No one will be allowed inside the gates of the estate except the inner circle; this already has been explained to the new commanding colonel of the guard.

"Pablo also has made it known that he doesn't want the lives of the other residents of the estates in Baja to be disrupted. Tonight he provided the presidential guard and Alberto Rodriguez with a vetted list of the estate owners. They won't be bothered with searches or invasions of their privacy. This is, of course, important in order to safeguard the Peña identity. At my direction, the presidential security office will inquire about any travel plans the other estate owners may have during the week the president is with his mother. Señor Peña, through me, will make it known that he intends to leave Baja the day the president arrives and will be gone the entire time the president is visiting his mother. We will, of course, use this as our means to leave Baja undiscovered.

"Eduardo will get word to Barega that Pablo wants to meet with him to share new information he has that will allow Barega to fill a power vacuum we're creating in Matamoros against the Butcher of Brownsville. Barega has wanted that for as long as he's been in the business. Whatever fears and doubts he may be having following the Vasso assassination attempt and his part in it, he won't be able to resist the meeting. After Pablo and I confront him about Francisco's murder, Carlo will see that he doesn't leave the estate alive. We'll return to Baja and then the city, where Pablo can conduct the people's business as the three of us continue to conduct our business in the shadows, helping him realize his dream."

"My friends," Alvarez said, speaking softly again as he looked about the group, "I understand and appreciate your concerns for my safety, but I must see Eduardo and Carlo one last time before not seeing them again for what may turn out to be years. I won't be dissuaded in this. My life is in God's hands now, and his will be done."

Sitting silently in shock, Ray used all that remained of his experience and training to maintain his fragile cover. He had fallen to pieces this morning under the accumulated stress of his nearly six months undercover as well as his guilt for having saved himself at the expense of so many others. In that moment of great despair, he had made his fateful call to Bennie. He believed all hope was lost because other than killing him, he couldn't see a way to stop Alvarez and was haunted by whether he even should. To kill Alvarez meant killing Raul as well and that terrible realization had pushed him over the edge of reason. Accepting the harsh realities of his situation and helping Raul and Alvarez seemed the only way forward, if he wanted to live—and he did, even if others did die. Ray never imagined that exposing and facing such a basic desire could turn out to feel so bad. What did that make him?

How was anything Alvarez or Raul doing any worse? It finally had been too much this morning, and he had made the call, effectively ending the life he knew. But maybe that all had just changed with the surprising announcement of this insane trip north. As Jacques Pablo Alvarez, president of Mexico, the man *was* untouchable. But as the Condor de Muerte, traveling clandestinely in the north with just his small inner circle, Alvarez would be exposed, vulnerable, and Ray knew it.

He was amazed by the twists and turns of his life in just a day. After everything that had happened, here it was unexpectedly—he was being given a chance to possibly keep his life, *if* he wanted to grab it. But there were still so many serious unanswered questions and doubts dampening this new realization as he watched Raul and Alvarez sharing a personal story. After all, what had his own ambitions and mission ever been about but to defeat the cartels? No one was in a better position to do that than Alvarez, and Ray knew if he just accepted his parallel life, as Alvarez had accepted his, and helped him, many of the cartels could be eliminated, and so much good could be accomplished. But he also knew that had been his reasoning this morning in Toluca, after his world had crashed down on him—what a difference a few hours and a possible way out to his old life could make.

As Ray watched the camaraderie around the table and thought about his call to Bennie and what he now knew, a big part of him wished he could take it all back and somehow tell Bennie about the upcoming trip. God, what Bennie must think about him! What his dad would think when Bennie told him! A life, however tragic it may have become, dies hard he was discovering, and from somewhere deep inside him, he was aware of a renewed desire to somehow contact Bennie and put things right. He suddenly needed to explain to him what had gone wrong and why he'd lost it. He also had new information, important intelligence that might change everything. Who knew? Maybe redemption was a traveler of many different roads. He sat quietly, just watching the others, his emotions spinning, until they slowly stopped, coming full circle once again. *Who am I kidding?* he thought, suddenly forlorn again. *I'll never get the chance to talk with Bennie, not after this morning's call. If I ever see him again, it'll be through the bars of a jail cell…I am truly lost.*

He took a drink of the fine Cognac that he'd selected, the slight tremors he'd first noticed in his hand the night following the killing of Guzman suddenly there again. To undo what he'd done this morning seemed impossible, for it meant somehow seeing and talking with Bennie face to face. The likelihood of that ever happening was now gone forever, he believed. The climax and collision of the many disparate events he'd been a party to—and the unbelievable, difficult choices he'd made as a result—might have been inexorably forced upon him, but to Bennie, Ray was now the enemy, just another name on the long list of traffickers and traitors Bennie kept track of and was duty bound to fight. Even if by some miracle he could arrange it, how could Bennie ever understand or trust him and then forgive him for everything he had done in the last twelve weeks in the cartel when *he* couldn't understand or forgive himself?

Ray thought back to the deeply spiritual lunch conversation he'd had with Alvarez in Baja, when Alvarez had spoken about God and how God must have brought them together, and it was their duty to understand why. Before this mission, he hadn't been sure what he believed spiritually, but he had to admit that from time to time over the last several weeks, as Alvarez had shared his deep beliefs with him, he couldn't help wonder if there wasn't some unseen force guiding him. How else to explain the fact that through the chaos that had so thoroughly engulfed him, there was still a life, still a mission with purpose, and friendships? With this new life, he could still accomplish a great deal of good; a good that his dad could understand and forgive. Did his life have a purpose beyond his reasoning? What secular rationale could ever explain all that?

Ray was beginning to see that Alvarez wasn't a metaphor for the majestic condor at all but rather the mythical phoenix, reborn from the ashes of his shattered life and risen to the presidency of his country. And with the awesome power he now controlled and his deep personal desire to rid the country of the evil that was consuming it, how could he fail? Was it Ray's destiny to help him, to be a phoenix too? What other answer could there possibly be?

Stealing a glance at Raul, who was laughing at something Alvarez had said, Ray thought, *It seems I'm destined to help you, my friend, and there's honor in that, even at the cost of the life I've known. Somewhere in time I'll see Dad again and make him understand. I may have burned my bridges with Bennie today, but in doing so, I hope I've saved us both from a worse tragedy. If I hadn't done what I did, I probably would have had to kill you in order to stop the Condor and end all this—but now, unbelievably, there may be a way.*

31

DEA Headquarters
Washington, DC
Early Tuesday Morning

It was just a few minutes after midnight when the air force major flying the executive jet carrying Bennie, Brigadier General Austin, and his senior staff feathered his approach and made a perfect landing at Andrews Air Force Base outside DC. As soon as the executive jet was taxiing toward the terminal, Bennie took out his phone and powered it up. He had been able to charge it during the flight and glanced at the screen as a beep alerted him to his voice-mail messages in the encrypted access part of the memory. He had a number of voice-mail-message drop numbers depending on the operation; he was flabbergasted when he saw one of the numbers listed was for Ray's mission, because there was only one other man who knew of it.

Brigadier General Austin was watching him closely in the tight quarters of the otherwise comfortable seating area they were sharing, but Bennie ignored him as he put the phone to his ear and played Ray's message. His spirits sank, and his countenance visibly changed for the worse as he listened and then relistened to the despair in Ray's voice when he told him his intentions. After all these weeks and finally receiving word from Ray, he was telling him he was needlessly throwing his life away.

"Everything OK, Bennie?" the pleasant brigadier general asked.

Bennie looked up, his face ashen, and shook his head sadly. "I'm afraid not. Sorry…I can't say more."

The general was quite familiar with the concept of "need to know" and didn't press him further. As the jet came to a stop near the terminal, Bennie gathered his few belongings and followed the general out the door. The general waited at the foot of the steps, his hand extended, and said, "It was nice to meet you, Bennie. Sorry you've received what appears to be bad news."

Bennie, his lips pursed, said, "Thanks for the lift, General. Sorry to have bumped your flag lieutenant off the flight."

"Forget about it," the general said, smiling. "Sometimes that's what young lieutenants need, and that one could use some humility. A night in the Bliss BOQ and a long, crowded commercial flight back to DC tomorrow will help achieve that objective. See you around."

The general clapped him on the back and headed for the senior-officer lounge as Bennie walked toward the civilian side of the terminal area, where he saw Charley standing inside the glass doors, waiting for him.

"Welcome back," Charley greeted him as they shook hands. "I've been concerned and uneasy since your call from Texas. What gives that you couldn't tell me over a secure line?"

"Not here, Charley," Bennie said glumly. "Let's get to your office, and I'll show you and tell you. Please tell me you have some decent booze hidden away. I could use a belt."

Charley could tell something was really wrong but said, "For you? You know I do. Car's out front."

It was a thirty-minute drive to the office from Andrews; the traffic was light because of the late hour. They hadn't said a word to each other since the first few minutes of the drive, when Charley had told him he'd done as requested and booked Bennie on the first available flight out of Dulles for Mexico City, but until Bennie could tell him why he wanted to go and convince him it was the right thing to do, he wasn't going to allow him to go anywhere.

Bennie had just coldly looked at him and said, "Suit yourself, Charley, but either with your ticket and in your employ or on my own, I *will* be on a fucking plane for Mexico City in a few hours."

Although Charley was surprised at his old friend's brusque tone and resolve, he knew better than to have it out in the car without knowing more. Bennie was deeply disturbed; that much was evident. Any further conversation could wait until he knew why.

Once they reached his office, Charley went to his desk and retrieved the bottle of fine single-malt Scotch that Bennie liked so much, along with two crystal tumblers, and joined Bennie on the couch. Bennie was taking his laptop out of his battered leather briefcase and setting it up on the coffee table. Finished, he reached into his pocket and retrieved a flash drive.

"After we spoke earlier on the phone," Bennie said, "and before I caught my ride to DC, General Rodriguez's aide, Colonel Romero, gave me this." He inserted the drive into a port and worked a few keys, then turned the laptop toward Charley.

"This is a copy of a video conversation we had with the general's cousin, Alberto Rodriguez, earlier today, after Fernandez's jet went down. The general fixed Alberto up with what he calls a see-tee, an encrypted laptop that talks only with a see-tee the general has. No one else has seen this."

Charley nodded and watched the video in silence, but he did lean forward, his elbows on his knees, his chin resting on his clenched hands, and he then glanced at Bennie with raised eyebrows at the part where Alberto revealed Ray's note. When the video was finished, Charley leaned back and ran a hand through his mussed graying hair and said, "Play it again, please—the part with the note and the Mayan stuff."

Bennie did as instructed, and Charley leaned forward again, watching the video carefully. When it was over, he turned to Bennie. "Alvarez is far more calculating than I ever would've imagined. All that crap about the calendars is brilliant."

Bennie was stumped. "I'm not following you."

"Don't you see? No doubt a bunch of their citizenry believes in the Mayan calendars. Alvarez's timing for this takeover isn't the least bit coincidental. Surely his timetable always has been predicated on this period, perhaps planned for years. An apocalypse of sorts has in fact taken place, albeit by his hand, and now he's the rising deity. Couple all that with a successful action against the Gang of Four, and he has the Mexican people in the palm of his hands. Brilliant and cold-blooded realpolitik, Bennie. His coup d'etat is complete. If not for Ray and the information he's provided us, Alvarez's plan would be flawless. I get why you're all bothered to go down there, but just hear me out on why you shouldn't go, OK?"

Bennie, who'd been drinking his Scotch, put his tumbler down and shook his head. "No, Charley. There's more."

He took out his cell phone, accessed Ray's voice mail, put the phone on speaker, and hit Play. Charley's look, which was already serious, turned grave as he heard Ray's voice for the first time in months, telling them what he had done and, worse, what he was going to do. When the message was done, Charley slowly sat back into the couch, looking at Bennie, and said, "My God, what have we done to that young man?"

Bennie nodded. "You see now why I have to be on a plane and right the hell now, Charley? It seems impossible, given where he's been and how connected Alvarez is, but Ray doesn't seem to fully understand what a colossal piece of shit that Fernandez was. I'm sorry others died in the crash, but their deaths and Fernandez's isn't something you let destroy your entire life. Ray did his job, at great personal risk, and doesn't realize it. He saved Alberto Rodriguez's life, for Christ's sake! It's not his fault that Alberto didn't discover the note until it was too late to save the others. Jesus Christ, shit happens! Ray hasn't failed this agency or me—I've failed him! How in the living hell am I supposed to live with that? I can't abandon him; I won't. I have to get down there and before he goes off and kills the fucking new president of Mexico!"

Without even realizing it, Bennie had been pounding his fist on the coffee table. Charley wasn't the least bit bothered by it; seeing Bennie's anguish, he reached over and patted him on the knee. "I agree, and I'm sorry about what I said earlier in the car." He glanced at his watch; it was just after 1:00 a.m. "Listen, it's clear you're running on fumes, and your flight is in six hours. That gives you about four hours to catch some sleep and for me to figure out ways to help you."

"Screw that, Charley. I don't want to sleep."

Charley could see Bennie's fatigue; his general pallor and the deep purple bags beneath his eyes were dead giveaways. Without another word he stood, went to his closet, came back with a pillow and a blanket, and tossed them on the couch.

"Don't make me throw my weight at you, Bennie. Sack out, and let me do my job to help you do yours. I want to help Ray as much as you do."

"What can you do in the middle of the night?" Bennie asked, his tone more conciliatory.

"Hey, give me some credit. I'm the DI—I can think of a few things. Now lie down and get some rest. Going where you're going, you'll need your wits if you want to be any help at all."

Bennie stared up at his old friend for a few seconds and said, "Two hours. Then wake me, OK?"

Charley smiled. "Sure. Anything you say."

Bennie lay down, but with everything he had learned today, and as bad as he felt, he didn't believe for a second that he could sleep. It turned out he was more tired than he had realized, however, for he fell into a deep sleep and then awoke with a start as Charley entered the office, the door closing noisily behind him. He was carrying a new black leather attaché case and set it on the coffee table in front of the couch.

Bennie was groggy and realized that he not only had dozed off but also had slept hard. "Jesus Christ, Charley," he mumbled as he slowly sat up, scratching his head. "How long was I out?"

"Almost four hours. I told you, you needed some rest. We need to leave in thirty minutes. A car and driver are waiting for us downstairs. Your suitcase is in my bathroom," he said, pointing to the door in the corner. "I sent one of my guys over to your place and had him bring back some fresh clothes; they're hanging in there. Grab a shower and a shave, and change. Then we'll go."

Bennie wasn't upset with Charley for letting him sleep. Rather, he was grateful, and it showed. He stifled a yawn and asked, "What's with the case?"

"Just a few things that maybe will help. It's the best I could do on such short notice. We'll get into that on the way to Dulles. Now go."

Bennie did as ordered, and twenty-five minutes later, they were in the backseat of an agency town car driven by an armed protective officer. Charley put the case between them on the backseat and opened it. As was typical for Charley, whom Bennie was always quick to point out was the real brains in the DEA, he obviously had spent the entire time Bennie had slept working on ways to help him in his mission. Not only did Bennie now have a first-class ticket, expense cash, and his diplomatic passport, but he also had some electronic goodies Charley had snagged from the DEA's technical branch. Included were some small listening devices, a few miniature transmitters and recorders, and a number of global encrypted cell phones preprogrammed with frequency-hopping burst transmitters designed to be difficult for normal radio-frequency monitors to pick up.

Bennie was impressed, not with Charley's thinking—that was never really a surprise—but with all the trinkets. He of course was familiar with some of the standard electronic gear used in their undercover work, but some of the stuff in this case looked as if it were right out of Q Branch in a James Bond film. Charley passed along some basic information regarding how to operate some of the sophisticated equipment as it had been explained to him by the technician he had ordered out of bed in the middle of the night to help him. He also had thought to include some technical instructions on their use, which he had the geek from the tech branch write out, just in case. Bennie's diplomatic passport, which Charley had pulled from his personnel file, would allow him entry into Mexico without being subjected to any inspections.

"Jesus, Charley, all this in four hours? Thanks. I guess there *is* a reason you're the DI."

Charley waved his hand dismissively. They were almost to Dulles, and neither had wasted any time discussing possible tactics Bennie might use to contact Ray or help Alberto Rodriguez; they both realized he would be improvising on the fly. The town car pulled up to the curb in the diplomatic drop-off area, and the driver got out and quickly walked around the car to open Bennie's door.

Bennie looked at Charley. "Listen, I need one last favor. Call Ray's dad in Sacramento and tell him, 'Our little project is going well.' That's our code phrase to let him know I've heard from Ray, and he's alive and well. It's been far too long; we need to tell him." He started to turn and get out, but Charley grabbed him by the arm. Bennie looked at his old friend and boss. "What?"

Charley's expression appeared mournful. "Bennie…Ray's alive, but he's sure as hell not well, and what in the world are you going to do once you get there? In trying to get to Ray, maybe all you'll do is expose him to Alvarez. With his totally screwed-up history, his demonstrated ruthlessness, and his new powers as president, you both could end up dead."

Bennie glanced out the windshield for a few seconds, then turned back to Charley, a steely look in his eyes, and said slowly and with determination, "What I'm going to do, Charley, is go down into that shithole, to use Ray's words, and with Alberto Rodriguez's help, find a way to get somewhere where Ray will see me. Then, without blowing his cover, I intend to convey to him somehow—with a look, a message drop, something—that he is *still* my guy, he is *not* alone, and I have *not* given up on him. Then, Charley? President Alvarez or no President Alvarez, I'm getting him the hell out."

Bennie got out of the car and didn't look back as he walked briskly into the terminal with purpose, all signs of the weariness he'd shown a short time earlier now gone. As Charley watched him, he shook his head as he thought, *If anyone can, old friend, you can.*

About the Author

Chris Thomas successfully practiced architecture after graduating from the University of Colorado in 1977. However, over the last twenty-five years, deep down he felt he should be writing stories. What began as an unrealized dream finally became a reality when at age fifty-five he semiretired from his architectural practice and fully committed himself to writing his first novels, *Until Philosophers Become Kings: Books One* and *Two,* and soon after a third, *The Last Good Samaritan.* He lives in Denver, where he's at work on his fourth novel.

www.ingramcontent.com/pod-product-compliance
Lightning Source LLC
Chambersburg PA
CBHW071143020726
47502CB00002B/243

* 9 7 8 0 9 9 6 5 6 0 7 0 2 *